P9-DHG-794

AUTHORS LOVE HIM

"Peter Robinson is an author with amazing empathy, a snare-trap ear for dialogue, and a clear eye for the telling detail."
—Michael Connelly

"Peter Robinson is a master, and *In the Dark Places* shows why. Thrilling, sophisticated, and emotionally involving, this is edge-of-your-seat, heart-in-your-throat suspense. A must-read."
—Tess Gerritsen

"Peter Robinson's *In the Dark Places* is wonderful—a cause for celebration. Brilliantly plotted, beautifully paced, it gathers speed and dread until I could barely stand it. Peter Robinson writes with compassion, with depth, with the assurance of a writer at the top of his game, and rewards us with a truly heart-pounding finale. All who adore great writing, and Inspector Banks, will find this a thrilling read."
—Louise Penny

CRITICS LOVE HIM

"The relationships between Banks and his crew and
the fascinating way that procedure and forensics
are used make for a solid read. Robinson belongs
on any P. D. James fan's must-read list."
—*Booklist*

"Deftly plotted. . . . Robinson is equally adept
at making murder on a small scale as compelling as
any serial killer hunt, and Banks continues to charm."
—*Publishers Weekly*

"Guaranteed to send new fans
to Robinson's back catalog."
—*BookPage*

"Peter Robinson should be a household name among
bibliophiles. . . . What Robinson promises and delivers
is solid plotting and first-class characterization,
presented in a package comprised of fine writing from
first paragraph to last. . . . Perfect for those dark and
rainy interludes that summer brings, a demonstration
that Robinson is yet again in top form."
—Bookreporter.com

"*In the Dark Places* gradually builds to a crescendo of suspense leaving you on the edge of your seat. Skillfully plotted, smart characters, astute dialog and attention to detail make this police procedural a thrilling read."
—Examiner.com

"Peter Robinson . . . has made this bleak, snowy, beautiful Yorkshire his own, and while Banks may be feeling his age, the crime stories are as fresh as ever."
—Fresh Fiction

"Well-crafted prose runs through Robinson's series. . . . So, too, do precise pacing and superior plotting. . . . Robinson is in full swing. . . . [Banks] is one of the most complex characters in crime fiction."
—*Richmond Times Dispatch*

"A welcome addition to the series. . . . Beautiful descriptions of the Yorkshire dales. . . . *In the Dark Places* is a complicated and intriguing mystery. . . . Robinson has again created a believable and entertaining world peopled by these characters."
—ReviewingtheEvidence.com

YOU'LL LOVE HIM

One of the world's most popular and acclaimed writers, **PETER ROBINSON** grew up in the United Kingdom, and now divides his time between Toronto and England. The bestselling, award-winning author of the Inspector Banks series, he has also written two short-story collections and three standalone novels, which combined have sold more than ten million copies around the world. Among his many honors and prizes are the Edgar Award, the CWA (UK) Dagger in the Library Award, and Sweden's Martin Beck Award.

IN THE DARK PLACES

BY PETER ROBINSON

IN THE DARK PLACES

AN INSPECTOR BANKS NOVEL

Peter Robinson

wm

WILLIAM MORROW

An Imprint of HarperCollins*Publishers*

This book is a work of fiction. The characters, incidents, and dialogue are drawn from the author's imagination and are not to be construed as real. Any resemblance to actual events or persons, living or dead, is entirely coincidental.

IN THE DARK PLACES. Copyright © 2015 by Eastvale Enterprises, Inc. Excerpt from *When the Music's Over* © 2016 by Eastvale Enterprises, Inc. All rights reserved. Printed in the United States of America. No part of this book may be used or reproduced in any manner whatsoever without written permission except in the case of brief quotations embodied in critical articles and reviews. For information address HarperCollins Publishers, 195 Broadway, New York, NY 10007.

HarperCollins books may be purchased for educational, business, or sales promotional use. For information please e-mail the Special Markets Department at SPsales@harpercollins.com.

A hardcover edition of this book was published under the title *Abattoir Blues* in 2014 by Hodder & Stoughton.

FIRST WILLIAM MORROW HARDCOVER EDITION PUBLISHED 2015.
FIRST WILLIAM MORROW PAPERBACK EDITION PUBLISHED 2016.

Library of Congress Cataloging-in-Publication Data has been applied for.

ISBN 978-0-06-224056-9

16 17 18 19 20   OV/RRD   10 9 8 7 6 5 4 3 2 1

For Sheila

"But look at these lonely houses, each in its own fields, filled for the most part with poor ignorant folk who know little of the law. Think of the deeds of hellish cruelty, the hidden wickedness which may go on, year in, year out, in such places, and none the wiser."

—Sir Arthur Conan Doyle, "The Adventure of the Copper Beeches," *The Adventures of Sherlock Holmes* (1892)

IN THE DARK PLACES

1

TERRY GILCHRIST CAME OUT OF THE WOODS OPPOSITE the large hangar, which loomed ahead of him like some storage area for crashed alien spaceships in New Mexico. Only he wasn't in New Mexico; he was in North Yorkshire.

It stood at the center of a large area of cracked and weed-covered concrete, its perimeter surrounded by a seven-foot chain-link fence topped with barbed wire. A large sign on the padlocked double gates read: PRIVATE—KEEP OUT. About a quarter of a mile beyond the hangar, a passenger train sped by on the East Coast line, heading for King's Cross.

As he usually did at this point on the walk, Gilchrist let Peaches off her leash. The space was open far enough that he could easily keep an eye on her, and she always came back when he whistled or called her name.

Peaches sniffed around the edges of the fence, and before long she had found a way in, probably the same hole the kids used when they went there to play cricket or smoke joints and try to feel up the local girls. This time, instead of continuing to sniff around the concrete and weeds, Peaches headed for the dark opening of the hangar and disappeared inside.

While he waited for her to finish her business, Gilchrist leaned his stick against a tree, stretched his arms out to prop himself up against the trunk and started doing a series of simple leg exercises the army medics had given him. They were already pleased with his progress: out walking, albeit with a stick, after only four months, when they had at first thought the leg was as good as gone. But Gilchrist wanted rid of the stick now, and the only way to do that was to build up the damaged muscle tissue little by little. His leg might never *look* the same, but he was determined that it would function as well as it ever had.

When he had done, Peaches had still not reappeared, so he whistled and called her name. All he got in reply was a bark followed by a whining sound. He called again, adding a bit more authority to his tone, and the whining went on for longer, but Peaches didn't reappear. She wasn't coming back. What the hell was wrong with her?

Irritated, Gilchrist grasped his stick again and made his way along the side of the fence, searching for the gap Peaches had found. When he saw it, his heart sank. He could get in, of that he was certain, but it would be a difficult, and probably painful, business. And messy. He called again. Peaches continued barking and whining, as if *she* were calling *him*.

To get through the hole, Gilchrist had to lie flat on the wet ground and edge slowly forward, sticking his arms through first and pushing back against the fencing to propel himself forward. There was an immediate familiarity in lying on his belly that flooded his mind with fear, more a cellular or muscular memory than anything else, and he almost froze. Then he heard Peaches barking through the haze and carried on. Standing up was another awkward maneuver, as he could hardly bend his leg without causing extreme pain, but he made it, hanging on the links of the fence and using them as climbing grips. Finally, he stood panting and leaned back against the fence, clothes damp and muddy; then he grabbed his stick and made toward the hangar.

It was dim inside, but enough light came through the large opening to make it possible to see once his eyes had adjusted. Peaches was standing about thirty yards to his right, near the wall; she was barking and her tail was wagging. Gilchrist made his way over, wondering what on earth was making her behave in such a willful and excited manner. Irritation slowly gave way to curiosity.

The floor of the hangar was concreted over like the surrounding area, and it was just as cracked in places, weeds growing through despite the lack of light. He could hear rain tapping on the steel roofing and the wind moaning around the high dark spaces. He felt himself give an involuntary shudder as he approached Peaches.

Even in the dim light, it was easy to see that she was sniffing around a dark patch on the concrete, but it took the light from Gilchrist's mobile phone to see that what interested her was a large bloodstain dotted with chips of bone and chunks of gray matter. Immediately, an image of blood on the sand flashed into his mind and he felt the panic rise like the bile in his throat.

Get a grip, he told himself, then took several deep breaths and bent to peer more closely in the light of the mobile. He didn't have Peaches's acute sense of smell, but close up, he picked up that rank and coppery smell of blood. It was a smell he remembered well.

The thought came into his mind unbidden: *Someone has died here.*

"A BLOODY stolen tractor," complained Annie Cabbot. "Would you merit it? I ask you, Doug. Is this why I put in all those years to make DI? Risked life and limb? Is this Homicide and Major Crimes? A stolen tractor? Is that why I was put on this earth?"

"It's rural crime," said DC Dougal Wilson, taking his eyes from the road for a moment to flash Annie a quick grin. "And rural crime is major crime. At least according to the new police commissioner."

"Christ, anyone would think it was election time again already."

"Well," said Wilson, "it's not as if it's the first piece of farm equipment gone missing over the past while, not to mention the occasional cow and sheep. And it *is* an expensive tractor."

"Even so . . . Is this farmer we're going to see a personal friend of the Commissioner's?"

"No, but I do believe his wife is a friend of Area Commander Gervaise. Book club, or something."

"Hmm. Didn't know Madame Gervaise was a reader. Hidden depths. She and Alan must have a lot in common. And where is DCI Banks when you need him? I'll tell you where. He's off in Cumbria for a dirty weekend with his girlfriend, that's where he is."

"I think you'll find it's Umbria, guv," muttered Wilson.

"Umbria? That's even worse. It'll be sunny there." Annie paused as Wilson negotiated a narrow humped stone bridge. Annie had always been nervous about such bridges. There was no way you could see whether someone was coming from the other side. The best you could do was close your eyes and put your foot down. She closed her eyes. Wilson put his foot down. They made it. "What is it about these Italiàns?" she went on. "First it was Joanna Passero, the one he went to Estonia with."

"She's not Italian. She's Scottish. Now she's got divorced, she's gone back to her maiden name. She's just plain old Joanna MacDonald." Wilson blushed. "Well, not exactly plain, perhaps, but you know what I mean. Works at County HQ in Criminal Intelligence. Quite the rising star."

"I've always thought there was something criminal about the intelligence at County HQ," said Annie. She shot Wilson a suspicious glance. "Anyway, how do you know all this?"

Wilson pushed his glasses up on his nose. "One of the perks of being a lowly DC. Privilege of low rank. You get to hear all the good gossip."

Annie smiled. "I remember. Vaguely. Still, a bloody stolen tractor. I ask you." She squinted at a road sign between the fast-beating windscreen wipers. "I think we're here, Doug. Beddoes Farm. Here's the track."

"I know. I can see it." Wilson turned so sharply that the car almost skidded into the ditch. The ground was sodden and the mud churned to the consistency of porridge. They hung on as the car bounced and squelched down the quarter mile of rough track that led to the farm itself, giving its shock absorbers a workout they probably didn't need. At least it was a car from the police motor pool, Annie thought, not her new red Astra.

Wilson pulled into the farmyard, where the mud wasn't any more welcoming, and parked beside a silver BMW. Beyond that stood a new-looking Range Rover. The layout was that of a typical courtyard farmstead: a two-story farmhouse, built of limestone with a flagstone roof, surrounded by farm buildings, including a barn, also of limestone with big wooden doors with flaking green paint, what looked like a garage built of corrugated steel, a pigsty, whose natives sounded happy to be rolling about in mud and worse, and a chicken coop so fortified that the local foxes had probably all slunk off with their tails between their legs.

The usual farm smells assailed Annie's nostrils when she got out of the car. No doubt the pigs contributed a great deal to it, she thought. And to the mud. You never knew what you were squelching through when you walked across a farmyard. The rolling fields of rapeseed, which would blossom a glorious bright yellow in May, now looked brooding and threatening under a lowering gunmetal sky. Very *Wuthering Heights,* Annie thought, though she knew that was miles away. Dark clouds lumbered overhead, unleashing shower after shower of rain, some heavy, some more like drizzle, and the wind whistled in the emptiness.

Annie had come prepared for a cold wet day in the country—it was only March, after all—her jeans tucked into a pair of red wellies, flower-patterned plastic rain hat, woolly jumper under a waterproof jacket. Doug Wilson looked a little more professional in his Marks and Sparks suit, trilby and tan raincoat with the epaulettes and belt. In fact, Annie thought, he looked a bit like a private detective from a fifties movie, except for the glasses. And when he took his hat off, he still looked like Daniel Radcliffe playing Harry Potter.

There was an arched porch over the entrance, where they removed their outer clothing. When Annie took off the rain hat, her chestnut hair tumbled around her shoulders. The blond was all gone now; she had let her hair grow out and return to its natural color. She could certainly testify that she had not had more fun as a blonde.

A tall, wiry man in his mid fifties, with a fine head of gray hair and a light tan, answered the door. He was wearing jeans and a red V-neck sweater over a pale blue shirt. Despite the casual clothing, Annie thought he looked more like a business executive than a farmer. There was an aura of wealth and power about him that she had never associated with farmers before. "You must be the police," he said, before they could pull out their warrant cards. He held the door open and stood aside. "Are your coats wet? If so, please don't hesitate to bring them indoors. We'll soon dry them out."

"They'll be fine," Annie said, rubbing her hands together, then reaching for her warrant card. "DI Cabbot and DC Wilson."

"I'm John Beddoes. Please, come in."

Most farms Annie had visited—admittedly not very many—smelled of mouthwatering baking, of pastry, marzipan, cinnamon and cloves, but Beddoes's place smelled of nothing but lemon-scented air freshener.

"I know you probably think this is a huge waste of your time," said Beddoes. "Not to mention a waste of police resources, but it's not the first such crime we've had around here this past year or so."

"We're aware of that, sir," said Annie. "That's why we're here."

Beddoes led them through to a cozy sitting room. First he bade them sit down on a three-piece suite that definitely hadn't come from DFS, then he called to his wife. "Pat? The police are here, love."

Patricia Beddoes walked in. Wearing figure-hugging designer jeans, trainers and an orange T-shirt, she was an attractive, elegant woman, with expensively coiffed dark hair, a good ten years or more younger than her husband. Even though she had been on holiday in the sun, her tan looked fake, from a can, like the kind that the young women all showed off on *Coronation Street*. She still looked a little chilly and severe to Annie, too many sharp angles, but her welcoming smile was genuine enough, her handshake firm, and she immediately offered them tea. Annie and Wilson said yes. Neither had eaten breakfast yet. Outside, the rain poured down and the wind blew it hard against the windowpanes and on the parked cars and tin garage. It sounded like someone chucking handfuls of gravel.

"Miserable weather, isn't it?" said John Beddoes. "And they say there's more to come."

Everyone was saying it had been the wettest March since records began, and Annie wasn't about to argue with that. Apart from a few days earlier in the month, it hadn't been all that warm, either. There was even snow in the forecast. And all this coming on the heels of a miserable winter, a particularly tough one for farmers, who had lost so many sheep in snowdrifts out on the moors. "You were away on holiday?" she said.

"Yes. Mexico. You might think it an odd time for us to go away—if there ever is a good time for a farmer—but we don't have any sheep or cattle, you see, so we have no need to worry about lambing or calving." He nodded toward the kitchen. "And Patricia needed a break."

"Very nice." Annie didn't think most farmers could afford to go to Mexico, not given the way they always seemed to be complaining about low prices of dairy produce, prohibitive EU tariffs and whatnot, but then with all the cheap flights and bargain all-inclusive holidays, it probably wasn't all that expensive these days. Not that Annie fancied the idea: a bunch of yobs in leopard-skin swimming trunks, slathered in coconut sunblock and pissed on weak beer had about as much appeal for her as a wet Sunday in Wales, or Yorkshire, for that matter. "I understand you only just got back," she said.

"Late last night. About half past eleven. We were supposed to arrive early in the morning, but the flight to New York was delayed and we missed our connection. Well . . . you know what it's like. Stuck in the airport lounge all day."

Annie had no idea, never having been in an airport lounge. "So that was when you found out?"

"Yes. I noticed that the garage had been broken into right away and telephoned the police. I must say you lot are quick off the mark. Much quicker than you used to be. That uniformed chappie who came around last night seemed very sympathetic, too."

"PC Valentine?" said Annie. "Yes, sir, he's a very sensitive young man."

"So what's being done?" Beddoes asked.

"We've got a description of the tractor out, sir—a green Deutz-Fahr Agrotron, if I'm not mistaken—and we've got people looking for it, keeping an eye open at ports and so on. We've been in touch with Customs and Excise. They have the details, description, number plate, engine serial number. Of course, the criminals will most likely have altered those by now, but sometimes they're lazy, or they slip up. It's our experience that most stolen farm equipment is shipped out of the country pretty sharpish."

John Beddoes sighed. "It's probably in bloody Albania by now, then. It's worth a hundred K at least."

His wife came in with a tea tray and served everyone. Annie could hear the radio in the kitchen. Ken Bruce playing golden oldies on Radio 2. "Runaway." She knew the song but couldn't remember who sang it.

"I don't suppose you have any idea exactly when the tractor went missing?" Annie asked. Doug Wilson pushed his glasses up again and bent over his notebook.

Beddoes shook his head. "We were only gone a week. We're not that big an operation, really, and it's mostly arable. Some cereals, vegetables, potatoes. Rapeseed's our biggest crop by far. We supply a specialist high-end oil maker. As you probably noticed, we also have a few pigs and chickens to keep the local quality restaurants supplied. Free-range chickens, of course, when it's possible. And the pigs are British Landrace. Excellent meat. So there really wasn't much to do last week."

"I've heard that certain breeds of pig can be valuable," Annie said. "Are yours?"

"Quite, I suppose."

"I wonder why they weren't taken, too?"

"I should think these people specialize, wouldn't you? There's a lot of difference between getting rid of a tractor and a pig. Also, you've got to know how to handle pigs. They can be nasty when they want to be."

"I suppose so," said Annie, though she knew absolutely nothing about pigs except they smelled and squealed and she didn't eat them. "Now the thieves know that the pigs are here, though, perhaps you should think about improving your security?"

"How am I supposed to do that, apart from standing outside the sty all night with a shotgun in my hands?"

"I'd forget about the shotgun, if I were you, sir. They only get people into trouble. There must be special fences, alarms, Country Watch, that sort of thing."

"I'll look into it."

"Where was the key?"

Beddoes looked away. "What key?"

"To the tractor. I imagine if it's modern and expensive it has various security features."

"Yes."

"So where did you keep the key?"

"Hanging on a hook in the garage."

"And the car keys? The Beemer and the Range Rover."

Beddoes patted his trouser pocket. "They're on my key ring. I carry them with me."

"But you didn't take the tractor key with you while you were away?"

"Are you here to interrogate me or to help me recover my stolen tractor?"

Annie and Wilson exchanged glances. "Well, sir," Annie went on, "at the moment we're trying to establish just how the tractor was stolen, and it would seem to me that being able to start it is a major issue. I mean, you could hardly push it into a waiting lorry, could you?"

"How could I know something like this was going to happen?" Beddoes had reddened and started waving his arms around. "We were running late. Pat . . . The bloody taxi was waiting. I just didn't think. The garage was securely locked when we left, for crying out loud."

"John," said his wife. "Calm down. Your blood pressure."

Beddoes smoothed his hand over his hair. "Right. Sorry." He turned to Annie again. "In retrospect I know it looks stupid, and I didn't want the insurers to know, but I . . . I mean, mostly we're around, so it's not a problem. I often just leave the tractor in the yard with the key in the ignition. When you get on a tractor, you want to just start it and get going, not search around for bloody keys. In this case, the garage was well locked, I had someone keeping an eye on the place. What more was I supposed to do?"

"I've no idea," said Annie. "Who took care of the place for you while you were away?"

"Frank Lane from over the dale said he'd feed the pigs and chickens and keep an eye on everything for us. Not that we blame Frank for what happened, of course. He can't stand on twenty-four-hour vigil any more than I can. Besides, he's got his own farm to take care of, and it's far bigger than ours." He laughed. "Frank's a *real* farmer, as he never ceases to inform us. And he's got that tearaway son of his to worry about. We're just grateful he was able to help at all."

"What makes you call his son a tearaway?" Annie asked.

"Oh, he's always been a handful, ever since he was a nipper. Mischievous imp. He got into some trouble with the police a while back."

"What sort of trouble?"

"Frank wasn't specific about it, but I think it was something to do with a stolen car. Joyriding. Got probation, community service, something like that. I didn't like to say anything to Frank, but to be honest, the lad always seemed a bit of a shiftless and mischievous sort to me, if truth be told. He doesn't live at the farm anymore, but he turns up now and again to see his father."

"Capable of stealing a tractor?"

"I'm not saying that. I don't think he's basically dishonest." Beddoes took a deep breath. "Just misguided. Frank calls me a hobby farmer. Laughs at me behind my back, like they all do. It's true, I suppose. But I was born on a farm and grew up on one, dammit, until I was twelve."

"I see," said Annie. "Is there any bitterness between you and the other local farmers?"

"I wouldn't really call it bitterness. More envy. They tease me, make fun of me, exclude me from their little cliques, but that's just their way. You know Yorkshire folk. God knows how many years before they finally accept you, if they ever do."

"Any recent disputes, arguments?"

"None that I can think of."

"Nor me," Patricia said.

Annie made a note to have a chat with Frank Lane and his "tearaway son" later. Intelligence had it that those responsible for the recent surge in rural thefts used "scouts," usually local delivery drivers, or itinerant laborers, who built trust by helping out the farmers with maintenance, crop picking or vermin control, as the seasons demanded. A tearaway son could easily get involved in such a racket if the price was right. Or if drugs were involved. There were plenty of cannabis farms around the region. Not that Annie saw any harm in having a few tokes now and then. After all, she had grown up surrounded by the stuff in the artists' colony outside St. Ives, where she had lived with her father and a constantly shifting cast of bohemian types and plain ne'er-do-wells, maybe even a minor drug dealer or two. But this wasn't just a couple of spliffs that bothered the police; it was big business, big profit, and that was what drew the nastier type of international criminals and gangs. It was hard to turn a blind eye to them.

"Do you have any security alarms?" Annie asked.

Beddoes snorted. "What, up here? Waste of bloody money, like I told the constable earlier. Any self-respecting criminal would be long gone before a patrol car got up here, even if one happened to be free when you needed it."

He was probably right, Annie realized. Once she had as much detail as she could get from John Beddoes, there seemed little reason to stay. Annie stirred herself and gave Doug Wilson the nod. "We'll be in touch as soon as we know anything," she said. "We'll just have a quick shufti around outside before we leave."

"Right you are," said Beddoes. "Please keep me informed."

"We will."

Patricia Beddoes lingered behind her husband, her hand on his shoulder. "Thank you for the tea, Mrs. Beddoes," said Doug Wilson, ever the polite young man.

"You're welcome. Good-bye."

Once they had put their rain gear on again, Annie and Doug Wilson squelched over to the garage where John Beddoes had housed the tractor. PC Valentine had examined it earlier, of course, and they saw nothing he hadn't mentioned in his report. It looked like a crowbar job, Annie thought. The entire metal housing had been prized from the wooden door, and the heavy padlock that lay in the mud was still intact. Annie took a photo of it in situ with her mobile phone, then dug a plastic bag out of her pocket and carefully picked up the lock using the end of a pencil and dropped it in the bag.

"A kid could have broken into that garage in five seconds," Annie said in disgust. "Come on, Doug. We'll send some CSIs to poke around in the mud when we get back to the station. There's no hurry."

"Poor Beddoes," said Wilson, as the windscreen wipers slid into action and the police Volvo shuddered to life.

"Oh, I wouldn't feel too sorry for him. That BMW over there looks new to me. And as you said, it's an expensive tractor."

Annie made herself as comfortable as possible in the passenger seat, rubbing at the steamed-up window beside her. Unlike Banks, whom she felt always needed to be in control, she didn't care who was driving. In fact, all the better if it wasn't her. She didn't like driving, especially in this weather. And there were too many arseholes on the roads these days, no matter what the weather. This week wasn't starting out well, she thought. It was only midmorning on Monday, but already her back was aching, and she wanted nothing more than to go home and have a long hot bath with a pile of trashy gossip magazines.

WHEN DS Winsome Jackman arrived at the abandoned airfield, there was already a patrol car parked at the gate and two uniformed officers, one of them enjoying a cigarette, were talking to a man through the chain-link fence. The man was tall and slim, wearing a camouflage jacket, waterproof trousers, sturdy walking boots and a baseball hat, black with a stylized white "A's" on the front. He was taller than Winsome, but stooped a little and leaned on a walking stick. Whether it was a rambler's prop or a genuine need, she couldn't tell. It was also hard to tell how old he was under the baseball cap, but he seemed too young to be needing a walking stick unless he'd had an accident. There was something vaguely familiar about him, Winsome felt, but she couldn't put her finger on it. A beagle sat quietly by his side, nose twitching as Winsome appeared.

The uniformed constable introduced herself and dropped her cigarette and trod on it as Winsome approached. Winsome had been told by dispatch that someone had reported seeing what he thought was a bloodstain in a disused hangar near the railway line. It was her job to go over there and assess the situation, weigh up the pros and cons of bringing in an expensive CSI team. The wind tugged at her hair and seemed to permeate the very marrow of her bones. The rain felt like a cold shower.

"What have we got?" Winsome asked.

"They're padlocked shut, ma'am," said one of the officers, pointing at the gates. "There's nothing urgent, so we thought it best to wait for you."

Winsome looked at the man inside. She couldn't help but see him as a man imprisoned in some sort of prison camp or compound. He had a military air about him—that was what had eluded her for the first few moments—though she would have been hard pushed to put her finger on what made her think that. "How did you get in there, Mr. . . . ?"

"Gilchrist. Terry Gilchrist. There's a gap around the side. I wouldn't recommend it, though. It's a tight squeeze, and it's mucky down there." He gestured to the mud-stained front of his jacket and knees of his trousers. Winsome was wearing black jeans and a belted winter coat, not exactly her best outfit, but not something she wanted to drag through the mud, either. She guessed that the uniformed officers also hadn't liked the idea of crawling through a hole in the fence and getting their uniforms dirty. "Do you know who owns the place?"

"Government, probably. You coming in?"

Winsome sighed. "A good detective always comes prepared," she said, and returned to her car. She opened the boot, took out a torch and a pair of bolt cutters and approached the gates. She handed the torch through the fence to Gilchrist, and with one quick hard snip of the bolt cutters she snapped open the padlock, which clattered to the concrete. Then, with Gilchrist's help, she pushed the gates open. They grated as they followed the semicircular grooves already etched in the crumbling concrete. They might not have been opened frequently, Winsome noted, but they had certainly been opened occasionally, and quite recently by the looks of the tracks.

Gilchrist smiled at her. "Thanks for rescuing me," he said. "I was beginning to feel I'd never get out of here."

Winsome smiled back. "You won't. Not yet for a while."

Gilchrist turned. "Follow me."

As he walked toward the hangar entrance, the dog trotting by his side, his stick clicked on the concrete. Winsome could see by the way he limped that the walking stick was no affectation. What had happened, then? An accident? A war wound?

Winsome paused in the doorway and took in the hangar. She imagined you could fit a few planes in here, at a pinch. She had no idea how many Lancasters or Spitfires there were in a squadron, or even if the hangar had been used during wartime. Her grandfather on her mother's side had fought in the Second World War, she remembered, and he had been killed somewhere in Normandy shortly after the D-Day landings. She doubted that there were a lot of fellow Jamaicans with him; he must have been very scared and lonely for his own people. A place like this made her think about such things.

Gilchrist stood by an area of the concrete floor and the dog's tail started wagging. Winsome went and stood beside him, taking her torch and holding it up, at eye level, shining the light down on the floor.

On the patch of cracked concrete Gilchrist pointed to, Winsome saw a large dark stain shaped like the continent of South America. It certainly resembled congealed blood. There was a familiar smell of decaying matter, too. She squatted closer. Just around where Brazil would have been, she saw fragments of bone and gray matter stuck to the scarlet stain. Brains, she thought, reaching for her mobile. Maybe they were both wrong, maybe it was paint, or a mixture of water and rust, but now that she had seen it for herself, she could understand exactly why Gilchrist had been concerned enough to ring the police. It could be animal blood, of course, but a simple test would determine that.

Winsome keyed in the station number, explained the situation and asked for AC Gervaise to be informed and for the forensics bloodstain analyst, Jasminder Singh, and DC Gerry Masterson to come out to check the blood at the hangar.

THE LANE farm seemed a lot less grand than the Beddoes spread, Annie thought, as DC Doug Wilson parked behind a muddy Rav 4 outside the front porch, a cobwebbed repository for inside-out umbrellas, Wellington boots and a couple of rusty shovels. The farmhouse was smaller and shabbier, with a few slates missing from the roof and a drainpipe leaning at a precarious angle, water dripping from the gutter. The yard seemed neglected, and the outbuildings were fewer in number. They looked old and in need of repair. One barn was practically in ruins. A couple of skinny chickens pecked at the wet ground inside their sagging wire coop. Annie doubted that Frank Lane had a

Deutz-Fahr Agrotron locked in his garage, if his garage even had a lock, and she wondered what the relationship between the two farmers really was. Beddoes hadn't given much away, but surely Lane had to envy the newcomer's obvious wealth? Or resent it? And was Beddoes patronizing or honestly supportive of his neighbors? Perhaps in their eyes he was merely playing at being a farmer while they were living the very real hardship of it. He had hinted at so much himself. These considerations might matter down the line, she told herself.

She and DC Wilson got out of the car and tried to avoid the worst of the mud, which seemed even squelchier than that at the Beddoes farm. At least the rain had abated to a steady drizzle over the short drive, and there were now a few patches of blue sky visible through the cloud cover. Not enough "to make baby a new bonnet," as her father used to say, but a small handkerchief, perhaps.

Annie knocked on the door, which was opened by a broad-shouldered man in his mid forties. Wearing jeans and a wrinkled shirt, he had a whiskered, weather-beaten face that conformed more closely to Annie's idea of a farmer. Satisfied by their credentials, he invited them in. There was a weariness and heaviness about his movements that told Annie he had perhaps been overdoing it for years, maybe for lack of help, or that the stress of survival was eating away at him. Farming was a hard physical job and often involved long hours of backbreaking work with little or no relief, though it was also seasonal and subject to the vagaries of the weather. But whereas Beddoes had seemed fit and fluent in his movements, Lane seemed hunched over and cramped up.

The living room smelled musty and stale, no scented air freshener. No offer of tea, either. Everything in the living area demonstrated the same quality of neglect and plain utility as the farmyard itself.

Frank Lane moved some newspapers aside and bade them sit on the worn sofa while he settled himself into what was no doubt his usual armchair by the fireplace. There were cigarette burns on the armrest beside an overflowing glass ashtray.

When everyone had made themselves as comfortable as possible, and Doug Wilson had taken out his pen and notebook, Lane looked at Annie as if to tell her to get on with it.

"We're here about your neighbor's tractor, Mr. Lane. I understand Mr. Beddoes asked you to keep an eye on his place while he and his wife were on holiday in Mexico?"

"Aye," said Lane, lighting a cigarette. "Bloody Mexico. I ask you. But you can't keep your eye on a place unless you're living there, can you, and I've more than enough to do here. I did my best."

"I'm sure you did," said Annie. "Nobody's saying it was your fault. But how did you manage it? What did your duties consist of?"

"I drove over there every day, fed the pigs and chickens, checked that everything was still under lock and key. He never told me to keep a particular eye on his tractor. I saw nowt amiss."

"That's very neighborly of you."

Lane gave a harsh laugh. "Neighborliness has nothing to do with it. Beddoes paid me well enough."

"Ah, I see."

"A man deserves to be paid for his labor. And it's not as if he can't afford it."

"When was the last time you checked on the place?"

"Saturday. Day before they got back."

"You didn't go over on Sunday?"

"No. They were supposed to be back by early morning. How was I to know they'd have problems with their flights? Nobody phoned me or anything."

"And everything was in order on Saturday?"

"It was. Or I'd have said something then, wouldn't I?"

Annie sighed internally. *Here we go again.* She was used to this type of cantankerous and patronizing Yorkshireman, but she still didn't have to like it. "What time was this?"

"Late afternoon. Around five."

"So the tractor was probably stolen sometime after dark on Saturday night?"

"It were still locked up at five when I left. Make sense to steal it after dark, wouldn't it?"

"Were you at home on Saturday night?"

"I'm always at home, unless I'm out in the fields. You might not have noticed, young lady, but it's lambing season, and with no help that means long days and even longer nights. Those young 'uns don't always know the most convenient time to be born."

"Did you notice anything wrong at all while you were over at the Beddoes place during the week? Hear anything? See anything?"

"No. But that's not surprising. If you've been up there, you'll know there's a fair bit of distance between us. Two miles, at least, as the crow flies."

"Yes, but I think you'd probably hear a tractor starting up, for example, wouldn't you?"

Lane's face cracked into a mocking smile. "You don't think they just got on it and drove it out of there, do you? They'd have needed summat to take it away, a flatbed lorry or summat."

"There would have been some noise," said Annie, blushing at her mistake. "A lorry, van, flatbed, whatever."

"Aye, but you hear lorries and cars from time to time. Even tractors. Nothing unusual about that in the countryside."

"In the middle of the night?"

"When your days are as busy as mine, you sleep like a log. I wouldn't have heard the bloody Angel of Doom blowing his trumpet. I said I didn't hear owt unusual, and I didn't. I'd have reported it if I had, wouldn't I?"

"What were you doing here on Saturday night?"

"Watching telly, when I finally got the chance. Not that it's any of your business. Then sleeping."

"Might Mrs. Lane have heard something?"

Lane snorted. "Not unless she's developed superhuman powers. She's stopping with her mother out Whitby way."

"Oh. Is her mother ill?"

"No. More's the pity. Old bag's as fit as a fiddle and twice as squeaky."

"So your wife's on holiday?"

"I suppose you could call it that." Lane snorted. "Extended leave."

Annie sighed. "Mr. Lane," she said, "I'm just trying to get some basic information here."

"Well, the basic information, if it's any of your business, which it isn't, is that she's gone. Left. Bolted. Buggered off. And good riddance.

Been gone two years now, and she still hasn't got out of the old bag's clutches. Serves her bloody well right, is what I say."

"I'm sorry to hear that, Mr. Lane."

"Don't be," Lane snapped, his face darkening. "I'm not. Though what it's got to do with Beddoes's tractor I don't know."

"We just try to gather as much background information as we can, sir," Doug Wilson chimed in. "It's perfectly routine."

Lane gave Wilson a withering glance. "Has anyone ever told you you look just like that bloke who plays Harry Potter?"

Wilson reddened.

"Watch them with your son, did you, Mr. Lane?" Annie said. "The Harry Potter films?"

"Leave my son out of it."

"Is he here? Can we have a word with him? Maybe he heard something."

Lane stubbed his cigarette out viciously in the ashtray. Sparks flew onto the upholstery. It was a wonder he hadn't burned the place down years ago, Annie thought.

"He doesn't live here anymore. He says there's nowt for a young lad in this life, around this place. Nowt to do, nowt worth doing. Nowt but hard graft. I just about reckon he might be right."

"So what does he do?" Annie persisted.

"Don't ask me. He lives in town. Wanted his own 'space.' I can't help it if he's drinking himself silly, like they do, or smoking Ecstasy."

Annie stopped herself from telling him that people don't usually smoke Ecstasy. It would only antagonize him further. "Is your son involved with drugs, Mr. Lane?"

"I've no idea. He doesn't confide in me."

"But you brought it up."

"It was just something you say. I didn't mean owt by it. Maybe he does, maybe he doesn't. Can't say as I care one way or another."

Annie didn't believe that. She sensed that under Lane's brittle anger and truculence were sadness, regret and guilt. Perhaps even love. But the anger and self-pity went deep, she felt. She knew from experience that people don't always have the patience, or the skill, to cut through someone's layers of aggression and unpleasantness to whatever kindness and vulnerability might lie below. Sometimes they might try for a while, then they realize life is too short, so they cut their losses and leave, move on to someone else, maybe, someone more open, someone easier to be with. Perhaps that was what both his wife and his son had done.

"What's his name?" Annie asked.

"We christened him Michael, but he goes by Mick. Why?"

"I understand he was in a bit of trouble some time ago. Something to do with a stolen car?"

"Silly bugger. It were nowt, really. Storm in a teacup."

"Even so, he got probation."

"They give kids probation as soon as look at them these days. It doesn't mean owt. Used to be ASBOs. Now it's something else. And community service."

"How old is he?"

"Nineteen."

"Where is he living in Eastvale?"

"I don't know the number, but it's one of them tower blocks. That rough estate. As if he didn't have a good home of his own. He's living with some tart, apparently."

Annie knew where Lane meant. The East Side Estate was the oldest and roughest housing estate in town. She ought to be able to find Mick Lane there easily enough. "He's living with a woman?"

"So he said."

"Who?"

"Dunno. He hasn't exactly brought her home for tea. But if she's living in a council flat, it stands to reason she's a slapper, doesn't it?"

Annie knew the East Side Estate and some of its denizens, but that didn't mean she agreed with Lane's opinion. "Do you still see Mick at all?"

"He drops by from time to time."

"Does he own a car?"

"A used Peugeot. Falling to bits."

"When was the last time he came here?"

"About two weeks ago."

"Does he have a job?" Annie asked.

"Hasn't mentioned one."

"Any particular skills?"

"Well, he weren't much use around the farm, that's for sure. Oh, he was all right with the manual labor, and he was good with the sheep, shearing and all. But he hasn't it in him to be a real farmer. Too lazy. He can draw and paint, I'll give him that, for all the use it is."

Annie was just about getting to the end of her tether with Frank Lane. Her father, Ray, was an artist, and drawing and painting had been a lot of use to him. Annie sketched and painted, herself, though only as a hobby, like Beddoes farmed. "How do you manage without your wife and son, up here all alone?"

"I get by. I don't mind being alone. I get plenty of peace and quiet. But I have to pay for help when I need it, don't I? Cuts into the savings, what's left of them. This isn't a one-man job, you know, especially when you get to harvesttime, or planting, or sheep shearing. Or lambing."

"It sounds like a hard life."

Lane grunted and lit another cigarette.

Annie coughed. He didn't react. "How do you get on with John Beddoes?" she asked.

For the first time, Lane seemed to think for some time before answering. "Beddoes is all right, I suppose," he said grudgingly. "For an amateur, that is. He's a bit full of himself, but there's nowt I can really fault him on. Or that wife of his. Patricia. Been good to me, they have, since Katie left. Not their fault they had more advantages in life."

"What do you mean?"

"Incomers, aren't they? City folk. Only been here seven years." He rubbed his thumb and index finger together. "Gentleman farmer. Hobbyist. Got a chip on his shoulder about it, too. Thinks we look down on him. Mebbe we do. I were raised to it. This farm was my father's, and his father's before him. Goes back as long as you like. John Beddoes bought his farm off Ned Fairbairn when it got too much for him to manage by himsen. Nowt wrong in that. Things change. And it meant a bit of extra land for me at a good price when I needed it. But it helps when you've got money behind you, doesn't it?"

"What money?"

"Beddoes were something big in t'City. Banking or stockbroking or whatever they do down there. Big finance. All a bunch of thieves, if you ask me. He paid me well enough for taking care of his farm, and I can use the money. I'm sorry about his tractor, but there really was nowt I could do short of stand guard over his yard all week. A fancy Kraut tractor and all. Asking for trouble around here, that is. God knows what he thinks he needs it for." He pointed a fat finger at Annie. "It's you lot should be paying more attention to crime around these parts. How often do we get a patrol car up here?"

"We do our best, Mr. Lane," said Annie. "But it's a bit like farming—good help's thin on the ground these days, and there's a lot of territory to cover."

"Aye, well . . . summat ought to be done."

"Do the Beddoeses have any children?" Annie asked.

"Not as they've ever mentioned."

There didn't seem much more to say. Wilson put away his notebook and they walked to the door. Lane remained motionless in his armchair, smoking and staring into space. He didn't say good-bye.

"Well, that was fun," said Annie as the car lurched back down the track to the road. Then she noticed something she hadn't seen on the way in: what looked like several rows of dead mice nailed to the wooden fence. At second glance, they seemed too large to be mice, she thought, and she gave a little shudder. Rats, perhaps?

"What the hell are those?" she asked Wilson, a well-known expert on all things Yorkshire.

"Moles," he said, turning to grin at her. "The mole catcher nails them there."

"Good Lord. Why?"

"To show he's doing his job," said Wilson. "And as a warning, of course."

"A warning to who?"

"Other moles."

TERRY GILCHRIST lived in an old farm laborer's cottage about a hundred yards west of the village of Drewick, from which he was separated by a patchwork field of allotments dotted with greenhouses and potting sheds. Gilchrist had his own garden, which Winsome could see through the window was well tended, even though everything was drooping under the weight of the rain, or bent by the wind. Beyond the allotments, apart from the square-towered Norman church and a couple of limestone and millstone manor houses, Drewick was almost entirely a postwar village with a few shops, a community hall and a pub, about halfway between Northallerton and Thirsk. Most of the houses were redbrick, with red pantile roofs, and consisted generally of bungalows and semis, with a few short terraces running off at right angles from the high street. The house was only a mile or so from the hangar, and she had thought it best to take him back home for a quick chat rather than stand out in the wind and rain. She had detailed the patrol car officers to guard the scene until Gerry and Jasminder arrived.

Gilchrist took her coat and offered her a cup of tea, which Winsome gratefully accepted. She could see him grimace with pain as he stood, and she offered to help. "Can I do it?"

"No. I'm used to it, thank you. Back in a jiffy."

Winsome took out her notebook and prepared some questions while he was away. He soon came back with the teapot and mugs, and as he poured, Winsome studied him more closely. She realized that he was much younger than his injury made him seem. War had aged him. The Blair Folly started in 2003 with the invasion of Iraq, and the Afghanistan fiasco had been going on even longer. If Gilchrist had been a young lad when he started out in, say, 2000, he could easily be somewhere between thirty and forty now. It was impossible to tell. He had a fine head of fair hair, a strong jaw and clear blue eyes. He was even taller than Winsome, and he had a soldier's bearing, but he also had a slight stoop, and the limp, of course. Though he seemed a little shy, there was something solid and dependable about his presence and Winsome felt safe in his company. Not that she normally felt unsafe, but it was a definite feeling, and one she wasn't used to. She found herself wondering whether the wound embarrassed him, if that was what made him appear awkward and shy. After a sip of Earl Grey, she got down to business. "Have you ever noticed anything odd about the hangar before?"

Gilchrist patted his dog. "I didn't even notice anything this time. Peaches was off the leash and wouldn't come back. That seemed unusual, so I went to get her."

"That's never happened before?"

"No."

"How long have you lived here?"

Gilchrist gazed around the room. "I grew up here. This house belonged to my parents. They died while I was overseas. Car crash. Ironic, isn't it? There am I dodging bullets and they get killed by a drunk driver who walks away without a scratch." He shrugged. "Anyway, I'm an only child. The mortgage was paid off. I inherited."

There seemed both anger and resignation in Gilchrist's sense of irony. Winsome had known one or two soldiers whose experience of combat had isolated them from their fellow man, but Gilchrist didn't seem like that—just wounded and angry. She picked up the threads of the conversation. "How long have you been back from . . ."

"Afghanistan. Helmand Province. It's OK to say it. Little over a year."

"How often do you take Peaches walking there, by the airfield?"

"Every now and then, maybe once a week or so."

"You knew about the hole in the wire, then?"

"Yes. I think it's always been there. I used to play there myself and I've seen the local kids crawling in and out. But kids can usually find a way to get in anywhere, can't they? They're all right. They don't do any harm. The younger ones play cricket and footie, and the older ones maybe down a few cans of cheap lager, kiss and cuddle with their girlfriends. They've nowhere else to go, poor sods. Where's the harm?"

"Was there anything else going on out there that you know of? I mean kids might get into fights, might even organize them. What about cockfighting, that sort of thing?"

Gilchrist shook his head. "I've never seen anything or heard any rumors of anything like that. I've seen lorries coming and going once or twice. Other than that, nothing."

"Lorries? Since when?"

"Just the past year or so. Since I've been here alone."

"How often?"

Gilchrist thought for a moment. "Maybe three or four times over the year. It's not a regular thing."

Gerry Masterson could always check on what companies had the use of the place, if any, Winsome thought. If it came to that. "You said you think the government owns the land."

"Just a wild guess. I've no idea, really. It's been like that as long as I can remember. All I know is it was used as an air force base during the last war. Nice and flat around here, see, edge of the Vale of Mowbray, and most of the trees weren't here back then. They were planted when Drewick was built in the fifties, to shelter it from the railway, I suppose. There was talk of building more houses on the airfield land a few years ago, but nothing ever came of that, and now it's supposed to become a shopping center. You ask me, people don't want to live that close to the train tracks. It's a busy line these days. London or the West Country to Scotland. And you can't go wrong with a shopping center, can you?"

Winsome had used the East Coast train line often enough. Plenty of people lived close to the railway lines, she thought, remembering gazing dreamily over backyards with their rabbit hutches, dilapidated brick outhouses, washing hanging on lines and old tires hanging from tree branches on train rides she had taken over the past few years. But perhaps Gilchrist was right, and such sites were becoming less popular for housing estates these days. A shopping center would make more sense. Out of the way, background noise no problem.

She couldn't think of anything else to ask Gilchrist for the moment, not until she had a better idea about what might have happened in the hangar. She stayed and chatted for a while longer, finishing her tea, then said she had better get back to the airfield to meet her colleagues. Gilchrist helped her on with her coat, and as she slipped her arms easily in the sleeves, she thought how pleasant it was to have someone do that for her.

2

BANKS WASN'T DUE BACK AT WORK UNTIL TUESDAY, but he felt restless and took a taxi to Eastvale police headquarters straight from Durham Tees Valley airport on Monday morning, dropping Oriana off at home on the way. He had enjoyed a wonderful weekend in a village on Lake Trasimeno, looking out over the Isola Polvese, with Oriana and her extended Italian family. Her parents lived in Yorkshire, as did Oriana herself, but there seemed to be a whole village full of aunts, uncles, nieces, nephews and cousins in Umbria. Most of the time Banks and Oriana spent eating fresh fish from the lake, talking and drinking the local Montefalco wines and going for long walks by the lake or in the nearby countryside, by olive groves, vineyards and winding brooks.

And now they were back in wet and windy Yorkshire.

He dumped his bags and hung up his raincoat in his office. He had taken with him only a small weekend bag for clothes and toiletries, along with his battered leather satchel, in which he carried his essentials—iPod, mobile phone, a book, notebook, pen, a couple of magazines, wallet and keys. There were no messages for him, and everything was as he had left it last Thursday. He walked along the unusually silent corridor to the squad room and found only DC Gerry Masterson there, tapping away at her computer.

"Gerry, what's up?"

"You're back early, sir. Everything all right?"

"Everything's fine. I'm fresh from the plane. Seeing as I'm back, I thought I might as well come by and find out if anything's been happening in my absence."

"You're a glutton for punishment, sir."

"Where is everyone?"

"At this very moment? I'm not exactly sure."

"In general will do. Is there some sort of flap on?"

Gerry leaned back in her chair and linked her hands behind her head. Her luxuriant red Pre-Raphaelite hair was tied back so it stayed out of her eyes as she worked. "No flap," she said. "Basically, we've got a stolen tractor, which DI Cabbot and DC Wilson are investigating, and a mysterious bloodstain, which DC Jackman is attending to."

"Major crimes, indeed." Banks grabbed Doug Wilson's empty chair and sat facing Gerry's desk. "Do tell me more."

"Not much more to tell, sir. You've just missed Doug. He was back briefly checking out some names in connection with the stolen tractor. They're searching for a lad called Mick Lane."

"Never heard of him."

"His dad's a neighbor of Mr. Beddoes, whose tractor was stolen."

"It just gets more and more exciting, doesn't it?"

Gerry laughed. "Yes, sir. Maybe you should have stayed in Umbria?"

"I should be so lucky. And the bloodstain?"

"A chap called Terry Gilchrist claims he came across it walking his dog. The AC decided to send DS Jackman to check it out."

"Is AC Gervaise in her office?"

"Meeting at County HQ." Gerry's telephone rang. "Excuse me, sir."

"Of course." Banks stood up and went back to his own office, wondering which of the major crimes that had occurred in his absence required his immediate attention. Stolen tractor or possible bloodstain? The tractor wasn't the first piece of expensive farm equipment to go missing over the past few months, and they had nothing resembling a lead so far. Perhaps this Lane boy Gerry said they were looking for would provide the break they needed.

Moments later, Gerry Masterson popped her head around the door.

"That was dispatch, sir. DS Jackman just called in from that aban-doned airfield near Drewick, on the other side of the A1."

"I know the place," said Banks.

"It seems our amateur bloodstain expert was right on the mark. Winsome's found what she thinks is a pool of congealed blood in the old hangar there. They've already sent more patrol cars, and Ms. Singh is on her way."

"Right," said Banks, grabbing his raincoat and satchel. "It's proba-bly a fox or something, but I'll take a possible human bloodstain over a stolen tractor any day. What are we waiting for?"

ANNIE DISCOVERED that Mick Lane had been arrested eighteen months ago for stealing a car and taking it for a joyride that resulted in more than two thousand pounds' worth of damage. Not a fancy German tractor, just a knockabout Honda, but even so, Annie thought, young Lane merited further investigation. He had got off with com-munity service, supervised by a probation officer, as he had been only seventeen at the time, and it had been his first offense. He seemed to have acquitted himself well and had not reoffended. Or he hadn't been caught. It was early days yet. Also, Annie had learned that, according to his probation officer, Mick Lane was living in a flat on the East Side Estate with a twenty-eight-year-old woman called Alex Preston. She had a four-year-old shoplifting charge on her record and an eight-year-old son called Ian to care for. Whether she was still up to her thieving tricks, the probation officer didn't seem to know, but her name wasn't known around the station. Maybe Mick Lane had made an honest woman of her?

Rain suited the East Side Estate, Annie thought, as Doug Wilson pulled up outside the block of flats. It looked too dirty, too bright and too brittle in sunlight. Along with its twin, it had been rushed up in the first Wilson era, that flush period when "progress" and "the white heat of technology" were the buzzwords. Architecturally, the best that could be said about the buildings was that they hadn't fallen down yet. Socially, many people wished they had. Luckily, there were only two tower blocks, and they were only ten stories high. As beautiful a market town as it was, and as attractive to tourists, Eastvale was slightly outside the borders of the Yorkshire Dales National Park, so not subject to its stringent building rules, or there wouldn't have been any East Side Estate at all, let alone tower blocks. Mustn't trouble the tourists with eyesores like that.

"Shall I put the Krook lock on?" Wilson asked.

"Nah," said Annie. "Don't bother. What's the point? It's not likely to stop anyone around here if they want to drive off with a police car. Bolt cutters come with the territory."

"Watch it, guv," said Wilson. "I grew up on an estate like this. You're maligning my social background. You can get done for that. It's not politically correct."

"Sorry. Is that right? I thought you grew up in the country. You seem to know plenty about mole catchers and so on."

"Just familiarizing myself with the territory. I like to take an interest in many things."

"You really grew up on an estate like this?"

"Worse." Wilson adjusted his glasses. "In Sheffield. It's not something I'd lie about, or brag about, either. Actually, it wasn't as bad as people think. We were lucky. We had decent neighbors. Give you the shirt off their back, they would. Or off someone's back, at any rate."

Annie laughed. "Come on."

They walked toward the lift and Wilson pressed the button.

"You know, if this were on telly," Annie said, "the lift would be out of order, and we'd have to walk up eight flights of stairs through a gauntlet of drugged-up hoodies flashing knives."

"Or if it worked," said Wilson, "it'd be covered in graffiti and stink of piss."

The lift shuddered to a halt, and the doors slid open. The inside was covered in graffiti and stank of piss. They got in anyway. Annie held her nose and pressed the button for the eighth floor. The doors closed, but nothing happened. She tried again. Still nothing. After a moment's panic—Annie had always been claustrophobic in lifts—the "doors open" button worked, and they got out and walked. In the fifth-floor stairwell, they had to push their way through a gang of hoodies. Someone made a remark about Harry Potter after they had passed, and they all laughed. Wilson turned beet red and reached up to take off his glasses. Annie grabbed his elbow to stop him going back and thumping the one who had spoken. "Not worth it, Dougal. Not worth it. Easy does it. It's probably just the glasses, you know."

"Yes, guv," he said through clenched teeth. "Think I'll make an appointment with the optometrist tomorrow and get fitted with some contact lenses."

"That should help," Annie said. "And maybe if you could do something with your hair, and lose the wand . . ."

Wilson turned and started to glare at her, then his face broke into a smile. "Right. I'll do that, too."

"Here we are," said Annie. "Eighth floor."

They walked along the balcony between the windows and doors and the midriff-high fence, past bicycles without wheels, a pram and an abandoned fridge almost blocking their path. It was a hell of a view, Annie had to admit. If you turned to the west, you could see over the railway tracks to Eastvale, the castle ruins, the market square, the river falls, and beyond that, Hindswell Woods and the rising slopes of the dales farther on, all tinged gray by mist and rain. She could also see Eastvale's "millionaires' row," where Banks's new girlfriend Oriana lived and where people paid a fortune for the same view. And a big house, of course. Perhaps a bit more peace and quiet and less crime, too.

Annie knocked on the door. A few moments later a young woman answered it on the chain and frowned at them. "Yes?" she said, nervously touching her cheek. "What is it? Can I help you?"

"Alex Preston?"

The woman nodded.

"Police," said Annie, flashing her warrant card. "Mind if we come in for a chat, love?"

"Is it about Ian? Nothing's happened to him, has it? Or Michael?"

"Nothing's happened to anyone as far as we know."

"That's a relief." The woman took off the chain and opened the door. It led directly into the living room.

Annie realized that she was probably as prejudiced as the next person, except Frank Lane, when it came to life on the East Side Estate—you got a blinkered view of such things when you were a copper—so she was surprised to see how clean and tidy the small flat was inside. Alex Preston clearly did the best she could with what little she had. The furniture, if inexpensive, was relatively new, polished and well kept, the walls a tasteful pastel, with small, framed photographic prints strategically placed here and there. The air smelled of pine freshener. The flat-screen TV didn't dominate the room, but sat peacefully in its corner, out of the way until it was needed. An electric fire with fake coals stood in the fake fireplace, and framed photographs of a smiling young towheaded boy stood on the mantelpiece. There were also a couple of shots of Alex with a young man, whom Annie took to be Mick Lane.

Of course, Annie's prejudice hadn't vanished entirely, nor had her suspicious nature. She found herself wondering just how and where Alex Preston and Mick Lane had got the money for all this.

"Can I make you a cup of tea?" Alex asked. "I'm afraid we don't have any coffee. Neither of us drinks it."

"No, thanks," said Annie. "Maybe a glass of water? Those stairs . . ."

"I'm sorry about the lift. It's got a mind of its own, hasn't it? Sometimes it works, sometimes it doesn't. We've been trying to get the council to fix it for weeks now, but you know what they're like. Especially when it comes to this estate."

Annie could guess.

Alex fetched them each a glass of water and sat down in the armchair, leaning forward, clasping her hands in her lap. She was wearing jeans and a T-shirt, showing to advantage her shapely figure. Fluffy blue slippers with pink pompoms added a homely touch. Her blond hair, which looked natural to Annie's trained eye, was tied back in a ponytail. Young and fresh-faced, she wore hardly any makeup and needed none. Her complexion was pale and flawless, she had a slightly upturned nose, a wide mouth and big eyes, a dark, beguiling shade of blue. Young Doug Wilson seemed smitten, at any rate. Annie gestured for him to stop gawping and get out his notebook. He fumbled with his ballpoint pen.

"What is it you want?" Alex asked, sitting forward in her chair, the small frown of concern still wrinkling her smooth forehead. "Are you sure nothing's wrong? It's not Ian, is it? Has something happened to Ian?"

"Ian? That's your son, isn't it?"

"Yes. He's eight. He's supposed to be at school."

"Then I'm sure that's where he is. This isn't about Ian, Ms. Preston."

Alex Preston seemed to relax again. "Well, that's good to know," she said. "And call me Alex, please. Kids. You never stop worrying. The older kids mostly leave him alone, but now and then they tease him a bit. They're not so bad, really." Then the frown reappeared. "What is it then? It's not Ian, and you said nothing's happened to Michael."

Michael, Annie noticed. Not Mick, as his father had called him. "Not as far as we know," she said. "But we would like to talk to him. Do you know where he is?"

"That's just it. That's why I was worried when you knocked at the door. I haven't seen him since yesterday morning. I'm starting to get worried."

"He does live here, though, doesn't he?"

Alex smiled. It was a radiant smile, Annie thought. "Yes. I know you all probably think I'm a cradle snatcher, got myself a toy boy. Don't think I haven't heard it all. But . . . it's hard to explain . . . we're . . . well, you know, it's the real thing." She blushed a light pink and made a self-mocking expression. "True love."

"None of my business," said Annie.

"I just wanted you to know. That's all. And he's really great with Ian. The two of them just get along so well."

"Where do you think Michael might be?"

"Well, he said he was going to meet someone about a job, and after that he might go and drop in on his dad later. They aren't on the best of terms, and it worried Michael. He knew he'd upset his father and let him down, especially after his mum left. He acted up, stole a car and all. I'm sure you know all about that, being police. They had a serious falling-out. They got over it to some extent, but things are still . . . well, difficult. I think it's partly my fault, you know, being older, having a child. His father doesn't approve."

"Did he say *where* he was going on this job?"

"No."

"Was that unusual?"

"No, not really. He doesn't always give a full account of his comings and goings. I don't expect him to. I find that sort of thing can stifle a relationship, don't you?"

Chance would be a fine thing, thought Annie. "And he said after that he might drop in on his father, even though they were on bad terms?"

"Yes."

"Has he done this before? Stopped out all night?"

"No. Not like this. I mean, once or twice he's stopped over at his father's, if they've had a few drinks, like, and got to talking, or if it's really late. But he always phones or texts."

"Not this time?"

"No, nothing. I've tried ringing him, and texting, but I got no response."

"No need to worry," Annie said. "His mobile's probably run out of power."

"It's always doing that. Like his camera. He's not very good with keeping his stuff charged."

"Which mobile provider does he use?"

"Virgin pay-as-you-go."

"Did you phone the farm? I noticed Mr. Lane has a landline when we were there earlier."

Alex glanced away. "Yes. His father just grunted, like, said he hadn't seen him. Then he hung up."

"You said that Mick Lane and his father still have a problematic relationship."

"Michael. Yes." Alex paused. "I can see you're both a bit confused. I think I know what you're thinking. I don't mean to be rude, but you're police, and you have a very narrow way of seeing things. You saw that Michael was on probation, that he did community service for the stolen car, and then you found out he was living with me, an older woman in a council flat, with an illegitimate child and a conviction for shoplifting. Well, you put two and two together and make . . . I don't know what. Bonnie and Clyde, maybe? It's only natural. I don't blame you. Michael's dad's the same. But it's not like that at all. I don't deny I've done some bad things, and I got caught. I don't know how I sank so low, but I did. I've had to face up to that. But people can change."

"What happened?"

"Ian's father walked out on me when Ian was little. I was flat broke. Lenny took everything, even emptied Ian's piggy bank, the miserable bastard. We were hungry. They were taking ages to process my benefits. So I went to the Asda in the shopping center and started filling up my pockets. It was either that or sell my body, and I hadn't sunk that low, though don't think I hadn't received a few offers from people who should have known better. You soon find out who your friends are when you reach rock bottom. I thought I was being careful, you know, but they had CCTV, store detectives, the lot. Took me in a room in the back and scared the wits out of me, pushed me about a bit, threatened me but stopped short of hitting me, then they called the police. Wanted to make an example of me." She gave a harsh laugh. "A couple of hundred years ago they'd have sent me to Australia, and there's some countries in the world today where they'd chop my hand off, but all I got was probation. I was lucky, I suppose. Child Care were round like a shot, of course, but I managed to hang on to Ian, if only because his dad had no interest in taking custody of him. God knows what I'd have done if I'd lost Ian. It was a bad time in my life. A very bad time. But it's over now. I only needed the one lesson."

Pity that doesn't work for everyone, Annie thought, feeling some of her skepticism slough away. "And now?" she asked.

"I'm doing a part-time course. Travel and tourism. Eastvale College. Ever since I was a little girl I've dreamed of seeing the world. I've got a part-time job at GoThereNow—you know, the new travel agency in the Swainsdale Centre—just taking bookings for stag weekends in Prague or Tallinn and stuff. There's not much money in it right now, but when I've finished the course, if I do well, I'm hoping to start leading some tour groups of my own. Today's my day off." She picked up a thick book about the history of Rome from the low coffee table. "Just doing a bit of homework. The history of the Coliseum."

"Won't you be away a lot?" Annie said. "If you're leading tours. What'll happen to Ian?"

"I'll take care of Ian, don't you worry about that. Michael and I will. We'll work it out. Maybe they can come with me? Michael can take photographs for travel magazines."

"Sounds ideal."

Alex shrugged. "Besides, there's school, and the neighbors are great. Well, most of them. Michael helps a lot, too, of course."

"How did you meet Michael?"

"It was a year ago. He was up at the college seeing if he could get into a photography course through the back door. He likes taking pictures. Drawing, too. He's very good at both, got a real eye. He did those." She gestured to the photographs and drawings on the wall that Annie had thought were bought prints. The castle ruins at night. Someone, Mick's father perhaps, shearing a sheep. The river falls in full spate. A charcoal head-and-shoulders sketch of Alex. Annie had an eye for good art and photography herself, and these were very good indeed. She told Alex so.

"Thank you, but to be honest, he might have the talent, but he doesn't have the qualifications, not even A levels, so they turned him down. He spent too much time off school helping out around the farm when he was a young lad. He doesn't have the right equipment, either. All Michael has is an old Cyber-shot. About six pixels. They're up to sixteen or more these days. He needs a better camera, a DSLR, with all the lenses."

"You understand about that sort of stuff?"

Alex cocked her head and gave Annie an appraising glance. "Of course. I'm not stupid. Look, we're poor but we're not destitute, you know. We both work, when we can. We're careful with what we have—have to be—but he'll get a new and better camera soon, especially if he gets into college and I make some progress in my job."

"So you met at the college?"

"Student pub. He was a bit depressed when he came in, and I was serving behind the bar—my previous part-time job. The place was nearly empty. I was revising for my exams. We got talking over a couple of drinks. He told me about his mum leaving and how miserable he was up at the farm with his dad, how he'd gone off the rails a bit, stolen a car, he didn't know why. Didn't know why he was telling me, either. Neither of us really came on to the other. . . . It just . . . you know . . . happened. It felt totally natural. I was lonely, too. I've been here with Ian now for about six years. We got the place when I was still with Lenny and Ian was two, but these past four years we've been on our own. One thing led to another. Funny, but we never thought about the age thing. People say I look younger than I am, and Michael looks older than he is, more mature."

Annie glanced at the photos on the mantelpiece again. Alex was right. They made a handsome couple, seemed natural together, and no casual viewer would notice an age difference. "Where's Lenny now?" she asked.

"God knows. Or cares. Last I heard of him he was working on the ferries from Immingham to Rotterdam. Up to something, no doubt, some scam or other. Lenny was a loser, but it took me a long time to realize it."

"I presume that if Michael does a lot of digital photography, he's got a computer, right?"

"We share mine. I've had it for ages, since before we met. He's just about computer illiterate. I pretty much had to teach him everything he knows. He hadn't used a computer before we got together."

"Not even at school?"

Alex shrugged. "Maybe. He never spoke much about school. He certainly didn't know his way around a computer, anyway."

"We might need to examine it later." It was a delicate situation. Annie knew the rules on computers. No one but a qualified techie was supposed to touch one, and only then after it had been photographed from every angle, including what was showing on the screen and where the various devices were plugged in at the back, front or sides. Although this wasn't a crime scene, if any information gleaned from Michael Lane's computer indicated that a crime, or crimes, had been committed, then its value in court would be greatly diminished if Annie and Doug Wilson had been interfering with it first. On the other hand, she wasn't at a point in her investigation where she had any reason to bring in the CSIs and have it removed. If there was incriminating information on it, there was nothing to stop Alex from erasing everything after Annie left. She decided to have a quick look before then, with Doug Wilson and Alex Preston present as witnesses. She asked Alex if that was all right.

"It's fine with me," said Alex. "Now?"

"Later will do. We have a few more questions first. Does Michael have a steady job at the moment, or has he managed to get into a photography course?"

"He's doing his A levels at night school, so he has a better chance of getting in college next year, if he does well, but he's still unemployed. And it gets him down sometimes. He does odd jobs to help make ends meet."

"What sort of odd jobs?"

"Farming stuff, mostly. That's all he knows, apart from drawing and photography. But there's plenty of it about, depending on the time of year. A lot of it's unskilled, of course. Casual manual labor. Harvesting and such like. But he's got a real knack for sheep shearing, and that makes good money sometimes. But it's all so seasonal. Why are you asking me all these questions? Has something happened to him? Has he had an accident? Or done something stupid?"

"Why would you think that?"

Alex studied the backs of her hands. Annie noticed how long and tapered her fingers were, how nicely manicured and clean the nails. "He can be a bit hotheaded sometimes, that's all. When he gets frustrated. I don't mean with me or Ian. He'd never lay a finger on us, and I'd never stand for it. Not after Lenny. So what is this all about?"

"It's nothing to worry about, really," said Annie. "His father's neighbor's farm was broken into on Saturday night. A valuable tractor was stolen."

"Beddoes?"

"That's right. Do you know him?"

"I've never met him, but Michael mentioned him sometimes."

"In what way?"

"He said Mr. Beddoes never liked him. Used to chase him off his land. Called him a layabout and a retard. Michael said Beddoes seems all right on the surface, but he can be a nasty piece of work when he's got a mind to be."

"Like?"

"He told me Beddoes hit him once."

"John Beddoes hit Michael?"

"That's right. Clipped him around the ear, was how Michael described it. Said it didn't hurt. He didn't even bother telling his dad. And once Beddoes thought Michael had been upsetting his precious pigs, chucking stones at them or something. Beddoes threatened to drop him in the sty and said they'd eat him. Michael was just thirteen or fourteen. He was terrified."

"I see," said Annie. "But that was a long time ago, wasn't it?"

"Not to them, I don't think. Long memories. They bear grudges." Her eyes widened. "Maybe he's done something to Michael? Beddoes. Maybe he blamed him for stealing his tractor?"

"It's unlikely," Annie said. "Mr. and Mrs. Beddoes didn't get back from holiday until late last night. The first thing they did when they noticed the tractor missing was call the police."

"Well, maybe you should talk to them again? Search the premises, or whatever you do."

"Don't worry," said Annie, "we'll be thorough. Has Michael ever threatened Beddoes? You said John Beddoes terrified him when he was younger. Do you think he might have wanted revenge?"

"You think—"

Annie held her hand up. "I don't think anything yet, Alex. I'm only asking. Michael's father was tending to the farm while the owners were away. I talked to John Beddoes, and he mentioned a 'tearaway' son. His words, not mine. Frank Lane didn't speak so highly of his own son, either. Or of you. He said he'd never met you, that Michael had never brought you home for tea to meet him."

"Ha!" said Alex. "As if we were ever invited. He knows nothing about me. To him I'm just the scarlet woman. A tart."

Annie let a few seconds go by. "I just want to talk to Michael," she said. "That's all."

Alex gave Annie a disappointed glance, and for some reason, it hurt. "You're all the same, you lot. Just because someone's made a mistake once, you think they can never put things right, don't you? Well, me and Michael are doing just fine. OK? And he was here with me on Saturday night, all evening and all night, but I don't suppose you believe that, do you?"

"Why wouldn't I believe you?" said Annie. "You say you last saw him on Sunday morning?"

"That's right."

"Do you think he might have another girlfriend, and that's where he is?"

Alex reddened, and her lower lip trembled. "No," she said, squeezing her fists together and putting them to her temples. "What are you saying? Why are you saying horrible things like that? What are you trying to do to me? I'm already going out of my mind with worry. Stop this."

"I'm sorry," said Annie, "but we have to know what's going on."

"Why don't you just do your job and go out and find Michael? He might be lying hurt somewhere."

"Where?"

"I don't know. Just somewhere."

"OK, I'm sorry. Calm down, Alex. We'll get to the bottom of this."

"You're more interested in a missing tractor than in what's happened to my Michael. Admit it."

"That's not true."

Alex leaned forward and clasped her hands together. "Then help me," she said. "Please help me find Michael."

THE FRONT gates stood wide open and a young uniformed constable waved down Banks and Gerry Masterson as they approached the air-field. Gerry came to a halt, and the officer asked for their identification. Banks didn't blame him. The young PC wasn't from Eastvale HQ, and there was no reason he should know who they were. The officer noted their names down carefully on his clipboard and waved them through. Three patrol cars and Winsome's Polo were parked willy-nilly on the cracked concrete outside the hangar, five officers leaning against them chatting, two of the men smoking. When Banks and Gerry flashed their warrant cards, the officers all straightened up, and the smokers trod out their cigarettes. Banks glanced down at the smudges on the wet concrete, then back at the culprits, who looked at him sheepishly.

"Sorry, sir," one of them mumbled.

"That's all right, son," said Banks. "You can explain the contamination of the scene to the CSIs when they get here."

The officer turned beet red.

"In the meantime," Banks went on, "don't you think you could be doing something useful, like organizing a house-to-house of the immediate area?"

"What for, sir?" asked one of the female officers.

"What for? To find out if anybody heard or saw anything. What do you think?"

"But we don't know what happened yet," said one of the others.

"That's right, sir," the woman said. "It's probably just a dead dog or a badger or something."

Banks sighed. "Well, how do you think you'll find out? Standing around the car smoking, contaminating the scene?"

"Besides," added the female officer, clearly a bit miffed at being bossed about, "I can't see any houses around here. How are we supposed to organize a house-to—"

"Just bloody get cracking and find some," snapped Banks, then he and Gerry turned away toward the hangar. Banks shook his head slowly. "Where do they get them from these days, Gerry?"

Gerry smiled. "Don't forget, sir, you were young once."

Banks flashed her a surprised glance, then shoved his hands in the pockets of his raincoat. She was coming along nicely, he thought; she wouldn't have dared talk to him like that six months ago.

They found Winsome inside the hangar, to their right, taking photos with her mobile. The crime scene photographer, if one were to be required, would cover every inch of the place soon, but many detectives liked to take their own set of pictures before the experts arrived, to capture the scene as freshly as they could. The photos sometimes came in useful. Banks took in the vast hangar, sniffing the air. Nothing specific registered with him. The wind sounded like a bassoon.

Winsome turned at their arrival, and her eyes widened when she saw Banks. "Sir?"

"I know, I know, I'm supposed to be on holiday. I just couldn't resist the lure of a bloody crime scene. Tell me all about it."

Banks listened closely as Winsome told him the story of her morning. "Where's this Gilchrist now?" he asked, when she had finished.

"I drove him home, sir."

"You didn't—"

"As if I would. I left two patrol officers guarding the scene. Gilchrist's ex-army. Seems to know what he's about, has his head screwed on right."

"Not an alarmist, then?"

"I wouldn't say so."

Banks looked at the stains on the ground. "Soldiers make good killers," he said. "It's what they're trained to do."

"He was wounded," Winsome said. "In Afghanistan. Walks with a stick."

"Did he have anything interesting to tell us?"

"Not really, sir. Just that he grew up around here and the airfield's always been like this as far as he remembers. Kids play there. He's also noticed a few lorries coming or going over the past year or so."

Banks knelt by the stains on the ground, hearing his knees crack as he did so. "It certainly looks like blood and brains to me. Let's say it is human. What happened? Someone shoots him, and he falls and bleeds out on the ground?"

"Possibly," said Winsome. "Or stabs him. Then leaves the mess but takes the body away. If it were just an animal, I couldn't really see anyone having a reason to do that."

Banks glanced at the stain. "There's not really all that much blood, is there? Have you—"

"I thought I'd better leave it to the CSIs."

Banks frowned at her. "Winsome, you're developing an annoying habit of answering my questions before I've asked them."

"Yes, sir. You were going to ask if I'd searched for a bullet or shell casing. I must be getting to know the way your mind works."

Banks stood up. "Do you know how frightening that thought is?"

"My dad always said I was a bit of a mind reader. Could have had a career on the stage."

Banks smiled. They heard another car pull up in the yard, and moments after the door slammed, Jasminder Singh hurried in with her bag of tricks. "All right, where is it?" she asked.

"Nice to see you again, too, Jazz," said Banks.

Jazz made a face. "DCI Banks. What a pleasure! And DS Jackman, how are you? Well, I hope? Will that do? Now can you show me where it is? No, don't bother, I can see it for myself."

The new forensics bloodstain analyst and DNA technician was a petite attractive brunette in her early thirties. She didn't usually attend crime scenes with the CSIs unless her specific services were required, and the squad always had a hard time finding protective clothing that fit her. She looked lost inside the baggy overalls as she squatted by the stain on the concrete. She quickly mixed a small sample of the congealed blood with a delivery agent and added it drop by drop to the collection tube. She looked up at Banks as he watched her work. "You've seen this trick before?"

"Uh-huh. It's still voodoo to me, but I understand it works."

Jazz showed her white teeth in a broad grin. "Pretty much," she said, getting to her feet. "We just wait for two or three minutes and— Jap's your uncle—we get an answer."

"Jap?"

"I didn't have an Uncle Bob, but I did have an Uncle Japjot."

Banks just stared at her.

"It was a family joke," Jazz muttered. "You had to be there."

They both turned to the tube, and a minute or so later two pinkish-red lines appeared.

"Human blood," said Banks.

"Don't jump to conclusions. It might be from a gorilla, or maybe a weasel or a badger. Nothing's perfect, is it? But I'd say there's a very good chance it's human, yes."

"Any chance of a quick result on the DNA?"

Jazz gave him a look. "Always in a hurry."

"Pretty please?"

"You want to jump the queue, is that what you're saying?"

"Yes. I mean, what's the point of having a forensics lab attached to the police station if we can't get a rush job on something? Besides, we need to know if this is something we need to call the team in for."

"Well, at least you admit it. I'll see what I can do. Tomorrow, perhaps."

"You're a treasure."

"Do you think we should call in the rest of the team, guv?" said Winsome.

Banks looked at her, at the blood on the ground, then back at Jazz.

"It's your decision," Jazz said. "But you know as well as I do that a positive in this test usually means human blood."

"Yes," Banks said, after a brief pause. "Yes, I really think we should." He felt the tremor of excitement start to dislodge the lazy, relaxed feeling he had been enjoying over the past few days. He wasn't sure that he didn't like this frisson more.

"WE'LL DO our best to help you," Annie said, "but you have to remember that Michael isn't officially listed as a missing person yet, so we can hardly pull out all the stops. He's nineteen, and he's only been away from home for one night."

"You'd pull out all the stops if it was Ian."

Both Annie and Doug Wilson gave her puzzled looks. "Well, yes, of course we would," Annie said.

Alex paused, seeming to understand the implications of what Annie had said, and of her own faux pas. "Of course you would. A child. Forgive me. It's just me opening my mouth before my brain's engaged. I'm sorry. I don't know what I'm talking about. I'm beside myself with worry."

"That's all right," said Annie. "I can understand your distress, especially if you say he hasn't done anything like this before. I'm not saying we won't look for him. We will. After all, we'd like to talk to him ourselves, so that's a bit of extra motivation, if you like. A touch of self-interest never goes amiss."

Alex nodded. "All right."

"Let's get back to Sunday morning," said Annie. "What time did Michael leave the flat?"

"He went out at about half past nine. Ian and I were just getting ready for church—well, Ian's in Sunday school."

"Michael doesn't usually go with you?"

"Michael's not religious. I can't really say I am myself, but I do find a bit of comfort in it sometimes. And it's tradition, a habit, isn't it? I mean, my mum and dad used to take me to Sunday school when I was little. Those are good memories. I loved the Bible stories and illustrations. Ian seems to like them, too."

"Did Michael receive or make any texts or phone calls that Sunday morning?"

"He got a text just before he went out. I was getting Ian ready, but I heard it, you know, that tinkling sound the phone makes when a text comes in."

"Did he tell you who it was from?"

"No. He just said that there might be a job on."

"On a Sunday morning? Doing what?"

"He didn't say."

"Did he say who with?"

"No."

"But he said he might drop in on his father later?"

"Yes. His dad's been unwell lately. And Michael's a good son, despite their differences. There was a cancer scare, but it turned out to be his gallbladder. He still had to have an operation. His health's been a bit fragile lately, and he's been a bit depressed. And he frets so about the farm. I mean, they have their problems, right, but they get on OK most of the time, as long as they avoid certain subjects—like me, and what Michael thinks he's doing with his life."

"Sounds like most of us," said Annie. "Then what?"

"He kissed me and Ian, like he usually does, then he left."

"Did he have any money with him?"

"He usually carries a bit of cash, but he's very careful with the credit and debit cards. We both hate the idea of being in debt and paying interest."

It didn't matter how careful he was, Annie thought. If he used them, they'd be able to find out where, should it come to that. "Does he have a passport?"

Alex walked over to the sideboard drawer and rummaged through it for a few moments, then returned bearing a passport. Annie opened it and saw the photo. It was the same person as in the picture on the mantelpiece. There were no stamps in the passport, which was only two years old. That meant he hadn't been outside the EU.

"Has anything out of the ordinary happened in your lives recently?"

"Not that I can think of."

"Did you have an argument or anything like that?"

"No."

"Did he seem worried, frightened, nervous, anxious? Different in any way?"

"No, he was the same as normal. But you're frightening me, asking all these questions."

"Sorry, it's just routine," said Annie. "We have to ask if we're to try and find him. Did he take the car?"

"Yes, of course. We can walk to church, but you need the car to drive up into the dale. Maybe that's it! I wouldn't be surprised if that old banger broke down somewhere. Maybe that's where he is? Up on the moors in the middle of nowhere with a dead mobile and a clapped-out car, hoping the AA might just happen to pass by."

"Can you tell me the number plate?"

Alex told her and Doug Wilson noted it down. "It's an old Peugeot. Dirty gray."

Alex was clutching at straws, Annie thought. Even if Michael Lane had been at home on Saturday night, there was still a better chance that he was now in a lorry helping ship a stolen tractor over to Albania than stranded on the moors in a clapped-out Peugeot hoping for the AA to turn up. But Alex didn't need to be told that. To Annie, Michael Lane was still a prime suspect, but to Alex he was a missing loved one. Somehow or other, Annie would have to sort all that out as gently as she could, or she risked losing any valuable cooperation she might need from Alex. It was a tricky balancing act.

"Could Michael be with a friend?" Annie asked. "And I don't mean a girlfriend. Do you know any of his mates?"

"He doesn't really have very many. His life was pretty isolated when he lived up at the farm, you see, and since then, well, most of the friends he did have have moved away, and we've sort of spent most of our time together. We don't socialize a lot. Going out can be expensive."

"You never go out for a drink or anything? Or to a party?"

"Sometimes we go to the local for an evening out, if we can afford a sitter for Ian, but not very often. Neither of us is a big drinker, and we just enjoy our own company. It's cheaper to get a few cans or a bottle of wine in and watch telly than it is to go out for the night. It sounds boring, I suppose, but we're happy."

"Can you think of anyone else at all Michael might have communicated with?"

"There's Keith, I suppose. He's still here. They went to school together, and they meet up for a game of darts once in a while. But Keith hasn't seen him. I phoned. Graham, too. He's married to Angie, who's my best friend, really. But Graham's a photography nut, and he and Michael get along well. They go off taking photos at various scenic spots around the Dales every now and then. Graham's been teaching Michael his way around a camera. As I said, Michael's a natural in some ways, but he doesn't know much about theory and techniques, or the history. I can't say I do, either, but Graham does. There's Morgan, too, I suppose. Michael works with him up on the farms sometimes. But I don't like him. He's too flash and full of himself. Wears a gold chain and has a spider tattoo on the side of his neck. Head shaved like one of those BNP types, though he isn't. He's half black. His dad's from Barbados. And he's always flirting with me."

"Does Michael like him?"

"They work together, and they go for a pint together, too, sometimes, after a day's work. They get along all right. Talk about any work that might be coming up. Morgan's managed to get Michael in on a couple of decent-paying jobs, and vice versa, so I don't suppose I should be so down on him." She gave a little shudder and pulled a face. "You know, it's just like, if you're a woman, he makes you feel like a piece of meat."

"I know exactly what you mean," said Annie. "I've met a few of those in my time. What kind of jobs do they do?"

"Anything that comes along, really. Morgan does small removals, you know, houses and flats and stuff. He's got a large van. Michael usually helps him out on jobs like that. They also do a lot of farmyard maintenance, like I said, roofing work, drainage ditches, helping bale hay for forage, that sort of thing. It's really a matter of who you know, who you've worked for before, where you've got a good reputation."

"And this Morgan has a good reputation?"

"I suppose he must have."

"Could he be the one who texted Michael about a job yesterday morning?"

"It's likely," said Alex. "It's what he usually does. Last minute, as often as not."

"Have you rung Morgan?"

"No. I don't know his number. But I know where he lives. He's got a caravan at that site down by the river, you know, near Hindswell Woods."

"Riverview?"

"That's the one."

"Well, it's a start, I suppose," said Annie, nodding toward Doug Wilson, who was busy scribbling in his notebook between stolen glances at Alex.

"Can you give me Michael's mobile number?" Wilson asked. "And tell me the full names and addresses of the friends you mentioned, Miss Preston, including this Morgan character? Phone numbers, too, if you have them. And do you have a recent photograph of Michael we can borrow?"

"Please, call me Alex," she said, smiling.

Annie could see that Doug was hers forever. He carefully wrote down the names and addresses, mostly just a street name, occasionally a telephone number Alex retrieved from her mobile's contacts. It was enough to be going on with. Back at the station, they could put DC Masterson on it. Nobody could track down a name, address or phone number as fast as she could. "We'll check again with them all," said Annie. "Just in case. One of them might remember something he said, something that might not have seemed important at the time."

Alex disappeared into the other room and came back with a photo of Michael posing casually on the balcony, with the view of Eastvale spread out in the background. "That was taken two weeks ago," she said. "I took it myself. You remember, that nice weekend near the end of last month?" She handed over the photo, then put her hands to her face. "Oh, God, what can have happened to him?"

"I know you're worried, Alex," Annie said, "but I've had a lot of experience with this sort of thing, and there's almost always no cause for concern. I bet you we'll have Michael back home with you in no time."

"It's true," added Doug Wilson. "Leave it to us. Is there anywhere you think he might have gone? A favorite place, a hideaway? You know, if he got upset about his father, or you had an argument or something? Somewhere he'd go to be alone, to think things over, feel safe and secure?"

Annie thought it was a good question to ask, and she watched Alex as she worked her way through it and framed an answer.

"I don't really know. I mean, he always feels safe and secure here, with us. He doesn't need an escape. We haven't really had any fights, not serious fights where either of us has gone off alone. Michael does like long walks by himself, though. I think it's a habit he developed in his childhood, you know, growing up on the farm." She laughed. "You had to walk a long way to get anywhere, where he lived."

"Anywhere in particular?" Wilson asked.

"Just around the dale in general," said Alex, "though I'm sure it's not something he'd do in this weather."

"We have to cover all the possibilities, Miss— Alex," said Wilson.

Alex favored him with another smile. "I know," she said. "If I could think of where he might be, don't you think I'd tell you? I can't go looking for him, myself. I don't have the car, and there's Ian . . ."

"Don't worry," Annie assured her, standing and giving Wilson the signal to close his notebook. "It's our job. We'll take care of it. Can we have a look at that computer now?"

They drew a blank on Michael's computer. Nothing but a lot of spam and a few harmless emails from friends—nothing from Morgan, no references to tractor-thieving sprees, as far as Annie could gather— and his photo collection, along with various software programs for manipulating images. The photos, mostly landscapes and people at work around farms, were as good as the framed ones in the living room. There was no porn, and no record of porn sites in his book-marks or browsing history. Either he was happy with what he had or he had gone to great pains to erase his tracks. Annie guessed the former. Most of the bookmarks were for travel-related sites and photo-posting services such as Flickr. If this business went any further, of course, the computer would have to go to Liam in technical support for a thorough examination, and if there was anything dodgy on it, or ever had been, he would find it, but there was no reason to suspect that it was hiding deep and dirty secrets just yet.

"You'll ring me as soon as you find him?" Alex asked at the door.

"We'll ring you," said Annie. She took out a card, scribbled on the back and handed it to Alex. "And I hope you'll call me if you hear from Michael. My mobile number's on the back."

They didn't even bother trying the lift. On their way down the stairs, Annie heard a cry of pain as they passed the fifth-floor gauntlet. Doug Wilson was behind her, hands in his pockets, looking as if butter wouldn't melt in his mouth, and behind him one of the hoodies was bent over, hands cupping his groin. The others were too shocked to move.

"Tut-tut, Dougal," said Annie, smiling. "Who's been a naughty boy, then?"

3

MORGAN SPENCER LIVED ON A CARAVAN SITE across the River Swain from Hindswell Woods, about half a mile west of town. The Riverview Caravan Park wasn't anywhere near as attractive as its name suggested. There was a river view for the first row of caravans, but as the meadow they were parked in was flat, all the rest could see was other caravans blocking the view. Most were permanent fixtures, up on blocks, though there were a few spaces for temporary sojourners. Of the permanent caravans, by far the majority belonged to people in Leeds, Bradford, Darlington or Teesside, who used them for weekend getaways. It wasn't far to travel, and it was the Yorkshire Dales, after all, river view or no river view. At least you could see the trees and hills on the other side and go for long bracing walks in the country. Quite a few people lived in the park year-round, the site manager told them, and Morgan Spencer was one of them. Annie had already heard the rumor that many of those who lived in Riverview Caravan Park were what the Americans would call "trailer trash." "Caravan trash" didn't sound anywhere near as apt a description, she thought, perhaps because it lacked the alliteration. The park's only attraction for occasional holiday visitors was that it was cheap.

The caravans were set out in neat rows stretching back from the riverbank across the meadow, each with a parking space beside it, though none of them was big enough for a large van. Some of the

homes looked well maintained, with a fresh paint job, awning over
the door, a window box or hanging basket. Others looked more neglected, resting unevenly on their concrete supports, sagging at one
end, windows dirty and covered on the inside with makeshift moth-
eaten curtains made of old bedding or tea towels. Because of the rain
over the last few days, the field was a quagmire, and any grass there
may have been before had been trampled into the mud. It reminded
Annie of the time she went to Glastonbury as a teenager. It had rained
the entire weekend. Even the Boomtown Rats weren't worth getting
that wet for.

Annie and Doug Wilson left their car at the paved entrance, beside
the site office, which was deserted at the moment, put on their wellies
again and went the rest of the way on foot. They found Spencer's caravan on the third row back from the riverbank. On a scale of one to ten,
it was about a six, which is to say, not bad, but a little on the run-down
side. There was nothing parked beside it. Annie's first knock produced
no reaction, only an empty echo from inside. She strained to listen but
heard no sound of movement. Her second knock produced an opening
door, but in the neighboring caravan, not Spencer's.

"He's not home, love," said the man who stood there. "Police,
you'll be, then?"

"Are we so obvious?" Annie said.

The man smiled. "You are to an ex-copper, love."

"You're . . . ?"

"I am. Rick Campbell's the name. Come on in out of the rain, why
don't you? Have a cuppa."

Annie and Wilson pulled their wellies off by the front steps, which
were sheltered from the rain by a striped awning. "Don't mind if we
do," Annie said.

"Leave the boots out there, if you could," Campbell said, pointing
to a mat outside the door.

The caravan was cramped but cheery inside, with a bright flowered
bedspread, freshly painted yellow walls, polished woodwork and a
spotless cooking area. The air smelled of damp leaves. At one end of
the room was the bed, which could be screened off by a curtain, and
at the other a dining table with a red-and-white-checked oilcloth. In

between, a sofa big enough for two sat opposite a television and stereo. Some quiet music played in the background. The sort of thing Banks would know about, Annie thought. Bach or Beethoven, or someone like that. Campbell told Annie and Wilson to sit down at the dining table as he busied himself filling the kettle.

"Do you live here alone?" Annie asked.

"Live here? Oh, I see what you mean. No, we don't live here. We just come here for our summer holidays, and weekends now and again. We live in Doncaster. When I retired, it was a toss-up between the Dales and the coast. The Dales won. Ellie and I had some fine holidays around these parts in our younger days. Keen walkers, we were. We don't do so much now, of course, especially after Ellie's hip replacement, but we still get around a fair bit, and there's always the memories. It's God's own country to us."

"Is your wife around?"

"She's visiting the son and daughter-in-law this weekend. Down Chesterfield way. I just came up to do a bit of fixing and patching up. The old dear—the caravan, I mean, not Ellie—needs more maintenance every year. That's the trouble with these things. They don't age well."

"The rain can't help."

"I'll say. Mostly, it's just general wear and tear. And they're not exactly built for the elements in the first place. Certainly not the kind of elements we seem to be getting these days." He looked toward the window and grimaced. "I've patched the worst leaks and strengthened the floor. So what is it I can do for you?"

"You said you're an ex-copper."

"Yes. I did my thirty and got out fast. South Yorkshire. Mostly uniform, traffic, a brief stint with Sheffield CID. Sergeant when I retired. Desk job the last four years. It was a good life, but I'm not a dedicated crime fighter like those TV coppers. Why keep working any longer than you have to, eh?"

Annie thought of Banks. They'd have to drag him kicking and screaming out of his office soon. Or would he get a newer, bigger office and an extra five years' grace if he got promoted to superintendent, as Gervaise had promised last November? "We're here about your neighbor, Morgan Spencer," she said.

"You know, that's what I thought when I heard you knocking on his door." He tapped the side of his nose and laughed. "I haven't lost all my detective skills yet, you know. So what's he been up to now?"

"Now?"

"Just a figure of speech, love, that's all."

Campbell made the tea and set it on the table along with three mugs, a carton of long-life milk and a bowl of sugar. "Biscuits? I can offer custard creams or chocolate digestives."

Both Annie and Wilson declined the offer.

Campbell settled into a chair opposite them. "Well, I can't say I know Morgan very well," he began, "but I must say, as neighbors go, he'd be hard to beat. Keeps some odd hours, hardly ever home, in fact, but he's considerate, polite, and he's even helped me out on a couple of tricky jobs around the place. Held the ladder, so to speak. He's a good hard worker."

Annie glanced at Wilson, who raised his eyebrows. It wasn't what she'd expected to hear after talking to Alex Preston. Campbell didn't miss the exchange. Once a copper always a copper. "What? Did I say something wrong?"

"Would you describe him as honest?"

"I wouldn't know about that. All I can say is it wouldn't surprise me to hear he's got a fiddle or two on the side. Probably sails a bit close to the wind. He likes to talk big sometimes and I'd say he reckons he's God's gift to women, but at the bottom of it all he's harmless enough. Why? Is there a problem?"

"No," said Annie. "Not at all. We just want to talk to him in connection with a missing person, that's all."

"Missing person?"

"Yes." Annie knew she was exaggerating more than a little. Michael Lane was not yet an official missing person. As she had told Alex Preston, he was a nineteen-year-old lad who hadn't been home since yesterday morning. And what nineteen-year-old hadn't done exactly the same thing more than once? But what other reason could she give for wanting to talk to Morgan Spencer? That he had flirted with Michael's girlfriend and had a spider tattoo on the side of his neck?

Campbell added a drop of milk and sipped his tea. "What connection might Morgan have with this missing person?"

Wait a minute, mate, Annie thought, *I'm supposed to be the one asking the questions.* But she said nothing. She realized that a heavy-handed approach wouldn't work with an ex-copper who also happened to be a pal of the person she was looking for. "Does Morgan have many visitors?" she asked.

"Not many," said Campbell. "There are no wild parties, if that's what you mean. At least not while I've been around, and I've heard no complaints from Ted in the office, or from the people on the other side. Word soon gets around about antisocial behavior, a place like this. We might not be the Ritz, but we're not some backstreet fleabag hotel, either."

"I didn't assume you were," Annie said.

Campbell ran his hand over his hair. "Sorry, love. You get a bit tired of some of the comments about us lot from Riverview up in the town. I'm just pointing out that we're decent folk, most of us. We're not Travelers, and most of us aren't on benefits."

Annie laughed. "You said Morgan doesn't have many visitors. Does he have a girlfriend?"

"If he does, she doesn't live with him, and he hasn't introduced me to her." He winked. "Maybe he's scared she'll run off with me, eh?"

"Not if he thinks he's God's gift. Do you know where his parents live?"

"No. He hardly ever mentions them. I seem to remember him saying his dad went back to Barbados, or some such place. And I don't think Morgan's from these parts. He's got a slight Geordie accent."

"Did you ever meet a lad called Lane? Mick or Michael Lane."

"I met a lad called Mick once or twice. Morgan introduced him. In fact, he was another good worker. Nice lad. They both helped out with the new siding last summer. I gave them a tenner each. Well worth it for me. I believe they work together, doing odd jobs on farms out in the dale. He a farmer's son, this Mick?"

"That's the one," Annie said. "We're trying to locate Michael Lane, and as he's one of Morgan's friends, we thought he might be able to help."

"I'm sorry but I haven't seen Morgan at all this weekend."

"How long have you been up here?"

"Since Saturday evening." He glanced at his watch. "I'm supposed to be heading back in a couple of hours."

"Don't worry. We won't keep you. Is Morgan often away for long stretches of time?"

"I wouldn't really know. I haven't paid much attention to his comings and goings, and Ellie and me aren't always up here. He's often gone for the weekends when we do come. Maybe he does have a girlfriend hidden away somewhere. It's been such a miserable spring so far that we haven't been up much at all this year—hence the leaks. We were just as well off staying in Donny and getting a few jobs done around the house there."

Campbell was obviously one of those cheerful DIYers who spent all their time at B & Q comparing spanners, toolboxes or bathroom tiles. Annie could understand doing your own maintenance to save a few bob, maybe, but clambering up a ladder and hammering in nails for fun, or laying tiles? That, she couldn't grasp. Even Banks enjoyed it from time to time, and he seemed proud of the little fixtures and alterations he had made around Newhope Cottage. He'd done a lot of work on the conservatory himself, for example. It must be a bloke thing, she thought, like hogging the TV remote, not asking directions or insisting on doing the barbecue when they didn't even know how to boil an egg.

When Annie's roof had sprung a small leak in the worst of the summer rains last year, the roofer she called said it was too small a job for him and suggested that perhaps she could do it herself with a spot of lead and bitumen. She had almost suffered an anxiety attack on the spot. Luckily, she had found a local handyman who was eager and more than happy to clamber up on the roof and do the work for fifty quid, cash on the nail, no questions asked, and no ladder, either, Health and Safety be buggered. Ah, the underground economy. "When did you last see Morgan?" Annie asked.

Campbell sucked on his lower lip. "Let me see . . . it'd be a while back. Two or three weeks. Remember, we had a nice spell of sunshine in late February, early March?"

"What does he look like?"

"Look like?"

"Yes. Morgan. His appearance."

"Well, he's a bit shorter than me, about five foot eight, and stockier, I'd say, curly brown hair cut very short, and a sort of round face. More oval, maybe. Light colored, or light brown, enough so you can tell one of his parents is black. His dad, I suppose. No facial hair. He should have, though. Bit of a weak chin. There's nothing that really stands out about him, except he's got a slight limp in his left leg. Fell off a roof once when he was a kid, or so he told me. Oh, and he's got one of those spider tattoos on his neck. Tends to be a bit flash with the bling, too. Gold chains, rings and what have you."

"Do you keep an eye on his place when he's not around?"

"I keep an eye on things for anyone who's not around. When I'm here, that is. The others do the same when we're not here. It's not exactly a crime hot spot, but we get the occasional break-in, as you probably know."

"Notice anyone noseying around lately?"

"Only you."

Annie laughed. "How old would you say Morgan is?"

"Early twenties. Thereabouts. Not much more."

"Clothes?"

"Usually jeans and some sort of work shirt, or T-shirt if the weather's warm. Baggy jeans. Not those with the crotch around the knees and belt around the thighs, but just . . . you know . . . baggy. Relaxed fit."

"Plenty of wiggle room?" said Annie.

"That's right."

"Does he need it?"

"Morgan's not fat. Just stocky, like I said."

"Hat?"

"Sometimes. Baseball cap, wrong way around. A red one. I don't know if it's got a logo. I'd have to see him from the back."

Doug Wilson jotted the description down.

"Do you know where he keeps his van?"

"What van?"

"I understand Morgan's in the house removal business. He has a large van."

"I didn't know that. Sorry, but I've no idea. I do know he rides a motorbike. A Yamaha. He usually keeps it parked beside the caravan."

Annie could think of nothing more, but when they got to the door she asked on impulse, "Do you have a key to Morgan's caravan?"

"No. Why? Do you think something's happened to him?"

"We have no idea. As I said, we're just trying to find his mate, Michael Lane."

"Sorry I can't help."

"Do you think we could have a look around his caravan?"

"Got a search warrant?"

"Come on, Rick. You were a copper once."

"It might just be a shitty old caravan to you, love, but it's home to Morgan. Come back with a warrant and Ted'll probably let you in. But, I warn you, he's as much a stickler as I am. We look out for one another around these parts."

"In adversity, solidarity," said Annie. She didn't know where she'd heard that before, but it sounded good. "I'll bear that in mind. No problem. Thanks for your time."

They struggled back into their wellies on the steps. "I really bollixed that up, didn't I?" Annie said to Doug Wilson as they squelched back to the car. She could feel Campbell's eyes on them as she walked.

"In what way?" Wilson asked.

"The phony camaraderie. Didn't fall for it, did he? I was hoping for a look around Spencer's caravan."

"Not your fault, boss," said Wilson. "If you ask me, the way things are going we'll be back with a warrant tomorrow if we want."

ANNIE CABBOT watched the door as Banks and AC Gervaise walked into the boardroom, deep in conversation, for the late briefing. The team was already assembled: Annie herself, Doug Wilson, Winsome Jackman, Gerry Masterson, Stefan Nowak and Jazz Singh, along with a couple of other CSI officers, Peter Darby, the police photographer, and PCs Kim Trevor and Derek Bowland. They all sat around the polished oval table under the gaze of the old wool magnates with red and purple bulbous noses and tight collars. Legal pads and styrofoam cups of tea, coffee or water sat on the boardroom table in front of them. A plate of biscuits stood at the center.

Banks and AC Gervaise took their positions by the two whiteboards and the glass board, which was looking to Annie more and more like something out of an American cop program. She kept expecting it to light up with pictures and charts and blowups of fingerprints whenever Banks touched it, or moving and talking images he could shift around with a simple wave of his hand. But it wasn't *that* good. Right now, there wasn't much on any of the boards, except the names of the various players and the times of significant events, along with a few of Darby's photos from the hangar, about which Annie had heard only recently, having been away most of the day. Apparently the CSIs had found some human blood, but they were still short of a body. A manned mobile crime unit had been set up on the compound just outside the hangar, and half a dozen or so CSIs were still at work out there. Shifts of uniformed officers would be guarding the scene until further notice.

Annie looked at the whiteboard while Banks and Gervaise settled down. Two hand-sketched maps were tacked up there, one of the area around Beddoes's farm and the other of the hangar area. They identified access roads and footpaths. From what Annie could see, there weren't many in either location. Rural crime at its best.

Banks shuffled his papers, stood up and opened the briefing. "I think we'd better start off by pooling our information. As you all probably know, I just got back from leave this morning, so the only case I'm current on is an apparent killing, or serious wounding, at the old abandoned aerodrome near Drewick, though the AC has filled me in briefly on one or two other developments that may possibly be related." He looked at Annie. "I understand you and Doug have been working on a stolen tractor and missing person?"

Annie rolled her eyes. "So it would appear," she said. "Not officially 'missing,' but we haven't been able to locate him yet. Or his mate." Then she went on to explain about John Beddoes and Frank Lane, not leaving out Michael Lane and Alex Preston, or Morgan Spencer. When she had finished, she leaned back in her chair and tapped her pen on her notepad.

"Do you think this Michael Lane character could be involved in the tractor theft?" Banks asked.

Annie seemed to deliberate a few moments before answering. "It's possible," she said. "I mean, he got probation and community service for joyriding eighteen months back, after his mum left his dad, though I don't think that means much. He was upset at the time. He also sometimes works as an odd-job man on the local farms along with his mate Morgan Spencer. It's likely that they are in a good position to know who's at home and who isn't. Maybe Michael Lane couldn't look a gift horse in the mouth? Maybe him and Spencer are both on their way to Romania or wherever with the tractor? But Lane has an alibi, for what it's worth. His girlfriend swears he was with her all Saturday night, until about half past nine Sunday morning."

"Any ideas?"

"Well," said Annie, "I wouldn't overlook the possibility of insurance fraud."

"You mean Beddoes himself?"

"Why not? He's got a City background, apparently. Knows finance. On the surface of it, he seems well off. But the farm can't be all that profitable. All he does is raise a few pigs and free-range chickens for local restaurants and several acres of rapeseed for high-end cooking oils. He might have got into something over his head. Or maybe he needs to supplement his income? And the idiot did leave the ignition key hanging on a hook on the wall."

"Worth thinking about," Banks said. He glanced toward AC Gervaise. "I understand you know Patricia Beddoes, ma'am?"

"Slightly."

"What do you think?"

"Their finances? Insurance fraud? I couldn't really say one way or the other. She always seemed like a comfortably-off person to me. Nice clothes. Designer labels. I think she was a bit bored with the country, missed her exotic travel. Hence the Mexico trip, I suppose. And I do believe they have a little pied-à-terre in Holland Park. Other than that, all I know is that she likes Kate Atkinson and Khaled Hosseini."

That drew several chuckles from the room. "You know," Annie

said, "if we're considering a local candidate being involved, what about Frank Lane? By the look of his farm he could do with an injection of cash, and he felt resentful toward the successful incomer. It was obvious in his tone and what he said. He was also in a position to organize the theft easily enough. He had the keys to Beddoes's farm, and he probably knew that the tractor keys were hanging on the wall of the garage. Just a possibility."

"And we'll bear it in mind," said Banks. "Maybe father and son were in it together? Did Michael Lane know that Beddoes was on holiday?" Banks asked Annie.

"More than likely. And Frank Lane also seemed a bit contemptuous of the Mexico trip. Or maybe he was just envious."

"You said Michael Lane's relationship with the victim, John Beddoes, was strained?"

"Yes," said Annie. "I suppose it could have been some sort of misguided revenge, an old vendetta. Also, Frank Lane said he thought Beddoes was full of himself. He played it down, said there was no bitterness, but there could be something in it. Lane's a professional farmer, making a hard living the hard way. Beddoes is an amateur, a hobbyist. That sort of thing. If Michael had something against both of them, then he'd know that stealing the tractor would probably hurt his father, Frank Lane, too, as he'd been given the responsibility of looking after the Beddoes farm. Two birds with one stone. And Michael does have the joyriding incident in his background. Trouble is, we don't really know Michael Lane, what sort of person he is. His partner thinks he's wonderful, but she's biased. Is he the vengeful sort, the type to harbor a grudge? We don't know. We also need to have a more extensive search of the Lane farm premises, just in case he's hanging out there for some reason."

"We'll schedule that for tomorrow morning," Banks said. "I'd like to talk to Beddoes and Lane myself. I'm not sure about the vendetta angle, though. These tractors are worth a lot of money, and it takes a great deal of organization, not to mention expense, to steal one. Do you think Michael Lane, or even his father, was capable of organizing such a theft?"

"No," said Annie. "I shouldn't imagine they were. I certainly don't think Michael Lane could have stolen it by himself, but he could have been involved with whoever did do it. As I said, Beddoes left the key in the garage. Michael Lane might have known about that, too. He could also have been the one who gave the tip-off about the Beddoeses' Mexico trip, for example." Annie became silent, as if she were realizing something for the first time.

Banks noticed the hesitation. "What is it, Annie?"

"Probably nothing, really." Damn it, Annie thought, she hated this. Talking to Alex Preston had affected her. Like most of the Eastvale police, Annie had written off the East Side Estate, mainly because the only times she had ever been there were to the scenes of domestics, drug deals turned nasty, fights, stabbings, even murders. On such experiences were a copper's judgments based. But Alex Preston not only kept a clean house and loved her young son, she had put her mistakes behind her—mistakes that could have set many a soul well on the way to more of the same—and pulled herself up by the bootstraps. She had a positive, optimistic outlook that Annie admired, and she had dreams. Perhaps Annie also envied Alex a bit, she was willing to admit. Alex seemed to have got herself together and found a good man. Annie had no one to look after her and make her happy. She didn't have many dreams left, either.

It was rare that Annie felt sentimental about people she didn't really know, and maybe it was a sign that she was leaving behind some of the depression and cynicism that seemed to have invaded her mind since the shooting. That was a good thing; she hadn't liked the person she was becoming. Loneliness was turning her into a moody and sharp-tongued bitch. If she got much worse, she wouldn't be able to find anyone willing to put up with her, let alone love and cherish her. She just hoped that she didn't get so soft she couldn't see the hard truth when it was staring her in the face. Any good copper needs at least an ounce or two of skepticism, even cynicism. But Annie also realized that she had not completely lost her copper's mistrust of the world, that some of what she had learned from Alex Preston had made her more suspicious of Michael Lane.

"Lane's girlfriend, Alex Preston, works part-time at that travel agent's in the Swainsdale Centre," she said. "GoThereNow."

"The same one Beddoes used to book the trip?"

"Dunno." Annie glanced at Doug Wilson. "We haven't had a chance to check it out yet. We've been splodging around in the mud most of the day."

This drew a titter from the audience. Banks glanced at his watch. "First thing tomorrow. Then we can scrounge up a few bodies and give the Lane farm a thorough once-over, just to make sure Michael Lane isn't there. That would be embarrassing." He paused. "Do you think this Preston woman could be involved?"

"She's worried sick," said Annie. "She thinks something's happened to Lane."

"And you?"

"I'm taking her seriously."

"Is anyone actually looking? I mean, he's not officially listed as missing yet, is he?"

"No, sir," said Doug Wilson. "But DI Cabbot and I got a recent picture and we've circulated it within the area. We've also been in touch with the airlines and railway stations, and we've asked to be informed of any activity on his mobile phone, debit or credit card. Nothing yet, not since last Friday."

"Makes sense if he's being careful." Then Banks turned back to Annie. "And Morgan Spencer?"

"He wasn't in when we called."

"Do you think there's a connection with the blood found in the hangar?" Banks asked. "It does seem a bit of a coincidence. Do you think the victim could be Lane? Or Spencer?"

"No. I . . . I mean . . . I don't know. Maybe. I was just making a point," Annie said. "I'm taking Alex Preston seriously. But now you come to mention it, an expensive tractor is stolen while the owner's away in Mexico, a neighbor's son with a criminal record goes walkabout, he's living with a woman who works at a travel agent's and his mate owns a removal van. It all seems a bit fishy to me. And someone texted Michael on Sunday morning, just before he went out. It could have been Spencer. It's not as if we get such a collection of coincidences every day, is it?"

"Let's see if we can find out anything about Morgan Spencer's removal van and that text he sent," said Banks. "And we'd also better look into who owns the aerodrome property. Does Morgan Spencer have a record?"

"No," said Annie. "He's clean as far as we're concerned."

Banks glanced toward Winsome. "Did you follow up on what Gilchrist told you about the lorries, get anything more, any confirmation?"

"Not yet, sir. We've still got officers out asking questions in the general area. Maybe someone else noticed these lorries, too. Though Mr. Gilchrist did say it was only three or four times in the past year or so."

"If our thieves were using the hangar as part of a route for getting stolen farm equipment out of the country, or even across it, they would probably only have needed it for larger items, like tractors and combines. As far as I know, they'd slaughter any stolen livestock locally and dispose of it here through illegal channels. Dodgy butchers. Abattoirs that don't ask too many questions. Quickly. Rustlers aren't in the business of grazing stolen sheep and cattle. And the airfield and hangar were ideal for large transfers. After all, the place was padlocked and signposted private. It looked official, even though it was neglected. People would most likely assume that whoever ran the lorries in and out were the owners, using it for legitimate business, or at least had official permission to be there. We could be onto something here."

"It's possible."

"Have another word with this Terry Gilchrist, Winsome. Could he be involved? After all, he is ex-army, and he did find the bloodstains."

"His dog did," Winsome said. "I don't really see why he'd follow it under a chain-link fence in his condition, with the weather the way it was, and then phone us if he was responsible for it in the first place. Do you, sir?"

"Perhaps not, when you put it like that, but we have to consider the possibility."

"Without Gilchrist and his dog, the crime scene could have gone unobserved for days, or weeks."

"True," Banks agreed. "Unless one of the lorry drivers noticed."

"But if they had something to do with the blood," Winsome argued, "then they'd hardly report it, would they, sir?"

"But Gilchrist does have a military background, doesn't he?"

"Yes, sir."

"So he's no doubt conversant with ways of killing?"

"I suppose so."

"And military operations and criminal operations have several features in common, including a certain level of organization. He also knows the area well. It shouldn't be too hard to track down his military records. You say he was injured in action?"

"Yes, sir. In Afghanistan. His legs."

"But he's still mobile?"

"I'd say he's pretty nifty on his pins, sir, yes."

Banks smiled. "'Nifty on his pins.' I like that." He turned to DC Masterson. "Gerry, can you see about tracking down Terry Gilchrist's military record? You know the sort of thing, any suspicions he was up to anything illegal while he was serving, black market activities, looting, whatever. And while you're at it, have a look into John Beddoes's finances. As Annie said, we can't rule out insurance fraud."

"Yes, sir," said Gerry, scribbling fast on her pad.

"And we'll need to know exactly who owns the abandoned airfield."

"Consider it done, sir."

"Excellent. Stefan, do you have anything for us? Tire tracks?"

"We're still working the scene," Nowak said, "but there's not much chance of tire tracks on the concrete. From the mess they trailed in, though, I'd say there could have been two or three vehicles at the scene, but I can't say when or what they were."

"Fingerprints?"

"There's no decent surface to get fingerprints from. Not the concrete floor and not the corrugated metal walls. The lock and the wire mesh gate are clean. We're still dusting around the general area, but don't expect too much with all the rain we've had. We might get a few partials or smudges, if we're lucky. We're also going to do a thorough luminal search. If blood was spilled there recently, there's always a chance that the hangar was used before as a place of execution. There might be traces of previous crimes, and they might lead to DNA."

"Good work, Stefan. Anything new on the trace evidence, Jazz?"

"You'll have your DNA analysis sometime tomorrow, as promised," Jazz Singh said. "And I want you to know it's got me in trouble with Harrogate. They thought they had priority. In the meantime, all I can tell you is that the blood type of the sample is A positive. Not very exciting news, as it's the same as about thirty-five percent of the UK population. But if you look on the bright side, it rules out sixty-five percent. I've sent the brain matter and bone fragments for outside analysis. We don't have the facilities for that. I'm not sure what that'll tell us, or how long it will take, but the odds are that it'll be very expensive and you'll probably have solved the case by then." She smiled sweetly and rested her hands on the table. Annie made a note of the blood type.

Banks glanced toward PC Trevor. "Anything from the house-to-house?"

"Nothing, sir," said a sulky PC Trevor. "Len and Dave are still out knocking on doors in Drewick."

Banks turned to Wilson. "Doug, I noticed the hangar's very close to the railway lines. Do you think you can check with East Coast and any other companies who use it about whether anyone saw anything there recently?"

Wilson nodded and made a note. "I'll see if I can get a request on the news as well."

Banks let the silence stretch for a moment, then addressed the room at large. "How do you get from the airfield to the A1?" he asked. "Is the only way the way Gerry and I came? From what I could see, all there was around there were bumpy overgrown tracks until you got to the village."

"You'd have to get back to the Thirsk road, a mile or so beyond Drewick," said Doug Wilson. "From there you could go north to Northallerton or south to Thirsk. Either way, it's a few miles."

"There is another way," said Winsome. "If you continue south on that track that runs by the airfield gates, you go through the woods parallel to the railway lines, and when you get to a village called Hallerby, you can turn right on a B road leading to the A1. That cuts off Thirsk and saves you a bit of time. There's also a lot less traffic and only the one village to drive through."

"Is there anything in this Hallerby?"

"Usual stuff, sir," said Winsome. "Few houses, couple of shops, village hall, chapel, a pub."

"And you'd have to pass through there either way if you were taking that shortcut to or from the A1?"

Winsome nodded. "It's where the bumpy lane starts and heads north. The B road from the A1 continues to Thirsk."

"Maybe you could pay a visit to this Hallerby tomorrow, Winsome, and see if anyone saw lorries, or any other traffic, heading to or from the A1 via that road this weekend. Someone must have seen or heard something coming out of the woods. It might have appeared odd or rare enough to remember."

"Sir," said Winsome.

"Is that all?" Banks asked, glancing around the room.

"There is one more thing, sir," Doug Wilson said.

"Doug?"

"When DI Cabbot and I went to talk to Morgan Spencer, he wasn't home, like DI Cabbot said. His neighbor hasn't seen him all weekend. We didn't have a search warrant, and he's ex-job, so he wouldn't have us taking a butcher's. We'll be needing a search warrant."

Banks looked toward AC Gervaise.

"Get back there tomorrow morning and have a good look around," she said. "Talk to his other neighbors on the site, too. I'll see to the warrant first thing. But make sure you ask the site manager beforehand and explain your predicament. If he doesn't have a key, then you'll have to break in, but only if, and only after, you have the warrant in your hand. OK?"

"Yes, ma'am."

Gervaise looked at her watch and stood up. "Why don't you all go home now and get some rest? Tomorrow looks like a busy day. We've got a stolen tractor, two young men we'd like to find and talk to and the makings of a suspicious death at an abandoned airfield. For the moment these are separate cases, and I'll see that actions are issued accordingly. But for crying out loud, keep open minds, all of you." She pointed toward the timeline on the whiteboard. "You know how I feel about coincidences. If you come across one shred of evidence you think links the cases, then report it to me immediately, and we'll change our strategy. Clear?"

Annie and the rest nodded, then they made their way out of the boardroom. After one or two brief conversations in the corridor, the team dispersed. At last, Annie thought, as she picked up her coat from the squad room, it was time to go home. Now she could enjoy what she had been wanting all day: that hot bath and stack of trashy magazines.

BANKS GOT home to a cold house at about eight o'clock. He turned up the thermostat, promising himself yet again that if he ever got a pay increase, the first thing he would buy was a better heating system. He dumped his bag and satchel on the floor, hung up his coat and picked up the post from the inside mat. It consisted mostly of bills, subscription renewal forms and a box set of Janet Baker CDs that had only just fit through the letter box.

There was also a postcard from his parents, who were cruising the Amazon: a picture of the Manaus opera house. Banks turned it over and read his mother's small neat handwriting. His father didn't like to write, Banks knew, because he was self-conscious about his spelling and grammar. His mother, with her typical economy, had crammed as many words in the small space as she possibly could. "We thought you might like this, being an opera fan and all. It's very hot and muggy here, so bad some days your poor dad can hardly breathe. The food is good on the ship. Some of the other passengers are really rude and stuck-up but we've made friends with a couple from York and some nice people from near Stratford. We went for a boat ride around some islands yesterday and saw a sloth, two iguanas and a conda. Your dad caught a piranha off the side of the boat. He's proper chuffed with himself!"

Banks puzzled for a moment over "and a conda," then guessed his mother meant an anaconda. She was in her eighties, after all. He could just imagine them in their sun hats and long-sleeved shirts, sweating in the heat, busy spending their inheritance. Good for them, he thought. They had never got much out of life, and they had had to suffer the death of their favorite son, Roy, not so very long ago. Spend it while you're alive to enjoy it, Banks thought, admiring them for their adventurousness. When he'd been young and excited by all the strange faraway places in the atlas, he could never have imagined his father—a beer and fish-and-chips sort of bloke if ever there was one— or his mother—homemaker, queen of the overcooked roast beef and soggy sprouts—venturing far beyond Skeggy or Clacton. But there they were, cruising the Amazon, something he had never managed to do. Banks had inherited his brother's Porsche, and for a long time he had tried to convince himself to sell it. Now that it felt lived in, he found that he sort of liked it. And it was a link with his dead brother, a link he hadn't felt when Roy was alive.

He put the postcard down beside his computer and walked through the hall to the kitchen, where he poured himself a couple of fingers of the Macallan 12 year. He was still working his way back to Laphroaig. He took a sip and sat at the breakfast nook to open the Janet Baker package, then went into the entertainment room and put on the disk that started with *Les nuits d'été*. He found the second disk of Oriana's *Tosca* in the CD player and put it back in its jewel case. There was a small pile of her CDs beside the amp, mostly opera and early music— Hildegard von Bingen, Byrd, Tallis, Monteverdi—and those damn U2 CDs she had insisted on bringing. Banks couldn't stand U2. All their songs sounded the same to him, and Bono and the bloke with the woolly hat and silly name got on his nerves. He turned up the volume on Janet Baker a notch, went to collect his whisky from the kitchen and went through to the conservatory, where he settled in his well-worn wicker armchair.

Oriana's wide-brimmed straw hat lay on the other chair, and on the low glass-topped table stood two stem glasses, the red wine crystallized at the bottom. One of them had lipstick stains on the rim, a faint pink semicircle that made Banks think of Oriana's lips and her kisses. They had been running late on Thursday, he remembered, and had left in such a hurry that she had forgotten her hat and he had forgotten to clear away the glasses. There were fragments of her life all over the house, Banks realized, though they didn't live together. Oriana was still at the Chalmerses' place. It suited her—her second family, the two daughters like younger sisters, people she'd known all her life, and her job as PA to Lady Veronica. And Banks liked his solitude. No reason to change things, he thought. If it ain't broke . . .

He felt a sudden urge to phone her. She was leaving for Australia in a couple of days on a book tour, accompanying Lady Veronica Chalmers, who wrote romances under the pseudonym Charlotte Summers. Then he remembered they had agreed not to phone. They both hated protracted good-byes, and he knew that if he rang her, it would hurt after the call was over. Best stay with the music, whisky and memories of the weekend.

It was only the second time he had met Oriana's Italian family, and he could tell that they were still suspicious of him, Oriana's older man, but they also knew that she was special, that she wasn't one for the callous young boys of the neighborhood, who were only interested in one thing, or even in the more serious youths, who wanted to marry her and tie her to home and kitchen and keep her barefoot and pregnant. The family knew that Oriana was a free spirit, so they respected her choice and tolerated Banks. Besides, he thought the Italians were far less concerned about age differences than the more stuffy English, though he didn't know where he got that idea from. One of her uncles even called him *commissario,* usually with a humorous glint in his eye.

Finding the privacy to make love had been difficult, as the relatives insisted on separate rooms for their unmarried guests, but Banks and Oriana had managed to circumvent the problem once or twice in the early hours. Banks was sure an aged aunt on her way back to her room from the toilet had spotted him once. She had glowered at him the rest of the weekend but said nothing, perhaps because she couldn't speak a word of English. Whether she had spoken to Oriana or one of her uncles, Banks had no idea. Oriana never brought up the matter, and he thought it best to let things lie.

The Macallan was going down nicely and the sensuous music of "Le spectre de la rose" flowed over him. It was dark outside, still a couple of weeks before putting the clocks forward, and all he could see was the black shape of Tetchley Fell, its ragged top a dark borderline with the lighter sky. Deliberately edging away from thoughts of Oriana, Banks let his mind drift back to the meeting he had just left.

A number of things puzzled him, not least of all whether there were any links between the tractor and the two missing boys. It was now Monday evening, and Michael Lane had not been seen since Sunday morning, thirty-six hours ago, or thereabouts. They didn't know yet when Morgan Spencer had last been spotted, and would have to carry out more inquiries at the caravan park to find out, but if Spencer had texted Lane about a job on Sunday morning, and they had met up, then it looked as if they might both have disappeared around the same time. Thirty-six hours was not a long time for lads their age to be gone. But then there was the human blood in the hangar and the signs of recent activity there.

Les nuits d'été finished and Banks didn't feel like listening to the two arias from *Les Troyens* that followed. He topped up his Macallan and went back in the entertainment room to pick something else, finally deciding on Gwylim Simcock and Yuri Goloubev: *Reverie at Schloss Elmau,* jazz piano and stand-up bass.

Another thing about the meeting struck him as odd, he thought as he sat down again. Winsome had seemed very defensive toward Terry Gilchrist, though as a soldier with combat experience he couldn't be easily dismissed as a suspect, even though he had found the blood and called in the police. Plenty of murderers reported their own crimes in the hope that doing so would discount them from suspicion.

And Annie had seemed defensive concerning Alex Preston and Michael Lane, though she had admitted that Lane might have been involved in the theft of the Beddoeses' tractor. What was it all about? Was his team going soft on him? Or was he just getting more cynical and hard-bitten as time went on? He didn't like to think so, and he returned to thoughts of Oriana as he worked on the Macallan. Halfway through "A Joy Forever" it started to rain outside, gently at first, then hammering on the roof and blowing against the windowpanes.

ALEX HAD just put Ian to bed and turned on the TV to watch a repeat of *New Tricks* when she heard a knock at the door. Curious, she went over and opened it on the chain. She was greeted by an identity card quickly thrust toward her, then returned to the inside pocket of its owner, a heavyset man in a navy blue raincoat.

"DC Meadows," he announced himself.

"You're not the one who came before," Alex said, feeling a little nervous. "Where's DI Cabbot?"

"Her shift's over. We can't all work 24/7, you know. Besides, she's a DI and I'm a lowly DC. Can I come in, love? It's a bit parky out here."

Alex closed the door, took off the chain and opened it for him. "Sorry," she said. "It's just . . ."

"I understand."

DC Meadows stepped into the living room. Alex took his raincoat and hung it on the hook behind the door. She noticed that he was sweating. "That lift still not working?"

He shook his head. "I'm not used to so much exercise." He dabbed at his brow with a white handkerchief.

Alex had noticed that DC Meadows was a bit overweight. He was also either bald naturally or he had shaved his head, and his bare skull gleamed as red and greasy as his face from the effort of climbing the stairs.

"Sit down," Alex said. "Catch your breath. Cup of tea? Or a glass of wine?" She turned down the volume on the television, assuming this visit wouldn't last long and she could get back to her program. TV helped her forget her problems for a while, and she felt exhausted with worry about Michael since DI Cabbot's visit. She also felt apprehensive about Meadows calling by so late. Had something happened to Michael? Had he done something wrong?

"Just some water, thanks," Meadows said, patting his chest. "I'll be fine in a minute."

Alex brought him some water, poured herself a small glass of white wine and perched at the edge of her chair. "What is it?" she asked. "Have you found out something?"

"In a manner of speaking."

"I don't understand."

"We were wondering if Mr. Lane has been in touch with you at all."

"Mr. Lane? Do you mean Frank Lane?"

"Michael Lane."

"Michael. I see. No, he hasn't. I was hoping *you'd* be able to tell *me* something about him."

"Well, we don't know anything yet, you see, love. That's the problem."

"Problem?"

"Yes." He scratched his scalp. "It's rather delicate. We'd like to talk to him—urgently, as it happens—and we thought that if he went anywhere, it would be to you, or if he got in touch with anyone, it would be you."

"I've been here all day, except when I went to pick Ian up from school, and I haven't seen or heard a thing from him. I wish I had. I'm still worried sick."

"I can understand that," Meadows said. "But you have to see it from our point of view. I mean, people aren't always, they don't always come clean with the police."

"Are you suggesting I'm lying?"

"We wouldn't blame you for protecting him, love. We understand. We get that a lot. Only natural, after all. People care about one another."

"Protecting him? From what? I reported him missing. I don't understand this. I asked you lot to find him."

"Now hang on a minute, miss—"

"Don't you 'miss' me. And you can knock it off with the 'love,' too. Have you found him or haven't you?"

"Well, obviously we haven't, or I wouldn't be here asking you where he was, would I?"

"It's not obvious to me. For all I know, you could be holding him in a cell and not telling me."

"Why would we do that?"

"I've no idea. I just wouldn't put it past you, that's all. It's the sort of thing the police do."

"You don't have a very high opinion of us, do you?"

"What does it matter what opinion I have of you? I want you to find my Michael. What do you want? Why are you here?"

"Don't get your knickers in a twist, love—"

Alex jumped to her feet. She spilled some wine on her T-shirt. "What did you say? What did you say? Get out of here. Go on. Get out. If you've nothing to tell me about what's happened to Michael, get the hell out. And before you go, show me that identification card again. I want your details. I'm going to make a complaint against you."

Meadows stood up and pushed her back down with surprising speed, then he sat down again himself, leaned back in the armchair and smiled. It was a chilling smile, Alex felt, revealing crooked, stained teeth, the incisors just a little larger than normal, like a vampire's. It was a cynical, arrogant and cruel smile, and it sent a shiver up her spine. The mask was off.

"You're not a policeman at all, are you?" she said.

"And I was hoping we could deal with this in a civilized manner," Meadows went on. "It seems not." He cracked his knuckles. "No matter. What I want to know from you is where Michael Lane is hiding."

"Hiding? Why should he be hiding?"

"Never you mind. Just tell me what I want to know, and I'll be on my way."

"I've told you, I don't know where he is." Alex's mind was racing around, trying to think of some way of getting rid of him, or of incapacitating him while she called for help.

He clasped his hands on his lap. Their backs were covered in thick reddish hair. "It seems we're at an impasse, then."

Alex remembered that her mobile was in her handbag on the bed. If she could just get to it, make a 999 call . . . "Look," she said. "I need to go to the toilet. I won't be a minute."

He scanned the room, then said, "All right. I'll wait."

Everyone knew these flats had only one way in and out.

Alex slipped into her bedroom. If she could only dial 999 before he guessed what she was up to, she would be safe. They could probably trace the call if she just left the line open. Her hands were shaking as she took the mobile out of her handbag in the dark room, then headed toward the toilet. Then she felt his presence looming over her. She hadn't heard him, but there he was, standing in the hall, leaning against the wall, arms folded. "The toilet's over there, I think," he said, pointing.

As she moved toward the door, he said, "What's that in your hand?"

"What do you mean?" Alex tried to shove the phone in the pocket of her jeans, hoping he wouldn't notice in the semidarkness. But her jeans were too tight; she missed the pocket, and the phone fell to the carpet.

"Oh, dear," he said, not moving. "Keep going. I think I'd better stay with you, though. You're a tricky one, you are."

Alex went into the toilet, and when he blocked the doorway behind her, following her inside, she realized the full extent of what he meant.

"You can stand outside," she said.

"I don't think so. You've already shown you can't be trusted." He shut the door and leaned back on it. "Go on, then, get your jeans down. Tinkle, tinkle. Chop chop."

Alex reached deep for the last shreds of defiance. "No," she said, hoping she sounded firm. "Not with you standing there, you sick bastard."

An odd smile crossed his face, not like the other one, but just as chilling in its way, then he opened the door for her. "All right," he said. "Piss yourself, then, if that's what you want."

Alex edged out, careful not to brush against him. She thought they were going back into the living room but her blood froze when he opened Ian's bedroom door. She rushed toward him. "What are you—"

He pushed her aside and blocked the open doorway, turning to look in on the sleeping child. Alex tried to get past him, to stand between him and Ian, but it was no good.

"What a sweet scene," said Meadows. "It's all right. Calm down, love. No one's going to get hurt."

"You dare lay—"

"Enough melodramatics. You know every bit as well as I do that if I wanted to lay a finger on him there's nothing you could do to stop me."

"I'll scratch your fucking eyes out." Alex launched herself toward him, arms outstretched, but he dodged aside and pushed her back. She hit the wall with such force that it stunned her, and she slid to the floor. Even then, as she was falling, she saw the dropped mobile phone and tried to reach for it, but Meadows was too quick. Before she could get a grip on it, he trod on it with all his weight and crushed it, then he shifted his foot to the index finger that she had almost managed to hook around it and trod hard on that, too. She screamed in pain. He put a finger to his lips. "Ssshhh," he said. "The boy's sleeping. We don't want to wake him right now, do we? No telling what might happen."

Ian stirred in bed but he didn't wake up. Alex bit back her pain and remained silent. She didn't know what would happen if Ian woke up now and saw Meadows in his doorway, but it wasn't something she dared contemplate.

Meadows squatted, his knees cracking loudly, and put his face close to hers. His breath smelled of Polo mints. "Look, Miss Preston. We don't want any trouble. We just want Michael Lane. Your lad looks like a decent kid. It'd be a tragedy if anything happened to him, wouldn't it? An accident walking by the river or falling out of a tree. Or on the roads. Not safe, these days, the roads. Kids get up to all sorts of dangerous mischief, don't they. Know what I'm talking about?"

Alex nodded, cradling her throbbing finger.

"So let's keep it simple. Tell us where Michael Lane is, and everyone lives happily ever after."

"I . . . don't . . . know," Alex gasped.

Meadows stood up and scratched his temple. "Know what?" he said. "I believe you. But I'm also sure that if he hasn't been in touch already, he will be very soon, and when he is, I want to know. Understand?"

Alex nodded.

Meadows walked toward the front door.

Alex held her breath. "How do I get in touch?" she asked.

He turned. "That's more like it." He handed her a card. On it was a printed number. "And there's no use handing it over to the police," he said. "They won't get anywhere with it, and it'll only make things worse for you. And your son." He glanced at Alex's hand. "Don't forget. You've still got seven fingers and two thumbs left. Not to mention the boy." Then he took his raincoat off the hook and left.

4

ABOUT THE LAST THING BANKS WANTED TO BE DOING
so soon in the mucky gray light just after dawn on a mizzling
March morning was stand around the Riverview Caravan Park looking at the smoldering remains of Morgan Spencer's caravan. His days
ended late, but they didn't usually start so early. If there were any jus-
tice in the world, he'd be lying in bed listening to *Today,* waiting for
"Thought of the Day" to shift him into the shower. Or better still,
he'd be cuddling up to Oriana's warm naked body beside him with
the alarm clock set on snooze. He shivered. No sense making things
worse for himself.

DC Gerry Masterson stood beside him. She had been first in the
squad room that morning, keen newcomer that she was, and as
usual, first to read through the nightlies, which detailed all the
police-involved incidents that had occurred in the region overnight.
Usually it was a matter of drunk drivers, the occasional domestic or
late-night pub brawl that got out of hand, but this time, she told
him, she had noticed one interesting item: a fire at Riverview Caravan Park. That rang a bell, and when she inquired further of the desk
sergeant, she was able to discover that the caravan belonged to one
Morgan Spencer. Now Banks stood beside her at the scene while the
fire investigation officer Geoff Hamilton and his team sifted through
the wreckage. Annie Cabbot was on her way. Winsome and Doug

Wilson could be safely left to take care of everything else for the time being.

The air smelled of wet ash and burned rubber, in its own way almost as bad as the smell of human innards at a postmortem. The area was roped off, but people stood outside their caravans or crowded around the edges of the prohibited area. Some were wearing only dressing gowns, having been woken by the blaze; others were already dressed and ready for the day. A number of uniformed officers made their way through the crowd taking statements. So far, nobody had seen or heard anything. More like they didn't want to get involved, Banks thought.

Banks spotted Annie arriving and waved her over.

"Bloody hell," she said, when she saw the devastation.

Of the neighboring caravans, fortunately, only one had been damaged by the flames, which was a small miracle in itself. Still, Annie told Banks, ex–police sergeant Rick Campbell would be mightily pissed off about his siding.

"Do people insure these things?" Banks asked her.

"I doubt it. The ones who live here year-round probably can't afford it, and the rest can't be arsed."

Hamilton conferred with his team and ambled over. He was never a man to be hurried, Banks remembered from the time they had worked together on a narrow-boat fire. He greeted Banks, Annie and Gerry with his usual courtesy and pointed toward the ruins of the caravan. "Not much left, I'm afraid. Firetraps, most of these things, no matter how much folks try to fireproof them."

"Anyone inside?" Banks asked.

Hamilton shook his head.

"Cause?"

"Well, we can't be certain yet, but the sniffer dogs have found no trace of accelerant, and the burn patterns would seem to indicate the Calor gas burner."

"You mean someone left it on?" Annie said.

"Mebbe," said Hamilton.

"But you doubt it?" Banks prompted him.

"You know me, Alan, I'm not one for wild speculation in the absence of any real concrete evidence."

"But . . . ?"

"Well, all I can tell you is that the rubber pipe had come out at the burner end. It's very much the same principle as a barbecue, if you know how that works."

"I know," said Banks. "I've got one." He had even managed to use it once or twice, between rain showers.

"I'd be careful, then."

"Don't worry, Geoff. I keep it in the garden."

"Even so . . . as I said, it looks as if the rubber hose had come free at the burner end, but was still attached to the Calor gas supply."

"Which turned it into a flamethrower?"

"Aye, more or less."

"And this happened how?" Banks pressed on.

"Well, these things do happen by themselves sometimes," said Hamilton. "Say, if the connection gets blocked by spiders' webs, or something else gets stuck inside and the rubber burns through. But from the remains I've seen here, it looks very much as if someone set a little pile of paper on fire on the floor of the caravan, near the burner, ripped out the end of the hose, turned on the Calor gas and got out fast."

"Arson, then?"

"A near certainty."

"Professional?"

Hamilton pulled a face as he appeared to think it over. "Doubtful. A pro would probably just have lit a fire underneath the caravan itself. Easy to do. And it would have had the same effect eventually."

"But someone was inside?"

"I'd say so. The lock area was splintered, the latch broken off. Fire doesn't do that. Someone had put his shoulder to the door and pushed. It wouldn't have taken much strength."

"Any signs of a search?" Annie asked.

Hamilton glanced back at the damage. "As you can see, nothing much has been spared. I must say, though, that while the cupboards and drawers might have come open and spilled their contents because of the fire, one thing a fire can't do is cut open a mattress and pillows."

"So someone went through the place thoroughly before starting the fire?" Annie said.

"Looks that way. And then pulled out the connecting hose and did as I said."

"Damn," said Annie. "If we'd searched the caravan last night . . ."

"You can't blame yourself," Banks said. "You followed correct procedure. How were we to know someone else had the same idea as we did? We still don't know whether it's connected to anything else we're looking into. Besides, no one was hurt."

"Morgan Spencer was certainly connected to Michael Lane," Annie said. "And Michael Lane was the son of Frank Lane, John Beddoes's closest neighbor and the man who was keeping an eye on his farm while he was in Mexico. Michael Lane lived with Alex Preston, who works in a travel agency. Those are the only connections we know about for sure."

"I know," said Banks. "And I don't like coincidences any more than you do. But what on earth could they have been looking for? Something he had of theirs? Or something that connected them to him? And who are *they*?"

"We won't find out standing here," said Annie. She looked at Hamilton. "Thanks, Geoff. If anything else comes up . . ."

"I'll let you know."

"Where are you going?" Banks asked.

"To see Alex Preston again, pick up Michael Lane's toothbrush or hairbrush for a DNA sample. After that, I think young Dougal and I will have a trip to the seaside."

Banks gave her a quizzical look.

"Denise Lane, Frank's ex, Michael's mother. She might know something."

Banks nodded. "Keep an eye out for any signs of Lane while you're out there. And keep in touch. I may see you at the station later today. Jazz might have something for us by then. Otherwise, report in when you get back from the coast."

Annie hurried back to her car, head down.

"Know anything about Morgan Spencer, Gerry?" Banks asked.

"I did a quick background check when I saw whose caravan it was," said Gerry Masterson. "His mother lives in Sunderland, and no one knows where his dad is. Back in Barbados, most likely. And *he* does have a record. GBH and breaking and entering. I'm still working on this removal van Morgan might have owned, but rumor has it he had a lockup somewhere. I'll be tracking it down when I get back."

"Soon as possible, if you can, Gerry," Banks said.

"Will do."

Banks turned back to the ruins of Morgan Spencer's caravan. The fire would have burned up any traces of DNA. If Michael Lane's DNA wasn't a match for that in the hangar, it could mean that Morgan Spencer was the victim, though there seemed to be no easy way to verify that. The only evidence was circumstantial. According to Alex Preston, Morgan often called or texted Michael Lane about jobs, and Lane had received a text on the Sunday morning he went missing. If both Lane and Spencer were involved in the tractor theft, which wasn't outside the realm of possibility, and if they had both turned up at the airfield that morning, were they both dead? Only Jazz Singh could solve that one when she came back with the DNA analysis. If not, had one killed the other and done a bunk? Alex Preston had told Annie that Michael Lane was home all Saturday night, but then she would, wouldn't she?

Too many questions, Banks realized. They could give a man a headache. He was reading too much into too little. It was time to get back to the station and start trying to gather his thoughts down on paper, put a few ideas together before heading out to the Lane farm.

ANNIE WANTED to find out if Alex Preston knew Michael Lane's blood type. She knew she could probably ask her over the phone, but that might prove tricky, taking into account the questions it raised and Alex's anxiety, so she decided to go in person, even if it meant climbing up to the bloody eighth floor again. Besides, she needed something that would yield a sample of Michael's DNA to take to Jazz.

By some miracle, the lift was working again, and Annie was spared the climb to the eighth floor. The smell was just as bad as last time, and she was glad when the doors finally opened. After a deep breath, she made her way along the balcony to Alex's flat. It was still early—she'd come straight from the caravan site—and she was hoping to catch Alex before she went to work. As it turned out, Alex had just got back from taking Ian to school, and she was making a cup of tea when Annie called.

"What happened to your finger?" Annie asked, noticing the bandages. She also noticed that Alex was looking tired, with bags under her eyes.

"I think I broke it," Alex said. "Trapped it in the door."

"You should see a doctor."

"I've got an appointment for later this morning. I don't think it's so bad I need to go to A and E."

"You never know." Annie accepted a cup of tea and settled down in an armchair. "Is everything else all right? Ian?"

"Yes, of course. Why shouldn't it be?"

"Nothing. You just seem a bit jumpy this morning, that's all."

"Well, wouldn't you be a bit jumpy if your partner had disappeared off the face of the earth?"

"He hasn't disappeared off the face of the earth, Alex. There's a simple explanation for all this. We'll find him. Have you seen or heard anything of him?"

Alex looked away. "No."

Annie wasn't certain whether she was lying. But why would she? "What about Morgan Spencer?"

"No."

"His caravan was burned down during the night."

Alex's eyes widened. "Burned down . . . you mean it caught fire?"

"*Was* burned down. As in, it was deliberately set on fire."

"And Morgan?"

"He wasn't home. There was nobody inside. The place was ransacked first. Any idea why?"

"Me? Why should I have any idea?"

Annie leaned forward, put down her mug and rested her elbows on her legs. "Because I don't believe you're telling me everything."

"Of course I am. What on earth do you mean?"

"Michael and Morgan were up to something, weren't they? Maybe they were mixed up with some seriously dangerous people. We don't know yet. But perhaps you do?"

"I don't know what you're talking about. I don't know anything. Surely you don't believe Michael could have had anything to do with this fire?"

Annie could see the fear in her eyes, hear it in her tremulous voice, smell it like a particularly heavy perfume in the air. "I'm not sure I believe you," she said. "Are you afraid of someone, Alex? Who is it? Morgan? Someone else? Michael? Has someone threatened you?"

"No," said Alex, just a fraction too quickly. "Don't be silly."

Annie glanced down at her finger again. "What was that? A down payment?"

"I told you, I trapped it in the door."

"Oh, yes."

"I don't care if you don't believe me. You can't prove otherwise."

"You're right." Annie settled back and picked up her mug again. "You don't have to tell me anything. And why should I care? But I was hoping you'd realize I'm trying to help you."

"I . . . I . . . there's nothing you can do."

"You're wrong about that. There's a lot I can do. I'm on your side, Alex, but I need something to go on. Anything. I'm in the dark here. What's Michael mixed up in?"

"Nothing. I told you."

Annie sighed. "OK. If that's the way you want to play it. Do you happen to know Michael's blood type?"

"Blood type? Why do you—"

"Can you just answer the question, please, Alex."

"Well . . . not offhand. I have it . . . I think. . . . " She excused herself and went over to the sideboard, where she rummaged through a drawer and brought out a small ring-bound notebook. "This is where I keep all the important information like that, passport numbers and so on," she said, flipping through the pages. "Here it is. A positive. Why do you want to know?"

Annie tried to show no reaction to the news. "It might help us find him."

"You mean you think he's been bleeding? Someone's hurt him? Is he badly hurt?"

"Alex, do you have anything here that I might be able to get a sample of Michael's DNA from? A toothbrush, hairbrush, perhaps?"

"Yes. He didn't take either of those things with him. But why? Why do you need his DNA?" She grasped the collar of her blouse and held it as if she were cold. "You have a body or something, don't you? You think it's Michael."

Annie walked over and rested her hands on Alex's shoulders. "Alex, calm down. You're letting your imagination run away with you. It's routine. It's not only dead people who leave traces of DNA, you know, or bodily fluids that can give us their blood group."

"I don't know what you mean." Alex ran her hand through her hair. "Can't you see I'm at my wits' end here?"

"Just give me what I ask for," Annie said. "Please. And believe me, it will help."

When Alex came back from the bathroom carrying a toothbrush and a hairbrush, she looked even worse. "You might want to tell your doctor you're run-down when you go and see him this morning," Annie said. "He may be able to give you a tonic or something. Are you due at work?"

"Not today, thank God."

Annie stood up and took two bags from her briefcase, placed the toothbrush in one and the hairbrush in the other and wrote neatly on the labels to identify the contents, asking Alex to sign as a witness. Still looking stunned, Alex did as she was asked.

Annie stopped at the door. "Just one more thing," she said. "Do you remember if John Beddoes booked his trip to Mexico through GoThereNow?"

"Yes. Yes, he did. I took the details myself. But what—"

"Did you tell anyone?"

"Why would I?"

"I don't know. Just in passing, you know, in general conversation. After all, Michael knows him. It might have come up."

"I suppose I might have. But I don't understand. Surely you're not suggesting that Michael had anything to do with that tractor, are you? I told you, he was here all night Saturday."

"Until Sunday morning?"

"Yes."

"When he got a text, probably from Morgan Spencer, and said he had to go out and do a job and might call in on his father?"

"Yes."

Annie grasped the door handle. "I'm sure everything's fine, Alex. Don't worry. And be sure to keep your doctor's appointment."

"You'll stay in touch?"

"As soon as we find anything out, you'll be the first to know."

"WHERE'S THAT bonny young lass and wee Harry Potter," said Lane, when Banks showed him his ID and a warrant to search the premises.

"DI Cabbot's on other business, and Harry couldn't come today," Banks answered. "He has an important Quidditch match." He thought Annie would be pleased to hear that she had been called a bonny young lass, though she might not be so thrilled when she heard the source. Lane wasn't that much older than she was, probably only in his mid forties, Banks guessed, though the years of hard physical labor had taken their toll on him: his shoulders sloped, his skin was leathery and weather-beaten, his complexion rough and raw.

Lane snorted. "I suppose you'd better come in." He glanced over Banks's shoulder at the uniformed officers, who were already setting about their search of the outbuildings. "What about them?"

"They won't be long, Mr. Lane. And they'll be careful. Don't worry."

"I'm not worried. Let 'em look to their hearts' content. I can't imagine what they expect to find."

Banks followed Lane into the living room. "We won't take up much of your time," he said, "only we've been around asking a few questions about your son, and the thing is, we still can't seem to find Michael."

"Oh."

"You're not worried about him?"

"Our Michael can take care of himself."

"You said you last saw him about two weeks ago?"

"A little over. Two weeks last Friday. He was doing some work at a farm over the dale, and he dropped by for a cup of tea."

"So you're on speaking terms at the moment?"

Lane's expression hardened. "We have our disagreements, but I've never shunned him. He's my son."

"Alex Preston said Michael told her that he might drop in on you last Sunday."

"Well, he didn't. And who might she be when she's at home?"

"Alex is your son's partner."

"Partner." Lane spat the word. "Scarlet woman, more like."

"Have it your way. I'm not interested in your petty family squabbles. I want to find your son, and I want to find out what happened to your neighbor's tractor." Banks didn't want to mention the blood just yet, the more serious reason for his questions, not until they knew a lot more about what had happened in the old hangar.

"You think he's here, don't you? Our Michael. That's what yon woodentops are looking for, isn't it?"

"We're interested in finding your son, Mr. Lane. It would hardly look good on us if we overlooked the obvious, would it?"

"I told you. I don't know where he is."

"Do you think he could be in trouble?"

"What sort of trouble?"

"Any sort. He's been in trouble with the law before, hasn't he?"

"That was when . . ." Lane stopped himself and subsided in his chair, reaching for a cigarette.

"When what, Mr. Lane?"

"When he was upset. His mother left. It was just a phase he went through, that's all."

"Do you know Morgan Spencer?"

"Aye. And I know Denise always blamed him for Michael's problems. Bad influence. She wouldn't have him in the house."

"He seems to be missing, too. Any idea what might have happened to him?"

"None at all. Why would I? I haven't seen him in nigh on three years."

There was a knock at the door, and the leader of the search team said they'd finished outside and would like to search the interior now. Lane had all three of them take off their muddy Wellington boots before letting them in the house, but they had come prepared with indoor slip-ons.

"Mind if I have a look around with them?" Banks asked.

"Please yourself. You will, anyway. You've got the warrant."

Banks followed the officers around the inside rooms. It wasn't a thorough search, the kind they would make if looking for drugs, for example; at the moment, they were just looking for any signs of someone else living on the premises. There were none that Banks could see. Only one of the three bedrooms was in use, with clothes strewn here and there over an unmade bed. One room was completely empty, even down to the bare floorboards, and the other, the smallest, had a single bed and a small pile of boxes in one corner. That would be where Michael slept if he stopped over, Banks guessed. The boxes held a few childhood toys and books. There was nothing to indicate that the room had been used or the bed slept in at all recently. The house was clean, including the bathroom and toilets. There was only one shaving brush, one twin-blade razor, one toothbrush and one tube of toothpaste. Banks watched a uniformed officer check the cabinets, too, where he found nothing but common pain relievers, cold remedies, indigestion tablets, a prescription for blood pressure medication, plasters and Germolene.

When they had finished, they returned to the living room. Lane looked up and said, "Told you there was nobody here." Then he lit a cigarette and turned on the TV with the remote control. An old episode of *Midsomer Murders,* the ones with John Nettles, came on. Some sort of village fete interrupted by a pagan ritual. It must have been ITV-3, Banks thought; they showed mysteries all day. He looked at the back of Lane's head for a while, then gestured to the three search officers to put their wellies on again and headed back to the police Range Rover. Michael Lane wasn't at his father's farm.

DENISE LANE'S parents, Henry and Ilva Prince, lived in a retirement bungalow on the coast between Whitby and Sandsend. As Annie

and Doug Wilson crossed the North Yorkshire moors, through patches
of thick fog and deep puddles, they chatted every now and then, but
they were also comfortable in silence, just watching the landscape go
by, when they could see it. Annie reflected on how nice it was not to
have to listen to Banks's music, which could be dreadful sometimes.
At the coast, the weather did another about-face and the sky was clear
out to sea. The sun blazed down from a deep blue sky, but there was a
sharp icy wind off the water.

The slight, gray-haired lady, who answered the door with a suspicious and alarmed expression on her face, examined their warrant
cards and let them into her sparsely furnished living room, explaining
how you couldn't be too careful these days, especially as her husband
was out. A picture window faced the North Sea across the slope of a
well-trimmed lawn. The waves rolled in, bright white streaks against
the blue of the sea, finally crashing in a haze of foam on the beach
below. Several tankers or merchant ships edged slowly across the horizon. Sunlight sparkled on the whitecaps.

"Lovely view," said Annie.

"Henry always wanted to retire to the seaside, so here we are," said
Ilva Prince. Her voice sounded like a sigh. Another woman disappointed with her lot in life.

Annie and Doug Wilson continued to enjoy the view as Mrs.
Prince made a pot of tea, then they sat down on the burgundy velour
three-piece suite, complete with wing arms, gold-braided cushions
and white lace antimacassars.

Annie had already explained that they hadn't come bearing bad
news, and Mrs. Prince seemed more at ease. At least, her hand didn't
shake as she poured the tea. "What we were wondering," Annie
began, "was whether you've seen your grandson Michael lately."

"Michael? Not for a few months now," said Mrs. Prince. "The last
I heard, he was shacked up with some floozie on a council estate in
Eastvale."

"That's right," Annie said. "Alex Preston. But you must have got
that from your son-in-law, Frank. Those were his very words. I've
met Alex, and she's not a floozie at all. As far as I can gather, she and
Michael are very much in love. Alex is worried about Michael. She

hasn't seen him since Sunday morning. She says it's not like him to go off without saying. She thought he might have been visiting his dad. I'm just wondering if maybe he was visiting his mother?"

"Our Denise? Well, he isn't. Maybe he's come to his senses and left this woman?"

"I'm being serious about this, Mrs. Prince."

"So am I. Besides, our Denise doesn't live here anymore, and Michael certainly hasn't been here visiting us. He's just like his father, never had much time for Henry and me. Not that we haven't tried. Oh, he'd drop by now and again when his mum was here at first, like, but—"

"Do you know if your daughter has seen him in the past few days?"

"She would have said."

"So you do still see her?"

"Yes, of course. It's just that . . . well, she met a fellow, you see. Lives in Whitby. And she . . . they . . . well, she's moved in with him. He's a nice chap, mind you, is Ollie. It's short for Oliver, you know. I always thought Oliver was a lovely name. Very distinguished. Like Oliver Cromwell. Not that he's got any airs and graces, mind you. But he's a decent lad. He's got a university degree. Got a good job, too. He works in the council offices. They were here for tea just this last Sunday."

"And she didn't mention Michael?"

"No. Why should she?"

"We'd really like to talk to her about him," said Annie.

Mrs. Prince looked at her watch. "Well, she won't be home now. She'll be at work. That big Tesco's down by the railway station."

Doug Wilson stood up. "Mind if I use your toilet, Mrs. P.?" he said. "Long car ride from Eastvale."

Mrs. Prince pointed across the room. "It's through there, on the right. And leave it as you find it."

"Yes, ma'am."

"Denise and her husband have been separated for two years now. Is that correct?"

"About that long, yes."

"Do you have any insight into what happened?"

Mrs. Prince pursed her lips. "Well," she said, "you never really know with marriages, do you? People don't open up to you about private matters like that, do they? All they ever talk about is being incompatible, or things not working out. Only they really do know *why*, if they're honest. I mean, Henry and me were against the marriage right from the start. She should never have married a farmer, I told her. She was throwing herself away on him. She could have made a good career for herself in business or something, married a nice accountant, or even a lawyer. You should have seen her then. She was a lovely girl. Clever, too. She did really well at school, got three A levels and all. She could have gone to any university she wanted, but no, she had to get a job straightaway and start earning money so she could enjoy her freedom. That's how she put it. 'I want to enjoy my freedom while I'm young.' Money for clothes and makeup and CDs and nights out clubbing in Leeds." Mrs. Prince snorted. "A long time *that* lasted. Her freedom."

"She married young?"

"Young enough. She was nineteen. Worked at the NatWest down on Eastvale market square back then. Henry and I were living in Middlesbrough for his work, like. It wasn't all that far away. And she'd learned to drive, had a little car of her own. Then Frank Lane had to walk in and apply for a loan. I ask you, what woman in her right mind would fall for a man who goes into a bank to apply for a *loan*?"

Wilson came back into the room and sat down again.

"How long were they married?" Annie asked.

"Twenty years. She's still a young woman. Takes good care of herself, too. Always down at that gym, working out."

"And she has a job at Tesco's?"

Mrs. Prince paused. "Well, it's just temporary, like, until she gets on her feet. She'll be back in banking before long, just you wait and see. Manager, I wouldn't be surprised."

"So she's not working in the Tesco office now, in management?"

"Not exactly."

"When she split up with Frank, did she come straight here to live with you and your husband?"

"Yes. She was in a terrible state. He kicked her out and chucked her clothes after her. I told her right from the start she shouldn't have married him, that life as a farmer's wife would never agree with her. She was like a beautiful bird in a cage. She liked nice things and parties and going to restaurants, holidays in Spain, trips to London and Paris. She was a virtual prisoner up at that farm. I don't know how she stuck it out for so long. It must have been for the sake of the boy."

"You think that's what did it in the end? The farm, her life up there, the isolation?"

"'Course it was. And there was never enough money. They were always scrimping and saving to make ends meet. I'm not saying her Frank was tightfisted or owt, not really, but there were times when she could hardly afford to put a meal on the table. I ask you. And he was working all hours God sent. They had no life, never went anywhere. Not even London. No, it's a wonder it didn't happen sooner." Mrs. Prince folded her arms.

"You mentioned the sake of the boy. Do you think she waited until Michael grew up before leaving?"

"I suppose that was partly it. I mean, she does care for the lad, give her her due. She was a good mother. But I'm sure it had been in the cards for some time. Michael was seventeen when our Denise finally left. I reckon she thought he was old enough to take care of himself by then. Not that he had a clue, like. Another one who didn't want to stay in school and go to university. Didn't know what he wanted to do, if you ask me. Still doesn't."

Annie didn't think she knew what she wanted to do when she was seventeen. Mostly just get drunk on Bacardi Breezes and hang out with the boys. Doug Wilson probably didn't know, either, she thought, glancing sideways at him. She thought Winsome knew, though, that she always wanted to be a police officer, just like her dad back in Jamaica. He was her hero, or so she had once confessed after a vodka and tonic too many. But Annie had no idea. Even now she sometimes wondered whether she had made the right decision.

Doug Wilson tapped his pen on his notebook and looked over at Annie. It was the kind of look that said what are we doing wasting our time here, and Annie realized he was right. They had found out as much as she wanted to know about the Lane family, and they would get nothing but more bile out of old Mrs. Prince. Christ, what a miserable bloody family, Annie thought. At least the two members she'd met so far were hardly bundles of joy. Maybe Michael and Denise had a better attitude. Well, she'd soon find out.

Just as they were leaving, she turned and asked Mrs. Prince, "Do you know any of Michael's friends?"

"I can't say as I do."

"A lad called Morgan Spencer?"

"Can't say as I've heard of him."

"Is there anything else you can help us with?"

"I don't see how. As I said, I don't have anything much to do with the Lanes, not since our Denise moved out."

Annie nodded to Wilson, and they left. They stood by the car for a moment and looked out to sea. The ships were mere dots on the horizon. The wind was chill but the water was blue, the sun bright.

"There was no one else in the house," Wilson said. "I had a good look around. Clean as a whistle."

"Not surprising," said Annie. "So what do you think?"

"She doesn't know anything."

"I've a feeling you're right. Fancy a bit of lunch before we tackle the ex-wife? I mean, one can hardly come to Whitby and not have fish and chips, can one?"

5

BANKS THOUGHT HE MIGHT AS WELL CHECK IN WITH Beddoes while he was out that way, and while he did so, the three search team officers could have a good rummage around the outbuildings. He didn't think Michael Lane would be hiding out there, but you never knew. Besides, he hadn't met John Beddoes yet and wanted to get the measure of the man.

Annie had told Banks that Beddoes looked more like a business executive than a farmer, and it was true. He was suave and distinguished looking, a man used to being in charge. Either way, Banks certainly couldn't see him mucking out the stables or cleaning out the pigsty or whatever farmers did. Maybe he employed someone else to do that for him. Gerry had also dug up a bit of background and found out that he had been one of the City boys in the mid-1980s, making huge amounts of money on the stock market when they threw out the rule book. Banks had been working in London then, but he had been fighting a losing battle with Soho gangs rather than making money hand over fist. Everyone was at it, though, and he knew that more than a few of his colleagues were on the take. Heady times.

The Bang & Olufsen sound system was top of the line, Banks noticed, and a quick glance at the stack of CDs on his way to sit down indicated a taste for Bach, Mozart and Handel.

"So you're the famous DCI Banks. I've heard all about you. The wife is in a book club with your boss, you know."

"I know," said Banks, who found it hard to imagine Area Commander Gervaise talking about him at her book club. "I hope what you've heard is all good."

Beddoes smiled. "That would be telling. Sorry. Pardon my manners. Can I get you anything? Tea, coffee, something stronger, perhaps?"

Banks held his hand up, palm out. "Nothing, thanks. This is just a quick call. That's a nice sound system you've got there."

"An indulgence of mine. Would you like to hear it in action?"

"Please."

Beddoes got up, flipped through the discs and put on a Bach cantata. Every instrument, every nuance of voice, came through loud and clear, yet the music was low enough that they could easily talk over it.

Beddoes gestured toward the window. "I notice you've brought the troops."

"Oh, them. I hope you don't mind. I asked them to have a good look at the scene, see if they could find any more trace evidence. We have so little to go on."

"I sympathize," said Beddoes. "And I don't mind at all. They'd better not get too close to the pigs, though. They're in a bit of a bad mood today."

"I'm sure they won't disturb your pigs."

Beddoes crossed his legs the other way. "So what can I help you with? I must say, everyone I've talked to so far has been very thorough. Most commendable. I don't imagine I'll be able to add anything to what I've already told your officers."

"I just wanted a look at the place, really," said Banks, "and as I was over talking to Mr. Lane I thought I'd drop by and introduce myself."

"Checking out the scene of the crime, eh? Have you seen anything of Patrick's son yet? I understand the lad's gone walkabout."

"Nothing yet," said Banks. "You didn't have much time for Michael Lane, did you?"

"I can't say I did. He was a juvenile delinquent just waiting to happen, as far as I was concerned," said Beddoes. "Or is that a politically incorrect term these days?"

"More dated, I'd say. Was there anything specific that caused your falling-out?"

"We didn't fall out, per se. We were never close to begin with. No, the boy was a pest, that's all. But that doesn't mean I'm hoping something's happened to him. I know Frank loves his son, despite their differences. He's just a man who finds it hard to talk about his feelings."

"Like most men, according to most of the women I know. Are you sure it wasn't just youthful high spirits with Michael Lane?"

"Perhaps it was. He was mouthy, mischievous. I don't suppose that makes him a criminal. Come to think of it, I was probably a bit that way, myself."

"Did he ever steal from you, commit any acts of vandalism?"

"No, nothing like that. You've heard about the joyriding, I suppose?"

"Yes. Do you think that makes him a suspect in the theft of your tractor?"

"Michael Lane?"

"Why not?"

"I never really considered that. I don't think he'd be capable of the level of organization needed to pull off such a job. There must have been more than one of them, wouldn't you think?"

"Possibly. Though I heard the key was readily available."

Beddoes reddened. "Yes, well, I've learned my lesson from that."

Something about bolting stable doors came into Banks's mind, but he didn't give voice to it. "Could Lane have known you were going to be away?"

"I suppose so. His father knew, naturally."

"Did you know that Lane's girlfriend works in the GoThereNow in the Swainsdale Centre?"

Beddoes frowned. "No, I didn't. I know nothing about his private life."

"Isn't that where you booked your trip?"

"Yes. Are you suggesting that she told Lane, and that he and some pals made off with the tractor?"

"It's just a possibility, that's all. I can't say it's one I take very seriously, though. As you say, there's a level of organization to all this. Of course Lane might be a cog in a much larger wheel. But it wasn't just something a mischievous kid does on the spur of the moment. Steal an expensive tractor. How would he get rid of it, for a start, assuming he could have made away with it?"

"That's exactly what I said."

"Do you know a friend of Lane's called Morgan Spencer?"

"I can't say as I do."

"The two of them do odd jobs on farms around the dale."

"Not here they don't. I wouldn't trust Lane anywhere near my property. Do you think this Spencer character was involved?"

"I don't know anything yet," said Banks. "Only that there are too many loose ends and too many coincidences." He slapped his thighs. "No doubt it'll all become clear before long. I've taken up too much of your time already. Thanks for the music, Mr. Beddoes."

"John, please," said Beddoes, holding out his hand to shake when they reached the door. "My pleasure."

"John, then," said Banks. "And don't worry, we'll do our best to find your tractor."

He headed back to the Range Rover, where the three uniformed officers were waiting for him. The looks on their faces told him they had found nothing of interest.

AFTER A hearty lunch of fish and chips and mushy peas in the Magpie, Annie and Wilson made their way to Tesco and found Denise Lane working at one of the checkout counters. Annie persuaded her to take an early break and accompany them to the little coffee shop near the supermarket entrance. They found an empty table by the plate-glass window that looked out on the car park and the inner harbor beyond. Wilson went to fetch a latte for Denise. Neither Annie nor Wilson wanted anything after their lunch. Besides, Annie thought, there was something obscene about drinking latte straight after fish and chips. A couple of unruly children were running around unattended, but other than that the coffee shop was quiet, and their table was far enough away from the others for privacy. Annie glanced out of the window and saw flocks of seagulls circling above an old wooden sailing ship moored in the harbor. It was something historic, she thought, something she should know about but didn't. Hornblower, Nelson or Captain Cook or someone.

Denise Lane had a heart-shaped face under a tidy cap of streaked blond hair, a smooth complexion and attractive features, all in the right proportions. She was also long-legged and looked slim and shapely under her uniform. Mrs. Prince had been right about the fitness center. Denise Lane would hardly be forty, Annie reminded herself, not much more than ten years older than Alex Preston, and maybe five or six years younger than her ex-husband. If those hard years on the farm had taken their toll on her, she had certainly worked at regaining her good looks and youthful glow. Perhaps her weakest feature, Annie noticed, was her fingers, which were short and stubby, with bitten and broken nails.

"What's wrong?" she asked Annie, before Doug Wilson had even returned with the coffee. "Has something happened to Michael?"

"Why would you think that?"

"It's not every day I get a visit from the police. I haven't done anything wrong, so I assume it must be bad news."

"Just routine inquiries," said Annie, kicking herself immediately for coming out with the most obvious police cliché. "I mean, we're just here to ask you a few questions, that's all. As far as I know, nobody's come to any harm, and nobody's done anything wrong."

"You must have *some* reason for seeking me out."

Wilson came back, handed her the latte and took out his notebook.

"When did you last see Michael?" Annie asked.

"Not for a while."

"How long ago?"

"A few months."

"You're not close?"

"I suppose not. At least, not since . . ."

"The separation?"

"Yes. It's been difficult for everyone. I mean, Michael stayed at the farm with his dad. What could he do, really? He was only seventeen. Oh, he used to come and see me at Mum and Dad's sometimes, at first, but we argued. I think he blamed me for what happened. And Mum can be so . . . judgmental. I suppose I felt betrayed, abandoned.

Then when I met Ollie things changed. I saw less and less of Michael. He and Ollie didn't get on at all. Maybe in time . . . ? I don't know."

"So you don't know much about his recent life, what he's doing, how he's living?"

"I know he moved out about a year ago and he has a girlfriend who's older than him, but that's about all."

"Your mother calls her the 'floozie.' Doesn't that bother you?"

"What? That Mum calls her a floozie? That she's older than him? Why should it? Men take up with younger women all the time. As long as they're happy, I don't care. Look, I wish you'd get to the point. My break's not long enough to waste on idle chat about Michael."

Annie wished she knew what the point was. "We're trying to find him, that's all," she said. "A neighbor's tractor was stolen while he was away on holiday, and Michael's father was supposed to be looking after the man's farm. Mr. Beddoes mentioned Michael, that's all."

"And you think he did it? On John Beddoes's say-so?"

"We don't think that at all, but we do want to talk to him. It seems there was some bad blood between your son and Mr. Beddoes, and Michael does have a conviction to his name."

"You never let go, you lot, do you? Oh, I know all about the stolen car. The joyride. One silly mistake and he's in your sights forever."

"It's not like that," Annie protested, though perhaps without too much conviction. "Michael's disappeared. Alex is worried about him. We want to find him, that's all."

"Don't make a mountain out of a molehill. It's not a disappearance. That's so melodramatic. Is that what this floozie told you? Alex. That he'd disappeared?"

"Do you know a friend of his called Morgan Spencer?"

Denise looked toward the harbor through the window. "Morgan? Why do you mention Morgan?"

"Your mother said you don't think very highly of him. He's made himself scarce, too."

"Well, there's someone you should keep in your sights. I always thought he was a bad influence on our Michael. He's older, for a start. They've known each other for a few years, since before I left. I suspect Morgan was behind the joyriding business, for a start. It was only Michael who took the blame, but I'll bet you anything Morgan was behind it. He was older. He'd probably have got a harsher sentence. I also blamed him for putting ideas into Michael's head."

"What ideas?"

"Oh, about what a waste of time education was, how you should just make your own way, that there was plenty of easy money to be had if you knew how to get it. Christ, I wish to bloody God I'd gone to university when I had the chance."

"Why didn't you?"

Denise gave a harsh laugh. "I wanted money in my pocket, the flash life. I couldn't see the sense in learning some subject I didn't care about. I wanted holidays abroad, sun and fun. What I got was Frank bloody Lane and the farm. Only myself to blame. But that's behind me now."

"So Morgan was a bad influence on Michael. Is that all you know about him?"

"He's . . . I think . . ." She looked away.

"What is it, Denise?"

"I think he's dangerous, too." She glanced around the coffee shop, as if to make sure no one could hear. Annie didn't think anyone could. Then Denise lowered her voice. "Or he could be. One time, about three years ago, before things really started to fall apart, Morgan came up to the farm looking for Michael. He wasn't there. Neither was Frank. I was by myself. Morgan didn't seem bothered by that, and he started to . . . I don't know . . . chat me up, I suppose. Then he got more explicit. Said why didn't we go upstairs, we could have some fun. That I wasn't bad looking for an old woman, and he could give me a good time. That sort of thing. Thinks he's God's gift."

Annie felt herself turn cold. "Did he touch you?"

"Just, you know, he put his hand on my breast, but I slapped him away. I thought then for a moment from the expression on his face that he was going to force me. He looked so angry at being rejected."

"But he didn't do anything?"

"No. He just left."

"And that was the only time?"

"I wouldn't have him in the house after that."

"Did you tell your husband or Michael?"

"No. I haven't told anyone. I felt so dirty, so ashamed, and things were already bad between Frank and me. But I want you to know what kind of person he is. If there's any trouble, if Michael's in any sort of bother, then you can bet Morgan Spencer is behind it."

"THANKS FOR agreeing to see me at such short notice," Banks said to Detective Inspector Joanna MacDonald as they sat in a pub on the outskirts of Northallerton waiting for lunch.

"Any excuse to get out of the office," Joanna said, smiling. "And you did say you were buying."

"How's it going?"

Joanna shrugged. "What can I say? The career's fine. The personal life's still a bit of a mess. It gets a bit lonely sometimes."

Banks knew that Joanna had recently separated from her husband after she had discovered that he was involved in a number of affairs, or flings, as she had called them. He remembered how much it had hurt him when his own ex-wife, Sandra, had left him for someone else, the betrayal, the sense of being played for an idiot for not seeing it coming, the shame and humiliation.

"You miss your husband?"

"Like a bad smell. But to look on the bright side, I'm not in Professional Standards anymore, so everyone doesn't hate me."

Somehow, Joanna didn't seem so much the icy Hitchcock blonde she had been when Banks had first met her. She was still blond, and still a very attractive woman, but now instead of wearing her hair piled on top, she let it hang straight over her shoulders. She wore black-rimmed glasses, which suited her and gave her the aspect of a college professor. There was also something warmer and more open about her manner. When they had been on a case in Tallinn together, she had been remote, edgy and quick-tempered. It was probably a lot to do with working for Professional Standards, Banks knew, and suspecting her husband of infidelity, and he had to admit that he hadn't exactly welcomed her with open arms. She was the enemy, after all. In fact, he had treated her cruelly, and he now felt childish when he remembered the silly practical jokes he had played on her.

"You did a damn good job," Banks said simply.

Joanna laughed. "Thanks. It might have helped if you'd told me so at the time."

"Well, no one likes being under the microscope."

"Oh, I was never out to get you. You know that. You just had an exaggerated sense of your own importance, like most men."

"Now there's a generalization if ever I've heard one. I wasn't that bad, was I?"

Joanna wrinkled her nose and held her thumb and forefinger slightly apart. "Maybe just a little bit. Anyway, you haven't come all this way only for the pleasure of my company." She tucked her hair behind her ears. "What can I do for you?"

Banks waited while the server brought their plates of food, warning them to be careful, they were hot. It was typical modern pub grub, haddock and chips and a beef and mushroom pie, also with chips. Banks sipped a pint of Timothy Taylor's and Joanna stuck to Diet Coke.

"You're still working on Operation Hawk, aren't you?" he asked.

"I spend most of my waking hours on it. Ever since our new police commissioner made it a priority. Why?"

Banks explained a little about the missing tractor and the blood found at the abandoned hangar.

"And you think they're linked?" Joanna asked.

"Yes. Not officially, of course, not yet. We don't have the DNA results, for a start. But we do have a stolen tractor and two people of interest who seem to have disappeared. And the timing is just too close to be coincidence."

"Are these two local?"

"Yes."

"Can you give me their names?"

Banks told her, and Joanna wrote them down in her notebook. She ate some more fish, then put her knife and fork aside and rested her arms on the table. Banks noticed that the cuffs of her white blouse were a little frayed around her wrists. That wasn't like the Joanna he had known. Had she let things go? Was she hard up? Perhaps the divorce was costing her in more ways than one. Or maybe she was just working too hard. "As you probably know," she said, "what we do on Operation Hawk is try to keep track of criminals on the move who strike at rural communities around the country. We also link up with various farm and border watch groups, along with the National Parks Commission, Country Watch and the Farmers' Union, to spread awareness of the problem. I don't really see how we can help you much if it's a local matter. You'd be just as well equipped to deal with something like that as we would."

"I understand," said Banks. "But it's the national angle I'm interested in. Maybe even international. Who knows? I mean, if someone steals a few sheep, the odds are he's going to slaughter them locally in an illegal abattoir and sell the meat off the back of a lorry, especially with the price of lamb these days. But if he steals a tractor worth a hundred thousand quid or more, he's going to whisk it out of the country sharpish. And for that you need organization. Remember Tallinn?"

"I do remember," Joanna said, with a tilt of her head. Then she laughed and touched his hand. "Whatever happens, Alan. We'll always have Tallinn."

Definitely not the Joanna Banks he had known. She *had* changed. She would never have said something like that before.

"But that was different," Joanna went on. "It was people we were dealing with, not sheep or pigs. Or tractors."

"We think the hangar might have been used as an exchange point," Banks went on. "You know, somewhere the local thieves deliver their goods, whatever they are, make the transfer, and get it on transport brought in specially for the purpose. Then it goes on its way to Bulgaria or wherever. For that, some of the people involved have to drive up and down the A1. I understand you're using ANPR to track the movements of suspects?"

"You've been reading the papers, I can tell," said Joanna, leaning back in her chair and sipping her Coke. "OK, yes, that's a part of what we do." ANPR stood for automatic number plate recognition, a system of software able to collect number plate data from converted CCTV units on all motorways, major roads and in town and city centers.

"So you must have some names for me."

"What do you mean?"

"Some of your regulars. And don't tell me Operation Hawk has yielded no results so far. There's organization involved here, Joanna. Palms to be greased, papers to be forged, that sort of thing. They might use locals for the jobs and for the scouting, but the whole operation's got to be run by an organized gang. There has to be a brain behind it somewhere. And money."

"Fair enough. There's a few people we're keeping an eye on, though they're hardly the ones who drive lorries up and down the motorways. We do liaise with the NCA, too, on a regular basis, as well as with other county forces." The NCA was the National Crime Agency, what the media referred to as the British FBI, which had replaced the Serious Organised Crime Agency. They weren't primarily concerned with rural crime, as was Operation Hawk, but they were interested in almost everything else except counterterrorism, which remained within the Met's remit. Slowly but surely, the technology was catching up with the criminals. "The problem is," Joanna went on, "that we'd need specific locations to know if a certain car or lorry has been regularly spotted on that route. And, as you can imagine, on somewhere like the M1 or the A1 there's a hell of a lot of normal traffic flow to rule out."

"I see what you mean," said Banks. "But if I give you the location of the hangar, and the closest access points to and from the A1, can you find out whether anyone's been visiting the place regularly over the past year or so?"

"We keep the ANPR data for two years, so yes, we can do that. I don't know about the actual location itself, but certainly the general area. Have you thought, though, Alan, that if some organization is using that corridor, as you suggest, then they'll be smart enough to know about ANPR, and maybe even about Operation Hawk—it's hardly a classified operation, after all. They could avoid detection by using different vehicles. Or different number plates. Or varying their route."

"Surely even you lot can spot a false number plate?"

Joanna laughed. "Sometimes. But there's a lot of traffic. Not to mention all the foreign vehicles. We can liaise with Interpol and Europol if we need, as well as with forces in specific countries, but that takes time and a finely honed sense of what you want. What you're talking about just sounds too vague to me. I'm not saying we can't help. Don't get me wrong. Just telling you not to expect miracles."

"I never have," said Banks. "Not unless I've laid the groundwork for them." He finished his pie and sipped some beer, then swirled the pale gold liquid in his glass. "If I'm thinking along the right lines," he went on, "someone might have driven up on Sunday morning. At least that's when one of our suspects received a text and left his flat in a hurry."

"Or down," said Joanna. "How do you know they didn't come from Newcastle, or Edinburgh, Glasgow?"

"Point taken. Or down. But one way or another we're looking at placing a vehicle, or vehicles, at the abandoned airfield between, say, half past nine and ten o'clock, which means they would have come off the A1 about a mile from the village of Hallerby five minutes earlier. Or from the junction at Thirsk or Northallerton."

"You'd be surprised how much data that involves, but I'd say we could probably do it, yes. Remember, though, we're only interested in specific vehicles. We've got a definite location and a specific time frame. What exactly are you looking for?"

"In the first place, anyone on your list, any of your specific vehicles, anyone suspected of having even the remotest involvement in rural crime on a large scale being spotted at that place and time. Second, anyone you've been tracking for some time, anyone who seems to have made an inordinate number of trips up there for no apparent reason. Also, anyone with a criminal record of any kind, especially for violent offenses."

"That latter request might be difficult," Joanna said. "It's not really within our parameters to check all number plates for convicted criminals. Needless to say, we can't actually tell you who was driving the car or lorry at the time, just that it passed such and such a location. And it's not as if we're out there writing down the numbers of all the cars that pass by. It's a very specific operation, precise, targeted."

Banks slipped out his notebook and gave her Michael Lane's number plate. "It would help if we could know whether he'd been in the area or not, too," he said. "And we're tracking down another number, a large van used for removals. We think it may have been involved in the theft of the tractor."

"I'll see what I can do," said Joanna. "But, remember, some of these people are clever."

"Everyone slips up sometime. And it's just possible that someone might have been in a hurry. It looks as if there was a shooting at the hangar, Joanna. It's not just a stolen tractor or a few missing sheep now. It could be murder."

TERRY GILCHRIST had just put his feet up for an hour's reading before dinner when the doorbell rang. His leg hurt and he cursed mildly as he got to his feet and went to answer it. He could see only a blurred figure through the frosted glass, but when he opened the door he saw the beautiful black detective standing there. At least he thought she was beautiful. He hoped his mouth hadn't dropped as far as he felt it had. Since he'd been to war, then invalided back home, he seemed to have lost whatever facility he had ever possessed with the opposite sex. He had certainly had no interest in the brothels of Helmand Province, and opportunities to meet other kinds of women outside the armed forces themselves had been few and far between. Now here stood a woman who probably suspected him of murder. He had been friendly with one of the military investigators out in Helmand, who had worked on the Met as a detective, and he knew they always suspected the person who reported the crime. Still, she was smiling, and that was a good sign. She was casually dressed in jeans and black polo-neck jumper. Perhaps that was a good sign, too.

"Come in," he said, standing aside and gesturing toward the living room.

"Hope I didn't disturb anything," she said. "I have a few more follow-up questions for you."

"Not at all. Just having a sit-down." *She has an intriguing voice,* he thought. At first he had hardly noticed it, as she appeared to speak unaccented English, but if he listened closely he could hear intermingled undertones of Jamaica and Yorkshire. It was a unique blend, and he'd challenge any actor, however skilled, to reproduce it.

She sat down gracefully, crossing her long legs. He noticed her glancing at his leg as he walked by and used his arms to lower himself back into the armchair.

"I suppose it could be worse," she said. "I mean the leg. Worse things than ending up with a slight limp." He got the impression from her awkward tone that he had embarrassed her by catching her looking at his disability.

"Much worse. The alternatives hardly bear thinking about. Believe it or not, I'm on the mend. The doctors assure me the stick will go completely soon, but they fear the limp will persist. I don't mean to complain, but the devil of it is that I'm used to outdoors pursuits. I used to love long-distance running, golf, tennis, even a little fishing and potholing now and then."

"Potholing?" Winsome said. "I used to do that."

"Used to? What happened?"

"I got lost once, and the water was rising. I'm afraid I panicked a bit. It sort of put me off."

"I suppose if you stop to think what you're doing when you're lost in a cold wet cave a hundred feet under the ground, it might seem like a sort of crazy thing to do."

Winsome laughed. He liked her laugh, and that he could make her laugh. "I almost came a cropper," she went on. "I was in the narrowest section, you know, worming my way through to the ledge overlooking the big cavern at Gaping Gill. When you panic, of course, you just get yourself more stuck. They found me and got me out, of course, but I think I must have lost my nerve after that. I thought there could be a sudden shower and I'd just drown like a . . . well, drown."

"It can be very dangerous down there." Gilchrist sipped his coffee. "I'm glad you didn't."

"What?"

"Drown."

"Oh, yes. Me, too."

They both laughed.

"Perhaps we could go together?" Gilchrist said. "Potholing, that is. When all this is over." He tapped his leg. "This wouldn't be much of a hindrance. Maybe I can help you get your nerve back?"

"Maybe. We'll have to see." Her tone sounded clipped, as if she were cutting off the possibility. Gilchrist felt disproportionately disappointed. After all, he hardly knew her. Was it forward to ask a woman you found attractive to go potholing with you? He no longer had any idea about the propriety or etiquette of such things. Best shut up about it and get to the questions she had come to ask him, stick to the point of her visit. To do otherwise would only be to invite grief.

"Do you remember anything more about those lorries you mentioned?" she asked. "Any markings or anything?"

Now they were back on familiar terrain, but even this Gilchrist found painful. He used to pride himself on his keen powers of observation and memory—he would probably have made a good detective himself, his CO had once said—but since the explosion, his memory seemed to have gone the same way as his leg. He only hoped it would recover as well in time. "I don't think they had any markings," he said. "I don't remember any."

"When you saw them, what did you think they were doing there?"

"I must admit, I had no idea. It's like when you see all those juggernauts by the roadside at Scotch Corner. Drivers having a nap or something. They have their routines. I know they're only supposed to drive a limited number of hours per day. They have to sleep somewhere, and it saves on B and B money if they sleep in the cab. These were smaller, so sleeping in the cab was probably out. In the back, maybe."

"I suppose so," said Winsome. "Did you ever get the impression they were delivering something, or picking something up? Ever see anyone loading or anything like that?"

Terry shook his head. "I think I would remember if I had," he said, feeling far from certain that he would.

"What about the children you said you saw playing there? Do you know any of them?"

"I've thrown their ball back to them once or twice, but I wouldn't say I know them. Not by name. They're from the village. As I said, they're all right, really, but the older ones do tend to be antisocial, or just suspicious of strangers. Maybe rightly so."

"Do you know where any of them live?"

"I've seen a couple of them coming or going from houses when I've been shopping."

"It might help if you could let me know the addresses."

"I'm afraid I don't remember. The streets are all named after trees, and I get confused. I could probably point out some of the houses."

Winsome nodded and Terry watched her make a note in her black book. "We'll send someone over when it's convenient for you," she said. "Maybe tomorrow morning, if that's OK? We'd like to have a word with some of them."

"I'm not going anywhere. I don't suppose they'll be able to tell you much, though. After all, they wouldn't have been there when the lorries were."

"No, but even so . . ."

"Yes. You have to be thorough." Again, Terry felt disappointed that she wasn't going to accompany him on a walk around the village to identify the children's houses. He could point out the highlights of Drewick, such as they were. As it happened, he could only remember where one or two of the children lived, so it probably wouldn't do her any good. They could canvass the whole village if they wanted. It wouldn't take long. He also realized that it probably wasn't a job for someone of her rank; she'd send a patrol car, most likely, and at most a DC to question the kids. But she had come to see him again in person. That was something to hold on to.

Before he hardly noticed, she was putting away her notebook and preparing to get up and leave. He was trying to think of a way to get her to stay when he had forgotten to offer her basic hospitality. "Forgive me," he said. "I forgot to ask if you wanted anything to drink. Would you like something? Tea? Coffee?"

Winsome smiled. "No, thanks. It's getting a bit late. I ought to be off. We're not only in it for the perks, you know."

He started to protest that wasn't what he meant when he noticed the cheeky grin on her face. "Got me there," he said.

He grasped the arms of the chair to heave himself up and follow her out, but she said, "No, that's all right. Stay there. I can find my own way. Don't worry about it." Then she smiled again and the next thing he knew the door had closed behind her.

He sagged back into the chair feeling like an abject failure. He banged the chair arm with his fist, then thumped his gammy leg, too, just for good measure.

6

CALEB ROSS HAD BEEN DRIVING AROUND THE DALES farms for thirty-five years, thirty of them for Vaughn's ABP, always the white vans with the high sides, covered and leakproof, in their various incarnations. He wouldn't say he knew the roads the way he knew the gnarled veins on the backs of his hands, but he knew most of them well enough that he didn't have to drive every inch; he could usually let the internal cruise control take over for a while. He was also used to people overtaking him. Everyone wanted to overtake him, no matter what speed he was traveling, so he had learned to stay at a reasonable fifty and to wave drivers on when he could see that the road ahead was clear. If anyone honked a horn at him, he never heard it because he was always playing his loud music, usually of the kind known as progressive rock, from Rick Wakeman to Genesis and Emerson, Lake & Palmer. He liked the operatic structures of the concept albums and the fantastic stories they told—*The Six Wives of Henry VIII, Journey to the Centre of the Earth, The Rime of the Ancient Mariner*—they kept him interested as he did what was, most of the time, an extremely dull job. And an occasional puff or two on the old wacky baccy didn't do any harm, either.

Early that Tuesday afternoon, he was driving south over Belderfell Pass from the western end of Swainsdale, listening to Pink Floyd's "Grantchester Meadows." It was not as progressive as some of the music he liked, but it suited his mood. He loved the drive for its panoramic views, no human habitation but for an occasional abandoned farmhouse, a distant dot on the vast landscape. Even in March, the greens were rich on the lower pastures and contrasted sharply with the patches of sere grass higher up. Belderfell Beck ran far below, a thin silver line winding along the narrow groove of the valley bottom, and squiggly lines of rills meandered down the daleside.

But Caleb didn't enjoy the journey so much on days like this. On days like this, only the experienced, the foolhardy and the lost ventured over Belderfell Pass. It had been clear when Caleb had made his way up the hill out of Swainsdale, but now heavy clouds massed and threatened from the north and west, and the wind was getting up, changing direction every few seconds, buffeting the high sides of the van. Caleb gripped the steering wheel tightly.

He lit a cigarette and shuffled in his seat to get more comfortable. Beside the road, which hugged the steep valley side, the land fell away on his left, a long sheer drop littered with rocky outcrops. It seemed especially dizzying when you were driving south, magnetic, too, as if the edge were calling you over, drawing you to it. Caleb tried to stick close to the center of the road. Sheep grazed and wandered on and off the pavement, which was fenced only sporadically.

Caleb was driving carefully, but he had a schedule to keep, and he was already running late, so perhaps his foot was pressed down a little harder than it should have been. Then again, the faster he got over the pass, the less likely it was that the conditions would worsen while he was up there. At least it wasn't raining yet, and there was no ice on the road.

Then it happened, it seemed, with the change in direction of one rough blast of wind. The next thing Caleb knew, hailstones as big as marbles were pelting down on the van, almost hard enough to shatter the windscreen. He certainly heard them over the music, and he felt as he imagined a soldier might feel under fire. Instinctively, he found himself hunkering down in his seat, as if he were dodging bullets, wondering if he should pull over until it stopped. Sometimes these storms were blessedly brief. The soothing pastoral of "Grantchester Meadows" played on through the bombardment.

Before he could make his mind up, the hail pellets fell so thickly that for a moment he couldn't see a thing, only hear the unrelenting rat-a-tat-tat on the metal and glass, and then he saw a dark shadow looming toward him, a frightened sheep running in front of the van, right into his path. He was at one of the steepest points of the pass, and he knew he was still too close to the center of the road. He felt himself hit the sheep before he jerked the steering wheel to avoid what he now saw was an oncoming car, but the combination of hail, shock, speed and lack of visibility disoriented him so much that, before he knew it, he crashed right through the flimsy fence and became airborne.

For a split second, he had the strangest sensation of being free. He had no control. There was nothing he could do. He was floating, cut loose from all that bound him to the world, and it came as a great ecstatic rush of release. But the euphoria soon gave way to panic as the van nose-dived down to the valley bottom with the gentle music still playing and hailstones tapping their staccato rhythm on the metal, Caleb screaming as he scrambled to unfasten his safety belt. Maybe if he jumped . . . ? But he didn't have time. The van had almost reached the bottom when it hit a huge limestone outcrop square on. The engine block smashed through the dashboard, taking the steering wheel with it, and squashed Caleb in his seat as a wanton boy might squash a fly. Then the van shattered into pieces and scattered itself and its load over the valley bottom.

Before the last scrap of metal had stopped spinning, the hailstorm ended, and the sun lanced through the clouds.

WINSOME AND Gerry Masterson arrived in Hallerby after a morning of paperwork and phone calls, and parked outside the George and Dragon. Winsome glanced around the village. The houses lining the road were mostly modern semis or short terraces, built of redbrick, with a mix of slate and red pantile roofs, the occasional bay window and a touch of pebbledash in evidence. There was no country charm here, though one or two larger detached homes stood back from the road, closer to the riverbank, and seemed older and grander. There was no village green, as everything lay spread out along the roadside:

small foursquare chapel, the George and Dragon, a row of shops including a hairdresser, general store and outdoor gear supplier, a community hall and a fish-and-chips shop. The church was behind the
row of shops, reached by a narrow ginnel, and Winsome could just see
the tips of the tombstones in the cemetery. That was about it for
Hallerby. At least the sun was shining, even though there was a definite chill in the air, and on the eastern horizon Winsome could see the
Hambleton Hills catching light.

"Where should we start?" asked Gerry.

Winsome nodded toward the pub. "Why not here?" she said. "Let's
take a leaf out of the boss's book. These places are usually the hub of
village gossip. Besides," she added, "I hate knocking on doors. It
makes me feel like a commercial traveler. And the dogs can drive you
crazy."

Gerry smiled. "I remember from my uniform days," she said.

Winsome gave her an appraising look. Her "uniform" days weren't
far behind, but she was showing excellent promise as a detective, especially in the fields of intelligence gathering and computers. There
didn't seem to be any fact or snippet of information that was beyond
the touch of her fingers on a keyboard. It was the other, more human,
skills she needed to develop.

"It's a miracle the place is still open," said Winsome. "So many village pubs seem to be closing for good these days."

The interior seemed dark after the bright sunlight, but their eyes
soon adjusted. It was a modern pub, not one of those old-fashioned
places with lots of brass and heavy varnished wood. The tables were
square and made of some sort of black synthetic substance. The chairs
had tubular legs. There was even a carpet on the floor. Video machines flashed and winked on the far side of the room. The lunch
menu was chalked on a board on the wall and offered the usual pub
grub.

"What'll you have?" Winsome asked.

"Diet bitter lemon, please."

"Sure you don't want something a bit stronger?"

"You must be joking," said Gerry. "If the boss found out we'd been
drinking on the job he'd go spare."

Winsome smiled. "I do hear he's not averse to a tipple himself now and then."

Gerry laughed. "Doesn't matter."

Winsome ordered two diet bitter lemons and turned to the barman after he had taken the small bottles from the glass-covered refrigerated area. "Are you the landlord?" she asked.

"For my sins. Gordon Fullerton. At your service."

Winsome flashed him her identification card and introduced Gerry.

"I thought I recognized you from the papers," Fullerton said. "Aren't you the—"

"Mind if we ask you a few questions?" Winsome cut in. "Sorry, I don't mean to be rude, but it's not a social call."

"There's not been any trouble, has there? I keep a quiet pub, and you won't find any after-hours drinking here, either, whether the local bobby's in or not."

Winsome thought he was protesting too much, but she wasn't interested in after-hours drinking. "No, it's nothing like that. We're here because of your location."

"Location?" Fullerton scratched his head, and Winsome noticed a few flakes of dandruff float to the shoulders of his brown cardigan. His wispy grayish hair looked both uncombed and unwashed, though he was otherwise presentable. Clean-shaven, with a small nick on his chin, clear-eyed behind wire-rimmed glasses, not too much of a pot-belly, as far as she could see. There were only four other customers in the place, two couples occupying separate tables and engaged in eating their lasagne and chips. If business was always as bad as this, Winsome found herself wondering if the pub could last much longer. There couldn't be enough drinkers in the village to support it, and people were so scared of drinking and driving these days, they mostly stayed home to drink. Also, money was tight, the economy poor and people tended to buy their home supplies cheaply at Bargain Booze and drink while they watched telly in the evening, instead of going to the local anymore. It was a shame, really, she thought, though she had never been much of a pub-goer herself, a whole tradition slowly dying. But times change. Nowadays it was all city center wine bars and gastro-pubs, for those who could afford them, and a taxi home.

"That lane heading off the high street just outside, know where it goes?" she asked.

"Kirkway Lane? Aye. It's centuries' old. Roman, I think. It runs through Kirkway Woods, then across a few patches of waste ground beside an old airfield up Drewick way. I think it used to go all the way up to Northallerton years ago, but now it sort of peters out in the woods just past the airfield. Nobody uses it much these days. We just get the odd lorry now and then."

"Lorries? How often?"

"Not that often."

"How many times a week?" Winsome persisted.

"Certainly not every week. Far more irregular. I've seen them maybe three, four times in the past year or so."

"Coming or going?"

"Both. They come off the high street from the direction of the A1 and turn left up Kirkway Lane. Then later they come back down, turn right and head back toward the A1."

"How much later?"

"An hour, two. I don't stand around watching and waiting, you know, but sometimes it's devilish quiet around here. Mostly I've just heard them."

"What time do they usually arrive?"

"I don't really remember. Different times, I suppose."

"Any particular days of the week?"

"Not so as I remember."

"Did any of them have any markings? A company name or logo or something?"

"No, they're just plain lorries, as a rule."

"How big are they?"

"It varies. You can't get anything really big up there, like those juggernauts or pantechnicons, or whatever they call them. Just lorries."

"Big enough to hold a tractor or a combine?" asked Winsome.

"Not a combine, I shouldn't think," said Fullerton. "That road's too narrow. Tractors and other heavy equipment, though. Aye. Why?"

"Livestock?"

"Well, they're not your typical livestock transporters, but I don't see as to why they couldn't be used for that. What's going on?"

"When was the last time you saw or heard one?"

"Funny you should mention that. It were this last Sunday."

Winsome felt a surge of excitement. "What time?"

"Let's see. I were just bringing Fred and Barney—them's the whippets, like—back from their run, so it would have been just after ten."

"Which way was it going?"

"Coming down, heading for the A1."

"You didn't notice it going up earlier?"

"No. But it could have gone up while I was walking the dogs. I wouldn't have noticed anything."

"Can you remember what it looked like?"

"Just like a moving van, really, like I said. Not one of those really big ones, like a furniture van or something."

"Could you see the driver?"

"Just about. I think he was wearing a flat cap, and I do remember noticing something a bit odd." He touched his cheek, just beside his ear. "He has those long sort of sideburns that come halfway around the chin. Do you know what I mean?"

"Muttonchops?" said Gerry.

"That's right. I was close enough to see them."

"Did you notice what color the lorry was?" Winsome asked.

"Dark green. Racing green, I think they call it."

"Did this one have any markings, the name of a firm, phone number, anything at all distinguishing about it?"

"No, it were just a green lorry. I mean, it might have had a phone number and a name on the side, but I didn't notice it. It certainly didn't have any logos or anything. I'd remember that."

"I don't suppose you remember the number plate?" asked Winsome.

"It's a long time since I used to stand by the roadside scribbling down car number plates."

"Did you see anything else at all on Sunday morning?"

"No. I'm afraid that's all."

"Thanks a lot, Mr. Fullerton," Winsome said. "You've been a great help."

"I have?" said Fullerton, looking puzzled.

BANKS LOOKED through the window of the helicopter as the pilot took it slowly down as close to the wreckage as he could get. The moving dots soon became people, emergency services, crash investigators, even some CSIs, all of whom had laboriously made their way down the steep valley side via obscure and bone-jolting farm tracks gleaned from Ordnance Survey maps. Most of the tracks hadn't been used for years, as the farms had died and the farmers had moved away. The location, about halfway along the pass, had very few points of access, and that was no doubt one reason for the economic failure of the farms. There was no road that ran along the valley bottom. Nobody lived there anymore.

Banks turned to glance at Annie beside him. She was sitting straight up, arms folded, earmuffs covering her ears, eyes tight shut. He was going to tell her that they would be arriving at any moment, but he realized she wouldn't hear him. The noise of the helicopter was deafening, and the swaying, bobbing motion it made, as if it were being tossed on waves in a stormy sea, was probably what was responsible for Annie's pale face and the contents of the paper bag she clutched on her lap.

Banks could already see that the crash site was spread over a wide area. The valley bottom was narrow, not more than a quarter of a mile wide, and bits of white van and various pieces of engine metal glinted in the sun, which seemed to illuminate the scene with an almost gleeful garishness, as if to say nature doesn't care, the universe doesn't care, we move to our own rhythms, follow our own whims, and life on earth means nothing.

An abrupt landing jolted Banks back to reality. The rotor blades started to slow down; the noise diminished from a roar to a whoosh. Banks touched Annie's shoulder gently and smiled when she looked at him. He mouthed the words, "We're down," and they took off their earmuffs. The pilot opened the door for them, and they both scrambled out. Even Banks felt glad to standing on terra firma once again.

Annie stumbled, her hair blowing in the downdraft generated by the rotor blades, bent forward and put the bag over her mouth. The pilot reached back into the cockpit and came up with a bottle of spring water, which he kindly handed to her. When she had finished with the bag, she gave him a weak smile and drank the water. He reached out his hand to take the paper bag, too. "Wouldn't want you contaminating the scene, ma'am," he said.

Annie pulled a face and handed it over.

"I assume you want me to wait, sir?" the pilot asked Banks.

"Yes, if you would, Mal." Banks glanced at Annie. "DC Cabbot might hitch a ride back with the CSIs, but I'll be needing you. Others may, too."

"Right you are, sir."

Banks and Annie trotted off toward Stefan Nowak, whom they had spotted directing his men to mark the positions of various bits and pieces of wreckage. Neither spoke about Annie's reaction to the helicopter flight. Banks knew something of what she felt like. He had suffered from car sickness as a child, until he was fourteen, when all of a sudden it had simply gone away. But the combination of stark terror and nausea Annie had just experienced could be very disorienting, he knew. The farther they got from the draft of the slowly turning helicopter blades, the worse the smell of raw decaying meat became.

Nowak was standing beside something made out of metal and human body parts that resembled a Damien Hirst sculpture or some Giger-designed creature from the *Alien* series. That bits of it had once been a man, a car seat, an engine and a steering wheel was just about possible to discern, but it wasn't as easy to estimate where one began and the other ended. Both Banks and Annie stood with their backs to it as they spoke to Stefan. Banks wondered if Annie was wishing she still had her paper bag. He almost wished he had one himself.

"I know," Nowak said, looking at their expressions. "I've seen tidier crime scenes. We think it's the driver." He pointed up the steep daleside to a rocky outcrop. "It looks as if he plunged over the edge and hit that rock full on. Most unfortunate."

Banks winced, and Annie turned paler. "That's putting it mildly,"

Banks said. "But it's not why we were called out here. The chief super wouldn't authorize a helicopter for a road accident."

"Too true," said Nowak. "The investigators will do their jobs, of course, but it was an accident, all right. The fellow going the other way reported it. He wasn't hurt, but he's very shaken. The paramedics took him to Muker to get him some hot sweet tea and keep an eye on him for a while. You can talk to him there later if you need."

"What did he say?"

"There was a brief but heavy hailstorm. Our chap here was in the middle of the road. A sheep ran out, in front of both the car and the van, and when this driver hit the sheep and swerved to get out of the way of the oncoming car, he ran the van over the edge. Anyway, you're right, it's not him you're here about. Had to be a bit circumspect on the phone, but I don't suppose it matters much now." He looked up at the news helicopter arriving from the south. "Want to follow me?"

"Do we *have* to?" Annie muttered. "I just know this isn't going to be good."

Nowak favored her with a heart-melting smile. "Not if you don't want to, my dear," he said.

"It's all right," she said. "Lead on."

"Careful where you tread."

Nowak led them away from the driver's crushed and broken body, treading carefully between scraps of metal and bits of engine. Banks had noticed that the ground was also scattered with black bin bags, most of them broken or split open and spilling their loads. The flags of black plastic flapped in the wind that roared eternally along the narrow channel of the valley bottom. That was how the pass had got its name; *belder* was Old English for "bellow" or "roar."

Here and there, Banks could make out the carcass of a dead sheep, pig or calf, a stillborn lamb, some of them whole, some just parts, a head, torso, hindquarters. Most of the animal bodies had split open to reveal inner organs, trails of glistening intestines and snail tracks of blood. It was a gruesome and surreal sight, he thought, and for a moment he could have sworn they were all museum animals, like the lions and tigers that had ended up on the overhead tramlines when the Germans bombed Leeds Museum in 1941. But when he looked more closely, there was enough blood and gore to convince him that they were real. The scattering of animal body parts and van wreckage seemed to spread across the whole valley bottom, as if it were some sort of battlefield. The field at Towton, Banks remembered from a book he had read, had been so drenched in blood that the becks and rivers had run red when the thaw came. Annie wasn't showing any reaction, but Banks found himself feeling a bit sick. Mostly, it was the smell.

"As I told you on the phone," Nowak said, "the driver, Caleb Ross was his name, worked for Vaughn's ABP, so this"— he spread his arm in a gesture to take in the whole area—"is only to be expected."

Vaughn's Animal By-Products was a company that dealt in the removal and disposal of fallen stock. If a farmer had a dead animal on his farm, it was Vaughn's, or someone like them, that he called. Caleb Ross would have driven from farm to farm, following a list of orders to pick up, and when his van was full he would take his load to the incinerator out back at Vaughn's yard. Banks had seen the distinctive white vans often around Eastvale, and woe betide you if you got stuck behind one on a slow winding road.

Banks heard the sound of another helicopter and wondered if Mal had taken off for some reason. But when he looked up, he saw the logo of yet another news station. There was also a line of vans way up the steep valley side, parked on the pass road, which had been sealed off to regular traffic. The media were here already. Hardly surprising, Banks thought, when he considered the drama of the crash and the scene. They'd be getting great visuals from their helicopters, too, and there was no way to stop them short of calling out the RAF.

"Peter Darby here yet?" he asked Nowak.

"No. He's waiting for a mate to come over from Salford. Some specialist in crash scene photography. They should be here soon. Geoff Hamilton and his team are here, though, and Dr. Burns. In the meantime we've been asked not to touch anything, just put down markers where we think they're necessary. We're taking plenty of photographs of our own, though. We're also arranging to have some lighting brought in. It'll be dark before long, and it doesn't look as if any of us will be going anywhere for a while yet."

"The wonders of the modern mobile phone," said Banks. "These days, it seems everyone's a photographer."

"Just as well they're useful for something," said Nowak. "There's no reception down here. I had to get one of the local officers to call you from Muker, the lad who went with the other driver. I think one of the crash scene specialists has a satellite phone, though, if you need to use one."

When they found Dr. Burns, he was kneeling by something on the ground, obscuring it from Banks's view. When Banks got close enough to see around him, he wished he hadn't. It was half a human body, the left half, by the looks of it, both armless and headless.

"Oh, Christ," Banks said, tasting bile in his throat.

Dr. Burns looked up. "I don't think He had much to do with it."

"The crash did this?"

"The crash spilled the load and crushed the van driver," said Dr. Burns. "But this was just a part of it, wrapped in that black plastic bag there like some of the animal parts. I very much doubt it happened in the crash. The butchery is far too neat for that. You can see the—"

"I'll take your word for it, Doc. Since when did Vaughn's get in the human body disposal business?"

"They're not, as far as I know," said Dr. Burns. "This, you might say, was superfluous to the load."

"A stowaway?"

"If you like. You'll have to ask the dispatcher, but I doubt if he knows anything about it."

"Maybe he did it?"

"Maybe," said Burns. "That's for you to find out."

"Any idea who it is?"

"None at all."

"Found any other bits?"

"Not yet." Dr. Burns nodded toward a line of uniformed police officers. "They're still looking."

At that moment, one of the officers raised his arm and shouted, "Over here, Doctor."

Banks followed Dr. Burns, along with Annie and Stefan, and they found the other half of the human being, again armless. Still no head.

"What the hell's going on," Banks whispered, almost to himself.

"There is one thing I can tell you, Alan," said Dr. Burns, gently pulling away the fabric of the victim's shirt with tweezers. "Actually, you can see for yourself."

Banks looked at the exposed skin, which was a rich light coffee color, even in death, and he saw the bottom half of what was probably a spider's web tattoo on what was left of the neck.

"Bloody hell," he said. "Morgan Spencer."

7

IT WAS EARLY EVENING BEFORE DETECTIVE CHIEF
Superintendent Gervaise managed to gather the troops together for
another meeting in the boardroom. This time the whiteboard and
glass board were practically covered in names, circles, arrows and photographs. They showed just how much the case had escalated within a
few short hours. A lot of the information concerned the Belderfell Pass
crash, but there were more connections now, more circles linked by
arrows.

Banks and Annie had just got back from the crash scene. Annie still
looked ill, Banks thought, though he could hardly blame her. She had
been as keen as he was to get out of the flesh-strewn valley bottom, so
she had decided to take the helicopter back with him rather than wait
for someone to give her a lift along the bumpy, winding tracks back to
civilization. Dr. Burns had accompanied them this time. The ride was
less turbulent, and though Annie had held on to a fresh paper bag, she
hadn't needed to use it.

When Banks and Annie had left the scene, Morgan Spencer's head
was still missing, though his right arm had been discovered under
some of the van wreckage. The CSIs and crash scene investigators
were still searching. As soon as the rest of Morgan had been found and
photographed in situ, the pieces would be delivered to Dr. Glendenning, the Home Office pathologist, in the basement of Eastvale Gen-

eral Infirmary, where they would be assembled for the postmortem. Banks had agreed to attend the procedure, and he was not looking forward to it. The media had also arrived in force, and there were rumors on the evening news about human body parts being found among the animals.

Leslie Palmer, the driver of the oncoming car, had been able to add nothing to his statement. He was the proprietor of a secondhand bookshop in Swainshead, on his way back home after a visit to colleagues at the Grove Bookshop in Ilkley. All he could tell the police was that Ross had been too close to the middle of the road when the sheep ran out and Palmer turned the bend. Pure bad luck. Geoff Hamilton's team and the rest would continue to investigate the circumstances of the incident, and Peter Darby and his crash scene photographer expert from Salford would take photographs and videos, but Banks was more interested in the remains found scattered around the scene than in Caleb Ross's unfortunate demise. As far as Banks was concerned, the pass wasn't the real crime scene; that was still the hangar in the Drewick airfield, where he was certain that Morgan Spencer had been shot. All they needed now was more forensic evidence to back up these theories.

"Right," said Gervaise, as soon as everyone had settled down. "Can we get down to business? It's been a long day, and it isn't over yet. DCI Banks?"

Banks walked to the front as Gervaise sat down. A long day, indeed. Banks remembered standing beside Morgan Spencer's smoldering caravan in the gray dawn light. It seemed eons ago.

"It's true that a lot's happened," he began, "and we've learned quite a bit. But we're still missing some important pieces of the jigsaw. While Jazz has analyzed the DNA sample from the hangar and discovered that it's human, and it belongs to one person only, we haven't yet found any match on the database. That doesn't mean a lot, as you know, but it does mean that we need to get a move on and broaden our search. Specifically," he said, "we need to get a sample of Morgan Spencer's blood analyzed as soon as possible. Given that we just found him—or what we think is him—in pieces scattered over the bottom of Belderfell Pass, that shouldn't prove too difficult."

Jazz nodded. "I'm on it." She looked at Gervaise. "If someone could just get Harrogate CID off my back for a while, please? They're driving me crazy over a sample I'm late with. It's a rape case, so I can hardly blame them."

"I'll talk to Harrogate, Ms. Singh," said Gervaise. "Just do your best."

"Thanks. Well . . . one thing I can say for certain is that there was *no* DNA belonging to Michael Lane found in the hangar. The hairbrush DI Cabbot brought in gave us hairs with the follicle attached, which was just what we needed to check that out. No match."

"So the body in the hangar wasn't Lane's," Banks said. "And thanks to Gerry, we also know from the mobile records that it *was* Morgan Spencer who texted Michael Lane at 9:29 a.m. on Sunday morning. We don't know what he wrote, of course, as we don't have access to either his or Lane's mobile phones, but we were able to check with the service provider against the numbers of the itemized calls. According to his partner, Alex Preston, when Michael Lane received this text, he said he had to go out to do a job, and that he might visit his father later. He left his flat at the East Side Estate shortly after 9:30, and it would have taken him about ten or fifteen minutes to get to the hangar, if that was his destination. That puts him there at about 9:45. We can also assume that the job involved Spencer, as he was the one who texted, and he and Lane were known to work together on removals and farm labor. As far as we can gather, Michael Lane never got to his father's, and he hasn't been seen or heard of since Sunday morning. Alex Preston assured DI Cabbot that's out of character."

"But can we assume that this job Lane and Spencer had to do involved the airfield and the hangar?" asked Gervaise.

"We still lack any hard evidence on that. We don't know anything about Morgan Spencer's movements that morning, except that he sent Lane a text at 9:29. If he stole the tractor, he may well have spent the night with it at his lockup. A number of people from the site do remember seeing him as usual during the day on Saturday. We've questioned most of the people at the caravan park now, and nobody admits to really knowing Spencer, or to seeing anything suspicious during the night of the fire. At the moment I'm just assuming it was his blood at the hangar because we know it wasn't Lane's, and we'd have to be very unlucky to have two major incidents at once. We'll know whether Morgan was killed in the hangar when Jazz compares the blood sample with that from the crash site."

"But how is the hangar connected with the theft of Beddoes's tractor?" Gervaise asked.

"We don't know that it is. Not for certain. Whatever happened there might not be connected with Morgan Spencer or Michael Lane or the tractor theft at all. I mean, why kill someone over a stolen tractor? The owner, John Beddoes, didn't get back from Mexico until late Sunday night, so he's in the clear. He also doesn't need the insurance money. It's possible that Spencer intended to meet Lane somewhere else entirely to do an honest job, then he got snatched and taken to the hangar, but none of that explains Lane's disappearance. If he couldn't find Spencer at the intended job site, why didn't he just go home?"

"I still don't like it," Gervaise said, casting her eyes around the room. "Too much speculation. What about physical evidence?"

"Stefan found some traces of red diesel in the hangar," said Banks. "It could have come from the tractor or some other farm vehicle permitted to use the stuff. But there was nothing else to indicate that the tractor had been there. He also found traces of other vehicles having been there, but it's impossible to say when. We just don't know."

"Anything from the train companies or the news item we ran?" Gervaise asked Doug Wilson.

"No, ma'am. They said they'd check the online purchase records and put a few flyers on the route, but it'll take time."

"Rather like train journeys themselves," muttered Banks.

"Is there anything else to connect the hangar with the stolen tractor?" Gervaise asked him.

"I think Winsome and Gerry might have something to report on that."

Winsome cleared her throat and spoke without referring to her notes. "The landlord of the George and Dragon in Hallerby saw a racing green removal van large enough to carry a tractor come down the lane that leads from the airfield at just after ten o'clock on Sunday morning," she said. "Headed in the direction of the A1. He got a brief look at the driver and said he was wearing a flat cap and had muttonchop sideburns. The lorry had no markings. He didn't see the number plate."

"What sort of car does Michael Lane drive, again?" Banks asked Annie.

"A clapped-out gray Peugeot."

"Has it been seen?"

"Not since he went out on Sunday morning. And nothing from the airlines or credit card company. He's off our radar."

Banks thought he might need another chat with Joanna MacDonald. She was his key to the magic world of ANPR. Cars could be tracked anywhere in the country. "And do we know what Morgan Spencer drives?" he asked the room at large.

"A motorcycle," said Doug Wilson. "According to his neighbor, he's got a Yamaha. He usually keeps it parked beside his caravan, but it wasn't there when DI Cabbot and I visited yesterday, and we don't know where it is now."

"Maybe he rode it to his lorry and put it in the back?" said Banks. "It wasn't outside his caravan after the fire, either, perhaps because he was already dead. Which reminds me," he said, glancing at Annie. "Could you have a word with someone at Vaughn's ABP, where Caleb Ross worked? They must have a schedule of pickups or some such thing. There has to be some way of finding out how and where his body parts got mixed up with the fallen stock."

Annie jotted on her pad. "And where it got chopped up like that," she added.

"Let's see what Dr. Glendenning has to say about that at the p.m."

"Do you think Caleb Ross had anything to do with it all?" asked Gervaise.

"It's a definite possibility," said Banks. "The accident may have been beyond Ross's control, but that doesn't mean he didn't know that he was carrying Morgan Spencer's body. Or at least something not quite kosher. We'll be looking for a link."

"If it was an accident," Annie Cabbot said.

"You think the van might have been sabotaged?" said Gervaise.

"I'm just saying it's a possibility, ma'am. Maybe the crash site investigators will be able to tell us what happened."

"Maybe," said Banks. "But they don't have an awful lot left to go on. If someone did sabotage the van, there may well be no evidence of that left."

"Morgan Spencer had an oversize lockup on the Bewlay Industrial Estate," said Gerry Masterson. "Apparently his van is sometimes filled with the contents of someone's house overnight, and he's required for insurance purposes to keep it somewhere safe, not just on the street, so the estate rents him the garage. It's empty at the moment. We're waiting for some free CSIs to send over there, but . . ."

"I know," said Banks. "They're all busy at Belderfell Pass, or the hangar."

"Yes, sir. DS Nowak says he hopes he can get some experts over there by the morning. Until then, we've put a guard on the place."

"We'll put out a bulletin on the van and motorcycle." Banks glanced at Winsome. "And the gray Peugeot. The landlord of the George and Dragon only reported one lorry coming out of the woods that Sunday morning, didn't he?"

"Yes, sir. One racing green lorry."

"Nothing going in?"

"He didn't see anything. But if they were using the route for criminal activities, it would make sense to vary it sometimes."

"I suppose it could have been Spencer's lorry the landlord saw," said Banks. "Gerry, do you think you could attempt to tie reported rural thefts in the region to traffic observed at the hangar or passing through Hallerby from Kirkway Lane?"

"We'd need a lot more data to go on, sir," said Gerry. "I mean, it's easy to collate the incidents of thefts from our crime figures, but that's no use unless we have definite recollections from people who lived in Hallerby. Who's going to remember when a lorry came down the lane?"

"The pub landlord might if you push him a bit," Winsome said.

"If he does, see if you can make any connections," said Banks.

"Yes, sir."

"Do you know who owns the airfield property yet?"

"Venture Property Developments, sir," said Gerry. "I spoke briefly to one of their executives on the phone. I must say I couldn't get much out of him. He seemed rather abrupt. They're based in Leeds. Apparently they're still involved in legal arguments over zoning it for commercial use—a shopping center. There's some local opposition from the villagers in Drewick and Hallerby. They say it'll ruin their peaceful natural environment."

"Indeed it will," said Banks. "Unless they can find some particularly rare species of bird or a few bedraggled badgers to get it a protection order."

"The company doesn't expect it to drag on for too long," Gerry went on. "In the meantime, they haven't been paying much attention to it. Other fish to fry. I asked them if it was locked up securely, and they said it had to be to comply with Health and Safety. But nobody from Venture has actually *been* there in ages, so they have no idea whether anyone has been using it for their own purposes."

"According to Terry Gilchrist, the kids get in anyway," said Winsome. "He says while walking his dog he's seen them playing football and cricket inside the grounds there."

Banks remembered his childhood, when he used to love playing in condemned houses. Did Health and Safety exist then? He didn't remember ever hearing about them. If they had, he thought, there would probably have been no bonfire night and the old houses would have been more secure. But children are resilient and malleable. They can survive the occasional fall through the staircase of a condemned slum. "Talk to Terry Gilchrist again, Winsome. He's the one who lives the closest. See if he knows anything else about the place. Anything. It might be worth finding out who some of these kids are, too, if he knows. They might be able to tell us more. Kids can be surprisingly observant. And find out what kind of car Gilchrist drives, just in case it comes up."

"As a matter of fact," said Winsome, "Mr. Gilchrist showed a couple of patrol officers where some of the children live this morning. None of them reported seeing anything. And he drives a dark blue Ford Focus."

"Well done, Winsome. I'll visit Venture tomorrow, myself," Banks went on. "See what sort of outfit they are. Find out what they know about the properties they own. Rattle their cage a bit. There's money and brains behind this rural crime business. It's not just the Morgan Spencers and Michael Lanes of this world nicking tractors while the owner's sunning himself in Mexico. It goes deeper than that. It wouldn't surprise me if Venture's cut in for some of the action. After all, they own the land and they know the hangar's out there, empty. Anything else?"

Nobody had anything to add, so AC Gervaise closed the meeting.

"We've all got plenty to do," Banks said as they filed out of the room, "so I suggest we get to it. Annie, would you meet me in the office in half an hour."

AFTER ALEX had put Ian to bed—the poor lad was tired out—she went back into the living room and turned on the television, just for the company. She had kept the front door deadlocked and bolted, with the chain on, all the time she had been at home, and now she sat with her new mobile on her lap, fingers ready to key in 999 if anyone came to the door. Luckily, the SIM card hadn't been damaged, and the man in the shop had set up a new phone with the same number and same account as the damaged one. She couldn't risk not having the phone—and the number—in case Michael called.

Her broken finger was throbbing, but she decided against taking the painkillers the doctor had given her until bedtime. She needed to be vigilant. Meadows, the phony policeman, might come again if he didn't hear from her, and she didn't know how long her nerves could stand the stress of knowing there would be another visit, more threats, perhaps even more serious violence this time, or—God forbid—violence toward Ian, because she really had nothing to tell him. And if she did find out where Michael was, she could hardly give that information away to someone who wanted to harm him.

When the mobile jangled like the old black telephones used to do, she nearly jumped out of her skin. It was the first time it had rung, and she had had no idea what ringtone was set. She didn't recognize the number and was in two minds about answering it. It could be Meadows. Then she decided she would. It was only a mobile phone; what harm could it do her?

After she spoke her name, there was a silence punctuated by some crackling in the background. Finally, his voice came through: "Alex. It's me, love. Michael."

Alex almost dropped the phone with the surge of relief that flooded through her. "Michael! You're all right."

"Yeah. I'm just peachy."

"What's wrong?"

"I wouldn't know where to begin."

"Are you in trouble?"

"You could say that."

"Trouble with the police?"

"They're the least of my worries."

"What is it? Tell me, Michael. I've been frantic with worry here."

"I know, and I'm sorry. I couldn't . . . I didn't want . . . Oh, shit, it's hopeless."

"What do you mean?"

"I think they're after me, Alex. Some very bad people."

"What did you do?"

"I didn't do anything. I just saw them, that's all. I witnessed something I shouldn't have."

"When you went out on Sunday?"

"Yes. I went to meet Morgan. He said he had a job. He didn't say what it was, just that he needed my help. I drove out to that old deserted airfield out Hallerby way."

"What happened?"

"I can't tell you."

"Why not?"

"I just can't, that's all. Except it was awful."

"Where are you now?"

"I can't tell you that, either."

"Why not? You mean you don't know?"

"I mean it wouldn't be safe for *you* to know. If you don't know where I am, then you can't tell anyone, can you?"

Alex bit her lip. She wasn't so foolish as not to realize that if Meadows decided to torture her, she would have nothing to give up, nothing with which to save herself. People usually broke in the end, when they were tortured, and Alex didn't think she could stand much pain—physical or emotional. But if you really didn't have the information the torturer wanted, what happened then? Not that she would ever betray Michael, but such were the chaotic thoughts that spun around in her mind. She was on the verge of telling him about last night's visit and her broken finger, but she held off. What good would it do? It would only add to his burden of worries, and he didn't sound as if he needed that right now. "What are you going to do?" she asked.

"I don't know. I just wanted you to know that I'm all right. At least, I'm not hurt or anything."

"Why didn't you call sooner?"

"I couldn't. I didn't dare use my mobile. People can trace those things. They leave records of calls and stuff. And I've been lying low. I couldn't get to a pay phone."

He sounded far from all right to Alex. "Is there anything I can do?"

"I have to keep out of the way until it all blows over. I just wanted you to know I'm all right, that's all. I saw the news this evening for the first time since it happened. I was in a pub and they had a big screen. I know they're looking for me and Morgan, and I know that something happened at Belderfell Pass. A car crash. Animal parts. Perhaps a human body. It was all very vague, but I'm sure it's all connected, Alex. I just wanted you to know that I'm OK. I thought you might be worried, that's all."

"Of course I'm worried, you idiot. The police have been around. How could I *not* be worried? What do you think this is doing to us?"

"Don't be angry with me, love. I couldn't stand that. Not now. I'm sorry. What did you tell them?"

"Nothing. I don't know anything. And I'm not angry. I'm upset. I just wish you'd tell me what's going on."

"I can't, love. Not yet. It doesn't matter what you tell the police. Tell them what you want."

"When are you coming back?"

"I don't know. When it's all over. They'll have to get to the bottom of it without me, then it'll be safe to come home. How's Ian?"

"He's fine. We're both fine."

"Give him my love. And be careful, Alex."

"Why?"

"Just be careful, that's all. I've got to go now."

"Michael, don't! Please. Tell me where you are. Let me come to you."

"No. Stay there. Stay with Ian."

"But when will I see you?"

"When it's over. Remember I love you, Alex. Good-bye."

"Will you ring again?"

"I'll do my best."

Alex held on to the phone, tears in her eyes, but the other end went dead. She sat still for a while holding the phone, staring at but not seeing the meaningless images moving around on the TV screen, her heart pounding in her chest, stomach churning, head aching. This was worse than when Lenny had hit her. There was no end in sight. Just when she thought she had found something worthwhile, something she could hold on to, it had been snatched from her.

Alex threw the phone onto the sofa, where it bounced to the floor, downed the rest of her wine and poured another full glass. She knew that alcohol wouldn't help, but she could think of nothing else to dull the edges of her pain except perhaps a couple of those pills the doctor had prescribed. Maybe even the whole bottle. What the hell was Michael playing at, gambling with their future like this? She knew he must be in serious trouble or he wouldn't have left her and Ian the way he had. He loved them. She had to cling to that. It was all she had.

Finally, she could think of nothing else to do, and she could no longer stand doing nothing, or feeling so alone, so she picked up the phone, took out the policewoman's card and called the number DI Cabbot had written on the back.

"THE OFFICE" meant the Queen's Arms. If Banks had meant his office at the station, he would have said "*my* office." It was going on for eight o'clock, and the pub was starting to fill up, which no doubt brought cheer to the heart of Cyril the landlord. The usual oldies selection was a bit loud, so they had to raise their voices to talk. Still, Banks thought it was pleasant enough to hear occasional fragments of "Wouldn't It Be Nice" or "She's Not You" in the background. A lot of pubs used themed satellite radio feeds, but not the Queen's Arms. Cyril was an intrepid pop fan, still stuck in the late fifties and early sixties, and he played his iPod through the pub's music system. If anyone didn't like it, they were welcome to drink elsewhere.

Banks noticed that Lisa Gray was working that night. She had short hair now, and most of the facial metal was gone. He knew that Winsome had developed a close relationship with Lisa during their previous case, and that they kept in touch. She smiled from behind the bar and he gave her a quick wave. Annie came back with the drinks.

Annie sipped some of her beer. "I still can't see Michael Lane as the villain," she said. "All he ever did before was take a joyride because he was mixed up and upset after his mother left. Since then, he's found a serious relationship. He has a kid to think about, too."

"Maybe all that was too much for him?" Banks argued. "Maybe he felt stifled and had to get out? Or maybe he just cracked under the responsibility? You said they don't have much money, that they're struggling."

"Yeah, but at least they're trying. They weren't doing so badly. And if that was the case, if Michael suddenly couldn't take the pressure anymore, then Alex Preston wasn't aware of it."

"I never expected Sandra to walk out on me for another bloke," said Banks. "But she did. These things happen, Annie."

In the silence that followed that remark, Lisa Gray approached the table with two plates. "Who wanted the salad and who wanted burger and chips?"

Banks and Annie exchanged a few moments' small talk with Lisa until she returned to her position behind the bar. Once they had settled down to their food, Banks went on. "I know you're emotionally involved and you don't want to think ill of Alex Preston or Michael Lane," he said, "and I'm sure they are trying their best to make a go of it, but we're not in the business of rehabilitation." He nodded toward Lisa. "Sure, Winsome took a damaged young woman under her wing and worked miracles, but let's not get carried away with the social work. Don't you think Alex might be just a little naive, especially when it comes to Michael Lane? Don't they say love is blind? Let's not allow it to blinker your judgment."

"I'm not."

"All I'm saying, Annie, is that we can't always save their souls, and we shouldn't expect to. Half the time we can't even save their bodies. Believe me, I've met plenty of deserving cases in my time, and sometimes I've even helped them, but sometimes I haven't. Sometimes it even worked. Often it didn't, and they went on to commit more serious crimes. We're not psychologists or miracle workers."

"I'm not blinkered," said Annie. "I fully accept that Michael Lane might have made a mistake, that he was probably involved at some level. I realize that being perpetually short of cash might have pushed him into doing something illegal, no doubt with Morgan Spencer's encouragement. He may even have seen the tractor as just a one-off to get him back on his feet, and to thumb his nose at John Beddoes. I'm not dismissing those possibilities. But I'd also like to point out that right now he's a missing person, possibly in danger, or already come to harm, not a suspect."

"But he is a suspect as well," said Banks.

"In what? The bloody tractor theft?"

"In that, yes, and in Morgan Spencer's murder, until we prove otherwise."

"Rubbish," said Annie.

"Maybe so. All I'm asking is that you keep an open mind."

Annie returned to her salad for a moment. "It's open," she muttered, when she looked him directly in the eye again. "She's got a broken finger," she said. "Alex Preston has. All right?"

"You never mentioned this before. What happened?"

"She said she trapped it in the door."

"You don't believe her?"

Annie paused before answering. "No," she said, then washed a mouthful of salad down with her beer. "Something's going on. I could tell by the way she was behaving. She was lying. You asked me if I thought Alex was being a bit naive. Well, maybe she is. Or was. I think she's getting a few quick lessons in the harsh realities of life right now. She's frightened as well as worried."

Banks sighed. "All right. I want you to keep on top of Alex Preston," he said. "Short of shadowing her. You think she's holding something back. It's no good thinking you're protecting her by keeping it to yourself."

"She might have let slip to Michael about Beddoes being on holiday," Annie said. "She did know he was going. She booked the trip for him. And we know there's no love lost between Michael Lane and John Beddoes. Also, if Michael found out that Morgan Spencer had made a pass at his mother, that might have given him a motive for Spencer's murder, too. How's that for an open mind?"

"But you said that was what, three years ago? Why would he find out just now?"

"I don't know. I'm not saying he did. I'm keeping an open mind. Maybe it's so open the dust's blowing in. I'm just saying it's another thing to consider when you look at Michael Lane as a suspect. Or his father, for that matter."

"Frank Lane?"

"Yes. Have we checked his alibis? Do we know for sure he's telling us the truth about everything? He's certainly not rolling in money, and he's no great love for Beddoes. What if the father had something to do with the tractor theft? Have we forgotten about that possibility?"

"Hmm, not entirely," said Banks. "We'll keep it on the back burner. What do *you* think happened to Alex?"

"Dunno. I suppose someone might have been warning her to keep quiet, if she knew anything, or perhaps they think she knows where Lane is and tried to get it out of her. Maybe they saw me and Doug call by her flat the other day."

"You don't believe she does know where Lane is, do you?"

"No, Alan, I don't. The poor woman's beside herself. That much I accept as true. You can't fake that, not unless you're an exceptional actress. Tears, yes, but it's much more than that."

"OK." Banks held his hands up in surrender. "Let's assume she *doesn't* know where he is. Someone thinks she does and comes to ask her? Breaks a finger when she won't, or can't, tell?"

"Which raises another important question," said Annie.

"Oh?"

"How did whoever did it know who she was and where she lived?"

"Through Michael Lane, I'd guess."

"That's right. Meaning that Lane probably is involved with whatever's been going on. Involved enough that the people he works for know where he lives and who with."

"There is another possibility," said Banks.

"What's that?"

"That it's Alex they know, Alex who's working with them. And she's spinning you a line."

"No way," said Annie, looking down into her dish.

"The question is," said Banks, "do we put someone on her 24/7?"

Annie looked up again. "Do you think Madame Gervaise would authorize that?"

"Hell, we got to use the new helicopter today, didn't we? It seems since we got our new home secretary and police commissioner, we only have to ask. Enjoy it while you can. It won't last. What I'm saying is that if you think Alex Preston is in danger, then we obviously need to keep an eye on her."

"It was probably just a low-level thug, not the boss himself."

"Even so. And there's something in it for us. He could lead us to the boss."

"OK," said Annie. "I'll see what I can get organized. It's stretching things a bit thin, I know, but four officers should be able to manage a twenty-four-hour watch between them. I mean, we don't need anything too elaborate here. It's not exactly *Tinker, Tailor, Soldier, Spy*."

"OK," Banks said. "And in the meantime, after the postmortem, why don't we go pay Alex a visit before we check out Venture in Leeds. Winsome can take Gerry or Doug and have a chat with someone at Vaughn's about Caleb Ross's pickup schedule and who might have had access to it. Ross probably drove a circuitous route. How long had he had this particular load in his van? How long did his round take him? Once we have the list, we'll have to check every farm he called at, and even then there's no guarantee anyone will know anything. I don't know, but I imagine it's easy to sneak another black bin bag or two among the pile if you know where it's kept. Ross is also bound to have left the van unattended here and there, and it wouldn't have taken long for someone to add a few bags to his load."

"Have you ever thought that Ross himself might have done it?"

"What? The killing in the hangar?"

"Yes. Or at least prepared the body for incineration with the animals after the killing. Why not? He had the best access."

"It's an interesting possibility. And he certainly might have known what he was carrying in the back of his van. You're heading in the right direction. He could be more involved than we think. What more perfect cover than his job for tipping off criminals where to find unguarded livestock, or when farmers will be away leaving expensive equipment in their garages and barns? And if that's the case, he might have been co-opted to dispose of the body himself."

"As long as we don't have to go back to that bloody valley of death and help them look for the head."

"Not if I can help it," said Banks. He waved his empty glass. "Another?"

"Why not?" Annie handed him her glass. "And when you get back you can tell me all about your romantic weekend in Cumbria with the lovely Oriana."

"Umbria. It was Umbria." Banks felt himself blushing as he walked to the bar. Behind him, he heard Annie's mobile make a sound like a demented cricket.

WHEN ALEX finally stopped crying, Annie poured her another glass of wine and took a glass for herself. She'd been denied that second pint with Banks, leaving him alone at the table as she hurried out of the Queen's Arms after receiving Alex's phone call, so why not? He had wanted to come with her, given the subject matter of their conversation, but she had told him, no, this sounded like something she could do better on her own. Woman's work. And it was. It was more a matter of do-gooding, of giving comfort, than real detective work. At least he had seemed relieved to avoid having to tell her about his weekend in Umbria and she left him alone listening to the Springfields' "Silver Threads and Golden Needles."

Banks had been right about Annie's motives. She did want things to go well for Alex and Michael. They weren't exactly a project, the way Lisa Gray had been for Winsome, but she had pinned some hopes on them already, and she was damned if she was going to let them slip through the cracks. Maybe she was doing it more for herself than for them. Maybe it was even a part of her own rehabilitation, something she could enjoy vicariously, seeing as she seemed unable to find a man of her own. She didn't know, and she didn't care. The room was warm and cozy, the shaded lamplight soothing. Once in a while she heard a yell or a loud noise from outside. Kids, most likely. Then the muffled male and female voices of a burgeoning domestic sounded from above.

Alex managed a weak smile. "Don't worry about them," she said, looking up at the ceiling. "They're always at it. You should hear them when they make up."

Annie laughed. "The best part of breaking up . . ."

" . . . Is when you're making up. But we're *not* breaking up. Michael and me, that is. At least I hope we're not. I'm just a bit confused at the moment. And scared."

"I'm not surprised," said Annie. "Why don't you tell me about it?"

Alex gave her a suspicious glance. "I don't know if I should be talking to you. You're police, after all. He said . . ."

Annie spread her hands. "You rang me. It's your decision. If you want me to go . . ."

"No. Stay. Please." Alex sucked on her lower lip as she thought, then she said, "OK. It's not as if I've got anyone else I can talk to about it."

"Oh, thanks a lot."

"I didn't mean . . ." Alex patted her chest and laughed. "I'm sorry. I didn't mean for it to come out like that."

Annie waved the apology aside. "Doesn't matter," she said. "I'm thick-skinned. And you're right. I'm the only one who's here, not to mention the best one to talk to about it." She drank some wine. It was cold and tart. Lidl's cheapest, most likely.

Alex clasped her hands together and hung her head. "I don't know where to start," she said. "Well, I suppose I do. I mean, you already know the start, when you came to see me yesterday. I can hardly believe it was only that long ago."

Annie herself could hardly believe it was still only Tuesday evening. So much had happened in two days. "We've checked the DNA,"

Annie said, "and the blood in the hangar isn't Michael's. He shares the same blood type with the victim, but that's all."

"That's why you asked me about Michael's blood type?"

"Yes."

"And you knew all along it was the same, but you didn't tell me?"

"I was going to. I almost came back to tell you last night, but I knew it would only worry you, and it's not as if there was anything I could do about it. Besides, there was no need for it. It's a blood type that belongs to thirty-five percent of the population."

"That's all right. I suppose I should thank you. As it was, I had a sleepless night anyway."

"If you don't mind my saying so, you don't seem surprised or over-joyed to hear that Michael is alive."

Alex turned away, avoiding Annie's eyes. "That's because I know it wasn't him. I know it wasn't Michael." She fell silent, and for a moment Annie was worried that she wasn't going to continue. But she did. "He rang me tonight. Just before I called you. So he's alive. He's all right."

Annie leaned forward. "I should imagine he's far from all right, Alex. Where is he?"

"He's scared, I think. Worried about us. But he's alive."

"Where is he?"

"I don't know. He wouldn't tell me that. He said it was for my own good."

Annie looked Alex in the eye and decided that she believed her. She cursed under her breath. "That makes sense," she said simply. "But it doesn't help us."

"He was ringing from a pay phone, I think. You can probably trace it through my mobile. I don't know about those things. But it doesn't matter. He won't be there anymore."

"Will you tell me the number, anyway?"

Alex fumbled with the mobile and showed it to Annie, who picked up her own phone and called the station. "I have to do this," she said, putting her hand over the mouthpiece. "You do understand?"

"Of course."

"For what it's worth, you're probably right, and he's far away from there by now. Does he still have his car?"

"I don't know. I suppose so. He can't have much money left by now, though."

Annie left the number with Gerry Masterson, who was still in the squad room. Did that woman never stop? Had she no life? You're one to talk, Annie said to herself, sitting giving comfort to a murder suspect's girlfriend instead of drinking with Banks, wondering if that would lead anywhere. She wasn't sure whether she had given up on Banks. She couldn't compete against the likes of Oriana, but Annie guessed Oriana would last a while and then drift away, like the others. She was far too young for him, for a start, almost half his age, and from what Annie could tell, she didn't seem the type to squander her life on taking care of an old man, which was certainly what she'd be doing before too long if she and Banks remained together. She turned her attention back to Alex, who was refilling their glasses. "I know we're at odds over this," she said. "You probably think you're protecting Michael, that it's best for him to stay on the run, to keep hidden, to avoid us, but we really need to find him. We have to talk to him. We can help him. He knows something about what happened on Sunday that could help us find Morgan Spencer's killer."

Alex thought for a moment. "He doesn't know much," she said. "All he told me was that Morgan texted him and asked him for help on a job at the old hangar. Morgan was probably into all sorts of dodgy things Michael didn't know about. Michael said he drove out there and saw something he shouldn't have. Since then he's been on the run. He hasn't done anything wrong. He's scared. Can't you see?"

"Maybe that's the case," said Annie. "But we still have to talk to him. We don't know that he hasn't done anything wrong. A lot's been going on, Alex, and we need explanations. Surely you must see that?"

"But I don't know where he is! Can't you believe me?" She held out her finger. "Do you see that?"

Annie nodded.

"I didn't trap it in the door. A man came by last night. He pretended to be police. He even had an identity card, though I didn't get a good look at it. He wanted to know where Michael is. He threatened me. Me and Ian. I shouldn't even be talking to you now. He's probably watching me. He'll kill us. Both of us."

Annie leaned forward and put her hand on Alex's shoulder. "Calm down," she said. "Nobody's going to kill anyone. You did the right thing, phoning me. I can help."

"But he said he'd hurt Ian. He broke my finger and he said he'd hurt Ian. I didn't tell him anything because I *don't know anything,* but he still believes I do. Why won't you believe me?"

"I do believe you," said Annie. "And we won't let him hurt anyone. Can you at least give me a description?"

"As if I'd forget," said Alex, and proceeded to describe her unwanted visitor to Annie.

"If I introduce you to a police sketch artist," she said, "do you think you could help him work on a likeness?" There were computer programs far more complex and accurate than the old Identikit format now, but Annie still believed that an artist was the best chance of getting a reasonable likeness. She was willing to admit that it was a prejudice that came out of her background and her own interest in art, but it had always worked for her.

"I think so," Alex said. "But I have to go to work tomorrow."

Annie looked at her watch. It was too late to bring in the sketch artist tonight. "Don't worry. We'll work something out with your employers. We can be flexible. It's important."

"He gave me a phone number." Alex took the card out of her purse. "He said it would be untraceable, but I suppose you can try. You know about these things. Can you really find him?"

"We can do our best," said Annie, far more interested in any fingerprints that might be on the card than tracing what was more likely than not a pay-as-you-go mobile number. "Did anyone else touch this?" she asked.

Alex shook her head. "Just me. When he handed it to me. Then I put it away."

"So he handled it?"

"Yes. Of course."

"He wasn't wearing gloves or anything?"

"No."

"OK. That was stupid of him. Helpful to us, though."

"I think he believed he'd scared me so much I wouldn't dare talk to you. He was almost right, too."

Annie patted her arm. "But you did, though, didn't you? Talk to me. Have you got an envelope? Just an ordinary envelope will do."

Alex fetched her a white envelope from the sideboard drawer. Annie popped the card inside and wrote on the front, then slipped it in her briefcase.

"Did he have any kind of accent?"

"I thought I could hear a bit of Geordie in the way he talked."

"Was it strong?"

"No, but I think it was just there, in the background like. He just sounded ordinary. Not broad Yorkshire, not posh or anything, either, but just a touch of Geordie."

"Well, there's plenty of that around these parts," Annie said. She picked up her wine, leaned back and said, "Tell me what you think's going on."

"Me?"

"Yes. You must have some ideas."

"All I know is that Michael has gone and that he's scared. He saw it on the news, about the crash at Belderfell Pass."

"Really? What did he say about it? Why did he mention it? Can you try to remember everything he said?" Annie put the wine down and took out her notebook.

Alex did her best to recount the conversation she had had only an hour or so ago. "He said someone on the news was saying something about another body being found. Or parts of one." She shuddered. "Among the animals pieces, like. He said he thought what happened at the hangar and the crash in the valley were connected somehow."

"That's interesting. Did he say why?"

"No. I asked him, but he couldn't say. I don't know if he even knew. It's not every day you find a body around here, though, is it? Especially somewhere like that, and mixed in with dead animals. Is it true?"

Annie remembered the scene—the glistening intestines of animals burst out of black bin liners, the human body cut in half longways, the dreadful smell—and shivered. It was something that would blight her dreams for a while. And it wasn't information she was going to pass on to Alex Preston. But why would Michael Lane assume that the body parts mixed with the fallen stock in a Vaughn's ABP van should belong to Morgan Spencer? Did either of them have a connection with Vaughn's, with Caleb Ross? She made a note. "Did Michael give any explanation for assuming these rumors were about Morgan Spencer's body?"

"No. He never even really said that. Just that it was all connected."

"Connected how?"

"He didn't say."

"We think Morgan was killed at the hangar, Alex."

"Michael would never do—"

"I'm not saying he did, but you have to understand that until we find him and talk to him, he's still a suspect. Thinking about what you've just told me, I'm guessing that Michael may have witnessed Morgan's murder, and then he drove off in a hurry. Whoever did it knows he was there, knows who he is and where he lives. That's why that man came here last night asking about him. He could easily have been the man who killed Morgan."

Alex paled. "Here, in my home? With Ian in bed? But how could they know who I am, where I live? These people? These killers? How could someone like that know about Michael's life?"

That was a question Annie had discussed earlier with Banks. She had a few possible answers of her own, but none that Alex would like.

But Alex wasn't stupid. "You're saying that he worked for them, aren't you? That he did criminal jobs for them with Morgan. You're saying Michael was involved."

"I wouldn't go that far," said Annie. "What I *would* say is that it's possible that Michael might have been about to get involved. On the fringes, perhaps, on the threshold. You say he wanted a new camera—"

"He wouldn't do that. Not Michael. You just don't understand. You don't *know* him."

"No, I don't," Annie said softly. "And that's what I'm depending on you for. But there's no point arguing. This won't be settled until we find him and talk to him ourselves."

"You'll put him in jail."

"Don't be silly, Alex. Why would we do that? I think it's time you realized that he stands a far better chance with us than he does with whoever's after him. People who would break a woman's finger and threaten her child. What do you think they'll do to Michael if they find him?"

Alex put her hands over her ears. "Don't. Please, don't."

"Be realistic, Alex."

"I can't tell you any more. I don't know any more. I would if I could."

"That's OK. I believe you. It's late now, but what I want to do first thing in the morning is get this man's card checked for fingerprints. If he's a habitual criminal, there's every chance we have his prints on file. I'll also need you to come in and give us your own prints for elimination purposes. Then we'll see about the sketch artist. I'll come over early and drive you to the station after we've taken Ian to school. And we'll fix it with your boss. Will you do that? Maybe you can help us with Morgan Spencer, too? We don't have any photos or good descriptions of him."

"OK."

"In the meantime, I'll see if I can get a family liaison officer to come over right now—"

"No. I don't want a stranger in my house. Why can't *you* stay? It's a let-down sofa. You'll be comfortable. Or you can take the bed, if you want. I've even got a spare toothbrush. Never been used."

"I can't do that, Alex."

"Why not?"

"I . . . just . . ." Annie could think of no real reason, except that she wanted to go home and be alone. She realized how selfish that was. Here was a young woman in need, and all that Annie had to do was agree to stop the night and settle down on the couch. Besides, she knew she had drunk a bit too much wine to be driving safely. She could always get a taxi home, but that would be expensive.

Alex refilled their glasses. "Seriously," she said. "I'm really scared. It'll make me feel a lot better if you'll stop. I don't want to be a victim anymore, but I need help right now."

Then the hall door opened, and a little boy stood there in his striped pajamas rubbing the sleep from his eyes, his hair tousled. "I can't sleep," he said in a pathetic little-boy-lost voice. "I had a bad dream. Can I sit up with you and watch TV?"

8

IT WAS FAR TOO EARLY IN THE MORNING FOR A POST-mortem, Banks thought as he walked down the high green-tiled basement corridor of Eastvale General Infirmary.

It would always be too early in the morning for a postmortem like this one, he thought, when he entered Dr. Glendenning's recently modernized domain and saw the pieces arranged on the stainless steel autopsy table: two sides of a human being, like two halves of a pig in a butcher's cold room, roughly aligned. The arms had been placed where they should have been joined to the body, and the head, which had been found after dark under a split bin bag containing a stillborn lamb, sat on top. Between the eyes was a ragged hole.

"Ah, Banks," said Dr. Glendenning. "Glad you could come. Decided to have a lie-in, did you? You almost missed the show."

"Pity," said Banks. For a moment, he longed for the old days, when Dr. Glendenning bent over the body, a cigarette dangling from his lips, spilling ash in open incisions. The days when he could enjoy a cigarette himself, anything to mask the smell of decayed flesh and take his mind off violent death.

No chance these days. Both he and Glendenning had stopped smoking years ago, and a lit cigarette would probably set off every alarm in the building. It was almost unthinkable today how much they used to be able to get away with. Dr. Glendenning didn't believe in a dab of Vick's under the nose, either. He thought anyone who did was a sissy, and you didn't want to be thought a sissy by Dr. Glendenning. Still, this time there wasn't much of a smell at all. At the crime scene, most of the stink had come from the dead animals, not from Morgan Spencer's butchered corpse.

"You look a bit pink around the gills," Dr. Glendenning went on as they approached the body. "Been sitting around brooding and boozing again?"

"Not sleeping very well," said Banks. "Or not enough."

"It's the demon drink. I thought so. Plays havoc with your sleep patterns. Now, what do we have here?"

"A jigsaw puzzle?" Banks suggested.

"I'm not normally a fan of TV crime dramas, but did you ever see that Swedish program—or was it Danish—the one about the body on the bridge? That was in two halves, but in that case, it was top and bottom. This is much more unusual. And see how clean the cuts are. Look at those arms, taken off right at the shoulder joints, just like chicken wings. What does that suggest to you?"

"A chef?"

"Be serious, man."

"A professional?" Banks ventured.

"But what kind? What kind?"

"Doctor, perhaps? A surgeon?"

"Hah. Apart from the personal insult implied, you couldn't be more wrong. The body's been jointed and split, Banks. Now, why on earth would a surgeon do that?"

"I don't know. A butcher, then?"

"Possibly." Glendenning scratched his bristly mustache. "Closer, at any rate." He bent over the remains and poked and prodded for a while, at one point lifting up the right arm and examining it from various angles. He then put it down and picked up the other arm. "No sign of defensive wounds, but there's some light bruising on the arms," he said. "Premortem."

"Somebody held him by his arms?"

"Well, laddie, he might not want to just stand still and get shot. Some people would take objection to that, you know."

Banks noticed as he looked at the naked body that there were no genitals. "Was he castrated?" he asked.

"The genitalia were certainly removed," said Glendenning. "As were all the internal organs and viscera. He was also exsanguinated. But all that was carried out postmortem. There are no incisions on what's left. Each part is intact in itself, except the head."

"Be thankful for small mercies," Banks muttered.

"Aye." Dr. Glendenning pointed to the head. The eyes were closed. "That's what killed him, I'm almost certain. That bloody great hole in his head, to be technical about it. And you can see if you look carefully that the throat was cut before the head was severed. There are signs of two different incisions." He selected a scalpel from the tray of instruments on the side table. "Now, let's see what else we've got here. There's no sign of lividity, no blood settled in the muscles or tissue." He put down the scalpel and conferred with his assistant quietly for a few moments, then he turned back to Banks.

"The victim was shot in the forehead. And I'm glad you haven't asked about time of death, because I'm afraid it would be very hard to tell."

"We think it probably happened on Sunday morning."

"Now look at this." Dr. Glendenning pointed toward the ankles, where Banks could see the deeply cut groove of some sort of binding.

"Rope?" he asked. "Leather? Metal?"

"We'll settle that later when we check the wound for fibers. For the moment, though, I can tell you that the throat was cut and the body was drained of blood, most likely while hanging upside down. The arms were expertly removed at the shoulder joints—no cutting of bone involved—and finally, the body was sliced in half by a very sharp blade and eviscerated. Scraped out. Look at the cleanness of those cut lines. There's little tearing, no raggedness."

"What was used? A chain saw or something?"

"Certainly *something*." Glendenning nodded toward his assistant. "But probably not a chain saw. At least not an ordinary one. There would be much more tearing. Karen over there has a theory. Tell DCI Banks your theory, my dear."

Karen gave Dr. Glendenning a daggers-drawn look at the sexist endearment. Not that it would do any good, Banks thought. Glendenning loved to tease and play the politically incorrect male chauvinist pig, and he was too old to change now. "Taking everything together," Karen said, "it very much looks to me as if this body was dressed in a working abattoir."

"An abattoir?" Banks repeated.

"Yes." Karen glanced at the remains, then back at Banks. She was a petite, serious brunette, most of her hair hidden under the surgeon's cap, and she looked far too young and innocent to know such things. "That's my opinion, DCI Banks. Your victim was shot first, and then taken and cut up in a slaughterhouse."

"Of course." Banks scratched his head. "Goes without saying. And the gunshot wound, the cause of death?"

"I just said *shot*," Karen explained. "I did not say gunshot."

"Christ," said Banks. *"No Country for Old Men."*

Dr. Glendenning gave him a surprised glance. "It certainly isn't," he agreed, "but this is hardly the time or place for a discussion of age and society."

"It's a movie," said Banks. "The killer uses a bolt gun."

"Give the man a cigar. I'll bet you a grand to a bucket of slops that when I go inside I'll find the frontal lobes scrambled, and no stray bullet. It's rare in human murder cases, but as you can see it does the job. The way it usually works is a gas cylinder is used to power the bolt, which enters the skull to a certain point, causing massive and irreversible brain damage, then the bolt retracts back into the gun. Used on a cow or a pig, you couldn't guarantee that death would ensue—the animal may just be stunned—so you'd probably have to be prepared for exsanguination on the spot, but with a human being . . . well, our skulls aren't as thick, no matter what some of us might think. This man was shot with a penetrating bolt gun, the kind that a professional slaughterman would use."

"So he would have died on the spot?"

"Most likely," said Glendenning. "Though he might have survived for a short while, as his system was shutting down. Death is not always immediate from such wounds. Though he would most certainly have been incapacitated."

"And the loss of blood?"

"Apart from the amount he lost at the scene—there's usually a lot of blood with head wounds—the rest was drained later. Judging by the straps and the split carcass, I'd suggest that he was hung upside down and his throat was slit. All you need to bleed out then is gravity's help. It doesn't even matter if your heart's stopped. After that, he was cut up, disjointed, eviscerated, and from what I can gather packaged up like a stillborn lamb and shipped off for incineration. No one would be any the wiser."

Banks looked at the gruesome remains of Morgan Spencer on the steel table and felt the taste of hot acid bile in his throat. *Christ,* he wondered, *what, and* who, *were they dealing with here?*

ANNIE FELT disoriented when she woke early on Wednesday morning, and for a moment she experienced that terrifying sensation of not knowing where she was or how she had got there. It didn't last long, thank the Lord, until the dry mouth and the throbbing headache told her she was on Alex Preston's let-down sofa and she had a bloody hangover. It was the strangest sensation, she reflected as she sat up and stretched, that split second when you don't recognize the place you're in. Maybe that's what you felt when you woke up dead, she thought, then chided herself for being so stupid as to think you could wake up dead. It must be the hangover thinking.

It was just starting to get light outside, and nobody else in the flat was up yet. Then she heard an alarm ring and stop suddenly. A few moments later, Alex padded down the hall in her dressing gown and, without stopping to check on Annie, went into the kitchen to put the kettle on. Annie lay on her back and pulled the blanket up to her chin. When Alex came back, she stopped in the half-light by the sofa and looked down at Annie.

"You're awake," she said. "I wasn't sure. Mind if I switch the light on?"

Annie rubbed her eyes. "Not at all."

"The kettle will come to a boil in a minute. Stay where you are, if you like, and I'll bring you a cup of tea. Right now I have to go and get Ian up. Believe me, it can be quite a job."

She seemed far too brisk and chirpy for so early in the morning, thought Annie, not at all a morning person herself. Especially a morning after the boozy night they'd had. At least it was quiet in the flat. No kids screaming next door. No domestics from upstairs. Maybe Ian would be quiet. And a cup of tea in bed. Now, that was a rare treat.

She checked her watch. Half past seven. She had better get a move on; there was a lot to do today. Banks would already be at the postmortem. Then she remembered last night's conversation, the card with the number on it. She still had it in an envelope in her bag. She would have to get it fingerprinted as soon as possible. And Banks would want to know everything Alex had told her. She reached for her handbag and checked her notebook. Thank God she had written it all down. Then she realized another thing. From this moment on, she couldn't leave Alex and Ian alone. Until she could organize a shift of watchers, she would have to stick with them herself, or get someone else to do it. Her unexpected visitor didn't sound the sort who would stop at a broken finger.

When Alex came back, Annie asked if she could use the bathroom.

"Of course," said Alex. "It'll take Ian half an hour to get out of bed, and I've got breakfast to make. Take your time."

Annie luxuriated in a hot shower and then brushed her teeth so long that she probably wore off most of the enamel. She had forgotten to do it last night, so she was making up for it now. Luxury. When she looked for some paracetamol in the bathroom cabinet, she noticed a strip of contraceptive pills. So there were to be no more children, at least not for the time being. It was none of her business, and she felt vaguely guilty about even finding them. But it was her nature to pry, and when she did, she found nothing more of interest. No prescription drugs. No illegal drugs. No guns.

She hated dressing in yesterday's clothes, but she had no choice. She thought of asking Alex for a loan of clean underwear but felt too embarrassed. The best she could do was turn her knickers inside out and pretend they were fresh. The bra was fine, and her jeans, but she could do with a different top, and she had no time to go home before she went to the station.

Things progressed slowly through tea, cornflakes and toast and marmalade, and eventually they were all ready for off. Though she felt she was perhaps being paranoid, Annie went out of the door first and glanced up and down the landing. Nobody around. She held her breath as they went down in the lift, half expecting the doors to open at six or four and for some heavies to get in. But they had it to themselves the whole way down.

She had been a bit anxious the previous evening about leaving her car parked in the street, expecting the wheels to be gone, or worse, but Alex had told her not to worry, and it was just as she had left it. Though Ian's school was hardly more than a couple of hundred yards away, they dropped him off there first and made sure he was through the doors before driving to the station. If Winsome, Doug or Gerry noticed that Annie was wearing the same clothes as yesterday when she entered the squad room, they were too polite to say anything. She remembered once in her early days she had turned up at the station in yesterday's clothes, and all the blokes had nudged one another and whispered and smirked. They wouldn't let her forget for the rest of the day. And if she had compounded the error by turning up with an attractive female civilian in tow, their imaginations, and comments, would have known no bounds. Annie introduced Alex to her colleagues, then took her over to the annex.

She could see Alex's eyes wandering everywhere, an expression of intelligent curiosity on her face as they walked among the lab-coated techies and the various machines and computer stations.

"I hadn't thought it would be so high-tech," Alex said.

"No expense spared for crime fighting," said Annie as they entered the Fingerprint Development Laboratory, Vic Manson's domain. "Except when it comes to our wages, of course."

Manson was at his desk already, poring over a stack of photographed fingerprints. He covered them with a folder when he saw there was a civilian present. Annie wondered why. It wasn't as if Alex would recognize someone's fingerprint from a photograph. Normally, of course, no one would go to Manson's office for fingerprinting; that would be done down at the custody suite. But Manson had all the latest technology, and instead of ink and paper, he simply scanned Alex's prints, leaving out the broken one, into the computer after

Annie had explained what they were after. "These will be erased as soon as we've finished," Manson assured Alex, who said she didn't really care, as she had nothing to hide.

"Getting fingerprints from porous surfaces is much easier than it used to be a few years ago," Manson explained as he held the card by its edge between his thumb and forefinger. "But the quality still depends on how much the handler secreted. Paper and cards such as this one are absorbent, you see, so we need to use special chemicals to make them visible. It may take a little time."

"He was sweating, if that helps," Alex said.

Manson looked curiously at her.

"The man who gave the card to me," Alex explained. "He'd just had to walk up the stairs to the eighth floor, you see. The lift's on and off, and it was off when he came. He didn't look very fit, either."

"Excellent. That should help a lot," said Manson. Then he waved his hand. "Now if you'll give me a little time, I'll get back to you later. I've still got a mass of work to get through from the hangar and the crash scene first, but I should be able to find time to fit this in sometime later today."

"When do you think you'll have a result?" Annie said. "It's all connected, we think. The crash. The hangar. This man."

"I'll do my best to have something by the end of the day," said Manson.

"Can you run it against NAFIS, see if you can come up with a name?"

"NAFIS? You're a bit out of date, Annie. We're more advanced than that now. I can run it against IDENT1, Eurodac, Europol and Interpol databases, too."

"Well, I suppose that gives us one good reason to stay in the EU."

Manson laughed. "We can even check with the FBI, if you like."

"You know me and technology, Vic. I'm just a silly slip of a lass. Europe wouldn't be a bad idea, but I don't think we need trouble the Feds just yet."

"Will do," said Manson. "I'll give you a bell."

Annie thanked him and shepherded Alex out of the lab. She looked as if she wanted to stay and watch, but Annie knew Manson wouldn't like that. Like many a scientist, he wanted to preserve the mystique, the magic, mystery and secrets of his profession, like the conjuror who won't reveal how he pulls a rabbit out of the hat.

"What now?" said Alex as they walked back down the corridor toward the squad room.

"Work for you, after the sketch artist. Me, too. I have to go to Leeds this morning."

"What about—"

"Don't worry. I'll make sure you're well taken care of before I go anywhere." There was no point now, she thought, in keeping the surveillance from Alex. Especially as knowing that there would be someone watching over her might ease her stress levels. Doug Wilson could take care of it for today, he said. She knew that Banks would approve, as Alex had now become a priority, if not a major witness. She was the best lead they had to Morgan Spencer's killer and to another member of the gang. "Ian will be fine at school, and you'll be fine at work, but I'll make sure there's someone keeping an eye out for both you, and someone to take you to pick up Ian and go home."

"But how will I know he's real?"

"You've already seen him. In the squad room."

"The one who looks like Harry Potter?"

"Don't you dare say that to him," said Annie. "He's very sensitive. He also has a black belt in karate."

Doug had no such thing, of course, but Annie felt the lie would reassure Alex more than knowing that he had grown up on an estate like the one where she lived, and that he could handle himself.

"Will you—"

"Don't worry. I'll be around to check that everything's all right later. We should have some results from Vic by then. And we'll also have some other officers to keep an eye on you. I'll make sure you're introduced to them. If you hear anything at all from the man who came to see you, call me." They turned into the squad room. "Now wait here with Doug. I'll go and arrange for the artist."

WINSOME TOOK Gerry Masterson with her to Vaughn's ABP after Banks had given them all the quick version of Morgan Spencer's postmortem results. She thought it could be too important an interview to carry out alone, and it would be good experience for Gerry.

They pulled up at the gate of the fenced compound and got out of the car. The place wasn't very large, Winsome noticed, just a few metal storage structures, aluminum most likely, an area for parking the fleet of collection vans, two temporary office buildings on blocks and a windowless structure with a tapered chimney, which Winsome took to be the incinerator. It was a fair day, weatherwise, if a bit cold and gray, but the ground was still muddy from the recent rains. Winsome and Gerry put on their Wellingtons before getting out of the car and heading for the nearest office trailer. A faint smell of decay hung around the compound—an occupational hazard, Winsome imagined, no matter how well you packaged up the dead meat. She also noticed that there were no other farms or businesses for some distance.

Another thing Winsome noticed as they climbed the steps to the office was a total lack of activity. There was no one in the yard, no sounds at all, only the pale smoke drifting from the chimney of the incinerator and dispersing in the chill air. She wondered if there was anybody around at all. It was Wednesday, so it should be a regular workday. She knocked on the flimsy door.

Almost immediately it was opened by a tall and slightly stooped man in jeans and a polo-neck green jersey. He had a head of bristly gray hair, which matched the bristles around his jaw. Winsome put him in his mid fifties. "Mr. Vaughn?" she inquired.

"One of them. Neil. It's a family business."

Winsome and Gerry showed their warrant cards and Neil Vaughn invited them inside. The side of an old cardboard box served as a doormat, and they wiped their feet as best they could without reducing it to shreds. Vaughn seemed to be the only person around. After he asked them to sit down, he returned to a desk littered with papers and swiveled his chair to face them. The inside of the trailer was bleak, as such places usually are, and on the pasteboard walls were hung with a girlie calendar curling at the edges, a large chart with written-in squares and an Ordnance Survey map of the immediate area. The floor didn't feel stable, and the chairs were lumpy. The office smelled of pipe tobacco, and Winsome guessed they didn't bother much about nonsmoking regulations in the workplace out here. A small electric fire stood against the far wall. Both elements were on, but the heat wasn't reaching where they were sitting.

"We're all gutted by what happened to Caleb," said Vaughn. "I gave everyone the day off. I can't imagine how anyone would have had the heart for collections today. I do most of the hands-on business now my father's incapacitated. My brother, Charlie, helps out sometimes." Vaughn paused. "When he can be bothered, that is."

Winsome didn't miss the edge in his tone. Nor did Gerry, judging by the way she frowned.

Neil Vaughn looked from one to the other. "What can I say? We all follow our own paths. Charlie's doesn't involve fallen stock collection and disposal."

"What does it involve?" Winsome asked.

"Horses, mostly. And not dead ones."

Winsome thought it would be a good idea to have a chat with Charlie Vaughn, and she saw Gerry writing in her notebook. Somehow, she sensed that was exactly what she was jotting down.

"Was Caleb with you for a long time?" she asked.

"Thirty years. I've known him since I started in the business. He taught me practically all I know."

"But he never sought promotion? Or got it?"

Vaughn gave a harsh laugh. "There's not a lot of promotion to be had around here. No, Caleb liked driving. He was his own boss, in his own world. Put him in the van with his music and his fags, and he was happy as a pig in . . . well . . . the proverbial."

"He worked alone?"

"That was one concession he earned over the years. And there weren't many as would want to ride with him and put up with the smoke and the music. That prog rock stuff, I think it's called. Old-fashioned, at any rate. Gives me an earache. And I know smoking's not strictly legal on the job, but . . . well, it was Caleb's cab. We usually have a team of two on collections, of course, but the local farmers were happy to help Caleb if they had to. Everyone knew him. He hadn't a bad word to say for anyone. And he was strong. It wasn't often he needed a hand with a load."

Winsome was getting the picture. Caleb Ross was a saint. Well, saint or sinner, it didn't matter that much; Ross wasn't the victim who interested them, unless he had played a part in the events of his own demise.

"Do you know if Mr. Ross had any financial problems, any money troubles at all?"

"Caleb? Good Lord, no. At least, he never complained. He lived a simple life. Had a little cottage in Lyndgarth, just off the green, lived there with his wife, Maggie. The kids had grown up and flown the coop. Maggie . . . has anyone . . . ?"

"She's been informed, sir," said Gerry.

"That's a relief. I must pay her a visit. Soon as I . . . well . . ." He waved his hands over the mess of papers. "I thought there was no sense in me staying at home. I couldn't bear it, just pacing and thinking of poor Caleb. So I came to work. Thought it might take my mind off things."

"And has it?" Winsome asked.

"Not really. Something like this, it's hard to get your mind around it. We all have to go eventually, I know that, but Caleb was fit and strong, and about the same age as me. I suppose I assumed he would always be around."

"From what we can gather, it was just a tragic accident," said Winsome. "The perfect storm. Though I don't suppose that's much consolation."

One of the elements made a crackling sound, as if a fly had just landed on it. "Then why are you here?" Vaughn asked. "Is it a matter of insurance?"

"Nothing like that, sir," said Winsome.

"Neil, please. Then what?"

Winsome and Gerry exchanged glances. "You haven't been watching the news?"

"A constable came to the office," Vaughn said. "All I know is that he told us Caleb had died in a crash due to severe weather conditions. I didn't want to go home and see it replayed endlessly on the news. Is that not what happened?"

"That's exactly what happened," Winsome said. "A freak hailstorm, a stray sheep and an oncoming car. There's no question of blame or anything."

Vaughn looked puzzled. "Then what . . . ?"

"It's what Mr. Ross was carrying that interests us."

"I don't understand. Carrying?"

"There was another body found at the scene."

"Another body? You mean a *human* body? Whose?"

"Among the animal parts, sir . . ."

"Good God! I don't believe it. How could a human body be mistaken for a fallen animal?"

"We don't think it could, but all the parts were wrapped in black bin liner."

"Parts?"

"The body had been cut into several pieces. I must ask you to keep this information to yourself for the moment, sir. All the press and TV have are rumors so far."

"Of course. My God. And you're saying someone put it there? This human body?"

"It looks very much that way. I can't imagine it got there by accident."

"But why?"

"We don't know why. Right now we're more concerned about *how* and *who*. Obviously, it was meant to be disposed of." Winsome glanced out of the window. "It would have ended up in your incinerator, most likely, and nobody would have been any the wiser."

"Except for the crash?"

"That's right. So what we need to know is what farms Caleb Ross visited yesterday morning, where he might have stopped, say for a tea break, or lunch, and who might have had access to his schedule."

"I can certainly supply you with a copy of Caleb's pickup schedule, but surely you can't think anyone here had anything to do with what happened?"

"We don't think anything yet, sir. We're still gathering facts and evidence. Can you help?"

"Certainly." Vaughn riffled through the papers on his desk. "That's easy. Our copies of yesterday's pickup schedule are here somewhere.

Caleb's is . . . ah, here it is." He brandished two sheets of paper stapled together. "Of course," Vaughn added, "he didn't finish his rounds, so he didn't get to all these places. I think the last one was Alf Wythers, Garsley Farm, just outside Swainshead. He'd probably have had his lunch in the village, then set off over Belderfell Pass to where his next collection point was. But, of course, he never got there."

Winsome took the list Vaughn handed her, looked it over and passed it to Gerry, who slipped it into her briefcase. "It seems like a long list," Winsome said. "Was he always so busy?"

"It's lambing season," said Vaughn. "Sad to say, but it's a time of high mortality on the dales farms."

"Could someone have added to the load at any of the places Mr. Ross visited?"

"It wouldn't have been that easy. At least not always. Sometimes the fallen animals are kept at some distance from the actual farm buildings, you understand, in which case it probably wouldn't have been very difficult for some interloper to swap a bag."

"Is there no record of the numbers? Bags, packages, you know?"

"Of course. Record keeping is essential when you're dealing with fallen stock. Any carcasses sent off farm for disposal—which is the only legal way to do it, most of the time—must be recorded, and all carcasses must be accompanied by a commercial document while in transit. In triplicate." Vaughn swallowed. "Of course, in this case, the documents would have . . . well . . ."

"I understand," said Winsome. "But the farmers would have a record of what stock they had had taken away?"

"Yes. They should." Vaughn scratched under his collar.

"Is there a problem, sir?"

"No, not really. I mean, ninety-nine percent of the time everything's shipshape and aboveboard, but sometimes, well, human error can creep in."

"Even in something as important as fallen stock records?"

"People don't like to admit it, of course, no more than the police like to admit they make errors, I'm sure." Vaughn smiled, but neither Winsome nor Gerry Masterson returned it. "But it happens sometimes," he went on. "Records don't always match the numbers."

"Why would that be?"

"Oh, perhaps another animal has died after the list was made up and before pickup. Caleb and the other drivers would usually change it on their copies of the commercial documents, even though they're not really supposed to."

"There's no black market in fallen animals, is there?" Gerry asked. "No profit to be made?"

Vaughn looked puzzled. "No. How could there be? I don't understand."

"Oh, I don't know. Perhaps food produce? You know, like the horse meat in the burgers."

Vaughn laughed. "No. That horse meat business was a direct result of the banning of DSM in meat products."

"DSM?"

"Desinewed meat. It's what left when all the good cuts have been taken. It's used in processed meats."

"The nostrils and eyelids?" Gerry said.

"It might include them, but that's not the point. When its use was banned, producers had to find other sources of cheap meat products to make up the shortfall. Hence the horse meat business."

"What about wild animals, game?"

"The law's complicated on that subject. You can blame the EU for that, too, of course."

"Why?" Gerry persisted.

"It's a matter of disease, infection. Wild animals can carry disease, even though they haven't been tended or fed by humans. Often it's best to make sure. But in many cases, you can't, and if it's apparent the animal has died of natural causes, it's permissible to bury it without calling us. On the other hand, there's a requirement to carry out BSE/TSE tests on all fallen cattle over forty-eight months. That's mad cow disease to you. The rules are stringent on most matters."

"Do you get many infected animals?"

"We're not approved for over-forty-eight-month-cattle sampling and testing. Too much hassle. It was mostly stillborn lambs At least that's what it would have said on the labels. But now we know different, of course. I'm still finding this hard to believe."

"Getting back to how these human remains could have been added to the load," said Winsome. "Would it have been possible for someone to add them to Mr. Ross's van, say, while he was having his lunch?"

"Officially, there's supposed to be someone with the van at all times."

"Only officially?"

"Caleb usually took his own lunch, just a sandwich and a flask of tea, but he liked his giant Yorkshire puddings. He might have stopped off in Swainshead for a quick bite at the White Rose, if the disinfectant or dead animal smell didn't clear out the whole pub. It depends on the kind of day he'd been having. But he wouldn't have had anything to drink. He was strictly teetotaler, was Caleb."

A tox screen on what was left of Caleb Ross would soon determine whether he had enjoyed a jar or two with his giant Yorkshire. "It sounds as if there's a great deal of laxity with the 'official' requirements around here," Winsome said.

Vaughn seemed unconcerned by the criticism. "It's not much different from any other business in that respect, I should imagine. We accept that biosecurity is essential. We also have some very strict controls on the incinerator. But if you obeyed all the rules handed down by the EU, Trading Standards and Health and Safety to the letter you'd hardly be able to breathe, let alone run a profitable business."

"So it could have happened that way? Someone could have added the body parts to his load while he was having his lunch?"

"It's possible. If they could gain access to the van. But if his paperwork was in order, it could also easily have happened anywhere on the route. Even if we were obeying all the rules."

"What do you mean?"

"I mean that Caleb wouldn't open any of the bags to check their contents, and they'd go straight into the incinerator here when he got back. Nobody would want to open . . . well, you can imagine. The idea is to dispose of fallen stock as quickly as is reasonably possible and, as I said, we don't do any testing here. If the farmer wrote down 'two dead lambs,' then Caleb would assume that was what was in the bags and the commercial document would bear this out. He's not going to open them and make sure that's what's in there."

"Assuming they were already bagged."

"Yes, of course. That *is* usually the case."

"And that's also assuming that one of the farmers Caleb visited must have known what was in the packages and passed them off as fallen stock?" Gerry added.

"Yes. Highly unlikely, wouldn't you think? They're all regular customers. All aboveboard."

Winsome didn't necessarily agree, but she nodded as she watched Gerry scribbling away. In fact, it seemed to her that the whole business was lax, and that it would have been unbelievably easy for someone to have slipped Morgan Spencer's body parts in with the load. "Someone could have made an exchange at one of the farms, if the fallen stock had already been bagged and listed. Swapped a couple of bags and labels. Then no one would have been the wiser, would they?"

"I suppose not," said Vaughn. "I really don't know. It's not something I've thought much about. It's not something that happens every day."

"How do you know?" Gerry asked.

Vaughn looked at her, openmouthed. "Well . . . I . . . I mean . . ."

"If you incinerate the bags without checking what's in them when they've been listed on the paperwork, it could have happened any number of times."

"Yes, strictly speaking. But you're splitting hairs."

Winsome thought so, too. They were hardly trying to make out that Vaughn was running a murder victim disposal service. One body was enough. She gave Gerry a curious glance and picked up the threads again. "I suppose it would make more sense if someone sneaked the body parts into Caleb's load while he wasn't looking. Most of the drivers are worried about theft, but we have the opposite here."

"You have a list of all the farms Caleb visited on his rounds before the accident. That's about all I can help you with. It's possible that someone invited him in for a cup of tea, and he left his load unguarded for a short while. None of us is perfect. If you can find out where he had lunch—if he did—you might get lucky there."

Winsome smiled. Nice of the public to tell them how to do their jobs, she thought, but she thanked him anyway. "If the other possibilities sound remote, is it likely that Caleb Ross loaded the body parts himself?"

"Caleb? You're suggesting that Caleb had something to do with this?"

"Well, he *was* driving a van containing several plastic bags of human remains."

"But like you said before, someone must have added those while he was away from the van, or at one of the farms. It's ridiculous to think Caleb—"

"Is it?" Winsome asked. "Is it, really? Mr. Vaughn, we think this murder is linked with a spate of rural crime in the area, involving not only livestock but expensive farm equipment. The latest victim was John Beddoes, who had a valuable tractor stolen over the weekend."

"Yes, I heard about that."

"Do you know Mr. Beddoes? Was he a client?"

"Not often. He keeps some pigs and poultry, doesn't he? I think we've been out there a couple of times over the past few years."

"Caleb?"

"I wouldn't know offhand. We have several vans and drivers. I can check if you really want to know."

"If you would, please."

Vaughn walked over to the large filing cabinet, opened the top drawer and flipped through the folders. "I'm afraid you're out of luck," he said after running his finger down the column for a few moments. "Mr. Beddoes's last pickup was November, last year, and Todd Griffin and Pat Bingley did the job."

"Was Caleb Ross working on Monday?"

"Yes. It was a normal workday for us all."

"Sunday?"

"Not this week. We do operate a skeleton staff on Sundays—you have to in this business—but Caleb had enough seniority that he rarely worked on weekends. What's all this about?"

"We think that whoever stole Mr. Beddoes's tractor must be in-formed as to which farms are especially vulnerable, where the rich pickings are, and when they're likely to be minimally managed, as John Beddoes's farm was last week. Now, don't you agree that

Caleb Ross would have been in a perfect position to know what was going on with all the local farms? After all, you've told us everyone knew him."

"Well, yes, I suppose so. But you didn't know Caleb. He was completely reliable. Surely there must be plenty of others in such a position?"

"Perhaps. But was he really so trustworthy? You've already admitted to us that he may have falsified official papers. Perhaps he did the same thing for someone else, no questions asked. Maybe he was doing a favor for someone and he didn't even know he was transporting human body parts? They say every man has his price. And the information he could give about local farms might also have been worth a fair bit. That's why I asked about financial problems earlier."

"But Caleb didn't lack for anything. He never needed much."

"Everything has got much more expensive over the past few years." Winsome glanced at the electric fire. "Just keeping warm, for example. Or the cost of cigarettes. Someone might have come up with an offer that made sense to him."

Vaughn shook his head. "No. I can't see it. Not Caleb."

"Did he have muttonchops?" Gerry cut in.

Vaughn turned to her as if she were mad. "Muttonchops?"

"Yes. Sideboards. You know." She touched her cheeks beside her ears.

"Ah, I see what you mean. What an odd question. No. No, Caleb didn't have muttonchops."

"Very well, Mr. Vaughn," said Winsome. "We'll take your character reference into consideration. Perhaps you might also care to give us the names and addresses of one or two of Mr. Ross's coworkers? Todd Griffin and Pat Bingley for starters."

"They'll only tell you the same I have."

"All the more reason for us to talk to them, then," said Winsome. "The quicker we'll be able to cross him off our list. By the way, do you know what a penetrating captive bolt pistol is?"

"A bolt pistol? Yes, of course. It's what the slaughterman uses in an abattoir to stun the animals."

"Do you own one?"

"Certainly not. Why would I need one? The animals are already dead when they come to us."

"Just wondering. Do you know of anyone who has one?"

"I can't say as I do."

"Caleb Ross, for example?"

"I very much doubt it. Why would Caleb have one? Where could he get hold of one? I take it you can't just buy them in the shops."

Winsome gave Gerry the signal and they stood up to leave. "Just one more thing, sir," said Winsome, pausing at the door.

"Yes?"

"As I said, the human remains had been cut into manageable pieces. It looked like a professional job, according to our pathologist. Would you have any idea how or where that might have been carried out?"

Vaughn rubbed his forehead. "Me? No."

"Don't know any dodgy butchers? Or slaughtermen?"

Vaughn was looking decidedly pale now. "No," he said. "Sorry. That's not a part of our business service." And it seemed to Winsome as if he couldn't wait to shut the door behind them.

VENTURE PROPERTY Developments was housed on the sixth floor of a redbrick office complex just south of Granary Wharf, overlooking the tangle of arterial roads south of Leeds city center. The mirrored lift was clean, fast and practically silent. Banks watched Annie "powder her nose" as they went up and was amazed at how quickly she applied a fresh coat of lipstick and brushed her hair into its natural chestnut glory. It had been windy outside, and even the short walk from their parked car to the office had been enough to reduce it to a messy tangle. Banks, of course, had no such problems. The wind hardly made a dent in his closely cropped dark hair. He did notice in the large mirror, though, that the touch of gray seemed to be spreading from his temples.

"You OK?" he asked Annie. She had been fidgety in the car and had phoned Doug Wilson on his mobile twice to check that Alex Preston was safe. She had told Banks on the way about her visit the previous evening, and about Alex's phone call from Michael Lane.

"I'm fine," she said, with a forced smile. "Ready to rock and roll."

The lift doors opened at the reception area of Venture Properties, where an immaculately groomed receptionist, whose name tag read BRENDA, sat behind a semicircular desk under the red company logo on the wall. The area smelled faintly of nail varnish remover.

Brenda smiled her patent smile of greeting, tinged with a hint of suspicion she no doubt reserved for newcomers, and said, "Good morning. Can I help you?"

Banks showed his warrant card. "We're here to see Mr. Norrington."

Brenda seemed unimpressed by the official identification. "Do you have an appointment?"

"Yes," said Banks.

"Please take a seat." She gestured toward a modular orange couch arranged around a glass table, on which was spread a selection of magazines: the *Economist, House & Home,* along with the *Financial Times* and a selection of the morning's papers, all looking untouched.

Brenda busied herself on the telephone, her voice reduced to a distant whisper. When she hung up, she said, "Mr. Norrington will see you in a few minutes. Can I get you something to drink? Coffee, tea, water?"

"Coffee, please. Black, two sugars," said Annie.

Banks asked for water.

Brenda disappeared and came back seconds later with a cup and saucer and a plastic bottle of fizzy water. Before Annie had managed to finish her coffee, Brenda's phone buzzed and she asked them to follow her.

Norrington's office was at the end of the corridor. It was larger than the entire Eastvale squad room, and the far wall was one giant picture window. The sky was gray, so the venetian blinds were up. Unfortunately, the window didn't look out over the city center, but toward the south, a flat and dreary wasteland of other office buildings, arterial roads, factory yards and retail warehouse outlets. Banks could even see the sprawling shopping park at Crown Point. Beyond that, lanes of traffic sped on the M621 as it coiled through the run-down urban areas of Hunslet and Beeston. Perhaps the view was an inspiration to property developers, Banks thought, a spur to bigger and better things. To most, though, he imagined it would be depressing.

Norrington himself had the look of a man who was comfortable with his environment. As he stood up and came forward to greet them, Banks noticed he had hung his suit jacket on the back of his chair, had his shirtsleeves rolled halfway up his arms and his tie loose at the collar, the way Banks liked to wear his when he had to wear one. His thinning gray hair was swept back and his nose slightly bulbous. His manner was open and polite. He even gave a little bow when Banks introduced Annie, and for a moment Banks thought he was going to kiss her hand. Instead, he offered more refreshments, which both Banks and Annie declined, then bade them sit. Their chairs were wide and comfortable, and faced the large window. At that angle, they could see only the sky, not the wastelands of south Leeds.

"One of our colleagues rang you yesterday, I believe?" Banks said.

"She talked to Geoffrey Melrose, not to me," said Norrington. "He's my partner, to all intents and purposes. I'm afraid he's had to go to London on business today, but I can help you with anything you need."

"I hope so. My colleague said she got rather short shrift."

"Geoff's a busy man. He told me it was something to do with the Drewick development."

"That's right. The old airfield with the hangar. How long have you owned the property?"

"About four years now. It was run-down for years, going cheap, so we bought it for the land. Ever since then we've been trying to get zoning laws and investors in line for a new shopping development. It's a long haul, I can tell you."

"Do such things usually take so long?"

"It depends. You certainly need patience in this business, though."

"While you're negotiating all this, who takes care of the property?"

"Again, it depends on the property."

"In this case."

Norrington leaned back in his chair and started stretching a rubber band. "In this case, nobody, really. There seemed little point in employing a night watchman or a security company, as there was nothing there to watch. The chain link and gates were already in place. We put up all the required signs and padlocks. I suppose some schoolkids might have managed to sneak in through a hole in the fence, but even a night watchman probably couldn't have prevented that. Kids get everywhere."

"Too true," Banks agreed. "And anyone can take a pair of bolt cutters and replace your chain and padlock with their own. Did you ever consider whether the premises were being used for criminal activity?"

"Why would I? We have many properties awaiting development, and it's never been an issue before." Norrington put his rubber band down and wagged his finger. "Now, I do hope you aren't trying to lay the blame for anything like that at our feet? Is this a matter of liability?"

"Well, as a legal issue, I suppose it might interest the lawyers and cost everyone else a fortune. But nobody's blaming anyone. That's not why we're here."

"I'm very glad to hear it."

"So what's the answer?"

"Of course we didn't know anything about criminal activities. I'm shocked to hear that you think we did."

"Not only that, Mr. Norrington," said Annie, "but the area is now also a crime scene, a possible murder scene, in fact. What do you think of that?"

"I don't know what to think. I find it very hard to believe, as a matter of fact. Besides, you can't blame any of this on us."

Banks stood up and walked over to the window. Norrington swiveled his chair so he could keep his eyes on him.

"Believe me, it's true," Annie went on. Norrington didn't seem to know who to look at. He finally decided on Annie.

"But what can I possibly do to help you?" he asked. "I've already told you, we've been involved in negotiations to develop that property for years now. It's not as if we stand guard over it or anything. Sometimes these things move very slowly."

"What's the matter? Not managed to grease the right palms yet?" said Banks, reclaiming his chair again. "Not found the right city councillors to enlist in the cause?"

Norrington reddened. "I resent that."

"Of course you do. But it happens in your business, doesn't it?"

"As a matter of fact," Norrington went on, "that's not the problem at all. Not that we'd resort to such a thing."

"'Course not. What is the problem, then?"

"Not that it's any of your business, but it's investors. Lack thereof. To put it crudely, we're still a bit short of the readies to make a start, even with the requisite planning permission, which we are on the verge of acquiring."

"I'm surprised you can't get anyone to invest in the building of a major shopping center where there isn't any competition for miles around."

"It surprises me, too, but that's the way it happens sometimes. Man plans. God laughs."

"I've had that feeling myself, often," said Banks. "Wouldn't it help if you rented the place out for some private venture in the meantime? Perhaps that would bring in the cash you need? Help you keep your heads above water until it's time to proceed?"

"Too much hassle," said Norrington. "Then we *would* have to hire security and worry about it all the time. We'll get the money. And by legitimate means." Norrington glanced from Banks to Annie and back. "What exactly is it that you want from me, Mr. Banks? I do have things to do, you know. Important things."

"I'm sure you do. And we'll try not to keep you much longer. For a start, I'd like to know if you have any idea who has been using the old airfield and hangar as a transfer point on a trafficking route."

"Trafficking? What do you mean? What trafficking?"

"Stolen farm equipment and livestock. Maybe other things. People. Drugs. We don't know the full extent of the operation yet. It's an ideal location, though. Isolated, unguarded, close to the A1."

"I have no knowledge of any such activity." Norrington seemed shaken. He stood up, took his jacket from the back of his chair and put it on. "Look, I think I'm going to have to ask our legal representatives to come in if our conversation continues in this vein."

"Why?" asked Banks.

"These insinuations you're making."

"I'm not making any insinuations. Do you have something to hide?"

"No, of course I don't. It's just . . . well, I don't know what you're after."

Banks scratched his scar. "You know, I'm not always too sure, myself, Mr. Norrington. I often feel as if I'm just digging around until my shovel hits something. I tell you what. Why don't you just take your jacket off, again, nice and informal like, then sit down, and we'll carry on. OK?"

Norrington hesitated, then seemed to relax and did as Banks suggested, though the suspicious expression remained on his face. "All right," he said, spreading his hands. "I've nothing to hide."

"Good. Can you give us a list of the investors who've signed up for Drewick already?"

"I'm afraid that's privileged information. I can't just go around giving out names. Some of these individuals might wish to remain anonymous. Surely you understand that?"

Banks leaned forward. "Mr. Norrington, perhaps it's us who ought to bring our legal representatives. In our case, it's called the Crown Prosecution Service, and they're very busy, but I'm sure we could persuade someone it's for a good cause. Next to the Internal Revenue, bankers, town planners and lawyers themselves, property developers are pretty low down in the popularity stakes, you know."

"We do an important and necessary job."

"Just as we do," said Banks. "So let's all do it. Accepting that you are an honest businessman, it doesn't have to follow that all of your investors are. One of them might have had an idea for putting the property to good use while he waited for a return on his investment."

Norrington ummed and aahed for a while longer, then rang through to his secretary and asked her to make a photocopy of the Drewick Shopping Centre investor list. "Just to show we've nothing to hide," he added. "Though I would appreciate your discretion in the matter."

"We'll prove the very souls of discretion, don't you worry." It would probably come to nothing, Banks knew, as anyone who was using the hangar for criminal purposes was hardly likely to be connected to the place on paper. But it all had to be checked; criminals get too clever and slip up, or they're just plain stupid to start with. The secretary knocked and entered with the photocopy, which Norrington directed her to give to Banks.

"Is there anything else?" Norrington asked.

"Have you ever visited the site yourself?"

"Once. Years ago, when we first acquired the property."

"2009?"

"Around then, yes."

"Do you always check out your firm's acquisitions?"

"I usually try to."

"Perhaps you could have your secretary make us a copy of the list of other properties your company is preparing for development before we leave, too?"

"Wait a minute. I've already given you the list of investors, against my better judgment. I really don't see why we should be expected to give you a list of our properties."

"I don't see why not."

"Again, it's private information, privileged."

"Mr. Norrington, your company owns a property on which a brutal murder has been committed, and which we believe to be a transfer point for stolen-goods shipments. How do we know you aren't using other properties you own for the same purposes? Absentee landlords or not, Venture Property Developments can't shirk responsibility entirely. Or the publicity that could come with it." Banks glanced at Annie. "I'm sure you can get a court order in an hour or less, DI Cabbot. I'll wait here with Mr. Norrington until you get back."

Annie stood up. Banks held his breath as she walked to the door. There was no way she could return with a court order within a couple of hours, so he could only hope his bluff worked.

"Wait. Wait," said Norrington, waving his hand as Annie grasped the door handle. "If it'll get rid of you once and for all, fine. I've got work to do." Slowly he picked up the phone and gave the instructions. After he had done so, he went on: "I would like to inform you, however, that I don't appreciate threats, and I will be talking to the company's legal department immediately after you leave. Any further intrusions into our time and our business records will be a lot more difficult to carry out and will be done in the presence of legal representation. And remember the names on that list are private property."

Banks and Annie got up to leave. "Thanks, Mr. Norrington, you've been a great help," Banks said over his shoulder. "You certainly sound as if you know the drill. No, don't bother to see us out. We'll pick up the list of properties from your secretary on our way."

9

THE TEAM GATHERED IN THE BOARDROOM AT THE END of the day, as the last rays of sunlight struggled in vain to blaze a trail of glory through the thickening clouds. Gervaise, Banks, Annie, Gerry Masterson, Stefan, Jazz Singh and Winsome were present. Only Doug Wilson among the major team members was missing, and as soon as he had organized his replacements to keep watch over Alex and Ian Preston, his job would be done for the day. He had already reported no progress with the train companies. Banks had guessed it might lead to nothing, but it was an avenue that had to be explored. Someone had sent to the canteen for a pot of coffee and a plate of digestive biscuits. Banks was thinking a bottle of wine or a barrel of beer would not have gone amiss. His mouth watered when he remembered the old Maigret stories his father had introduced him to: Maigret was always sending out to the local bar for beer and sandwiches from the Brasserie Dauphine. No such luck here.

The overhead fluorescent lights were turned off and a couple of tasteful shaded lamps provided a soft ambient glow that everyone seemed to need after the long and frustrating day they'd had. Banks knew they needed a break in the case soon, and the meeting was being held to try to determine from which direction that lead might come. Tacked to the whiteboard next to a sketch of Morgan Spencer and a picture of Beddoes's bright green Deutz-Fahr Agrotron were images of the penetrating bolt gun and the man Alex had described to the police sketch artist. There was no news from Vic Manson on the fingerprints yet, but Banks knew that Vic was a patient man, and sometimes these things took time to get right. He'd come up with something, even if they had to wait until tomorrow.

Jazz Singh was a bit faster with DNA, and she spoke first. "I won't bore you with the technical details," she said. "Not that you'd understand them. First, and perhaps most important, we have a match between the DNA extracted from the blood at the hangar near Drewick and that taken from the body discovered in the Vaughn's van crash. And to be clear, I don't mean the driver, but the other body, the one that was cut up and put in bin bags."

"So it *was* Morgan Spencer who was killed at the hangar," said Banks.

"Hold your horses," said Jazz. "I didn't say that. I simply said they were the same. We don't have a sample of anything we know to be Morgan Spencer's DNA, so I can't say for certain it's him. Everything he owned was destroyed when his caravan burned down, and he's not on any of our databases."

"OK," said Banks. "We recognized Morgan Spencer from the crash site, especially after the searchers found his head." He pointed toward the sketch on the board. "That's how everyone we know who's seen him says he looks. Especially Alex Preston."

"What about his parents?" asked Winsome.

"His father is proving difficult to contact," said Banks. "We understand he's somewhere in Barbados, but other than that . . . His mother lives in Sunderland. She's an ex-junkie and her mental health is precarious. She lives in a halfway house and has very few personal possessions, none of which include a photograph of her son. Apparently, she lost touch with Morgan some years ago, when she lost touch with the rest of the world."

"We've had a look around Spencer's lockup," said Stefan Nowak, "but I don't know if there's anything that can help you in there, Jazz. You're welcome to have a look. You might find a hair or something. No sign of his removal lorry or his motorbike, but we found traces of oil, petrol and red diesel."

"Thanks," said Jazz. "Maybe I'll have a look tomorrow. I have to go back to the lab now. Backlog. The Harrogate rape case. Is that OK?"

"Of course," said Banks. "And thanks for all your efforts."

Jazz skipped briskly from the room.

"And let's not forget," Banks said to the room at large in the silence after Jazz's departure. "Even though we think we've found and identified Morgan Spencer, we still have to find Michael Lane. Hopefully alive and well. He may well be our only chance of a witness to what happened. And we aren't the only ones who want him."

"I managed to trace the number he called Alex Preston from last night," Annie said. "It's a public telephone on Coppergate in York."

"We'll alert the York police," said Banks, "but I imagine he'll be far away by now."

After that, everyone submitted a brief summary of the day's activities, questions and responses, what they had learned and what they suspected. It didn't add up to a lot. The old wool barons on the walls looked sinister in the shadows, as if they were watching over the team, or sitting in judgment. A bloodred lance of dying sunlight managed to stab through a crack in the clouds and illuminate a particularly grim-looking specimen.

"Do you think Keith Norrington at Venture had anything to do with it?" AC Gervaise asked.

Banks glanced at Annie. "No," she said. "He's just a creepy businessman covering his arse, ma'am. It won't do any harm to check him out, though. Bound to be something dodgy in the company books."

Gervaise managed a thin smile. "Well, don't go too far," she said. "We don't want to be accused of harassing creepy businessmen."

"No, ma'am."

"What about Neil Vaughn?" Banks asked.

"I don't think so," said Winsome. "He seemed genuinely distressed about what had happened to Caleb Ross. He'd given his employees the day off. I know that doesn't mean much, and he could be merely trying to manipulate what we think, but I didn't notice any false steps. Gerry?"

"The one thing that struck me," said Gerry Masterson, "was how easy he made it seem to get around the rules. I mean, a business like his is highly regulated. Has to be, doesn't it? Stands to reason with all those animal carcasses and risks of disease and contagion. Vaughn himself might not be involved in anything, but he certainly gave the impression that it wouldn't be too difficult for someone who did want to bend the rules."

"I agree," said Winsome. "And something he said gave us cause for concern about his brother, Charlie Vaughn. Apparently he's not interested in the family business, which is nothing of itself, but he is interested in horses of the live kind. Live and running races."

"So he's a gambler?" said Banks.

"Yes. Winner or loser, I don't know, but that's the impression I got."

"I've never known a gambler who was a winner," said Banks. "They all win sometimes, even win big, but they lose it in the end. It's the nature of the business. And when they lose big, things can get tough for everyone around them. It's like a junkie in need of a fix. Know anything more?"

"Apparently, he's got an alibi," said Gerry. "He's been out of the country the past two weeks. Spain."

"Solid."

"I think so," said Gerry. "Want me to dig deeper?"

"No, not yet. We've got plenty to be going on with. Let's keep him in our thoughts, though."

"By the way, sir," Gerry added. "Caleb Ross didn't have mutton-chops."

Banks raised his eyebrows. "So he's not our Sunday driver? I must say, I never really thought he was. Good work, though, Gerry."

Gerry Masterson beamed.

AC Gervaise turned toward Stefan. "I understand you have something of interest to report, Mr. Nowak?"

"Yes," said Stefan, with a gentlemanly nod toward Gervaise. "One of our search team found some marijuana in a tin at the crash site. It was actually in the van, more a part of the carburetor when we found it, and we'll need to send it for analysis and do a number of tests to make certain. But the CSI who found it seems sure about what it was. He . . . er . . . he seems to know what he's talking about."

They all laughed.

Stefan smiled. "I believe him."

"Could it have been a contributing factor to the accident?"

"It could have been," said Stefan. "If he'd been smoking it at the time of the crash, it could certainly have interfered with his motor functions and his reaction times. All it would have taken in the conditions at that time would have been a momentary distraction. But we have no way of knowing whether he smoked it in the cab. Of course, Dr. Glendenning will order a tox screen on the remains and that might show up something, though I doubt it."

"But in a way, that doesn't matter, does it?" said Banks. "I mean whether he was sober or stoned when he crashed. Maybe to the insurance companies, perhaps even to the other driver and to Caleb's friends and acquaintances. But it doesn't matter to us."

"What do you mean, Alan?" said Gervaise.

"It's no great sin that Caleb Ross smoked a bit of marijuana now and then. In fact I'd be surprised to hear that he didn't. Apparently he was a big prog rock fan, and prog rock and marijuana use go together like fish and chips. I even remember seeing a few people smoking and listening to *Tales from Topographic Oceans* when I was a student. Of course, I never touched the stuff myself."

"Of course not," said Gervaise. The thin smile drew her Cupid's bow lips tight. "Or at least, if you did, you didn't inhale."

"I mean prog rock," said Banks, deadpan.

They all laughed again. Gerry played mother and refilled everyone's coffee cups. The biscuits were all gone.

"What I mean," Banks went on, "is that what might be interesting is where he got his dope, and whether his dealer had some kind of hold over him. Perhaps there were even other, more serious, drugs involved."

"We had a couple of local DCs search his house," said Winsome. "They didn't find anything. No drugs, no stash of money. Nothing of interest."

"I suppose it's still possible that Ross was somehow blackmailed into helping the gang," said Banks. "Or even willingly paid in marijuana. Maybe that was their way to make him do their bidding. If nothing else, he would certainly have lost his job had it come out that he was a habitual pot smoker."

"So we try to find his source?" said Winsome.

"We'll keep a lookout. And we might as well have a good look at Caleb Ross again. Winsome?"

"As far as I could gather from all his coworkers I talked to, no one had a bad word to say about him. Salt of the earth. Honest as the day is long. All the usual clichés. None of his colleagues could believe that he could possibly have been up to no good. 'Caleb? No way' was the general response."

"Maybe they just didn't want to be heard speaking ill of the dead?" Annie suggested.

"I'm sure there was a bit of that involved. I mean, even with this new information, we still can't say he was connected with the theft or the murder, can we? As the DCI says, it's hardly a major crime to smoke marijuana. Maybe he was a minor player? It's amazing how easily people can avert their eyes from what they just see as a harmless little fiddle, like nicking pens and writing pads from the office stationery, like it's something you're entitled to."

"Good point," said Banks. "But I still can't shake the feeling that Ross and Lane are involved at some level. Ross might not have known what was in the extra packages he accepted, and he might well have balked if he had, but if he knowingly accepted them, he knew that what he was doing was against regulations, and that it probably involved forging official documents. And finding the marijuana does cast a slightly different light on him. It seems he wasn't quite as honest and law-abiding as everyone makes out. Look a bit deeper, Winsome. Maybe talk to some of the farmers he regularly picked up from, see what you can find out there."

"Will do, sir. I'll draw up a list from the one Vaughn's gave us and make a few visits."

Banks turned to Stefan Nowak again. "Thanks, Stefan," he said. "Anything else?"

"Nothing to report, really. The accident lads will be there all night again, by the looks of it. They've found no traces of tampering and don't expect to at this point, but they still have a lot of other ground to cover. My lads are about done and should be able to get away tomorrow. It's bloody freezing out there."

"Anything more from the hangar?"

"Some partial prints. We might be able to come up with some matches, but nothing that would stand up in court."

Banks turned to Gerry Masterson. "Anything more on Beddoes's finances?"

"Nothing dodgy at all as far as I can make out, sir. All in order. He's not rich, but he gets by. He's got plenty of investments, mostly low-risk—he's no gambler—and the farm makes a small profit on paper. You ought to see the prices for some of those oils and pork chops!"

Banks laughed. "Maybe when this is all over, Beddoes can take us all out for dinner."

"Only if we find his tractor, sir. I can do a more thorough check, if you like."

"We'll see how things go. You're going to be busy tomorrow, Gerry. We need workups on Venture Properties, for a start. I've got a couple of lists to get you going there."

"Yes, sir. By the way, I did manage a brief glance at Terry Gilchrist's military record and it's without blemish. Quite the opposite, really. Most distinguished."

"Thanks, Gerry," said Banks. He looked at Winsome, who had her head down and her pen in her hand.

"Perhaps most important of all is this," Banks went on. He turned to the whiteboard and pointed to the image of the bolt gun. "I know it looks like one of those ray guns aliens use in old science-fiction movies, but it's not. It's what's called a captive bolt pistol, or gun, and it's used for stunning animals in abattoirs. There are essentially three versions. The first is nonpenetrating, in which a retractable bolt is fired either by compressed air or by a blank round. This bolt hits the animal's skull but doesn't penetrate it, causing unconsciousness. The second type is a penetrating bolt gun, in which the bolt is pointed and penetrates the skull, destroying brain tissue. There's also a noncaptive free bolt type, in which the bolt is actually fired like a bullet. In this case, we're dealing with the penetrating bolt gun. If it had been free bolt there would have been much deeper internal damage, and we would have found the bolt somewhere, unless the killers took it with them. Dr. Glendenning assures me that was not the case, and the wound indicates a typical penetrating bolt gun."

"Would the blow have been enough to kill Spencer?" asked Gervaise.

"Probably," said Banks. "We can't be a hundred percent certain, but such a blow is usually fatal to humans. The only thing that makes the bolt pistol a rather awkward weapon, and perhaps why it isn't used so often, is that you have to be close up to the victim to use it. You can't shoot from a distance because the bolt never actually leaves the gun. Which explains why someone had to hold Spencer's arms. He'd hardly be likely to just stand still and take it."

"How do you get hold of one?"

"Like many such things," said Banks, "you order it over the Internet."

"Don't you need a license?" Annie asked.

"No," said Gerry. "I checked. At least you don't need a firearms license. You'd need a slaughterman's license, though."

"And how do you get that?" Annie asked.

"Pass the course. The slaughterman course."

"Sick," said Annie.

"Penetrating bolt pistols are very much discouraged these days," Gerry went on. "Not because they're inhumane, but because by initiating contact with the animal's brain, they could become a conduit for disease. Mad cow, that is, for the most part. Free bolts are rare, only used in an emergency if you can't restrain the animal."

"I suppose the top and bottom of it is," said Banks, "that while they're not easy to get, and they can be expensive, they're a hell of a lot easier to get your hands on than a regular handgun." He looked at Gerry. "Again, it looks as if you're going to have to do a bit of tracking down here. Purchases. Thefts. The usual suspects. And I think first of all you should see if you can find out whether there have been any crimes with a similar MO in the last couple of years. Start locally, then move out to the rest of the country."

Gerry nodded.

"And we need to have a close look at the abattoir business in these parts," Banks said. "Everyone knows illegal and unregulated abattoirs exist, along with legitimate establishments, and they can take many shapes and sizes. It's true that the prime season for stealing lambs is August, when they're nice and plump and ready to eat, but someone has been picking off the odd field of sheep or cows around the dale for a while now, and I doubt they've all been shipped to Romania or Bulgaria, no matter what the *Daily Mail* would have us believe. Cattle are especially difficult to sell, as they have electronic ID tags and passports, whereas sheep only have easily removable ear tags. But if your intention is to get the animal cut up as soon as possible and sell it locally, off the back of a lorry, none of that matters too much. There's a big enough market at home for a bit of cheap meat, no questions asked." Banks turned to Annie: "Maybe you and Doug can start checking out the local abattoirs tomorrow? We want any hints of illegal operations, any objects stolen, especially bolt pistols, any disgruntled employees recently fired and maybe setting up on their own, that sort of thing."

"But I'm a vegetarian," protested Annie. "Yuck."

"I know," said Banks. "It's a dirty job, but . . ."

Annie pulled a face, and the others laughed, then there was a tap at the door followed by Vic Manson, a buff folder in his hand. "Thought you'd like to know," he said. "We've got a result."

WHEN TERRY Gilchrist opened the door, he looked surprised to see Winsome again. "DS Jackman," he said. "What a pleasant surprise. Come in. Please. Take your coat off." She hung up her coat on a hook in the hall and followed him through to the living room. He was walking without his stick, but he seemed able to manage all right unaided, though she noticed that he rested his hand on the back of the sofa to hold himself up for a moment when he got to the living room, and she thought she saw a grimace of pain flash across his features.

"Are you all right?" she asked.

"Fine. Just the occasional twinge. The doc said I'd get them for a while."

"I'm sorry to call so late. It's been one of those days."

"Then sit down. Take the weight off."

Winsome sat and smoothed her skirt. It was a chilly evening, with a brisk cold wind gusting outside, and Gilchrist had a wood fire burning in the fireplace. Peaches lay stretched out asleep in front of it. Winsome felt the warmth permeate and envelop her. "That's nice," she said, reaching out her hands to feel the heat.

"One of life's little luxuries. And you can see Peaches loves it. Drink?"

"Not for me, thanks. I'm driving."

"Tea, then? Or I can offer you a cappuccino."

"That'd be lovely, if it's no trouble."

"No trouble at all."

The room seemed different after dark. Perhaps it was the wood fire. Winsome absorbed the warmth and the sound of crackling logs as she listened to the hissing and grinding of what sounded like an espresso machine. Peaches was still breathing slowly and peacefully in front of the fire. She stirred and growled once, as if disturbed by a dream, then stuck out her tongue and settled back down again. Soon Gilchrist was back with two cappuccinos. He handed one to Winsome.

"Another of life's little luxuries?"

"The espresso machine? Rather a large luxury, I'd say. Actually," he went on, "you're lucky to catch me in. It's trivia night at the Coach and Horses tonight. Highlight of my week, usually."

"Don't be so cynical."

"Sorry. I really do enjoy it, though. The trivia, I mean, not the cynicism. We used to play it on the base."

"I almost signed up once," Winsome said after a pause.

"For trivia? You?"

"No. The armed forces. Why not? I'm fit. And it's in the family, like policing. My grandfather fought in the Second World War. I was a bit more mercenary. I thought I might at least get an education out of it later, if I survived. Maybe IT, or office administration, something like that."

"Dream on," said Gilchrist. "They were going to send me to university after my spell. Middle Eastern languages. I showed a bit of aptitude in the field, and they can always use someone who speaks the lingo."

"What happened?"

"Canceled. Decided to send me out there again instead." He tapped his leg. "Hence this. I suppose they thought I was a better soldier than a linguist."

"And now?"

"I don't know. I'm out for good. I might actually go to university. I'm still considering my options, as they say."

Winsome had read Gerry's report after the meeting, and she knew how Gilchrist had been injured while getting his comrades and some children out of a booby-trapped school before a second bomb went off. The Military Cross and an honorable discharge. There was no reason to mention it now and embarrass him. One thing she did know was that soldiers didn't like to talk about their wars.

"I don't suppose you came here to talk about my war wounds," he said.

"No. I was just wondering if you remembered anything more about Monday morning."

Gilchrist rubbed his forehead. "I've been thinking about it since the last time we talked, and I've been keeping up with the news. Did the victim really end up at the bottom of Belderfell Pass in pieces, or am I reading too much into the reports?"

"Yes, he did. But he was in pieces before that. How did you know it was him?"

"Is this where you do your detective thing? Tell me I couldn't have known unless I'd done it?"

Winsome laughed. "Good Lord, no. I don't think you did it. At least I hope you didn't."

"Well I'm grateful for that. Actually, it's elementary, my dear Jackman. It's just the odds. I've lived around these parts long enough to know that you don't get a pool of blood in a disused hangar and human body parts in a fallen stock lorry without some sort of connection. Stands to reason." Gilchrist shook his head slowly. "Just when you think you've got as far away as you possibly can from all that sort of thing. The only other thing I remember is the car."

"What car?"

"It was on Sunday morning, the day before I found the blood. I was just coming back from the newsagent's in the village with the papers, about a quarter to ten or so, and I heard a car pass by on that road just beyond the trees, heading toward the Thirsk road. I noticed because it seemed to be going unusually fast and you almost never see cars on that road. It's not very easy on the shock absorbers."

"You're sure it was a car, not a lorry or a van?"

"Yes, it was a car. I'm afraid I can't tell you what make, though. I'm not that good. And I didn't see it, really, just a flash of dull gray through the trees."

"Gray?"

"Yes. But not silvery. More a sort of dirty gray. It didn't sound too healthy, either, not at the speed it was going. I could tell that much at least."

Michael Lane, Winsome thought. Or whoever was driving his car if he had taken Spencer's lorry. But she didn't think he had. Fullerton had seemed pretty sure about the muttonchops and flat hat, and unless Lane was wearing a disguise, which Winsome doubted, then it probably wasn't him. The timing was right. He wouldn't have been worried about his shock absorbers if he thought he was fleeing for his life. Or if he had just shot someone. "Which way was it going?" she asked.

"Drewick direction. If it kept going straight on, it would have ended up on the moors. But there's the Thirsk road. It might have turned on there and joined up with the A1."

"Was anyone following it? Another car? A lorry, motorcycle?"

"No, nobody. At least not for as long as it took me to get back to the house and open the door."

It was something, at any rate, Winsome thought. They could get some patrol cars out to the moors villages and ask if anyone remembered seeing a dirty gray Peugeot last Sunday morning. A car like that might stand out in areas where there wasn't much poor weather traffic. Nobody in Drewick had mentioned it when first questioned by the patrol officers, but it might be a good idea to recanvass the village. Also, Winsome remembered that Lane's mother and grandparents lived over the moors, in Whitby. If Lane had continued across the Thirsk road, he'd have hit the A19 eventually. A little jog either way on there would have had him heading into the North York Moors. Or up to Teesside or down to York, she reminded herself glumly.

She made some notes, aware of Gilchrist watching her writing with a curious eye. "What?" she said, glancing up.

"Nothing. You're very meticulous, that's all."

"It pays to be, in my job."

"I'll bet."

"Do you know what a bolt pistol is?"

Gilchrist frowned. "Isn't it one of those things they use in abattoirs?"

"That's right. Have you seen one lately, heard anything about one?"

"No. Not just recently, but never. The only reason I know about them is the firearms course I took in my basic training. Not that we'd use them, but the instructor was thorough. He even covered air pistols and cap guns." Gilchrist stood up slowly. "Look, I've got to go now, but I've just had a great idea. Why don't you come to trivia night with me? I promise you'll enjoy it. The Coach and Horses is just on the village high street."

"I'm not much of a trivia person, I'm afraid."

"Don't worry about it, I'm good enough for the two of us."

Winsome laughed. "No, I still don't think so. Sorry. It's been a very long day, and tomorrow doesn't promise to be any easier. I'm tired."

Gilchrist looked disappointed. "If you say so. Is that all?"

"For now. Yes."

"OK, then. Let me help you with your coat."

Ever the gentleman, Gilchrist led her, again without his stick, into the hall, and helped her on with her coat. Winsome's Polo was next to Gilchrist's Ford Focus.

"Can I offer you a lift or anything?" Winsome asked. "Save you taking the car out."

Gilchrist tapped his leg. "No, thanks. The walk will do me good. The doc says I need as much exercise as I can get if I hope to return to my former Adonis-like physical glory."

"I'm sure if anyone makes it, you will. Good night. And thanks."

They stood there a little awkwardly, and Winsome felt confused by the waves of tension between them. Just when she thought Gilchrist was leaning forward to kiss her cheek, or her lips, she turned quickly and left. Back in the car, her heart was beating fast, and she had to tell herself to get a grip and calm down. Why had she refused his invitation? She wasn't *that* tired. And the potholing he had mentioned on her previous visit? What harm could that do? Was it because she still thought of him as a suspect, or at least as a witness involved in a case she was working on? Partly, she thought. But it was more than that. She didn't like the idea of sitting in an estate pub in what was little more than a modern country village. She would be the only black person in there, and she would stand out. She was used to that in her job, of course, but people knew her in Eastvale, and at least there was a college there. It attracted all colors and all kinds. In the pub, she would be an object of curiosity, and that would make her uncomfortable.

Oh, why, she told herself, after running through the list of reasons for turning down Gilchrist's offer, didn't she just admit the truth: that she was attracted to him, and that the feeling frightened her. Then she heard her mother's voice in her mind, as she so often did. "Get a grip on yourself, you foolish girl." It wasn't easy, but she made herself stop thinking of Gilchrist and concentrated on the road.

IT HAD been a useful meeting, Banks thought, as he tossed his briefcase on his computer desk, picked up the post and hung his coat up on the rack behind the door, but he still felt that he lacked a coherent picture of recent events. No defining pattern had emerged from the vast collection of data and pooling of ideas.

Vic Manson's contribution had probably been the most valuable: the identification of the man who had threatened Alex Preston. He would see the complete file in the morning, but he already knew the man's name was Ronald Tanner, and he had a string of arrests for breaking and entering, and one for GBH. He had served two prison sentences, one for six months and the second for eighteen. What his connection was with the rural crime gang and Morgan Spencer's murder remained to be seen, but they would certainly be a step closer to finding out when they got Tanner in custody. The local police had agreed to pick him up before dawn and deliver him to Eastvale. It was the most likely time to find him at home, and they would certainly have the element of surprise on their side, which could make all the difference if he were in possession of a weapon.

Banks walked through the hall passage to the kitchen. There was a small dining-table-cum-breakfast-nook that could seat four, in a pinch, and a TV on one of the shelves on the wall beside it, where he usually watched the news or listened to the radio as he drank his breakfast coffee. He flicked on the remote, found nothing of interest and switched it off again, then he poured himself a glass of wine and sat at the table in silence.

The post was uninteresting, apart from the latest issue of *Gramophone,* which he flipped through idly as he drank. Then he realized he was hungry again. The only thing he had to eat in the fridge was some leftover pizza with pork, apple and crackling saved from the quick lunch he and Annie had grabbed at Pizza Express at the back of the Corn Exchange in Leeds. He put it in the convection oven, where it would hopefully crisp up a bit, and went back to his magazine. When the bell dinged, he took his wine, pizza and *Gramophone* into the conservatory. Dense clots of black cloud fringed the top of Tetchley Fell on the horizon, but above them, the starry night was a clear dark blue, with a thin silvery crescent of moon. Banks sat in the wicker chair and watched its slow-moving arc as he ate his pizza. The crust was dry, and still a bit too cold. He decided he wasn't hungry anymore and put it aside. When he had finished, the moon had disappeared behind the fell.

The headache that Banks had first felt during the meeting began to get worse when he concentrated on thinking about the case. He left his wine for a moment and went into the entertainment room to pick some music, finally settling on Agnes Obel's *Aventine.* The gentle, repetitive piano figures and cello and violin accompanying her soaring voice would soothe him better than paracetamol.

But even with the music playing, he felt restless; random thoughts continued to swirl around his mind, and his head throbbed steadily. He thought of breaking the pledge and ringing Oriana to ask if she wanted to meet up for a quick drink, but soon changed his mind. They had a great relationship, he felt, as long as neither of them tried to push it too far. Right now, even if her body was still in Eastvale, her mind would already be in Australia.

He could always wander down to the Dog and Gun, he supposed.

There was bound to be someone he knew in there, maybe even Penny Cartwright. But he didn't particularly feel like company, he realized—other than Oriana's, of course. Ever since Sandra had left him and the kids moved out, he had become more and more attuned to his solitude—to the point where he actually enjoyed being alone. Maybe he didn't eat healthily enough or work out at the gym, and perhaps he drank and brooded too much, but on the whole, he enjoyed his life. It wasn't necessarily a psychologically healthy state of affairs, he thought, but there was a lot to be said for solitude. Some people even climbed distant mountains to be alone. The world was often far too much with him, the hustle-bustle always just around the corner. In the end, he decided to pour himself another glass of wine and go watch a DVD in the entertainment room. The latest James Bond movie had been lying around for a while unopened, mostly because Oriana didn't like James Bond.

Banks had just started attempting to remove the cellophane wrapping when his phone rang. It was Joanna MacDonald.

"Alan, I think I might have something for you."

Banks put the DVD aside, picked up his wine and sat down. "Fire away. Every little bit helps right now."

"I can't be specific about visits to the hangar, or anything like that, but basically we have someone on our radar who's come off or on the A1 at Scotch Corner or Darlington."

"It's a start."

"He made a visit to the area on the Sunday in question. We've had our eye on him for a while—Operation Hawk, that is. He's involved in international investments, but he's often seen visiting rural areas. He also has a lot of overseas contacts, Eastern European in particular. Some of them are not entirely wholesome. Frequent traveler to the Balkans and Baltic states. Knows all the palms to grease. He calls himself Montague Havers, but his real name's Malcolm Hackett."

"Maybe he's expecting a knighthood for services to crime?" Banks suggested. "I think the 'sir' would go better with Montague, don't you?"

Joanna laughed. "Much better."

"What time did he leave the A1 on Sunday?"

There was a pause as Joanna consulted her notes. "He came off at Scotch Corner and took the Richmond road at 2:35 Sunday afternoon. He drives a silver BMW 3 Series. Nice car, but not too ostentatious. Doesn't attract too much attention. And to be fair, he does have relatives in Richmond."

"That's not far north of Eastvale or Drewick, but it's a bit late for what we're looking at," Banks said. "Still, he wouldn't be the trigger puller. If he's southern based, the odds are he's one of the top brass and would want to keep himself as far away as possible from the rough stuff. And if for some reason he had to get there from London in a hurry, maybe he was there for the mopping up. Do you know when he set off back?"

"He entered via the Catterick junction at 3:05 on Tuesday afternoon."

"Tuesday? That's just after Caleb Ross's van went over the pass. Anything definite on Mr. Havers?"

"No. That's the problem. The NCA are working with us on this, too."

"Can I talk to him?"

Joanna paused. "Normally we'd say no, in case you scare him off. But Monty doesn't scare easily. We've questioned him on a few occasions, as have agents of the NCA, and he's always ended up as cocky and squeaky clean as ever. Maybe a fresh face would be a good thing. I doubt he'll give anything away, though. He's too canny. And don't beat him up. He knows his rights."

Banks laughed. "As if I would. Thanks, Joanna. Can you give me his details?"

"He works out of an office building just off the Euston Road. That dodgy part to the north between St. Pancras and Regent's Park." She gave Banks an address. "Apparently he used to be something in the City back when the Conservatives took away all the trading restrictions in the eighties."

"What a coincidence. Just like John Beddoes. How does rural crime come into it?"

"Through his contacts. They run the routes. But we haven't been able to pin anything on him. It's mostly guilt by association. He's the man standing over the road with his hands in his pockets, whistling when the building on the other side blows up. He's the one who visits Norfolk or North Yorkshire before or after a big job. It may mean nothing, but you asked, and he's all we've been able to come up with. We don't have time or the resources to scroll through the list of all the cars that left the A1 at the exit for your airfield, and nothing else has come up that sets off our radar. Sorry."

"That's OK," said Banks. "It was a long shot. But I like the sound of this guy."

"You're welcome. Only too glad to help. I'm thinking maybe I should have waited until tomorrow morning to tell you, and I might have got a free lunch out of it."

Banks laughed. "Maybe I'll take you to dinner when it's all over."

"And pigs will fly."

When Banks hung up the phone, he realized that he still felt some sort of connection with Joanna. The loneliness she talked about over lunch the other day was in some ways at odds with his own previous contemplation of the joys of solitude, but she made him consider that he really had no friends outside the job, either, and that he neglected the ones he had. He hadn't been to see ex-Superintendent Gristhorpe in ages, for example; Jim Hatchley had also retired and wasn't interested in anything but his garden, his kids, darts and Newcastle United; he saw Ken Blackstone only on sporadic visits to Leeds; and even Dirty Dick Burgess only turned up when the shit hit the fan, as a rule. As for his ex-wife, Sandra, she had her new family and her new life. His job had lost her to him. These days, it seemed, it was the job or nothing. He didn't even see his own grown-up children, Brian and Tracy, all that often.

Why did he seem to be letting everyone go? Why didn't he make more of an effort to keep in touch with his friends? Sometimes he felt he had nothing to say, nothing to add to the lively company of a boozy evening in the pub. It wasn't true, though; he always enjoyed himself when he made the effort; it had just got harder to make that effort.

Maybe he should have suggested that Joanna meet him for a drink tonight, he thought. Maybe he should ring her back and ask her. Then he thought of Oriana. They had spoken nothing of fidelity, commitment, or any of those big, difficult subjects. They had made each other no promises, but he knew that if he asked Joanna out and didn't tell Oriana, he would be cheating in a way, and she would be hurt. Even though she would be off to Australia, fighting away all those virile young journalists who wanted to interview Lady Veronica Chalmers. He also knew that if he rang Joanna back and asked her out for a drink, it wouldn't end there. The attraction had been obvious even when they had been at odds in Tallinn, and it was still there. With Oriana away for three weeks, there would be too many opportunities for mischief. The last thing he needed at his age was to be a two-timing bastard.

Besides, he needed his sleep if he was to be sharp for an early interview tomorrow.

He finished stripping the cellophane off the Bond movie and slipped it in the player. Easier just to give himself over to a fantasy world. While the preliminaries were showing, he went back into the kitchen and fetched the rest of the bottle of wine.

10

AS THINGS TURNED OUT, THE INTERVIEW WAS DE-
layed until Alex Preston had picked out Ronald Tanner from the
VIPER display, much relieved that she could go through the process
on a large TV screen instead of having to stand in front of him again.
After that, Tanner requested a second consultation with his lawyer.
Banks used the extra time to prepare himself for the interview, gathering all the evidence they had against Tanner in one folder and everything they suspected him of being involved in, in another. Alex's
identification certainly strengthened the case against him, so it was
worth the delay. The only new evidence came in the form of a partial
fingerprint found in the hangar. There weren't enough points of com-
parison to declare that it actually was Tanner's, but it was something
Banks felt he could use as extra ammunition in an interview.

According to his file, Ronald Tanner was forty-six, a car mechanic
by trade from Chester-le-Street. After spells in London, Bristol and
Birmingham in the 1990s and early 2000s, he had been living in Darlington since 2004. In addition to his arrests for breaking and entering, assault, theft and GBH, the local police were also interested in
him as part of a wide-ranging porn and prostitution investigation,
linked to some of the places he had worked as a club bouncer. Both
Tanner's prison sentences had been significantly reduced for good behavior. Apparently, he was a model prisoner. As Banks read over the

files for the fourth or fifth time, he yawned. He had stayed up too late watching the Bond movie, and even the double hit of espresso from AC Gervaise's private machine hadn't given him much of a second wind.

He selected Gerry Masterson to accompany him. She had the training but lacked the experience. After all, most interviews were carried out by detective sergeants and constables, and it was only at Banks's own insistence that he had managed to keep his hand in all these years. Nowadays, there was even talk about training civilians to carry out police interviews in order to free up officers for other duties and show more of a presence in the communities and on the streets. Banks wasn't too sure about that. Mostly, it was a matter of getting the experience, not being trained by a psychologist. He wasn't as skilled in all the fancy modern psychological techniques as someone like Gerry would be, after all the courses she had done, but he usually knew how to get what he wanted out of someone without resorting to torture, which was, after all, the point of a police interview. However he proceeded, there was no chance of using the casual, friendly approach in the hope of getting Tanner to admit to something in a weak moment; the man was far too experienced for that.

They walked into the interview room at 9:35 a.m. Tanner was sitting beside his brief with his arms folded, brow furrowed and a scowl on his face, wearing his disposable "Elvis" suit while his clothes were being forensically examined. Banks could hardly blame him for scowling after the morning he'd had. The locals had busted down his door at five o'clock and hustled him out in the cold predawn. Then he had sat in a holding cell in the basement while the various formalities, including Alex Preston's identification, were completed. The only advantage he had gained from all this was that it had given him time to get his solicitor there.

Her name was Cassandra Wakefield, and she was one of the better-known advocates in the county. No lowly legal aid lawyer for Tanner. Even so, Banks was surprised by the firepower he had managed to acquire, especially at such short notice. He was a habitual criminal, but how had he got to know Ms. Wakefield? And how could he afford her? Banks suspected the hand of a bigger player in this, but he knew it would be impossible to discover who was actually paying for Tanner's defense. Cassandra Wakefield was too good to let anything like that slip through the cracks. After all, how was she to pay for her trips to Harvey Nicks? She certainly wasn't a Primark sort of woman. Rumor had it she had more shoes than Imelda Marcos. She was a thoroughly professional lawyer in her mid forties, very attractive, always immaculately and fashionably turned out, with a great deal of charm and far more alluring beauty than an interviewing cop wanted sitting opposite him at a time like this. Distractions were all very well in their place, but Ms. Wakefield knew the value of what she had, and she wasn't afraid to exploit it. The extra button on the blouse undone, the full, shiny lips, long wavy auburn hair, slightly hooded green eyes and the entirely deceptive dreamy bedroom look. At least, Banks thought it was deceptive. She was good in court, too. Gone were the times when only a barrister could represent a client—now people like Cassandra Wakefield offered the full-service criminal defense. She had obtained her Higher Rights of Audience and could, theoretically, appear in any courtroom in the land.

Pleasantries out of the way, Banks turned on the recording machine and clearly stated the necessary details. Gerry Masterson seemed nervous—she was playing with her hair too much—but he had advised her to observe for the most part, unless she was struck with a sudden inspiration. He imagined she would settle into her role when the interview got going. The room was stuffy but bearable. Hot enough that Tanner's shaved head was damp and shiny with sweat and Banks felt like taking his jacket off. With its beige walls, a high window covered with a grill, one overhead light fixture similarly covered, scuffed concrete floor, it was meant to be neutral, but it erred more on the side of unpleasantness. It needed to be the kind of place that those not used to such institutional claustrophobia wanted to get out of quickly, thereby encouraging their willingness to talk. Sometimes it even worked.

"So, Ronald," he began. "What's your story?"

"I don't have to tell you anything."

"That's true. But you might want to help yourself a little by helping me."

"You lot always say that. Why would I want to help you?"

"Do you know why you're here?"

"Because a gang of coppers broke into my house at the crack of dawn and dragged me here."

"We've had a serious complaint about you," Banks went on. "A woman alleges that you talked your way into her home by impersonating a police officer, and that once inside, you threatened and intimidated her and her child."

"What a load of bollocks."

"She further alleges that you destroyed her mobile telephone and that you badly damaged her index finger by treading on it while she was lying on the floor, pushed there by you. How am I doing so far?"

"You tell a good story."

"She picked you out of a VIPER identification parade."

"What's that?"

"Come on, Ronald, don't play the innocent. How long since your last arrest? Move with the times. Video Identification Parade Electronic Recording. A bit awkward when you say it all out loud, but VIPER works quite well, I think. Most apt."

"Can you cut out the innuendos, DCI Banks," said Cassandra Wakefield, rolling her eyes. "I mean, really."

"We're not in court, you know," Banks shot back. "There's no jury."

"Even so. Let's all get along here, shall we?"

Banks turned back to Tanner. "How about giving me your version of events?"

"How about I don't?"

"Did you visit Alex Preston and her son, Ian, at flat eighty-one Hague House on the evening of Monday, the fourth of March? That's last Monday, in case you're confused."

"I'm not confused. I've never heard of the woman or the kid. Or Hague House, for that matter."

"I suppose you've got an alibi, then?"

Tanner just smiled. He might as well have said, "I can rustle one up if you want."

Banks shuffled his papers and slid over the sketch artist's likeness so that both Tanner and Cassandra Wakefield could see it. "Would you say this bears a reasonable resemblance to you?" he asked Tanner.

"Could be anyone. Lots of blokes shave their heads these days."

"I don't think so. It's not just the shaved head. There's the broken nose. Quite distinctive, that. And the shifty eyes. It's you, all right. This description was worked out between Alex Preston, the alleged victim, and a police sketch artist. I'd say, as these things go, it's a good likeness."

"I don't think you'd get very far with that in court, Mr. Banks, as I'm sure you know," said Cassandra Wakefield. "These sorts of concocted identifications can be incredibly unreliable. The witness could easily have been describing someone she'd seen in the street, someone she had a grudge against. And there's evidence that witnesses simply pick out faces they don't like from VIPER displays. My client can't help being . . . er . . . distinctive."

"It's *because* he's distinctive that we were able to identify him so quickly," said Banks. "And everything was done according to correct legal procedure, so I think it will be up to a court to decide, not you." He returned to Tanner. "There's the fingerprint, too. Let's not forget that. It was on a card Ms. Preston says you handed to her."

"Why would I do that?" Tanner said. "Give her a card? Assuming I'd ever met her, of course, which I haven't."

"Are you saying you didn't?"

"Of course I didn't."

"Can you explain the card with your fingerprints and a telephone number on it being in the possession of Alex Preston?"

"Maybe it was something I threw away in the street and she picked up? A handout of some sort. Did the number have anything to do with me?"

"We called the number. There was silence, then dead air. The number is untraceable. A pay-as-you-go cheapie, unregistered and disposable."

"Well, there you go," said Tanner. "The wonders of modern technology."

"Except for your fingerprints on the card."

"And I'm saying that maybe someone handed it to me in the street or something and I threw it away. Jehovah's Witnesses or someone. What are you going to do, arrest me for littering?"

"DCI Banks, do you have anything other than this remarkably circumstantial evidence for holding my client against his will?"

"I would think that when a young woman reports the events Ms. Preston reported and presents us with the evidence she has presented us, in the form of the sketch, a broken finger, the fingerprints and the VIPER identification, it's a little more than circumstantial. It's certainly something we all ought to take seriously."

Ms. Wakefield glanced at her watch. "As you will. But please hurry up. I have appointments."

"Don't let me keep you." Banks went immediately back to Tanner. "Where were you on Monday evening, Ronald?"

"Home, I suppose. I haven't been out much all week. The weather, you know. Plays havoc with my rheumatism."

"Can anyone corroborate that?"

"I'm not married, if that's what you're asking."

It was no alibi, but Banks knew that most alibis were thin. If you had someone who would lie for you, it helped, of course, but Tanner could just as easily have said he went for a walk on the moors, and it would have been as hard to disprove, unless he had been seen elsewhere. The damn thing was, they had only Alex Preston's statement to go on. Not that Banks doubted her for a moment, but it might not be enough when people like Ronald Tanner and Cassandra Wakefield were involved. Officers were still asking questions around Alex Preston's tower block, but Banks held out little hope that anything would come from that. The residents of the East Side Estate were hardly known for helping the police. "Are you currently employed?" Banks asked.

"Not at the moment."

"What do you do for money?"

"Benefits. The social. I'm entitled."

"Did you know a lad called Morgan Spencer?"

"Can't say as I did. Is he dead or something?"

He was lying, Banks could tell from his change in tone. Cassandra Wakefield knew it, too, but she was doing her best not to react. "Yes, he's dead," Banks went on. "Murdered. Were you anywhere near the Riverview Caravan Park on Monday night?"

"Why would I go there?"

"To burn down Morgan's caravan after you'd had a good look for anything that might incriminate you or your mates."

"Incriminate how? What mates?"

"What about Caleb Ross?"

Tanner looked just surprised enough at the question that Banks guessed he did know Caleb Ross.

"No," Tanner went on. "Funny name, Caleb. I think I'd remember."

"Mr. Ross used to drive for Vaughn's ABP. He is also deceased."

"Murdered?"

"We're not sure. What kind of work did you do before you became unemployed?"

"I'm a motor mechanic. Skilled, trained, experienced and all that, but it doesn't seem to matter these days when they can get someone half my age with half the experience for half the money. Last while I've been doing a bit of club work."

"Bouncer?"

"Crowd maintenance, noise control, that sort of thing."

"Odd that," Banks said. "About your being a motor mechanic and all. Caleb Ross died in a motor accident."

"Treacherous time of year on the roads."

"Have you ever worked in an abattoir?"

"You must be joking. Me? In one of those places. I couldn't stand the stink, for a start."

"But killing the animals wouldn't bother you?"

Tanner shrugged.

"Do you own a captive bolt gun?"

"What's that when it's at home?"

"It's a nasty little weapon. A special kind of gun used in an abattoir to stun or kill the animals. Mostly fatal on humans."

"Sounds cruel to me. No, I don't own anything like that. You'll no doubt have searched the house, so you'll know that already."

"You could have hidden it somewhere. Have you got a lockup?"

"Why would I need a lockup? I don't even need a garage."

"Do you take drugs?"

"Tobacco and alcohol, for my sins."

"Do you know anything about tractors?"

"I've worked on a few in my time. Stands to reason, if you're a motor mechanic on the edge of a large rural area."

"Where were you on Saturday night?"

"All night?"

"Yes."

"I went to the pub. I usually do on a Saturday night. Then I should think I went home and fell asleep watching telly."

Another flimsy but probably unbreakable alibi. Even if the people in the pub didn't remember him, it wouldn't mean much. One night was very much like another and most people, if pushed, didn't know what they were doing last week. Tanner was being smart in not coming up with anything too elaborate. Elaborate alibis were the easiest to break.

"What about Sunday morning?"

"Sunday morning's my lie-in time. Make a cuppa, read the *Sport* and the *Mail*. I don't usually do much on a Sunday. Maybe down the pub for a jar or two and a game of darts at lunchtime. Roast beef and Yorkshires if I can afford it."

"Are you sure you didn't go out last Sunday?"

"I don't think so. Where to?"

"An abandoned airfield near Drewick."

"I'd remember that."

"Do you know the place?"

"I've seen it from the train."

"Did you go there last Sunday morning about nine-thirty?"

"Why would I do that?"

But Tanner was getting worried, Banks could tell. He could see his mind working furiously behind the words. Banks wanted to push him. Tanner hadn't realized that they had already connected him to the airfield and Morgan Spencer's murder.

"No reason. Only our lads found another fingerprint there that's very much—"

"DCI Banks," Cassandra Wakefield cut in. "I'd like to know where you're going with this. But first of all I'd like to know about this fingerprint. There's no mention of it in my notes. If it was indeed Mr. Tanner's, why wasn't I informed? And if it wasn't, why bring it up?"

"It was brought to my attention just before this interview," said Banks. "It's only a fragment, not enough to be certain, but—"

"In that case, DCI Banks, I think we'll pass it by. Continue."

"Our men are still working at the scene."

"I still say you're fishing. Move on."

Banks paused to shuffle his papers and frame his words. "We believe that the hangar was used as a transfer point for stolen farm equipment on its way overseas. Possibly also for stolen livestock being shipped to illegal abattoirs around the country." Banks knew he was close to the edge, especially with Cassandra Wakefield present, but he needed a break.

"Sheep rustling, eh?" said Tanner, grinning. "Just like the Wild West, isn't it?"

"Perhaps even more important," Banks went on, "a man was murdered there. The one I mentioned earlier. Morgan Spencer."

"Yes, and I told you then I don't know him. *Didn't* know him. Never known any Morgans or Calebs. And I don't own a gun, even one of those abattoir ones you've been going on about."

It was true that police searching Tanner's Darlington home had found no trace of a captive bolt gun by the time Banks started the interview, though they had found a stash of weapons, including various knives and flick-knives, knuckle-dusters, a cosh and a crossbow. If Tanner had used the bolt gun on Spencer, there was a good chance that he had done the sensible thing and tossed it. On the other hand, according to ballistics, it was a formidable weapon, and would no doubt be expensive and difficult to replace.

As if reading his mind, Cassandra Wakefield said, "This is getting us nowhere, DCI Banks. I trust your search hasn't turned up a gun of *any* sort on my client's property?"

"Not yet."

She raised a perfectly plucked eyebrow. "Like the fingerprint that's not quite his but might be?" She scooped up the papers in front of her and stood up as if to leave. "Then I suggest we suspend this interview for the time being and review my client's situation. Pending the results of the house search, the fingerprint identification at this abandoned hangar, as I see it you have no evidence on which to base a charge. I also find myself confused about what it is exactly you want to charge Mr. Tanner with. Threatening this poor woman, murdering Morgan Spencer and Caleb Ross, sheep rustling? What is it to be?"

"We'll decide that later, Ms. Wakefield," Banks shot back. "With the CPS of course. And it may include possession of illegal weapons."

Cassandra Wakefield favored him with a sweet smile, tender lips curled at the edges. "Of course. And in the meantime . . ."

"Just a couple of final points. I'll keep it brief."

Tanner looked apprehensive.

"Have you ever heard of a man called Montague Havers?" Banks asked.

Tanner narrowed his eyes. "You do come up with some funny names."

"His real name is Malcolm Hackett."

"Means nothing to me."

"What about John Beddoes?"

"Isn't that the bloke whose tractor got pinched?"

"It is. Do you know him?"

"Only from reading about it in the paper."

"Why are you looking for Michael Lane?"

"Who's that?"

"Who wants you to find Michael Lane?"

"I don't know what you're on about."

"Why did you visit Alex Preston and ask her where Lane has gone?"

"I told you, I never did that. I don't know the woman."

"Is it because Lane witnessed something happen at the hangar on Sunday morning?"

"You've lost me."

"Me, too, I'm afraid," said Cassandra Wakefield. "I think we'll have to call it a day."

"Interview suspended at 10:05," said Banks. Tanner was rattled, he could tell. It wouldn't be such a bad idea to let him stew for a few hours while the team tried to dig up more damning evidence.

Cassandra Wakefield walked toward the door.

Ronald Tanner, however, lingered a moment, then said, "Look, I'm sure this will all be sorted out soon. In the meantime, please give my regards to Ms. Preston. Tell her I'm sorry she felt that she had to go to such trouble over a silly mistake and I hope her young lad's all right."

Cassandra Wakefield stopped in her tracks and turned, an alarmed expression on her face, then quickly shooed her client out of the interview room, where the custody officer was waiting to take him back to his cell.

Gerry Masterson looked at Banks openmouthed and said, "Was that what I thought it was, sir?"

Banks smiled. "Yes, Gerry," he said. "I'm afraid I very much think it was. We've got to get moving fast on this. Our twenty-four hours is running down. We've got to connect Ronald Tanner to Morgan Spencer and Caleb Ross. Finding Michael Lane would be a big help. And you might have a look into Tanner's known associates."

"What about Alex Preston?" Gerry said.

"I'll have a word with Annie and AC Gervaise, but I think we're going to have to increase security on Alex. She's in far more danger now that Tanner knows she shopped him. He obviously isn't in this alone."

"I DON'T like it," Annie said over an early lunch in the Queen's Arms with Banks and Gerry Masterson. "I don't like it at all."

"I'm sorry," said Banks, putting aside his bacon sandwich for a moment. "But it's done now. And you know as well as I do that it had to be done."

"But I'm the one who convinced her to talk in the first place, arranged the sketch artist, had Vic get the fingerprints from the card."

"None of this is your fault, Annie. You were only doing your job. And it was good police work. Alex Preston herself volunteered the information about Tanner's visit, even after he had threatened her to keep silent."

"I couldn't live with myself if anything happened to her. Or Ian." She gave a shudder.

"It won't come to that."

"You can't guarantee it, short of locking them in a cell. Even then—"

"There's no point jumping to worst-case scenarios," Banks snapped. "At the moment, Tanner's the one in a cell."

"Yes, but you and I know damn well how long that will last. That Harvey Nicks lawyer of his will have him out on the street the minute his twenty-four hours are up. What are you going to do then? Put Alex and Ian in the witness protection program? We don't have one."

"I'm sure something along those lines could be arranged, but it's not necessary yet."

"You mean you won't do anything until you've brought Tanner's accomplices into the open. You're using Alex and Ian as bait?"

"That's not fair," said Gerry.

Annie shot her a dark look and turned back to Banks. "It's true, though, isn't it? That's why you had Gerry here in on the interview and not me. You didn't trust me to keep my cool. These people are out there covering their tracks, and the closer we get the more danger all the people on the fringes are in. They've got rid of Spencer and perhaps Ross. They're after Michael Lane, maybe they've even got to him already, and now there's Alex and Ian, too."

"It's Lane they want," said Banks. "Not Alex or Ian."

"No, but they'll use her and Ian as a means to an end, won't they? And we've seen just how much respect for human life they have. I saw Caleb Ross's and Morgan Spencer's bodies in the pass, too, you know."

"I know," said Banks. "But this all started with Spencer. He wasn't killed as a part of any cleanup operation, or for information, as far as we know. We don't know why he was killed, but I think Michael Lane does. There's a different motive for his murder, and as far as we can be certain, there's been only one murder so far. We might suspect that Caleb Ross's van was sabotaged, but we have absolutely no evidence of that. The CSIs have managed to get the pieces back to the forensics garage and they're still working on it. Until they can tell us something definite, we're only investigating one murder: Morgan Spencer."

"Well, that makes me feel a whole lot better."

Gerry Masterson nibbled on her chicken in a basket and looked from one to the other. "I'll get back to the computer with the lists straight after lunch," she said. "We've got plenty of names from a number of sources. Maybe it's Venture Properties?"

"Venture?" said Annie. "What makes you think that?"

"Just that someone who has invested in the new shopping center development would be in a good position to know the state of negotiations and the lie of the land at the airfield. I mean, I doubt the place was chosen just at random."

"Good point," said Annie grudgingly. "I must admit I had a funny feeling about Venture."

Banks laughed. "I always have a funny feeling around property developers. It doesn't mean they're all murderers."

"I'm not saying anything about murderers," said Gerry, tucking a stray tress of red hair behind her ear. "It's probably just a business to them." She glanced at Banks. "And I'm not saying Venture is involved, only that their lists might provide a connection."

"Have you got anywhere with that name I gave you yesterday? Montague Havers?"

"As a matter of fact, I have," said Gerry. "It took a bloody long time and a lot of perhaps less than legal maneuvers, but I got the name."

"He's on the Venture list?"

"Indeed he is."

"Why didn't you say so before?"

Gerry blushed. "I just got it, the moment before we came out to lunch, sir."

"Well, go on," Banks urged her.

"It might not lead anywhere."

"But Havers is an investor in the shopping center?"

"Indirectly, yes. That's why it took so long. To cut a long story short, sir, he's connected with a company called Retail Perfection Ltd., or a smaller division of that, a company within a company."

"You're losing me, Gerry."

"High finance and corporate finagling aren't really my area of expertise, either, sir, but let's say he's on the board, a major shareholder, of a branch of Retail Perfection Ltd. that handles property acquisition and development. His main business is international financing, but he's got his finger in a number of pies, or companies, I should say."

"That's the connection we were looking for."

"Yes, but there are lots of other investors."

"It doesn't matter," said Banks. "Joanna gave me Havers's name as someone they were keeping an eye on for Operation Hawk. Apparently he's clever and slippery and they've not been able to get him for anything yet. He's obviously careful and makes sure he never handles anything that can be traced back to the thefts and transportation. But if he's also an investor in the Drewick shopping center development, then he's in a position to know that it would be a good place to use as a depot. All he has to do is know and pass on that knowledge. He doesn't have to organize anything himself, get his hands dirty. It's ideal. That's great, Gerry. Well done."

"Wait a minute," said Annie. "Gerry said there are a lot of other people involved in investing in the airfield. What about them? Shouldn't we check all of them out?"

"We could, I suppose," said Banks. "But I vote that Havers gets first attention. It's a double hit, Annie. He's invested in the airfield development and he's on Joanna MacDonald's Operation Hawk list. Also, he drove up here on the Sunday we think Morgan Spencer was killed at the hangar."

"I suppose that makes sense," Annie said. "What are you going to do?"

"Go see him. I was going anyway, but now I've even got a bit more ammunition, thanks to Gerry."

Gerry Masterson blushed, and Annie looked sulky. "While Alex and Ian just wait around for someone to kill them or abduct them?"

"Don't be absurd. They'll be well protected."

"Sure."

Gerry stood up. "I should get back to the squad room now, if that's OK? I've got the Venture stuff to finish, then a whole lot of abattoirs to look into."

"Absolutely," said Banks. "And dig up all you can on Montague Havers."

Gerry left, and they watched her go. "She's come on a lot," said Annie.

"Indeed, she has."

"Still a bit sensitive, though."

Banks smiled. "And you're still a bit acerbic."

"Whatever that is. I'm working on it."

Banks touched her hand on the table. "I know you are. And your concern for Alex and Ian hasn't gone unnoticed. We're going to make damn sure their security is tight and that neither of them is going to be damaged by this."

"But for how long?" asked Annie, banging her fist on the table. The glasses rattled and one or two people looked over. "I just feel so damn responsible."

"As long as it takes. As I said before, they're not interested in Alex. True, she's a means to an end, but as soon as that end no longer matters, neither does she. We've got to increase our efforts to find Michael Lane."

"So why not just kill her, then?"

"Because I think we're dealing with businessmen, and it wouldn't be to their advantage. They've no reason to. Look at Spencer. We don't know why they killed him, but it was hardly as a warning, an example or to hurt someone else. They were hoping his body would be incinerated, for crying out loud. All we've encountered so far has been the pond life—Tanner, Ross, Spencer, Lane. The man with the bolt gun, whoever that is. But there's someone else calling the shots, someone whose orders they obey, someone with brains. That's who we want to get to. And that's why I'm going to see Montague Havers."

"I don't think Michael Lane is pond life."

"Maybe not. But that's another question we want the answer to, isn't it? How deeply is he involved? And he's the focal point, too. They want Lane. We have to get to him first. Then Alex Preston becomes irrelevant."

"Unless they're the vengeful types," muttered Annie.

Banks's phone rang and he excused himself to answer it. The message was brief and he smiled when he ended the call and slipped the mobile back in his pocket.

"Well, at least we've made a bit of progress," he said. "We've found Michael Lane's car. Fancy a trip to the seaside?"

SCARBOROUGH IN season is a delightful and popular place to visit. The ruined castle towers over the seascape, its promontory splitting the town in two: South Bay, with its promenade of amusement arcades, pubs, casinos and fish-and-chips restaurants; and North Bay, with its holiday apartments, golf club and Peasholm Park.

But on a cold, blustery March day, even the inhabitants would admit, it is not a place in which you would care to linger long. Marine Drive runs around the base of the promontory and links the two halves. On a rough day, it is often flooded by waves that crash high over the solid seawall, and signposts warn of falling rocks from the steep cliff on the other side of the road. Unfortunately for Banks and Annie, Michael Lane's car had been found parked in a Pay-n-Display area close to the coast guard office, in the old Toll House, with its fairy-tale brick tower and its witch's hat of red tiles topped with a weather vane. And this was certainly the sort of day when you didn't need a weather vane to know which way the wind was blowing. It was blowing straight off the North Sea, wet and freezing, carrying with it a spray that immediately soaked anyone in the vicinity.

The local police had cordoned off the car when Banks and Annie arrived early in the afternoon. Ronald Tanner was still in his cell, and Gerry Masterson was slaving away over her computer with lists of names and companies beside her.

"Nice day for a visit to the seaside, sir," said one of the uniformed officers cheerfully, as Banks and Annie struggled to keep their raincoats on in the wind, which seemed to be trying to rip off every item of clothing they wore. "Isn't it funny," he went on, "the way people assume you're on perpetual holiday when you tell them you're stationed in Scarborough?"

"Indeed," said Banks. There was no point in even trying to open an umbrella. Banks could feel the salt spray on his face and taste it in his mouth. It was invigorating, at least for a moment or two, then it just became cold, uncomfortable and downright annoying. "So what have you got?"

The officer, an inspector named Martin Mills, led them to the front of the car, where they could clearly see the parking permit stuck in the window of the ancient gray Peugeot. It gave them the date, which was

Tuesday's, and the time by which the car was supposed to leave, which was 6:14 in the evening. Lane had put in enough money for three hours, which meant that he had parked there at 3:14 on Tuesday, two days after he had "disappeared." As he had paid until after six, when the parking charges no longer applied, he would have been all right there until eight o'clock on Wednesday morning. In season, the car would no doubt have been towed away quite early that day, but at this time of year, in this sort of weather, it had only attracted a couple of parking tickets before one of the more adventurous parking officers had become suspicious. Even so, it was Thursday now. Lane could be anywhere.

Banks tried the driver's door. Locked. He was eager to find out if there were any clues to Lane's whereabouts in the car. "Any chance of getting this open?" he asked Mills. The pounding waves and screaming wind were so loud they had to shout to make themselves heard.

Inspector Mills pulled a key from his pocket. "Thought you might want to do that," he said. "No point just standing around getting wet while we were waiting for you. It's an old car, no fancy locking mechanism. There's not even an alarm system. We also checked the fuel earlier with a dipstick. Empty."

Banks nodded. "Thanks. So he ran out of petrol and couldn't afford any more?"

"Not surprising at today's prices," said Annie. "And Alex said he didn't have much money with him. But don't you think it's a bit strange?"

Both Banks and Mills looked at her curiously. "What? Why?"

She pointed to the windscreen. "Well, that he's on the run and he dumps his car because it's run out of petrol and he can't afford any more, but he takes the trouble to pay and display a parking sticker?"

"People do odd things when they're flustered," said Banks.

"They also do what they'd normally do," said Annie. "Don't you think this is a sign of an honest man?"

"I'll grant you it's a little odd," said Banks. "Who was that famous killer who got caught because of a parking ticket?"

"Son of Sam," said Mills. "And he was caught because of a ticket he got for parking illegally. See, even serial killers don't pay for parking."

"But our Michael Lane does," said Annie. "I still think it's weird."

"Shall we have a look inside?" said Banks.

Annie took out her protective gloves.

Mills held up the key. "The garage assures me this should do the trick." He opened the door. "Voilà!"

"I'll do the front and you do the back," Banks said to Annie.

They got in the car and started looking and feeling around. It was a relief to be out of the wind and spray for a while, a haven of quiet and shelter. The interior smelled neutral, and the seats and floor weren't littered in sweets wrappers or discarded newspapers. The glove box yielded nothing but a dog-eared manual, a few old petrol station receipts and a pack of chewing gum. There was a dock for a mobile phone, but no phone, also no GPS, which might have been useful for plotting Lane's travels. There were no maps conveniently open at a particular page, either. There was a box of tissues and a few CDs in the compartment between the seats: Vampire Weekend, Manic Street Preachers, White Denim. Banks reached down the sides and under the seats. Nothing there but a dried-up chip, one of those long skinny ones from McDonald's, by the look of it, and a crumpled coffee container from the same establishment.

"Anything in the back?" he asked Annie.

"Couple of twenty p coins down the back of the seats. A Mars bar wrapper, copy of *Beano* from last month. Looks like Ian's been in here. Nothing else."

"OK," said Banks. "Let's get it locked up again and shipped to the forensics garage. See if they can get anything out of it. I'd like Vic Manson on it, too. Prints would help. We'll see if anyone other than Michael, Alex and Ian have been inside recently."

"You'd have to take Ian's prints for elimination purposes, then."

"He'll love it," Banks said. "I know I would have done when I was a kid. In fact, I remember getting my very own fingerprint kit for Christmas one year. I took everyone's. Even the postman's."

Annie rolled her eyes. "Why doesn't that surprise me?"

"Don't mock. They came in useful when we nicked him for receiving stolen property later."

"You never—"

Banks pointed at her. "Got you there."

They got out of the car, and a blast of cold wind laced with sea spray hit them again. It was the kind of chilly damp that penetrated deep into Banks's body and gave his bones an inkling of the aches and pains they would be feeling even on a normal day in a few years' time. When they had made sure the car was locked, Mills suggested they adjourn to a tea shop across the road and warm up. He even offered to buy.

When they were settled with their cups of tea, Banks rubbed a clear patch in the misted window and gazed out at the bleak gray North Sea heaving in the distance. His mind became lost out there on the almost imperceptible horizon where sea met sky, until he realized that Annie was asking him a question.

"So where do you think he is, then?"

"He parked here just after three on Tuesday and he rang Alex from a public telephone in York on Tuesday evening. You can catch a train to almost anywhere from York, even connect to the Eurostar. He could be on the bloody Riviera by now."

"Remember," Annie said, "he's got no money. And we'd know if he used any of his credit or debit cards. Besides, he doesn't have his passport with him."

"Somewhere still in England, then. Or maybe he took a train north to Scotland?"

"But what about the money, the abandoned car, the empty petrol tank?"

"Maybe they were designed to throw us off the scent. We're assuming that he had no money, but we don't *know* it for a fact, do we? We're just basing our assumption on Alex Preston's word. We're making a lot of guesses about his motives, too, but maybe it's just blind fear that's driving him, and there's nothing to be read into it. Is he just a scared kid or a seasoned criminal on the run? He could have money on him that Alex doesn't know about."

"A private stash?"

"Why not? Especially if he *was* involved in criminal activities."

"Happens all the time," said Mills. "People don't always tell their partners about financial matters, especially cash. Look at those blokes who spend a fortune on prostitutes. Do you think they use their credit cards?"

"These days, probably yes," said Banks. "It no doubt appears on the statements as dry cleaning or something."

Mills laughed.

"But seriously," Annie went on. "OK, let's say he does have money with him."

"I can think of three, maybe four ways he might have got it," said Banks. "First off, he was prepared to go from the start and took his own private funds Alex didn't know about. Second, he could have got it at his meeting with Spencer. We don't know what happened there except that someone's tracking him down because of it. Maybe it was a meeting to split proceeds, or a payoff? Couldn't he be on the run because he made off with someone's money?"

"But Alex said he was running because he saw something he shouldn't have seen at the hangar."

"But again we only have her word for what he said, and even if she's telling the truth, we don't know that he is. And don't forget, if Lane was involved with people who knew about overseas smuggling routes, he might not need a passport to get out of the country. If they needed to get him out, they'd get him out. And he'd hardly tell her about a pile of money he'd nicked, or received for criminal activities, would he?"

"What's the third and fourth?" asked Mills.

"He could have nicked it or someone could have given him it."

"Does he have any friends here in Scarborough?"

"Not as far as we know."

"There is one more possibility I reckon we should follow up on while we're in the area," said Annie.

"Lane's mother and grandparents?"

"Right. They live in Whitby, which is just a few miles up the road. We need to head over there and have a word."

Banks turned to Mills. "Thanks, Inspector. Sorry to put you to such trouble on a miserable day like this. Someone from forensics will be over for the car before long."

"You don't think we should leave it here and keep it under surveillance in case he comes back for it?" Mills asked.

Banks thought for a moment, then said, "Have a patrol car keep an eye out until our men come. But I don't expect he'll be back now. He's left it here for two days already. And like I said, it's a red flag. Even he must know that. He's not coming back for it. We'll learn more from forensics than we would by leaving it here."

"You're the boss. We'll guard it with our lives till they come."

Banks smiled. "I wouldn't go that far." Then he looked at Annie. "Come on, then, let's have a ride up to Whitby. With any luck it'll be teatime when we've finished and we can grab some fish and chips and salvage something out of this day."

11

I T WAS A DAMP GRAY AFTERNOON WHEN WINSOME SET out from Eastvale west into the dale to make a few inquiries at the farms on Caleb Ross's route.

She stopped in a lay-by just outside Helmthorpe and consulted her Ordnance Survey map. Through her potholing and walking experience, she already knew the area. She had also become adept at reading maps, and could visualize the landscape as it was laid out on paper, in contours, broken lines and arcane symbols. As she had suspected, the next call, near the hamlet of Mortsett, was halfway up the daleside to her left, then the farms grew fewer and farther between as she moved on past Helmthorpe and Swainshead into the high Pennines.

Thus far, she had heard nothing but praise for Caleb Ross and the job he did, and the fallen stock on the farmers' copies was just as it was described on Neil Vaughn's master document. On the surface, this was the sort of job Banks could have sent a DC or even a couple of PCs in a patrol car to do, but on the other hand, he had told Winsome he needed the instinct of a seasoned detective, someone who could read the nuances, give voice to the unspoken. Winsome was trying to dig, or see, under the surface, look for the unconscious signs and signals others might miss. There hadn't been any so far, and she didn't expect it to be any different this time as she pulled into yet another farmyard. Her boots were already caked with mud and worse, and she feared she would never be able to wash the farmyard smell out of her hair and her clothes, or scrub it from her skin. The farmer, Reg Padgett, according to Winsome's list, was working in the yard in his donkey jacket, flat hat and wellies, and he came striding over to Winsome as she pulled up.

"I know who you are," he said, beaming as she got out of the car and held out her warrant card.

Winsome smiled shyly. "So my fame precedes me?"

"I'll say it does. Rugby tackles and dropkicks. We could do with you on the England side."

"I don't think I'm quite up for that. And it wasn't strictly a drop-kick." Winsome was referring to the rolling push with which she had sent a three-hundred-pound drug dealer flying over a third-floor balcony on the East Side Estate a year or two ago. "The papers got it all wrong."

"Never mind, lass," said Padgett. "Whatever it was, it got the job done."

Indeed it had. Winsome's action had put the person in question in the hospital for nearly a month with numerous fractures and abrasions, and earned her a reprimand for excessive force, which she thought was excessive in itself.

"I've come about Caleb Ross," she said. "He had a pickup here last Tuesday morning, didn't he?"

"Indeed he did," said Padgett, lifting up his flat hat and scratching his head. "Poor Caleb. I heard about what happened. A real tragedy. Treacherous, that place, even on the best of days. But surely you don't think there's anything suspicious about the accident?"

"No, it's nothing like that," said Winsome, taking out her copy of Vaughn's list. "It says here that you were his fourth call of the day."

"I wouldn't know about that, but he did seem in a bit of a hurry."

"A hurry?"

"Yes. Usually he stands around and chats for a while, you know, just passes the time of day."

"But not on Tuesday?"

"No. He seemed to just want to get the job done and go. Two still-born lambs. Too many of those at this time of year. Keeping him busy, I suppose."

"Did he act as if there was anything bothering him?"

Padgett chewed on his lower lip for a moment, then said, "No-o-o, I wouldn't say that. He just seemed distracted. In another world, like."

"As if he was thinking about something else?"

"That's right. As if his mind wasn't on the job. He seemed cheerful, though. I mean, I wouldn't say he seemed anxious or depressed or anything like that. You don't think . . . ?"

"We're almost certain it was an accident, Mr. Padgett." But another thing that had occurred to Winsome since she started the job was that someone might have been following Ross, trailing him, chasing him between farms even, and that might have contributed to the accident. Palmer, the driver coming the other way, hadn't noticed any cars approaching from the same direction as Caleb after the crash, but he was probably in a state of shock for a while, and he had pulled over to the far side of the road, away from the drop. He could easily have missed something. "Did you notice any other cars around when Mr. Ross arrived?"

"No. But I wouldn't. You can see for yourself, this is a well-hidden track. We can't see what's happening down on the Mortsett Road from here, so I wouldn't have noticed even if there had been. We had no other callers here, I can tell you that."

"Could anyone have gained access to Mr. Ross's van while he was here?"

"No. We were standing out here, just like you and me are now, and the van was where your car is. I remember he had the window open and that blooming music he likes blaring out. Fair scared the wits out of my chickens. Put them off their laying, nearly."

"Could anyone have tampered with your fallen stock before it was picked up?"

"I don't see how," said Padgett. "I follow all the correct storage regulations. They were bagged, tagged and locked in the barn until Caleb came for them."

"No signs of illegal entry?"

"None at all. Where are you going with this, lass?"

"You'll have heard rumors that he was carrying more than he should have been. That's really all I can say for the moment."

"The human body parts, you mean?"

"You've been watching the TV news, then?"

"Well, you'll know the truth, I suppose."

"That I do, Mr. Padgett."

"Whatever it was, it didn't come from here. Mrs. Padgett's still very much alive and well."

"I'm sure she is. We're interested in Caleb's state of mind. Could he have been drinking, or anything like that?"

"Not Caleb. I happen to know he's a teetotaler, and he certainly didn't behave as if he was drunk. No, as I said, he was just a bit keen to get going, as if his mind was running ahead of him."

"What about drugs? We know that Caleb smoked marijuana from time to time. Did you see any signs of that in his behavior?"

"I wouldn't know what to look for. But he seemed normal to me. And if he did smoke that stuff, like you say, he kept it well to himself."

"What about a woman?" Winsome ventured. Some of the farms were isolated, and if Caleb had taken up a dalliance with one of the farmers' wives, or a milkmaid, if such creatures still existed, it might both distract him and cause him to hurry.

Padgett just laughed. "Caleb? If you'd have known him, lass, you wouldn't have said that. Devoted to Maggie, he was, for a start. And for another thing, he wasn't exactly your Brad Pitt or Tom Cruise, if you know what I mean."

Winsome laughed. "He wasn't really close to the end of his rounds," she said. "So it's unlikely he was in a hurry to get home. In fact he had a few hours to go. Was he late when he arrived here?"

"Not so far as I'm aware. It's not an exact science, his business, though you could usually depend on him to arrive close to when Vaughn's said he would. Dependable firm."

"Do you know if he ever made any unscheduled stops?"

"I wouldn't know about that. Shouldn't think so, mind you. Caleb was an honest man. He took his work seriously. I can't see him taking jobs on the side and trying to put one over on his employers."

Neither could Winsome. For a start, it wasn't the kind of job on which you could really take anything on the side, though she supposed he could accept untested animals over the age limit for a few quid and have some sort of out-of-the-way burial spot he used for them. And for the human remains he was carrying. The idea seemed a bit far-fetched to her, though. It must have been something else that made it appear as if his thoughts were elsewhere and he was in more of a hurry than usual. She didn't even know yet whether he had Morgan Spencer's body parts in with the load at that point, let alone whether he knew about them. Perhaps he was looking forward to picking up his marijuana later on the route?

Winsome thanked Padgett for his time and got back in her car. Only another six farms to go before Belderfell Pass. Just before she got to the next stop, her mobile rang.

"Winsome. Hello, it's Terry. Terry Gilchrist."

Winsome pulled over. "Terry. Have you remembered something?"

"No. It's nothing like that." He sounded disappointed. "Is work all you ever think of?"

"No, of course not. I'm just very busy right now. What is it? How was the trivia?"

"The trivia was fine. We won. 'In which country would you find the Simpson Desert?'"

"I don't know. America?"

"Australia. I got it."

"Congratulations. What is it, then? Is something wrong?"

"Not at all. At least I hope not. Why must something be wrong for me to just want to talk to you?" He paused. "Look, I was wondering if you'd like to have dinner with me tonight. There's a nice bistro on Castle Hill, or there's that Italian place, if you like. I can book us a table."

"What?"

"Don't make it so hard, Winsome. It must be obvious I like you. It took me long enough to pluck up courage to ask you out. I know I'm a bit of a gimp, but—"

"No, no. I'm just a bit stunned, Terry, that's all. Dinner?" Winsome didn't get many dinner invitations, and the whole thing had knocked her sideways. She wasn't at all used to being asked out. In fact the last time she had been out for dinner it was with Lisa Gray. But she couldn't think of an excuse to say no on the spot. And she didn't really want to say no. In the end, she said, "Well, yes. I mean, if you like. Yes, that would be nice."

"Seven-thirty OK?"

"That's fine."

"Bistro or Italian?"

"Bistro, please," said Winsome.

When she had ended the call and got back on the road, she felt apprehensive. Had she agreed too easily? Wasn't Terry still a witness? Could it affect their investigation? Then she put all the silly questions out of her mind and got on with the task at hand. She looked at her watch and realized she could manage at least another two or three farms until she had to go home and try to scrub the farmyard smell off her before her date. She could do the rest tomorrow.

BANKS'S PORSCHE rode the wind along the edge of the moors to Whitby. On the way he played some Nick Drake, and Annie didn't seem to object. She even said she thought "Northern Sky" was not bad at all. They remained silent for most of the journey, having run out of ideas on where Michael Lane might have gone after he had paid to park his car in Scarborough and disappeared.

They drove into the town, picturesque in its little harbor, the Esk estuary dividing it into two distinct halves. One consisted of old streets of cottages and gift shops specializing in Whitby jet, and 199 steps led up the hill to the ruined seventh-century abbey and St. Mary's church and graveyard, where Mina saw the long black figure bending over Lucy in Bram Stoker's *Dracula*. The other side of the bridge was a bit more commercial, with more bed-and-breakfasts, fish-and-chips shops, amusement arcades and a "Dracula Experience" on the front by the fish market, where the fishermen landed their catches. The tide was in and small fishing boats were bobbing up and down in the harbor. The sea didn't seem as wild as at Scarborough. Whitby had suffered dreadfully in the previous year's floods, when the water breached the seawalls and flooded the lower town, but it was quickly getting back on its feet.

It was Denise Lane's day off, they discovered at Tesco, and they found her on her own in a small house not far from the hospital.

"Do you remember me?" Annie said, when Denise opened the door. "Annie Cabbot? This is DCI Banks. Can we come in?"

Denise hadn't fully opened the door, and she was still hesitating nervously. "It might be important, Mrs. Lane," Banks said. "It's about your son."

"I guessed as much." She opened the door a few inches more. "You've found Michael?"

"Not exactly, no," said Annie. "But we've found his car. Can we come in?"

Denise stood back, looked up and down the street, and gestured to them to enter, then she led them through the hall to the living room. A mirror hung over the tiled fireplace, reflecting the candy-striped wallpaper and the gilt-framed painting of a little waif standing by the seashore on the opposite wall.

"I suppose you'll be wanting a cup of tea," Denise Lane said over her shoulder.

"No, that's all right," said Banks, sitting on one of the armchairs. "Just a quick chat. That's all."

Denise eased herself into a chair slowly, as if her bones were aching, and immediately started rolling and unrolling the hem of her unbuttoned cardigan. "Ollie's out," she said, "but he'll be back soon. You'd better be quick."

"Why?" said Banks, frowning. "Is there something you want to keep from him?"

"No. He just wouldn't like me talking to you, that's all."

"Why? Not a fan of the police?"

"You're twisting my words. He hasn't done anything wrong, if that's what you're getting at. He doesn't have a record or anything. He's just . . . well, private. We're both very private. We just want to get on with our lives."

"I can appreciate that," said Banks. "We're all entitled to a little privacy to get on with our lives. But this is a murder investigation, and I'm afraid that does call for more special circumstances." Banks could see why Annie had described Denise Lane as attractive after their first meeting. She was long-legged and shapely, looked good in the tight jeans she was wearing. She clearly visited the gym regularly, kept her blond hair neatly trimmed and layered and had a naturally pale, un-blemished complexion. Her blue eyes radiated suspicion and, if Banks wasn't mistaken, more than a trace of guilt. Though guilt about what, he had no idea. There was also a lack of confidence evident in her posture and body language. She slumped, slouched; her fingernails were bitten to the quick. Had life with Lane sapped all the energy from her, or was it life with the "private" Ollie? She certainly seemed nervous because he wasn't present, but Banks got the impression that she would be even more so if he were in the room.

"Why don't you want us to talk to Ollie, Denise?" Annie asked.

"Has he hurt you?" said Banks. "Does he hurt you?"

Denise's eyes opened wide. "Oh, no. It's nothing like that at all. Ollie wouldn't do anything to harm me. We love each other. You're getting me all wrong."

"Then why are you so on edge?" Banks asked.

"On edge? I'm not on edge. What makes you think that?"

"You're fidgeting, you can't sit still, your eyes are all over the place. Need I go on?"

Denise Lane looked even more self-conscious. Her complexion turned red and her upper lip quivered. Banks thought she was going to cry. "It's not fair to talk to a person like that," she said. "You come here, into my house and you . . . you bully me, insult me."

"How are we insulting you, Denise?" Annie asked, passing her a tissue. The waterworks had started now.

Denise sniffed. "By saying horrible things."

Banks leaned forward in his chair and clasped his hands on his thighs. "Can we start again, Denise?" he said. "Nobody meant to upset you. Far from it. DI Cabbot and I are concerned about you. We sense there's something wrong, but you won't tell us what it is. Now, wouldn't it be better all around if you told us? We can probably help, you know. I understand you want all this to go away, whatever it is. You have a lovely house, a partner you love and you want to get on with your lives. But Morgan Spencer can't get on with his life. He's dead. Murdered."

"Morgan Spencer." She spat out the name. "He's a creep. A pervert."

"Maybe so, but he didn't deserve what happened to him. DI Cabbot told me you had a problem with him. But that was a long time ago, wasn't it?"

"I still feel scared and angry when I think about it."

"I'm sure you do," said Annie. "Things like that don't go away." She paused. "Believe me, I know."

Denise looked at her, and for the first time the recognition of a kindred soul, or at least an empathetic one, came into her eyes. "You do? Really?"

Annie nodded. "But you're lucky. You fought him off. You made him leave."

"Yes."

"It's really Michael we're interested in," said Banks. "We found his car abandoned in Scarborough. We're worried about him. Scarborough's not far. We were wondering if you'd seen anything of him."

"Scarborough? Is that where . . . ?"

"Is that where what, Mrs. Lane?"

"Nothing. I . . . I meant is that where you found it?"

"You're not a very good liar, Mrs. Lane."

Denise Lane glared at him again, then burst into tears once more. Annie handed her another tissue and put a comforting arm over her shoulder. "Ollie will be back soon," Denise said between sobs. "Then you'll have to go."

Banks didn't want to get into the Ollie business again, and his patience was wearing thin. "What do you know, Denise? What is it you're not telling us? Have you seen Michael? Has he been here?"

"I'm not a bad mother. Really, I'm not."

"Was he here?"

Denise quivered and quavered a bit, then said in a barely audible voice, "Yes. Yes, he was here." She was tearing the tissue into shreds with her stubby fingers.

"That's better," said Banks. "See how it feels much better to get it off your chest?"

Denise gave him a weak smile. "I don't know about that."

"Tell us what happened," Annie said. "As much detail as you can." She took out her notebook.

"It was on Tuesday, lunchtime."

Before he phoned Alex from the pay phone, Annie thought, and shortly before he'd parked the car in Scarborough. "The day after my colleague and I visited you at Tesco?"

"Yes."

"Why didn't you call us?"

"I . . . I . . ." Denise Lane just shook her head.

"Was it because he's your son?" Banks said. "And no matter what he might have done, you'll take care of him?"

Denise looked heartbroken at that. "Yes," she said. "But I didn't. I mean, I don't think he's done anything. He's a good boy. I really believe that. But he was scared and cold. I think he'd been sleeping rough, maybe in the car on the moors. It gets cold out there. And he hadn't eaten. He said he didn't have much money with him, and he couldn't use his credit or debit cards because you'd be able to trace him. His mobile, too. He was just keeping it switched off."

"So what happened?"

"He asked if he could stay for a while."

"Did you tell him about my visit?" Annie asked.

"Yes. Well, I had to, didn't I? He deserved to know you lot were after him."

"How did he react?"

"He wasn't surprised. It didn't seem to bother him. I mean, he didn't run off or anything."

"How did he appear? Was he upset, frightened, worried?" Banks asked.

"Of course he was. All of those."

"Did you notice . . . I mean, did he have any blood on him anywhere?"

Denise's eyes widened again. "Blood? Good Lord, no. Why would Michael have blood on him?"

"Never mind," said Banks. "What did you do?"

"I gave him a cup of hot sweet tea and something to eat, some cake. He wouldn't say anything else—said it was better if I didn't know— but I could see he was in trouble. I said he should just go and see you, the police, like, and explain that he hadn't done whatever you think he has, and you'd sort it all out, but he wouldn't."

"We don't know that he has done anything," said Banks. "It's for his own safety, and that of his partner and her child, that we want to find him as soon as possible."

"Alex? And Ian?"

"You know them?"

"He mentioned them, that's all. I mean, I knew about them, but he'd never really talked before. This time I could see he was head over heels. He said he would bring them to see me one day Ollie was out, then . . . all this . . ."

"Well, as long as Michael's missing, they're in danger, too. Did you let him stay? Is he here now?"

Denise stiffened. "No. I couldn't possibly do that."

"Why not?"

"Ollie was home. He often comes home for his lunch. It's not far away and it . . . well, it saves a bit of money. You have to understand, Ollie doesn't *know* Michael. That's a part of my other life, and Ollie doesn't like to talk about that. That's why he had to be out if they were going to visit."

Banks was getting the picture. He glanced at Annie, and by her expression he knew that she was getting it, too. "Your other life?" he said.

"Yes. At the farm. We've drawn a line under that, Ollie said."

"And that includes Michael? Alex and Ian?"

Her eyes teared up, and she nodded. "It's not me. Honest. I would have taken him in in a second, but Ollie wouldn't have it. Said he wasn't having no outlaws on the run staying in his house, and Michael should think himself lucky we didn't just call the police right there and then and turn him in. Michael pleaded with him. I pleaded with him. But it did no good. In the end, Michael got mad and left. Just drove away." She wrung her hands. "I hope nothing's happened to him. I'd never forgive myself."

"We don't think so, Mrs. Lane," said Banks. "Not yet. But it's vital that we find him as soon as possible."

"Did he say anything about where he might be going next?" Annie asked.

"No. I'm sorry."

"He didn't get in touch again? Phone, or anything?"

"No."

"Is there anything else you can tell us, however insignificant?"

Denise thought for a moment. "When he was going, when we were alone at the front door, I managed to slip him some money we'd been putting by in the hall sideboard."

"How much money?"

"It was only a hundred pounds, but it was all we had. Our 'mad' money. When Ollie found out he went spare."

I'll bet he did, thought Banks. A hundred pounds wasn't very much these days. It might get you mediocre lodgings for three, perhaps four nights, if you didn't eat, or a couple of tanks of petrol. Lane abandoned his car even though he had the money to buy petrol. He had paid for parking because he wasn't thinking and had simply done what he would normally do. Had the car broken down? Everyone said it was on its last legs. The forensics mechanics would be able to tell him about that. Or was Lane planning to come back for the car later but something had happened to prevent him? He had phoned Alex that evening from York, so he had still been free then.

If he were to hazard a guess, Banks would have said that Lane left the car just to confuse everyone, took a train to York, wandered about there for a while plucking up the courage to phone Alex, then headed for London.

And Montague Havers lived in London.

THE DINNER was delightful, the service impeccable without being obtrusive, the crispy duck breast cooked just the way Winsome loved it, and Terry said his entrecôte and frites were spot-on. For starters, they shared chicken liver pâté, and instead of a sweet, they went for the cheese plate, which was served, as it should be, at room temperature. They drank a simple inexpensive Rioja, nothing outrageous or ostentatious, and Terry had only one glass because he had to drive. The small glass of ruby port he ordered for Winsome later went exceptionally well with the cheese. Their conversation flowed with an ease Winsome hadn't realized existed. Terry didn't talk about his experiences in Afghanistan, and Winsome largely avoided talking about her job. As they laughed a lot and told each other stories about their potholing experiences and areas they had explored, they found so many topics in common that they could have carried on talking all night. Terry had even been to Montego Bay on a couple of occasions, and had visited the area around Spring Mount and Maroon Town, where Winsome had spent her childhood as the daughter of a local police corporal. His own childhood, he confessed, had been that of an army brat, never staying anywhere long and finding it very difficult to make friends.

The only disagreement arose when it was time to pay the bill, and even that was minor. Terry insisted on paying for the two of them, whereas Winsome insisted on going dutch. In the end, Winsome won, and Terry was gracious in defeat. Winsome noticed that he wasn't carrying his stick, just an umbrella.

They walked out onto Castle Hill, and Winsome immediately felt the wind and rain bring a chill to her bones. In her mind there flashed a vision of the country they had been talking about, where she had been brought up. Banana leaves clacking in the wind, the long walk to and from church in her Sunday best in the searing heat, out-of-season days walking the deserted beaches around Montego Bay, looking for driftwood with her father. She felt herself shiver. For better or for worse, England was her home now.

Terry moved closer with his umbrella and gently put a tentative arm around her, sheltering the two of them under its broad black circle. She felt herself stiffen a little at his touch, but she didn't shake him off. She could hear the umbrella whipping about in the wind, straining at the metal spokes, and feared it would snap inside out or simply fly off into the sky. Maybe they'd go with it, like Mary Poppins. But Terry managed to keep a grip on it as they headed around the corner and down the cobbled road toward the lights of the town square, the castle behind them tastefully floodlit against the sky. The shops were all closed, but the pubs and restaurants were open and the sounds of conversation and laughter drifted up on the night air along with the sounds of high heels clicking across the cobbles.

"Can I give you a lift?" Terry asked.

"It's all right," Winsome said. "I don't live far."

"But it's cold. You're cold."

Winsome laughed. "I'm used to that. Thanks," she said. "It really was a lovely evening."

"My pleasure."

They stopped as they entered the top of the square. "Well, I'm parked over there, behind the shopping center," Terry said.

Winsome pointed the other way. "I'm up York Road a bit."

"Well, if you won't let me drive you home, then . . ."

Winsome felt rather than saw him moving toward her, his lips aiming for hers. She felt a surge of panic, of claustrophobia almost, and found herself turning aside, so that his lips grazed against her cheek, then she heard herself saying a curt "Good night" and hurried off toward home, heart palpitating.

She pulled her jacket collar around her throat to keep out the icy needles of wind and hurried along, head down, past the lit-up shop signs and window displays until she got to her street, on the fringe of the student area. There she turned left, walked up the slight rise for fifty yards and turned into the imposing detached house, with its gables, bay windows and large chimneys, where she had the top-floor flat.

Once she was inside, she leaned back on the closed door and took stock. What on earth was she thinking of? It was only a good-night kiss. Was that something to be so frightened of? But she had been. She remembered the tension that ran through her body when she saw him moving toward her, the tightness in her chest.

She made herself a cup of chamomile tea in the kitchenette and thought about what a pleasant evening it had been, how easily their conversation had flowed. When she curled up in her favorite armchair, with only the shaded lamp lighting the room, she realized that she had very little experience of talking to anyone outside her job. Most of the time she talked to other cops, criminals, forensic scientists or lawyers. She had been a shy child and had never found it easy to socialize, and that carried over into her adult life. Was this what her life had come to? But wasn't she too young to start wondering what had happened to all the promise, the dreams, the young woman who had walked down the jetway at Gatwick, excited as a little child at the life ahead of her in the new country she was about to discover? Marveling at the cars, the huge buildings, the fast motorways and even the unrelenting rain and a sky the color of dirty dishwater.

No, she decided in the end. She hadn't lost all that. She was still young and she had most of her life ahead of her. She was scared, she realized; that was all. Like so many people. Scared of commitment, scared of dipping a toe in the water. Scared of being hurt. It was a long time since she had had a serious boyfriend, someone there was a possibility of sharing her life with. Tonight had shown her that there could be other possibilities. That Terry liked her was obvious, and she knew she liked him. How could she get over her fear? How could she stop behaving like a silly little girl, probably making him think she was nothing but a tease? She was soon starting to feel really stupid about her behavior.

Winsome sipped her tea, brow furrowed and swore to herself that the next time she saw Terry Gilchrist, she would kiss him. On the lips. That thought made her smile.

12

BANKS ENJOYED TRAIN JOURNEYS ONCE HE HAD GOT through the station experience, found somewhere to put his luggage and laid claim to an empty seat. Fridays were busy days on the East Coast line, but he got a midmorning train that wasn't too full, and the seat next to his remained empty all the way to Kings Cross. He had decided to board at Darlington, though York would have been closer, because from Darlington the train would pass the airfield and hangar after Northallerton, and he wanted to have a look at the area from a train window. Doug Wilson had got the message through to the railways, and they had even put out a few flyers on selected trains, but so far nobody had come forward to report seeing anything out of the window on the Sunday morning in question. Banks was curious as to why.

The sky looked like iron, and he got the feeling that if a giant banged the rolling landscape with a hammer it would clang and reverberate. It was partly the stillness that caused the effect, especially after last night's wind, and the sudden dryness after the constant rains. Still, it felt like the calm before the storm. And the daffodils ought to be out by now.

It didn't take long to get to Northallerton and whizz through the small station without even slowing down. The only stop on this journey was York. Keeping his eyes fixed on the left, where the lighter gray of the Cleveland Hills broke the charcoal horizon in the distance, he finally saw the hangar coming up. There was a stretch of about a quarter of a mile of neglected pasture between the airfield and train lines, but he could see the huge hangar clearly. The problem was that all the action had occurred on the other side of the building, where the gate in the chain-link fence was. Banks could see a couple of patrol cars and a CSI van parked by the outside fence—Stefan's team was still working there—but it was all gone in a flash. Even if someone had been looking in that direction, he realized, they couldn't have seen anything going on inside the hangar, and any cars parked right at the front would have been obscured by the building itself. The only possibility would have been someone noticing a lorry or a car heading down the road in front of the gate, parallel to the train tracks, but the timing had clearly been wrong for such an observation.

Satisfied that they had probed that possibility to the end of its usefulness, Banks returned to his relaxation. There was no hot water on the train, which meant no tea or coffee and only cold sandwiches to eat. He decided he could manage the two-and-a-half-hour-plus journey on an empty stomach. He still had half his Costa latte left when he boarded, so he made that last for a few miles. He had brought his noise-canceling headphones, which meant he could listen to any kind of music he wanted, and not just the sort of loud rock that drowned out the train noise. He started off with the Bartók and Walton viola concertos. Other musicians made fun of the viola in orchestras, but he loved its sound, somewhere between the plaintive keen of the violin and the resonant melancholy of the cello, with a sweet elegiac strain all of its own. He had known a professional violist once, a very beautiful young woman called Pamela Jeffreys, but he had let her slip away from him.

The train rattled along and Banks was more aware of feeling the physical rocking than the sound. He was reading *Hangover Square,* but he looked up every now and then at the landscape. As they passed through flat green stretches of the English heartland, the flood damage was plain to see, whole fields underwater, streams and rivers overflowing their banks, and that terrible iron-gray stillness about it all. He even saw a tractor marooned in the middle of a deep broad puddle, and thought of John Beddoes, whose stolen tractor seemed to have started all this. Was Beddoes connected somehow? An insurance scam, as Annie had suggested, or in some way more sinister, through some vendetta with the Lanes, perhaps. Other than for insurance, though, why would a man have his own tractor stolen?

The train flashed through Peterborough, with its truncated cathedral tower, the river and its waterfront flats, looking a bit shabbier now than they had when Banks worked a case down there a few years ago. Banks had few friends left from his Peterborough childhood days. Graham Marshall had disappeared when they were all schoolboys, and many years later, when his body was found, Banks had helped with the investigation into what happened to him. They had been the famous five all those years ago: Banks, Graham, Steve Hill, Paul Major and Dave Greenfell. Steve Hill, the boy who had introduced the young Banks to Dylan, the Who, Pink Floyd and the rest, had been the next to go, from lung cancer a few years ago. And just last year Paul Major had died of an AIDS-related illness. That left two out of five. No wonder Banks felt his circle of friends diminishing.

He put down *Hangover Square* and switched the music to his playlist of Scott Walker singing Jacques Brel songs, starting with the beautiful "If You Go Away." Banks liked Brel in the original, though he couldn't understand all the words, but even he, with his limited French, knew that there was a big difference between "If You Go Away" and "Ne me quitte pas." Where the English version was sad, the original was a desperate plea.

The playlist lasted him all the way to London.

ANNIE KNEW she'd been putting off the abattoir trawl, and after visiting four of the places she knew why. She had intended her objection to the assignment at the meeting partly as a joke, but she was fast coming to realize that there was nothing funny about it at all. She was getting heartily sick of abattoirs. Almost to the point of being physically sick on more than one occasion so far. The affront to her vegetarian sensibilities was almost more than she could take.

Fortunately, the previous day she had headed off to the east coast with Banks and so postponed the task, but on Friday morning she had no excuse. All she could do to ameliorate things was to drag poor Doug Wilson along with her. She thought he'd provide a little comfort and amusement, but so far he had provided neither. If anything, he had been more disgusted than she was at the things they had seen, heard and smelled. If she hadn't been a vegetarian already, occasional lapses into fish and chicken aside, she decided, she would be one by now. Doug wasn't one himself, but Annie was starting to think that by the end of the day he might well be. If she were in the business of conversion, she knew now he was at his most vulnerable and it wouldn't take much effort.

For the most part, they had managed to avoid the working areas and have their conversations in offices that didn't smell of the rank horrors being committed on the killing floor. But you couldn't escape the stench entirely, or the screaming or bleating of the terrified animals. Nobody could convince Annie that they didn't know exactly what was coming. No matter how much you modernized an abattoir and tarted it up, it was still barbaric, in her opinion. You could paint the inside yellow and pin children's drawings to the wall and it wouldn't change a thing.

They were about to call it a day and head back to the station a bit early when Gerry Masterson rang Annie's mobile.

"Where are you?" Gerry asked. "Where are you right now?"

"Wensleydale," said Annie. "We're just packing in for the day. Why?"

There was a pause at the end of the line. For a moment, Annie thought she'd lost the connection. It happened often out here. "Gerry?" she said. "Are you still there?"

"Have you visited Stirwall's yet?"

"No. We're saving them for tomorrow."

"You're not so far away."

"No, but—"

"I'm sorry to do this, guv, really I am, but I think you should go there now."

"Gerry, what's going on? It's been a crap day, to put it mildly."

"I know, I know. And I'm sorry. But I've been checking reports and speaking on the phone all day, and Stirwall's reported a penetrating bolt pistol stolen about two years ago. We need more details."

Annie swore under her breath. "Can't you get them over the phone?"

"It needs an official visit. There's always something else comes up you'd never think of on the phone. Employee records, for example. Someone might have some names for us. Besides, you're a senior officer on the case."

Annie knew she was right. "OK, we'll go now."

"I'm really sorry."

"Forget it. Got a name for us?"

"Ask for James Dalby. He's the head supervisor, and he's there waiting for you."

As Annie turned the car around, Doug Wilson gave a heavy sigh.

"What's up, Dougal?" she asked. "Hot date tonight?"

"Something like that," said Wilson. "Actually, it's my sister's eighteenth-birthday do. We've booked a table at that new steak restaurant in town."

Annie looked at her watch. "Don't worry, you'll make it in plenty of time."

"Aye. Smelling like an abattoir, no doubt."

"Well, you'll be eating steak for dinner, won't you?" said Annie with a sweet smile. "If what we've seen so far today hasn't put you off, then why not watch a few more cows getting slaughtered first? Who knows, maybe you'll even see your dinner before it's dead."

"Ha-ha," said Wilson, then he scowled and looked out of the window at the dark gray moors.

Soon the long squat shape of Stirwall's loomed before them. There had been complaints that it had been built too close to the nearby village, and residents complained of the smell and noise at all hours of the day and night. But it was still there, still operating. Stirwall's was one of the larger abattoirs in the area, too, with vans coming and going at all hours, stacks of boxes on pallets in the yard.

They parked in the area marked VISITORS and asked the first worker they saw where they could find James Dalby. He pointed to the front doors and told them to turn left up the stairs and they'd find Mr. Dalby's office on the first floor.

They thanked him and walked toward the open entrance. The outside of the building was surrounded with lairages, as one of the workers at the previous slaughterhouse had called them, holding pens where the animals languished awaiting slaughter. At the moment, some of them were full of lowing cattle and others were being sluiced out according to health regulations before another batch was led in.

The smell got worse inside. And the noise. As each animal came individually through a chute from the lairage, it was rendered unconscious by a knockerman's bolt gun, then strung up by its hind legs on a line. Three monorails of dead animals slowly moved down the length of the abattoir. At each stage of the way, slaughtermen performed their specialized tasks, such as slitting the throat for bleeding, spraying with boiling water to loosen the skin, then the actual skinning and disemboweling, careful removal of valuable organs, such as the liver, kidneys, pancreas and heart. The stench was awful. Annie tried to keep her eyes averted as she climbed the metal stairs to Dalby's office, but it was impossible. There was something about ugly violent death that demanded one's attention, so she looked, she watched, she saw. And heard: the discharge of the bolt guns, the buzz of the mechanical saws, and the change in pitch when they hit bone as the head was cut off and the animal split in half. It was almost unthinkable that someone had done this to Morgan Spencer.

Annie knocked on Dalby's office door, and they were admitted just as a screeching noise far worse than fingernails on a blackboard rose up from the killing floor. Annie didn't know what it was, and she didn't want to know. She was glad to close the door behind her and find that the room was reasonably well soundproofed and that the air smelled fresh. No doubt Dalby's exalted position had its perks. Annie had been worried that he would have been patrolling the floor in a white hat and coat keeping an eye on the workers, and that they would have had to walk by his side to interview him, keeping pace with the line, as they'd had to do at the previous place they visited. But he was the one who supervised the supervisors.

Dalby was a roly-poly sort of fellow in a rough Swaledale jumper, with a ruddy complexion and a shock of gray hair. "Sit down," he said. "Sit down. I apologize the place is such a mess, but I don't get a lot of visitors."

Annie had wondered about that when she had parked in the visitors area. It certainly wasn't very large, she had noticed. There were two orange plastic molded chairs, and Annie and Doug sat on them. Dalby went behind his desk. Through the window, over his shoulder, Annie could see the moors rolling off into the gray distance. It was a calming view.

"I've just been speaking with a DC Masterson," said Dalby. "Nice lady. Terrible business, this, though. One wonders where to begin."

"How large is this operation?" Annie asked first, when Doug had taken out his notebook.

"Stirwall's is a large abattoir," Dalby replied, leaning back in his swivel chair and linking his hands behind his neck. "We employ about a hundred personnel, sometimes more when things are especially busy in autumn."

The lambs, Annie thought. *The Silence of the Lambs.* "That's a lot of people," she said.

"We manage to keep busy. We've a good number of meat processors to supply. Not to mention butchers and supermarkets."

"As you're aware," Annie went on, "we're interested in an incident of theft that took place here around two years ago."

"That's right," said Dalby, nodding gravely. "We did report the theft to the police at the time."

"What exactly were the circumstances?"

"It was a penetrating bolt pistol. This model." He took a loose-leaf binder from his desk and flipped to a picture for her. It was exactly the same as the kind the forensics people said had killed Morgan Spencer.

"Where was it kept?"

"There's a metal cabinet fixed to the wall down on the floor where we keep all our stun guns."

"Locked?"

"Of course."

"Who has keys?"

"Well, I do. The supervisors do. And the knockermen and slaughter-men, of course. I mean, to be honest, almost anyone down there can get to them if he wants."

"That sounds very secure."

Dalby gave her a suspicious look. She knew her sarcasm wasn't lost on him. Nor was it appreciated. "It worked," he said. "We've only had the one theft in sixty years."

"It's enough," said Annie, "if it was used to kill someone. A human being, I mean."

Dalby narrowed his eyes and peered at her. He didn't look so roly-poly anymore. "You don't approve of what we do, do you?"

"Whether I approve or not is irrelevant."

"Right. Yes. I thought so. You're one of them there vegan tree huggers, aren't you?"

Annie flushed. "Mr. Dalby. Can we please get back to the matter in hand? The bolt gun."

"Right, the bolt gun. Well, as I said, it's the penetrating kind." He leered. "Know what that means?"

Annie said nothing.

Doug Wilson looked up from his notes. "I wouldn't use innuendos like that with the boss," he said. "She's been known to get quite nasty."

Dalby looked at Annie and swallowed. "Aye . . . well . . . We don't use those much anymore."

"Yes, I know," said Annie. "You stopped using them because they can cause brain matter to enter the bloodstream, and these days people are all so worried about mad cow disease."

"My, my. You *have* done your homework. Anyway, we now rely mostly on the nonpenetrating kind, which stuns the animal. It works without puncturing the skull."

"The one that killed our man put a hole in his head," said Annie.

"Well, it would, wouldn't it? It was a penetrating bolt gun. In some cases, even a nonpenetrating gun can put a hole in a human's skull, if it's positioned correctly."

"I'll bear that in mind. Back to the stolen pistol."

"Yes, well, as I said, we reported it stolen at the time. Nothing happened."

"I'm sure the officers followed up."

"Oh, I'm sure they did, but it would be a bit like looking for a needle in a haystack, wouldn't it, if you didn't even know where to start."

"Could it just have been lost? Mislaid?"

"We might be a bit sloppy on occasion, but we're more careful than that. It was stolen."

"Did you have any suspects?"

"No. Well, not technically, at any rate."

"What do you mean?"

"Nobody saw anyone take it, and nobody knew anyone who had expressed an intent to take it. We don't even know exactly how long it had been missing before the loss was discovered."

"You don't check them often?"

"Once in a while. Stocktaking."

"So it could have been missing for some time?"

"Not more than a couple of weeks. After your boss called, I checked the files and discovered we had let two people go around that time, either of whom could have stolen the pistol. I'm not saying they did. That's what I meant by 'not technically.' For all I know, the person who did it could still be working here. But she said she was interested in disgruntled employees, perhaps with a grudge, and these two fit the bill."

"Thanks for doing that," said Annie. She meant it, and she could tell that Dalby knew she did. It seemed to embarrass him.

"Well, we take this sort of thing seriously," he said.

"She's not my boss, by the way."

"What?"

"The detective who called. She's not my boss."

Dalby glanced at Doug Wilson. "No, I should have gathered that much from him. You're the boss. My mistake."

"No problem. So why did you fire these two people?" Annie asked, feeling a bit silly. Was it really important enough to make a point of her rank with Dalby?

"Why do you usually fire someone?"

"There could be any number of reasons. In your business, I don't know."

"My business is the same as any other. You fire people for incompetence, for stealing, for persistent absenteeism, for failing to follow correct procedures, for insubordination."

"OK. So what did these two do wrong?"

"They weren't connected at all. It was two separate incidents, a couple of weeks apart. The first one was a skinner, and I suppose you could say he was just too sensitive. He shouldn't have been doing the job. This kind of work isn't for the fainthearted."

"Then how did he get it in the first place? I mean, don't you have psychological tests to weed out psychos who get their jollies from killing. So you can employ them, that is."

Doug Wilson gave Annie a horrified and chastising glance.

"Sorry," she said, holding her hands up.

Dalby paused and spoke slowly. "All employers make mistakes sometimes," he said. "Even the police, I should imagine. It's why we all have probationary periods."

"This worker didn't make it past his probation?"

"No. The official problem was absenteeism and drunkenness on the job."

"I imagine that would help in—"

"Yes, the drink helped him. He couldn't handle the job so he took to drink to dull his mind. But do you have the slightest idea how dangerous it is to be intoxicated around some of the equipment we have in here? And not only for the one who's drunk."

"I can imagine," said Annie.

Dalby grunted. "Aye. It worked, to an extent. Sometimes he'd be so badly hungover he didn't come to work for two days."

"So you fired him?"

"Yes."

"Wasn't there any counseling or anything available?"

Dalby gave her a scathing look.

"Can you give us his name and address?" she asked.

"Ulf Bengtsson. He was a Swede." Dalby read the name and address off a sheet of paper on his desk, and Doug Wilson wrote them down. "I don't know if he's still there—in fact, I very much doubt it," Dalby added. "But it's the last address we have for him."

"Do you have any idea what's become of him?" Annie asked.

"All I can say is I doubt he's working in the industry anymore. Maybe he's gone home to Sweden."

"Do you know of any other abattoirs that would have employed him after that?"

"No. We certainly didn't give him a reference, and he hadn't yet earned his slaughterman's license."

"What about an unregulated abattoir?"

"I'm not saying they don't exist. They tend to be small operations, with just one production line, and I can't see one taking in a drunk like Ulf. I mean, it was pretty much constant intoxication by the end. I can only hope he got professional help, or he's probably dead by now."

"Can you tell us where any of these illegal abattoirs are?"

"I don't know of any around here. I'm not saying there aren't any, but I don't know them. As you probably know, this industry is very strictly regulated, and since the various controversies, from mad cow to horse meat and rotten meat in your frozen burgers, it would be even harder to get away with anything. No doubt people do it. No doubt they succeed. But to be off the radar you'd have to stay out of the way and keep a very low profile. They're small operations, as I said. They supply some restaurants and hotels, unscrupulous butchers, the occasional old folks' home."

"And the other man? What was his problem?"

"Kieran Welles, with an 'e,' like Orson. He was a different kettle of fish entirely."

"Tell us about him."

"Kieran was with us for some time. Eighteen months, in all. He was a good worker, not troubled by nerves or drink. He was a slaughterman, and he was versatile. Mostly he did knocking work. It was his job to use the bolt gun on the animals when they came through from the lairage. But you could put him just about anywhere on the line and he'd get the job done. A good slaughterman is hard to find."

"And what was *his* problem?"

"He was a bit too keen, you might say."

"Too keen?"

"Cruel."

"What?"

"He was cruel to the animals. He kept it well hidden, but it came out often enough, and in the end we couldn't tolerate his working here anymore. I can tell by your expression that you think we're all a bunch of callous bastards in this business, but we have our lines, and Welles crossed one."

"What do you mean 'cruel'? What did he do that was worse than his job? I mean, it was his job to fire a bloody bolt pistol at their heads, right, penetrating or non. How more cruel could he be?"

Dalby leaned forward on his desk. "I'll tell you," he said. "I saw him stub a cigarette out in a pig's eye once, just for the fun of it. He'd kick and punch the animals sometimes. Again, for fun. Sometimes he'd deliberately fail to stun them correctly, so they were still alive and conscious when they were hung up on the line."

Annie felt her stomach churn. It was becoming difficult to hold the bile down. She noticed Doug looking into the gray distance out of the window, over Dalby's shoulder. Maybe he was reconsidering tonight's steak dinner. "And it took eighteen months to find this out? You weren't aware of it before?"

"I'm not here to answer to your censure. You can save your righteous indignation for your tree-hugging sisters in the pub. They do it when you're not looking, and you can't be looking every minute of every shift. But word gets around. Once somebody saw him. We found it hard to believe—Welles was a big lad, but he had a sort of farm-boy innocence about him—but we kept a closer eye on him, and that was that. He got warnings, but they didn't do any good."

"Was he intelligent?"

"He wasn't stupid."

"And do you know where Mr. Welles is today?"

"I neither know nor care," said Dalby, "just so long as he never shows his face back here again."

"Have you never considered the effect that doing this sort of work can have on people? Alcoholism, cruelty. You're creating these monsters yourself. Don't you think it desensitizes people, creates the kind of person you say you had to fire?"

"I'm not a psychologist, miss. I'm a simple abattoir worker. Maybe you're right. Maybe that does happen in some cases. As I said, this kind of work isn't for everyone. If they're not damaged to start with, maybe it damages them. All I can say, though, is that most of the workers are decent human beings doing an honest day's work, and the bad apples are few and far between. In that, it's no different than any other line of work."

"But why do people do it?"

"Somebody has to. You have to eat. It's a job, a decent wage."

"Is there no other way?"

"If there were," said Dalby, "believe me, we'd be using it. But as long as people want to buy their nice cuts of meat all nicely wrapped in cling wrap at the supermarkets, or laid out in neat juicy rows in the butcher's window, this'll go on." He pointed his finger at her as he talked. "You can think what you like about us, but we do try to be humane, and we don't countenance behavior like Welles's. The other guy, the Swede, maybe you can feel sorry for him. He couldn't cope, and it messed him up. I suppose it's our version of shell shock or battle fatigue, whatever the shrinks call it now."

"PTSD. Post–traumatic stress disorder."

"Whatever. Like I said, it's not for everyone." Dalby stood up slowly. "Now, I've got work to do. Have you got what you came for?"

Annie swallowed and looked at Doug, who put away his notebook. "I think so," she said. "There may be a few more questions later, if any of this leads anywhere."

"I'll be here. Just ask for me."

As they walked down the stairs, Annie knew that she should go and examine the metal cabinet the guns were kept in, but she couldn't face it. She didn't think it would be fair to send Doug, either. If it came to it, she realized, they could send someone over to examine it, but it was two years since the gun had been stolen, and they weren't likely to find anything of interest there now. She felt guilty for shirking her duty, even though she could easily rationalize her actions, but she held her breath, and her tears, all the way to the car, and only when she was inside with the engine running, reversing out of the abattoir yard, did she let out the stale air and breathe in again. But she kept the tears to herself.

IT WAS a pleasant winter afternoon in London, with temperatures just into double figures, so Banks decided to walk from Kings Cross to

Havers's office. It was a long time since he had visited the area behind and to the west of Kings Cross–St. Pancras, and he knew little about it. It was hard to categorize, he thought as he walked and looked around him, but as Joanna had pointed out, it was a bit dodgy. There were offices, houses, flats, garages and so on, but it lacked any coherent identity, at least any that was obvious to the casual visitor.

At one point he passed what was clearly a drug house. A tall, burly man with a shaved head blocked the reinforced metal door, hands clasped firmly over his bollocks, and beside him a hunched weaselly young fellow had his mobile glued to his ear. Banks was certain the Met must know about them, and they were probably under surveillance at that very moment. There seemed to be so much watching and so little catching and convicting these days. Montague Havers was obviously another case in point. Whatever it was he did, nobody stopped him; the police just watched. There was always the chance of a bigger Mr. Big around the next corner. And so it went on. What did you have to do these days to convince the CPS you had enough evidence for an arrest?

Banks's mobile rang just after he had passed the drug house. He saw the burly man cast a baleful glance in his direction as he answered. Did he look so obviously like a copper? He had never thought so.

"Banks here."

"Sir, it's me. DC Masterson."

"Ah, Gerry. What can I do for you?"

"Can you talk, sir? I mean, listen. I think I can do something for you."

"I'm on my way to have a chat with Montague Havers."

"Then I'm just in time."

Banks turned a corner and leaned against a brick wall. "Go on."

"I've found out a couple of things that might interest you, sir."

"What?"

"First off, there's an old murder with a bolt gun, eighteen months ago in East London. A man called Jan Wolitz. Polish. The investigating officers thought he was connected with a people-trafficking outfit and suspected he'd been taking more than his cut from them, not to mention helping himself to some of the girls' favors. Young girls mostly. Prostitution. Nobody ever arrested for it and no suspects named, as far as I can gather. The police did, however, find prints at the scene that didn't belong to the victim. They led nowhere. Not in the system. He wasn't cut into pieces or anything. Just dead."

"Can you get the prints sent up and check them against whatever Vic got from the hangar?"

"As we speak." Banks could hear the smile in Gerry's voice.

"You're too good for this world, Gerry."

"So they tell me, sir."

"Where was the body found?"

"Abandoned warehouse on the Thames. I mean, it's probably gilding the lily calling it East London. More like west Essex."

"Who owned the property?"

"Don't know yet, sir, but I can see why it might be useful to know. I'll get onto that as well."

"Any hint of a connection between this Jan Wolitz and anyone we know? Spencer, Montague Havers, Tanner, Lane?"

"No, sir, but DI Cabbot and Doug are running down a lead on a stolen bolt pistol. It was lifted about two years ago from Stirwall's Abattoir. But he's the one I wanted to talk to you about, sir. Montague Havers. Or Malcolm Hackett, as was."

"What about him?"

"He worked for the same stockbrokers as John Beddoes in the mid eighties. They were City boys together between the Big Bang and Black Monday. Both the same age, in their mid twenties at the time. There was a cocaine charge against Hackett back then, but it went nowhere. Small amount. Slap on the wrist. The point is, according to what I could find out from someone who also worked there at the time, the two of them were pretty thick. Socialized together and all that. Made oodles of money. When the bubble burst, Hackett went into international investment banking and Beddoes became a merchant banker before he moved to the farm."

"Well done. That's an interesting connection, Gerry," said Banks. "And your timing's impeccable. How are things back at the ranch?"

"Ticking along nicely. DS Jackman's still chasing down Caleb Ross's collection route."

"All well with Alex and Ian?"

"Everything's fine, sir. We've got surveillance on them. Nothing to report."

"Any news on Tanner?" They had had to let Ronald Tanner go when his twenty-four hours were up early that morning.

"He's still at home. We're keeping an eye on him. AC Gervaise is with the CPS as I speak, working on possible charges. I did a bit of research into his known associates and there's a bloke called Carl Utley looks good for the driver. Muttonchops, usually wears a flat hat. He used to be a long-distance lorry driver but he got fired when he was suspected of being involved in the disappearance of some expensive loads. Nothing proven, but enough to lose him his job. He drifted into nightclub work and that's when he met Tanner. They're good mates."

"Excellent. Follow it up. See if you can have this Utley picked up. No further sign of Michael Lane?"

"No, nothing."

"Keep at it. And thanks, Gerry. Get back to me as soon as you hear anything from Annie or the CPS."

Banks ended the call and went on his way, mulling over how he could use what he had just found out against Havers.

It was a dilapidated sixties office building with about as much charm and character as the shoe box it resembled. However well Havers was doing, he hadn't moved his business into better digs, somewhere nice and trendy down in Dockland, for example. But maybe this was his cover, and maybe it didn't matter to him. Banks had learned over the years that criminals had some very odd ideas about what was the best thing to do with their ill-gotten gains. Take Ronald Tanner, for example. He probably didn't make a fortune, but he could have afforded a larger house and a decent car. Instead he seemed to be broke and on benefits all the time. What did he spend his money on? Banks knew one safecracker who spent most of what he earned on expensive women's clothes, and they weren't gifts for a girl-friend, either. A cat burglar he had once arrested collected rare vinyl and lived in a small flat in Gipton on a diet of baked beans and toast. He didn't even own a record player. Maybe with Havers it was still coke, which could be an expensive habit, or the dogs? Or maybe he had a nice little nest egg hidden away offshore, and when the right moment came, he'd vanish to the Caymans for good. Anything was possible.

Banks took the rickety lift to the fifth floor and found the door marked Havers Overseas Investment Solutions Ltd. He'd heard that it was very much a one-man operation, so he wasn't expecting the receptionist who greeted him when he knocked and entered.

"Can I help you, sir?"

"I'd like to see Mr. Havers."

"Do you have an appointment?"

Banks showed her his warrant card.

She picked up the telephone. "If you'd care to—"

But Banks walked straight past her and through the next door, where he found Montague Havers sitting behind a flat-box Staples desk tapping away at a laptop computer. As soon as Havers saw Banks, he closed the lid on the computer and got to his feet. "What is this? You can't just come barging in like that."

Banks showed his warrant card again. Havers sat down and smoothed his hair. A funny smile crossed his features. "Well, why didn't you say? Sit down, sit down. Always happy to help the police in any way I can."

"I'm very glad to hear it," said Banks, sitting down on a very uncomfortable hard-backed chair. "It makes my job a lot easier." The view, he noticed, was of the railway lines at the back of the mainline stations. A trainspotter's wet dream.

Havers wore his wavy brown hair just a trifle too long for a man of his age, Banks thought. Along with the white shirt and garish bow tie he was wearing, it gave him the air of someone who was desperately trying to look young. Banks wondered, as he peered more closely, if his hair was dyed. Or a rug, even. It looked somehow fake. Maybe that was what he spent his money on: expensive rugs. The rusty mustache on his lip didn't do much for the youthful effect.

"So what exactly can I do for you, D . . . is it DI Banks?"

"DCI, actually. Am I to call you Malcolm Hackett or Montague Havers?"

"I changed my name legally six years ago to Montague Havers."

Banks tilted his head. "May I ask why?"

"Let's just say that in the business I'm in, it helps if you have an educated-sounding name. Malcolm Hackett was just too . . . too comprehensive school."

"And Montague Havers is more Eton?"

"Well, I wouldn't go that far, but that's the general idea. Yes."

Banks looked around the small office, at the crooked blinds, the stained plasterboard walls, the scratched filing cabinets. "And the office?"

"This? Nobody comes here. You're lucky to find me in. This is just a place to keep records and make phone calls. All my business appointments take place in fine restaurants around Fitzrovia or Marylebone High Street, or at my club. The Athenaeum. Perhaps you know it?"

Banks shook his head. "I never was very clubbable. What exactly is your business?"

"What it says on the door."

"That sounds like some sort of dodgy tax avoidance scheme to me. Offshore banking. International Investment Solutions."

"It's a complicated world out there, and taxation is only a part of it."

"What other services do you offer?"

Havers glanced at his watch. "I don't mean to rush you, but are you interested in becoming a client or are you just making polite small talk?"

"I'd like to know."

"Very well. I'm part of a larger network of companies, and we offer just about any financial service—legal financial service, mostly investment opportunities—you can imagine."

"All international?"

"Not all."

"Is property development investment one of your specialties?"

"We don't mind investing in property development occasionally, as long as it seems sound. But you have to remember that I'm in the business of investing British money abroad, not in domestic markets, and it's often difficult to get a clear perspective on overseas properties. The laws can be so complicated. That doesn't apply to my personal investments, of course."

"The Drewick airfield shopping center? Does that ring a bell?"

"Yes. I have a middling amount of my own money invested in the project, through a subsidiary."

"Retail Perfection?"

"That's the one. You have done your research. Anyway, I have a number of small investments in shopping centers. Can't go wrong with them in a consumer society like this one."

"As long as people have the money to spend."

"Oh come, come. That's hardly an issue. People will spend whether they have any money or not. That's the nature of capitalism."

"Maybe so. But I'm still interested in Drewick. Do you keep up to date on what's happening there?"

"I trust Venture Properties to keep me informed. As far as I know, there's been no movement for some time. Some minor problem with zoning laws. We expect it to be settled soon."

"But Venture would let you know as soon as any impediments to progress were removed?"

"Of course. I should think so."

"I see." That meant Havers would be in a good position to switch operations from Drewick to some other location if he did happen to be involved in rural crime. "I understand you visited North Yorkshire recently."

"My, my, am I under surveillance?"

"Don't tell me you didn't know."

"Well, I very much doubt you'd be here if they didn't know I know, if you see what I mean."

"Exactly. So who were you visiting up there?"

"My wife's brother and his wife live in Richmond."

"And you stayed with them?"

"Of course."

"All the time? Sunday to Tuesday?"

"Why wouldn't I? I happen to get on well with them, and I like the Dales."

"Did your wife accompany you?"

Havers looked down at his desk. "My wife is dead, Mr. Banks."

"I'm sorry to hear that."

"It's been some years now. But Gordon, Cathy and I have always been close. We still maintain strong family ties. Is there anything else?"

"Were you with them all the time?"

"Of course not. I did a bit of touring around by myself. The weather was bad, though, so that dampened my spirits. Still, it's a fine part of the world."

"Did you visit Belderfell Pass?"

"No. I know it, of course, but I'd avoid it in such poor conditions."

"Visit any farms in Swainsdale?"

"No. I didn't visit Swainsdale at all. What is it you're after? I just drove around a bit, went for a pub lunch here and there, looked in a few antique shops—I collect antiques—and I spent some time with my family. We had a trip to Castle Bolton. It's always been one of my favorite historical spots. Very manageable. What's your problem with that?"

"I have no problem with Castle Bolton, Mr. Havers. It's just the timing. Did you meet with a Ronald Tanner, Carl Utley, Michael Lane or Morgan Spencer?"

"I can't say I've ever heard any of those names."

"What about John Beddoes?"

"Doesn't ring a bell."

"Are you sure the name John Beddoes doesn't ring any bells?"

"I'm afraid not. Should it?"

"Indeed it should. You worked with him in the stockbroking business in the mid eighties. You were friends. You socialized together. Snorted coke. Drank champagne from the bottle. Painted the town red."

"Now hang on a— Just a minute." Havers snapped his fingers. "Of course! Bedder Beddoes. How could I forget? Yes, I knew him, back in the day. It was a long time ago, though."

"Bedder Beddoes?"

"Use your imagination, Mr. Banks. We were young and free."

"A lot of coke gone up the nasal passages since then?"

"That was one mistake. I don't do that sort of thing anymore. Even if I wanted to, I couldn't." He patted his chest. "Heart."

"Are you telling me you have one, or that there's something wrong with it?"

"Ha-ha. Very funny. I'm saying I've had two heart attacks. Cocaine would kill me. I'm allowed two units of wine a day. Do you know how hard that is?"

Banks could only imagine. "So we've established that you do know John Beddoes, and you did work with him some years ago, but you didn't visit him in Yorkshire last week? Did you know he now owns a farm there?"

"Bedder? No. I didn't even know he lived there. We were good mates once, it's true. But you know how it goes. You drift apart over time. And those times, well, they were heady indeed. Fueled by coke and champagne, as you say. The memory tends to fade quickly, if indeed it registers at all. It went by in a whirl, I'm afraid. I'm only lucky I still had my wits left when the bubble burst. I was able to get into international banking. That's where I learned most of what I know about overseas investments."

"So if we were to dig into your financial affairs, the financial affairs of your company and your movements over the past while, we wouldn't find any sort of intersection with John Beddoes and his interests?"

"I couldn't guarantee that, but they would be none that I'm aware of. He's not a client, if that's what you mean."

Havers sounded nervous at the prospect. It was obvious that he was lying, but Banks didn't think he was going to get any further with him. By denying that he knew Beddoes, though, Havers had unintentionally told Banks a lot. Why deny it unless Beddoes was involved? Or unless Havers himself was involved? Havers had pulled himself out of the hole quickly, but not quickly enough to convince Banks that he had forgotten "Bedder" Beddoes's existence. No doubt he had lied about other things, too. He wasn't going to admit to knowing any of the others, thugs like Tanner and Spencer, or to using the hangar at the airfield as a loading bay for stolen farm equipment. But by talking to him, and by letting him know that *he* knew, Banks thought he might just have ruffled things up enough that Havers, or someone in the organization, would make a mistake. He still didn't know how deeply Beddoes was involved—after all, it was *his* expensive tractor that had been reported stolen—but these two old friends certainly had the knowledge between them to run a sideline in stolen farm equipment. Beddoes knew something about farming, and he lived in a large rural area; he had also been a merchant banker, so he knew about financing. All they needed were connections to the illegal trade routes, and Havers's international contacts might easily have supplied those, according to what Joanna MacDonald had said. Banks decided to lay his cards on the table before leaving.

"Mr. Havers, I believe you're part of a group, or call it a gang, a criminal organization, involved in rural crime in a big way, and a part of your operation made a nasty mess on my patch. I believe you've been using the abandoned airfield and hangar at Drewick because it's a convenient transfer point for stolen goods from the north, and because you knew it was in limbo for the time being. Your men wouldn't be disturbed. Last Sunday, one of your underlings, Morgan Spencer, was murdered there, killed by a penetrating bolt pistol to the head. Either you wanted rid of him for some reason or some rival gang was muscling in. We don't know yet why he was killed. Either way, I believe you know something about it."

"This is ridiculous," protested Havers. "I don't know what you're talking about. I wasn't even—"

"In the area at the time? How do you know what time it took place? I didn't tell you."

"Oh, very clever. The old 'how could you have known' trick. Now you're putting words in my mouth."

"Well, how could you?"

"Because it was on the news on Monday, while I was still at my brother-in-law's. Ask him. They said it took place on Sunday morning. I didn't get to Richmond until Sunday afternoon, as you well know."

As far as Banks was aware, the media didn't know on Monday that the murder had taken place in the hangar on Sunday morning, but he decided he would keep that point in reserve until he had done a thorough check on Havers, including a visit to his brother-in-law. "Exactly," said Banks. "So where were you before then? How do I know you didn't find a way to foil Operation Hawk and the ANPR cameras and sneak up to the airfield earlier, for example?"

"This is absurd," said Havers. "I have nothing more to say to you. If you plan on continuing this charade I want my lawyer present."

Banks stood up to leave. "You'd hardly need a lawyer if it were a charade, Monty," he said. Then he paused at the door. "You know," he went, "if I were you, I'd take this as an omen, a bad omen. If I were you, I'd back off for a while, lie low and take stock. Disappear from the radar. No matter what you think, things aren't going to get any easier for you from now on."

"Is that a threat?"

"It's reality, Monty. The threats come later."

Banks closed the door gently behind him. The secretary scowled at him as he left.

13

"SO YOU DIDN'T NOTICE ANYTHING UNUSUAL ABOUT Mr. Ross when he came to pick up here on Tuesday?" Winsome asked. She was at the last farm on her list, the last place Caleb Ross had visited before heading for the Belderfell Pass and his death, and she had found out nothing new. He had arrived at a quarter to one and left just after one, so Mr. Wythers said. Some of the farmers thought Caleb was a bit distracted, in a hurry, whereas others thought his behavior just the same as usual.

Mr. Wythers, owner of Garsley Farm, had invited her in for a cup of tea, and Winsome was grateful for it. She felt as if it had been a long day, though it was still only midafternoon, and she had not stopped for lunch. The slice of Battenberg cake Mr. Wythers gave her with her tea reminded her how hungry she was. It would be back to the station, a quick report, then home for an early dinner followed by an early night.

"Caleb never said much," Mr. Wythers was saying. "I don't mean he was rude or anything, but we weren't mates, if you know what I mean. He was just a man doing his job, and I was the one who paid him for it. It was just like that. Businesslike, but polite, friendly, you know. I even asked him in for a cup of tea and a piece of cake, just like I did you, but he said he'd just had his lunch. We didn't chat or gossip or owt, so I'm afraid I can't tell you anything about him."

"That's all right," said Winsome. "I'm just collecting whatever bits and pieces I can to try to build up a picture of his last day."

"It's a terrible thing, what happened," said Wythers. "That pass has claimed more than one victim in my time here, that's for certain. And you couldn't see it coming. When he left here it was clear as anything. Clouds, aye, but there's nowt odd about that. Came like a bolt from the blue, it did. Weather's like that in these parts and it can be awful bleak out here. It pays to be careful, lass."

"I'll remember that," said Winsome. "But I think I'm just about done now." She ate the last small piece of cake, one of the pink bits with a marzipan border, washed it down with the last of her tea and stood up.

"Sorry I couldn't be more help, lass," said Wythers, walking her to the door. "Stay, boy," he said to the excited young collie who had started to accompany them. The dog sat down by the hearth. "Stay. There's a good lad."

Winsome said good-bye and stepped into the farmyard. She had seen, and smelled, enough farmyards over the past few days to last her a lifetime, she thought, but at least she hadn't drawn Annie's unenviable task of checking out the abattoirs. Still, Annie had come up with a viable lead in the stolen bolt gun and dismissed workers, and Winsome had come up with nothing except the possibility that Caleb Ross might have had something on his mind the day he died. Whatever it was, she guessed that it had lain at the other side of Belderfell Pass, and he had never reached it.

She started the car and headed back up the long drive to the B road. Instead of turning right to get back to the Swainshead and Helmthorpe road to Eastvale, she turned left toward the high moorland. She remembered this part of the dale well because the potholing club had visited it often. The hills that loomed ahead of her were riddled by one of the largest cave systems in Europe, with miles of underground passages linking huge chambers, some as large as the inside of a cathedral.

Thinking about her potholing days took her mind back to Terry Gilchrist. She still felt embarrassed about the previous evening. He had rung her that morning, before work, and asked her if she would see him, just to talk. Reluctantly—mostly because of her embarrassment, not lack of interest—she had agreed to have lunch with him on Saturday. How long could she go on behaving like a flirtatious virgin around him? Not that she would jump into bed with him—it was only lunch, after all—but she would make good on that kiss she had promised herself last night. It had been a long time since she had been romantically and physically involved with a man, that was all. It would take a little practice.

Beyond Wythers's farm, which was right on the edge of the high Pennines, the land wasn't much use for farming and was practically uninhabited. Sheep grazed there, of course, but that was about all. The road turned a sharp left toward Belderfell Pass, and Winsome could see it snaking up the hillside ahead. She pulled over in a passing place and got out to admire the distant view. She probably wasn't that far from the Lancashire border, she thought, or perhaps she was even far enough north to be neighboring on Cumbria, where the wild fells and moorlands of the Yorkshire Dales would slowly morph into the older, more rounded hills of the Lake District. It was a panoramic but desolate view before her, that was for certain, two or three large hills like long flat anvils, a disused quarry, stretches of moor and marsh. She got her binoculars from the boot and scanned the distance. There were one or two isolated hunters' lodges, owned by private clubs and used during the grouse season, but that was about all. She was already beyond the source of the river Swain, above Swainshead, and though becks and small waterfalls cascaded from the steep hillsides and meandered through the moorland, there were no rivers or tarns to be seen.

Shivering in the sudden chill breeze, she got back in her car and decided to take the long way back to Eastvale, over Belderfell Pass. Remembering Wythers's warnings about the weather, she scanned the sky as she made her way up the winding, unfenced road. Before long, she could feel her ears blocking and ringing, the way they did in airplanes at takeoff and landing. She yawned and felt them crack and clear. The pass wound its way high above the valley bottom over to the next dale. She got about halfway when she encountered the first signs of the accident, the dots of the investigators still working at the scene way below. She could see scatterings of black plastic bags. She slowed down as she rounded a promontory and stopped for a moment to watch the men below, but the perspective gave her vertigo. She never usually had a problem with heights, but even the hardiest of souls had been known to tremble at Belderfell Pass. Going the other way was a lot easier, of course. Then you hugged the hillside all the way. But in the direction she was going, the direction Caleb Ross had taken, there was nothing between her and the sheer drop.

Soon she realized she had started on the slow and winding descent into the tiny village of Ramsghyll, nestled at the bottom of the hill and famous for its pub, the Coach and Horses, which boasted real ale and gourmet food. Hungry as she was, Winsome didn't stop, but carried on through the village's narrow high street, past the pub and onto the road that, beyond Helmthorpe and Fortford, would take her eventually back to Eastvale. Perhaps it had been a wasted journey, she thought as she drove along admiring the scenery in the lengthening shadows, and perhaps it had been a wasted assignment altogether, but she still couldn't shake off the nagging feeling that the answer to Caleb Ross's role in Morgan Spencer's murder lay somewhere in the landscape she had just left behind. She was too tired and confused to do anything about it today, or even to know *what* to do, but she would approach the problem afresh tomorrow morning and work out just what it was that was niggling away at the edge of her consciousness.

THE DUCK and Drake was a popular old pub on Frith Street, in the heart of Soho, just a stone's throw from Ronnie Scott's. Banks had been there many times before, both when he worked in the West End and when he visited London or went down on business. Like this afternoon. The after-work crowd usually started congregating early, and there were already a few people standing outside smoking and quaffing pints when Banks got there at four. It was a small pub, long and narrow. Banks walked past the crowded bar through to the back room, which was furnished with a few ancient wooden tables and chairs, and found the person he was looking for right at the back table, scaring prospective punters away with his churlish expression.

Detective Chief Superintendent Richard "Dirty Dick" Burgess

stood up and beckoned Banks over, shaking hands vigorously. "Banksy, it's good to see you again. How's it hanging?"

Banks cringed. Burgess was the first person to call him Banksy since his school days. Not that he didn't admire the artist's work, but the nickname still rankled. Back at school there hadn't been the "other" Banksy.

Burgess had worked for just about every law enforcement agency there had been, every acronym imaginable, had been involved in counterterrorism, drugs, people trafficking, airport security, homicide and organized crime. Now he was high up in the new National Crime Agency, the NCA, which had been working on Operation Hawk with the local forces. Though Burgess wasn't the go-to man for rural crime, he oversaw a variety of operations, and Banks was willing to bet he knew as much about what was going on there as the team that had been assigned to it.

"I'm fine," said Banks, squeezing himself into the small space on a wobbly chair.

"I noticed the bar was getting busy," said Burgess, "so I took the liberty of getting the drinks in. Lager for me, of course, and one of those fancy real ale things for you. Can't remember what it's called— Codswallop or Cock-a-doodle-doo or some such thing—but the delightful young lady at the bar recommended it."

"Thank you," said Banks, and took a sip. It tasted good. Hoppy and full-bodied.

"So you got my message?"

"I'm here, aren't I?" Banks had received a phone call from Joanna MacDonald just after he had left Havers's office, telling him that she had been speaking with the NCA about his visit. They wanted to talk to him while he was in London and see if they could share information. She had no idea it was going to be Burgess who turned up. Banks doubted that she even knew him. But Banks wasn't greatly surprised. Burgess had a habit of turning up when you least expected him— which was, perhaps, when you should *most* expect him. He and Banks had many points of difference, but they got along well and never let a good argument get in the way of the job.

He had also received a call from Gerry Masterson to inform him that DC Cabbot and Doug had got two names of possible bolt gun thieves out of Stirwall's—Ulf Bengtsson and Kieran Welles. Annie believed that Welles was their best bet, but the team was working on tracking both of them down.

Gerry also informed him that the Kent police had phoned to report that Morgan Spencer's removal van had been found on some waste-land on the outskirts of Dover. Inside were a Yamaha motorcycle and a Deutz-Fahr Agrotron tractor. Both intact. The whole lot was being shipped up to North Yorkshire as soon as the locals could get transport organized. That came as a shock to Banks, but he filed it away for later.

"Well, it's good to see you down here again," said Burgess. "It's been too long. When was the last time? That gay spook murder, wasn't it?"

"Probably," said Banks. "I forget the exact occasion. You're well, I take it?"

Burgess looked more gaunt than usual, the belly that had been hanging over his belt the last time they met trimmed down, and the extra flab gone from his face, making his cheeks look hollow.

"Don't let appearances deceive you, old mate. I've been working out at the gym. Given up the evil weed—Tom Thumbs, that is—and cut back on the demon alcohol. A little. You should try it. I had a minor health scare a while back, meant they had to shove a camera up my arse on a stick. I must say, though, with the drugs they give you if you go private, you can't feel a thing. You can imagine my surprise when I found a note stuffed in my shoe afterward saying, 'I hope you enjoyed it as much as I did.' Still, such is life."

"It was a false alarm?"

"It wasn't the big C, if that's what you mean. A small operation soon put things right, and now it's the healthy life for me." He knocked back some lager.

Banks felt relieved to hear that Burgess's problem wasn't serious, and he realized that the man sitting opposite him was one of his few remaining friends, one of the few people he cared about, though he would never admit it. "It's that stuff'll kill you," he said, pointing to Burgess's quickly vanishing pint of lager. "All chemicals. You want something like this." He held up his own pint. "Organic. Good for you. Or red wine."

"Same old Banksy, it's good to see." Burgess clapped his hands together. "Anyway, enough of this banter. Let's get down to brass tacks, as you lot say up north."

Banks hadn't heard anyone say that for a long time, except on television satires of northern life, but he let it go by. It was best to do that with many of the things Burgess said, he usually found. "Montague Havers?" Banks said.

"Yes, good old Monty."

"Why is he still walking around free?"

"Because he's a devious bastard," said Burgess. "All right, I know. I'll say it before you do. I'm a devious bastard, too, and not above bending the rules when it suits my purposes. You and I, we're from the same side of the tracks. We should understand each other. Thing is, Monty is, too."

"But he's a crook. And he changed his name because he thought it sounded more posh."

"It was a business decision. Monty grew up in the East End, like me, when it really was the East End, if you know what I mean. Thing is, when Thatcher started putting the economy to rights and commies like you went off feeling sorry for the poor fucking miners and electricians and factory workers, some of us knew a gift horse when it kicked us in the face, and we took our opportunities where we found them. There were billion-pound privatizations, hostile takeovers, corporate raids, asset stripping. And very few rules. Great times, and open to all. You didn't have to be from Eton and Oxbridge to make it back then. All you had to do was throw out your lefty social conscience— something you could never do, old mate. Those City lads were practically printing money, and they came from the same place as you and me. The mean streets. Shitty council estates. Comprehensives. If I hadn't already been busy climbing the greasy pole of policing, I might have been one of them, myself."

"I'm sure you would have made a lot more money. But things have changed."

"Tell me about it. Bunch of wankers we've got in there nowadays couldn't manage a kid's piggy bank, let alone a fucking economy. But that's not our concern. If you want to understand people like Monty Havers, you've got to understand people like me. The barrow boys made good. We were young, we were quick-witted and we were cocky. Not a shade of shit different from the criminal classes you might say, and you'd be right. But we had vim and vision and stamina and, by God, that's what the country needed. We got things done. So what happened to them when the dream ended? Well, I imagine some of them were damaged for good by the lifestyles of excess, same way as the hippies who'd taken too much LSD. But the others, like Havers, wormed their way into legitimate businesses, like specialized banking, and learned the ropes and how to get around them. Like I said, we were bright and the rule book was out of the window. Now, if you ask me, there's not a hell of a lot of difference between most of your merchant banks and organized crime, so it shouldn't come as such a big surprise that Havers is bent. Thing is, he's learned his tradecraft. He knows intimately the ins and outs of money laundering, invisible transfers, hidden accounts, offshore shelters, shell companies and so forth. He's always one step ahead of the legislation. That's why we know him only by his contacts, and by what they do. Some of them do very unsavory things, but Havers never puts his name to anything that can get back to him, never gets his hands dirty. He knows the people who can ship you anything anywhere anytime, for a price. He knows where you can get your hands on fake passports, phony bills of lading, thirteen-year-old virgins, you name it. He knows which palms need to be greased, and he might supply the funds—from somewhere squeaky clean—but he doesn't do the greasing. See what I mean? He stays out of the world he helps to run, even socially. You'll find him at the Athenaeum, not some dive in a Soho basement."

"I suppose he just had to become a Montague, then. But why the rural crime? I mean stolen tractors, for crying out loud, when according to you Havers could make a million just by the blink of an eyelid. Where does that fit in?"

"Because there's a market for them, old son. Multiply one tractor by ten, twenty, whatever. Do you know how much those things are worth? They're not going to peasants in Bolivia, you know, Banksy. They're going to people who can afford them. It's not just tractors and combines and pitchforks and what have you, it's forklifts, backhoes, Land Rovers, Range Rovers, along with all the Beemers and Mercs from the chop shops. Seems country people are often a lot more sloppy about security than us city dwellers. It's easy pickings, and when you have the know-how to get it from A to B, you've got it made."

"There are a lot of people to pay off."

"Peanuts. I know where you can get an arm broken for twenty quid, two for thirty."

"Twenty quid? Them's London prices, then?"

Burgess laughed. "Yes. I'm sure you can get it done for half in Yorkshire." He finished his lager and set the glass heavily on the table.

"Another round?" Banks asked.

"Don't mind if I do."

Banks walked back to the bar. It wasn't too busy. He thought over what Burgess had said as he waited to get served. If Havers were even half as smart as Burgess gave him credit for, he would be very hard to bring down. On the other hand, Banks thought he'd put the wind up him by the end of their meeting. For one thing, he had let him know that the police knew the names of pretty much everyone they thought was involved. That ought to be cause for concern, even if two of them were dead and Havers believed none of the survivors would dare talk. Whether he would be cocky enough to carry on business as usual remained to be seen. In a way, it wasn't so much him as the northern branch of his operation that Banks was interested in, especially the person who had killed and cut up Morgan Spencer. If Beddoes was involved, Banks would also make sure he went down one way or another. Someone would talk, given the option of a softer deal.

When it was his turn, he ordered the same again. The barmaid had an American accent and hennaed hair. She smiled sweetly at Banks as she pulled the pint, but he didn't think she was coming on to him. It was just her style. Besides, she was young enough to be his daughter. Which reminded him, he had to get in touch with Tracy. They'd planned to go and see Brian's band the Blue Lamps at the Sage next week. Banks was excited about that, seeing his daughter and watching his son perform on a prestigious stage. He'd call her tonight when he got back home. If he got back. But he had to, he realized. There was so much to be done up there, he couldn't desert the team and enjoy an overnight in London. There were plenty of trains, and he wasn't far from Kings Cross. This would have to be his last pint.

Burgess was jotting something down in his notebook when Banks got back with the drinks. He put it away. "I knew Havers when I was growing up," he said. "Not very well—I'm a bit older than him—but I knew him. He lived in the next street over. That's why I'm taking more of an interest than usual, I suppose."

"Ever heard of a John Beddoes?" Banks asked.

"I can't say as I have."

"It was his tractor got stolen, but now I'm wondering if he isn't in it with Havers. They were close mates back in those good old days you were just talking about."

"It's entirely possible," Burgess said. "But he'd hardly steal his own tractor, or get someone to do it, would he?"

"No. I'm working on that. It's just been found outside Dover, so that should make him happy."

"That's a bit odd, isn't it?"

"I agree. The thieves must have run into some sort of a snag and had to abandon it. I imagine it was due to ship from somewhere near there. But we think the whole operation was a maverick job, or at least it's rated as one. A young lad called Morgan Spencer acting alone. It was probably what got him killed."

"He's the boy who was killed with the stun gun and cut up, right? I heard about that. No, the name hasn't come up in any of our investigations."

"Very low level, I should imagine," said Banks. "You had a murder with a similar MO some time ago, if I'm not mistaken?"

"A bolt gun? Yes. Very nasty. Polish bloke. It wasn't a case I worked on at all closely, but I took an interest. Anything out of the ordinary like that gets my attention. As far as I know, it was never solved. Maybe I'll have another look at the case file. Something might leap out. Didn't they find some prints?"

"They did. I've got someone working on them now, comparing

them with partials we found at the hangar. But if anything does jump out at you, let me know."

"Will do."

"We've got a couple of suspects in the theft of a penetrating bolt gun from a big abattoir up north. We're trying to track them down, of course, but any help you can offer . . ."

Burgess took his notebook out again. "Give me their names."

"Ulf Bengtsson and Kieran Welles."

"Scandinavian is he, this Bengtsson?"

"Swedish."

"Thought so. If my memory serves me well, he's dead. I'll check, but I'm pretty sure his name was Ulf something or other. Everyone knew him as 'The Swede.'"

"Oh?"

"Don't get your hopes up, Banksy. It was natural causes. He was sleeping rough, had a serious alcohol problem. One morning some tourists found him under a bridge near the Embankment. Lights out. Liver and heart failure."

"How do you know this? Surely there wasn't an investigation?"

"I try to keep up. It's my city. As a matter of fact, hypothermia was involved. It had been a very cold night, and questions were asked in Parliament. How could our society . . . blah, blah, blah . . . You ask me, people want to sleep out on the streets and beg instead of getting a decent job and somewhere safe and warm to kip down, good luck to them."

"You haven't changed much, have you?"

Burgess winked. "Governments come and governments go, but basic truths remain the same."

"And so does Dirty Dick Burgess. And the other? Kieran Welles."

"Don't know anything about him. Kieran's an Irish name, though, isn't it?"

"Sounds like it to me."

"Hmm. I'll see what I can find out." He sipped his drink. "Sometimes it's like pissing in the wind, this job. Christ, don't you long for the old days, Banksy? You were down here then. Out on the mean streets. You had a bit of a reputation. Took no prisoners, as I remember."

"Different times."

"Too true. But let's not get all nostalgic, hey?" He hoisted his glass and they clinked. "To old friends."

"You sentimental bastard."

"Go carefully," Burgess said. "I mean it. People like Havers, and perhaps even your Beddoes, for all I know, look harmless on the surface. They'd run a mile if you raised your fist to them. But they don't have to deal with that end of the business themselves. They use people like your Kieran Welles, and they don't care what damage they do. Do you think Welles is behind the killing?"

"Off the cuff?" said Banks. "I don't know Kieran Welles—don't even know if he was the one who stole the bolt gun. All I know about him is that he was cruel to animals in an abattoir, if that doesn't take the biscuit. There's a couple of others—Ronald Tanner, who threatened a witness, and a mate of his called Carl Utley, who we think might have driven the van with the tractor away from the scene and dumped it outside Dover. We're looking for him. I don't rate Tanner. He's a bruiser. He's never worked in an abattoir, and we've found no trace of a bolt gun at his house."

"He could have dumped the body."

"Oh, he's involved somehow, but the impression he gives me is that he's just low-level muscle. Bruises and fractures, maybe, but not whack jobs, to use the correct parlance. I hope not, anyway. We had to cut him loose today."

"Why?"

"Cassandra Wakefield."

"Bloody hell! Is that gloriously shaggable bitch still putting criminals back on the streets?"

"Indeed she is."

"Talking about shaggable, that DI MacDonald you've got up north on Operation Hawk is quite tasty, isn't she?"

"You know her?"

"We've met at a couple of meetings. Bit frosty at first acquaintance, but those types often turn out to be the loudest screamers. I'm not treading on your toes, am I, Banksy? She did mention your name. But I hear you'd got a bit of young Italian crumpet on the go."

Banks smiled. He hadn't heard the word "crumpet" for years. Trust Burgess. "I have a girlfriend, yes, and her family's Italian. I worked with Joanna MacDonald when she was Inspector Joanna Passero, that's all. Before her divorce. She was in Professional Standards then."

"Bloody hell. Now you come to mention it, I can just see her doing that job."

"She didn't like it. She's happier now."

"A happy divorcée. Just friends, then?"

"Just friends."

"Even after that dirty weekend in Tallinn?"

Banks gave him a look. Burgess held up his hands and responded with the closest he could get to feigning innocence. "OK," he said. "I'll be in touch on the names and anything I can find out about your John Beddoes. And remember what I said. *Adiós, amigo,* and be careful out there."

Banks finished his pint and stood up. "I will."

IT WAS just after dark when Alex decided to nip to the mini supermarket down the street. She was out of milk for the breakfast cereal, needed bread for toast, and there was no white wine left. Ian was playing *Call of Duty,* legs crossed on the armchair with his game console, and he didn't want to stop while he was ahead. As the two of them, and their flat, were being watched over by the police, Alex knew there was nothing to worry about. They had said she was free to come and go as she pleased, to carry on as normal. She wouldn't see them, but they would be watching her. Even so, she felt a bit nervous leaving Ian alone when she put on her leather jacket and picked up her handbag. It was the first time she had been out after dark since her visit from the man they had identified as Ronald Tanner. And she had seen on the local news just an hour ago that he had been released from police custody that morning, despite the fingerprint and her identification from the VIPER screen. Alex couldn't really get her head around that. She knew criminals were always getting off, but this Tanner had so obviously *done it*. She guessed that the police were looking for more evidence, and she imagined they would be watching him very closely. He certainly wouldn't want to give them any reason to put him back in jail by coming to visit her flat again.

Alex could hear hip-hop coming from one of the flats on the floor above as she walked along the balcony toward the lifts. She had never been able to understand hip-hop, though several friends and neighbors had tried to explain its virtues to her. She'd been to raves when she was a teenager, danced all night to pulsating, repetitive electropop, even popped Ecstasy on one or two occasions; she was open-minded, but she had never taken to hip-hop, even when it wasn't grime, or using ugly words to describe women and the things men should do to them. Still, she knew the kids up there, and they were OK. It was probably just a matter of taste. She liked Beyoncé and Rihanna; they liked Tinie Tempah and Dizzee Rascal.

The lift was working, thank God, though the smell of piss was as bad as ever. It was just as likely down to the incontinent old geezer on the tenth floor as it was to kids. He'd been told often enough but he said he couldn't help himself. It was quiet out on the street, the lamps giving out that eerie late twilight glow, just a few people walking about, heads down, the smell of someone's cigarette drifting on the damp night air, mingling with the hot grease and acrid hint of vinegar from the fish-and-chips shop. She glanced around but could see no signs of her police watchers. They were being very discreet. She stuck her hands deep in her jacket pockets, bag slung over her shoulder bumping against her hip. She could see the lights of the supermarket about fifty yards ahead, just across the street, could see people coming and going. She passed a woman who lived on the same floor as her, and they said hello. The night was still and cold. Cold enough to freeze the puddles, Alex thought, with a shiver.

The automatic doors slid open and she was bathed in the warmth and bright fluorescent lights of the supermarket. She picked up a basket and started wandering the aisles. There were a few other customers in, a mother trying to control two unruly children, a young couple loading up on beer and crisps, an old man in a woolly cardigan and a flat hat browsing the magazines.

Alex had just turned at the end of the aisle, opposite the frozen-goods section, when a hand came from behind, covered her mouth and pulled her back around the corner.

BANKS DROVE out to see Beddoes as soon as he got back to Swainsdale. The farmyard was frozen and rutted, and he wished he'd taken a car from the pool instead of the Porsche, though it managed the bumps well enough.

Inside the farmhouse was as neat and nicely appointed as before: only the best furniture and antique porcelain on shelves on the wall. The Bang & Olufsen was silent, and Beddoes himself was relaxing in an armchair drinking coffee and reading a book about economics, a subject Banks had never understood, as Patricia Beddoes led him in. He hadn't seen her before and noted that she was an attractive woman, a good decade or more younger than her husband, with a few sharp angles and a slightly hard, businesslike manner. It was hard to imagine her and AC Gervaise discussing Jonathan Franzen or Kiran Desai over a glass of wine and a plate of cheese and crackers.

"DCI Banks," said Beddoes, putting down his book and coffee and standing up to shake hands. "Nice to see you again. I hope you come bearing good news."

"We've found your tractor, if that's what you mean."

Beddoes's jaw dropped. His wife grabbed his arm. "John! That's wonderful news."

"You have?" said Beddoes. "I don't know what to say."

"You might like to ask *where* we found it."

"I would have imagined it in some Eastern European country by now."

"Dover."

"You mean it never left England?"

"Apparently not."

"Isn't that unusual?"

"Very."

"So what do you think happened?"

"We don't know yet. Clearly something went wrong with their plans."

"Lucky for me. I never thought I'd see the blessed thing again. When can I have it back?"

"Not for a while yet," said Banks. "There's a lot of tests we have to do."

"You mean fingerprints and stuff like that?"

"Yes. Stuff like that. On first inspection, however, it appears to have been wiped clean."

"Oh? Well, wouldn't you expect that, if the thieves had to abandon it and scarper. They wouldn't want to risk leaving their fingerprints behind."

"They can't have been in much of a hurry then, can they?"

"I suppose not. It's a real puzzle."

"Yes, but I'm sure we'll get to the bottom of it. Our fingerprints experts are *very* good."

"Do have any idea *when* I might get it back, how long your tests will take?"

"Do you need it now?"

"I *am* a farmer. If this damn weather clears up there'll be a lot of field work to do."

"Yes, of course. I forgot." Banks leaned forward. "Could be a while. You see, the problem is that technically it's evidence in a murder investigation, perhaps two murder investigations, and we're also examining it in conjunction with the lorry it was transported in and the motorcycle that accompanied it. Morgan Spencer's lorry and motorcycle, as it happens. And Morgan Spencer was murdered last Sunday morning near Drewick, as I'm sure you've heard."

"Yes . . . I . . . I didn't know there was any connection. I already told you I don't know this Spencer person. Do you think he could be the one who stole it?"

"We think he might have been part of the gang that took it, but that's as far as it goes. There's still an awful lot to sort out."

"Yes, I suppose there is. Well . . . Pat, darling, do you think you might fetch a cup of coffee for DCI Banks. I think there's some left. It ought to be fresh."

"Of course." Mrs. Beddoes went into the kitchen and brought back a tray with coffee, milk and sugar. Banks took his black, so he simply picked up the cup and thanked her. It was good coffee. Rich but not bitter, strong but not nerve-jangling. Probably cost an arm and a leg, he thought.

"Is there anything else I can help you with?" said Beddoes.

"Perhaps. Do you know a man called Montague Havers?"

"I can't say as I do, no."

Surely Havers had rung up Beddoes as soon as Banks had left the London office? Probably told him to admit to knowing him but to play their relationship down. "You might have known him as Malcolm Hackett."

"Yes, of course. Malcolm. We worked together in the City years ago. Why has he changed his name?"

"He thought Montague Havers sounded a bit more upmarket for the kind of work he does."

"That's typical Malcolm. Always was a bit of a snob. What's he up to these days?"

"Haven't you spoken with him recently?"

"We haven't been in touch in years. Not since the late eighties."

"I see. He's in investment banking. Specializing in international investment. That's his profession, at any rate. Personally, he's also interested in property development."

"But what has Malcolm got to do with my tractor?"

Banks leaned forward in his chair. "I was coming to that," he went on. "Leaving the various thefts, threats and murderers aside for the time being, I found out an interesting thing about Mr. Havers."

"You have my attention."

"Havers has invested in the abandoned airfield near Drewick, where Morgan Spencer was murdered. You may have heard it's slated for redevelopment as a shopping center. Should be quite lucrative, I'd think, in the long run."

"I've heard of it."

"Well, we think—I'd say we're pretty much convinced, thanks to the forensics buffs—that the hangar was used as an exchange point for stolen farm equipment on its way from North Yorkshire, and perhaps points north, to Eastern Europe."

"I see. Including my tractor?"

"We think so."

"That is quite a coincidence."

"Yes, it is. And this Montague Havers—Malcolm Hackett, as was—claims that he and you were best buddies in the eighties. You worked for the same firm of stockbrokers, drank in the same pubs, maybe even shared the same women, for all I know. They were heady times, and you were young lads on the way up fast."

"I'd hardly say we were best mates, and it was a long time ago. We did have some good times together, though."

"Funny, that," said Banks. "He didn't appear to remember you at all until I jogged his memory."

"Well, as I said, we weren't that close."

Banks sat back in his chair and made a note in his notebook. Beddoes didn't seem to like the look of that. "When he did remember, he said he used to call you 'Bedder' Beddoes. Is that right?"

Beddoes blushed and coughed. "Please, Chief Inspector."

"It's all right," said Patricia, in a voice like tempered steel. "That was long before John and I met. I never imagined he was a monk. I'm sure he had many romantic exploits." She paused. "I know I did."

"Look," said Beddoes. "What does this have to do with anything? You come here making remarks about my personal life, raking up the past. I haven't seen or heard from Malcolm Hackett in years."

"Are you sure about that?"

"Of course I am. Do you think I'm lying?"

"I'm not sure," said Banks. "There are too many coincidences, and we detectives don't like coincidences."

"Then you'll just have to learn to live with them like the rest of us." Beddoes stood up. "And now, if you don't mind, it's late. I think it's time you left."

"Of course." Banks got out of his armchair. "Do you know Caleb Ross?"

"Know him, no. But I know who he is. Was. You already know that. All the local farmers were acquainted with him. Look, you said leaving aside the thefts, threats and murder. A while ago, you said that. What do you mean? What has any of it got to do with me?"

"Nothing, I shouldn't think," said Banks. "Has it?"

"Of course not."

"Just a few more names to conjure with before I go, Mr. Beddoes. Kieran Welles, Ronald Tanner and Carl Utley. Ring any bells?"

"None at all."

"Thought not. But if you should suddenly remember that you did know one of them, no matter how long ago, or how well, do let me know. Thanks for your time, Mr. Beddoes, and thanks for the coffee, Mrs. Beddoes. Good evening."

And Banks left, smiling. That cat was well and truly among the pigeons now. As he turned out of sight of the farm, he pulled up next to a car parked in a lay-by and rolled down his window. "Keep an eye on them, Doug," he said, to DC Doug Wilson, who was sitting behind the wheel. "But don't get too close."

"No problem, guv," said Wilson, and wound up his window. Banks drove off.

ALEX'S HEART leaped into her throat and waves of panic swept through her. She was in a brightly lit supermarket, for crying out loud. There were people around. Why did no one come to her aid? This couldn't be happening. And where were the police? She tried to bite down on the hand over her mouth but she couldn't open it wide enough to engage her teeth. Finally he let go slowly, grasped her shoulder so hard it hurt and turned her around to face him. The hoodie confused her at first, but the eyes gave him away. It was Michael. She was looking at Michael. Her immediate desire was to hold him to her and never let him go, but her survival instincts took over. A young couple reached the end of the aisle and passed by them on the way to the next, hardly giving them a glance. She rubbed her shoulder. "That hurt."

"I'm sorry for the drama, love," Michael said in a quiet voice. "You never know how someone's going to react to a shock."

"Michael, you have to go. Right now. It's not safe."

"They can't look everywhere for me. And this is probably the last place they'd expect to find me. I've been careful. I've been watching, just waiting for a moment like this." They moved to the far back corner, by a rack of crisps. "I had to see you. I've missed you so much."

Alex ran her hands over his cheeks, tears in her eyes, and kissed him hard on the lips. "And I've missed you, too. More than I can say. I love you, Michael. But you really must hurry. You don't understand."

Michael smiled that heart-melting smile of his, but Alex noticed the hint of puzzlement and fear in his eyes. "I don't understand what?"

"It's not *you* they're watching."

The smile disappeared. "I don't—"

It all seemed to happen at once. A loud voice shouted for everyone to leave the shop as two armed police officers in protective gear appeared around the end of the nearest aisle. "Armed police!" a stern voice shouted. "Don't move. Stay where you are."

Alex cowered in the corner, knocking over the rack of the crisps. It acted as a signal for Michael to dash off down the aisle past the checkout. Alex couldn't move; her muscles were locked with fear. She wanted to shout after him, but she couldn't find her voice. The police officers didn't seem overly concerned about Michael running off. They put away their guns. One of them approached Alex and took her arm firmly, saying in a gentle voice, "Come on, love. Come with us. You'll be all right now."

She wanted to tell them she was already all right. That all she wanted to do was stay with Michael and go back to Ian, and the rest of the world could leave them alone. Slowly, she let herself be led, surprised that she could even walk. She heard a commotion at the front of the store, more racks being knocked over, crashes, loud voices.

When she got to the checkout area she could see flashing lights outside, through the windows. Then she saw Michael, his hands cuffed behind his back, being shoved into the back of a police car, one of the officers pushing his head down, just like they do on television. The supermarket doors slid open. She called his name, and he looked over his shoulder at her, such a desolate, lost expression, she thought. She just wanted to take him in her arms again, but the next moment he was gone, and the stern young policeman who had her in his grasp was talking about taking her home. She realized as she walked limply by his side, still in his friendly but firm grip, that she hadn't even had a chance to buy anything. She had no milk, no bread, no wine, and she hadn't the heart to go back. Next to Michael and Ian, she realized, she wanted to see Annie Cabbot. Wanted to rage at her, blame her, and to ask her for comfort and help, ask her to explain what was happening.

14

WINSOME AND GERRY MASTERSON WERE THE ONLY ones left in the squad room that Saturday morning. Annie Cabbot was with Alex Preston and her son, and Doug Wilson was back watching the Beddoes farm after being relieved by a PC overnight. Gerry had her hair tied back in a ponytail, her neck craned toward the computer screen and her fingers on the keyboard. Whatever it was she was up to, Winsome thought, it was certainly intriguing her.

Winsome looked again at Caleb Ross's delivery schedule spread out on her desk, along with her notes from her visits to the farms where he had collected on the morning of his death. She couldn't come up with any point at which a substitution could have easily been made or an extra load added. All the farmers had stood in the yard with Caleb and chatted and had helped him load the bags in the van. The bags themselves had been locked overnight, or longer, in secure buildings. There was nothing extra, nothing last moment, nothing suspicious, nothing that appeared to have been tampered with.

So where had Ross picked up his load of human remains?

Winsome knew she was missing something, and it irked her. Ross had started his round at nine o'clock and had visited ten farms before his crash at five past two in the afternoon. The distances between the farms accounted for most of the time, and the job itself, along with the few minutes of gossip at each stop, seemed to account for the rest. Except that, however often she added it up, Winsome was left with about one hour unaccounted for. She had assumed that Caleb must have stopped for lunch at one of the many watering holes along the way, whether it was discouraged or not, but inquiries at all the pubs he could possibly have called at for his giant Yorkshire puddings yielded not one positive response. They knew him, but they hadn't seen him that day.

Then she remembered as her finger touched the last name on the list. Mr. Wythers, of Garsley Farm, the last place Ross had called at before his accident, had let drop in passing that Ross had refused a cup of tea and a biscuit because he said he had just eaten his lunch. Winsome had checked all the places on his route, and he hadn't eaten in a pub, so he must have taken a sandwich and flask with him, as Vaughn said he often did. Assuming that Ross had already eaten before he arrived at Wythers's farm, which he left just after one o'clock, what was he doing between one and two? Garsley was the end of the road, as Winsome had seen for herself. "Beyond this point be monsters," she thought, remembering the old maps on the classroom walls at school. Well, perhaps there were. Or perhaps there was at least one monster who shot a young man with a bolt pistol and skinned and dressed him like a slaughtered lamb.

She headed for the station library, where they kept the Ordnance Survey maps of the county.

Alex: You've got to talk to them, Michael, tell them everything. A clean slate, it's the only way.

Michael: I can't. Don't you see? Whatever I say, they're bound to pin something on me. I've got a record. I'd be a perfect fit-up. Case closed.

A: Not if you tell the truth. I've spent a bit of time with one of them. Annie Cabbot. She was looking after me when you were away and . . . you know . . . that man came. She's not bad. She helped me. Talk to her. You'll get a fair deal.

M (snorts): That's what I love about you, Al. All the knocks life's given you, and you're still the eternal optimist. Pollyanna.

A: Don't, Michael. You know I don't like it when you call me that. And I'm not. I'm being realistic. If you've done nothing wrong, you've got nothing to fear from them. It's the others they're after, the ones that killed Morgan, that stole Beddoes's tractor. Not you. You were just in the wrong place at the wrong time. You saw something you shouldn't have.

M: You can say that again. And heard. But try and get them to believe that. Especially after I ran. (He reaches out and takes her hand. No physical object passes between them.) I'm sorry. It's my fault that man came and hurt you. I couldn't bear it if anything happened to you.

A (smiles): Nothing's going to happen, silly. Not if you tell them the truth. They already got the man who came to the flat. You can help them catch the others.

M: But they had to let him go, didn't they? I mean, he's still out there, on the streets. Maybe there is a court order against him coming anywhere near the flat again, I don't know, and maybe he is on bail until his trial, but that doesn't stop people like him, people like them. He'll be back.

A: And a fat lot of use you'll be if you're still in here. Besides, the police will get them.

M: And let them go, and lock up people like me. (Shakes his head.) No, love. My best chance is to keep shtum. Say nothing. Get a good brief. If I do that, they've got nothing on me.

A: Don't be childish. You're acting like a fool. You can't keep silent forever.

M: It's my right.

A: But they hold it against you now. I've heard that. And you know we can't afford a good lawyer. If you don't explain yourself and then you try to get out of it later, it looks bad in court.

M: It doesn't matter.

A: Don't be so negative. (She squeezes his hand.) Look, let's put all this behind us. A brand-new start. Me, you and Ian. We can go on a holiday or something first. I'm sure Mr. Evans at the agency will give us a deal on something. Then we can move if you want, a new life. Somewhere else. By the sea.

M: But we're just getting started on this life.

A (snatches back her hand): Oh, for God's sake, Michael. Anyone would think you didn't want us to be together again, that you didn't want things to be right again. Sometimes I even wonder whether you *weren't* up to something, whether you *don't* have something to hide. Is that why you don't want to talk to them? Afraid they'll find out your secret?

M: I don't have any secrets. I just think they'll do me for it anyway. That's what they're like. People like me, we're scum to them.

A: You're doing it again, behaving like a child.

M: And you're being all Pollyanna.

A: Pollyanna didn't get such a great deal, you know.

M: Whatever.

A: Stop sulking. Do you want to get out of here and be with us again? Wherever we are, it doesn't matter to me, as long as the three of us are together.

M: I . . .

A: Do you?

M: Of course I do. You know I do.

A: Then act like it. Talk to them.

M (hangs head. Seconds pass. Finally he looks up again, into Alex's eyes): All right. (resignedly) All right, I'll talk to them. I'll tell them what I know.

A (takes his hand): I'll stand by you, Michael. Whatever happens, we'll stand by you, Ian and me.

M (nods): I said I'll talk to them.

END

Banks turned off the computer display. After letting Michael Lane stew in a holding cell overnight, he and Annie had granted his request that he be allowed to talk to Alex and had listened to their conversation. Now they wanted to review the video recording for body language before starting the interview.

"Well," said Banks, leaning back in his office chair. "If they've got some kind of secret code, I'd have to say it's a damn good one. I didn't see anything in there that struck me as suspicious."

"Me, neither," said Annie. "Though I should imagine they knew we'd be listening, if not watching, too. It's hardly a hidden camera."

"True. But it didn't look like acting to me. He's obviously terrified. For himself, of course, but for her and the kid, too."

"Alex and Ian."

"What I meant. Sometimes he seems more afraid of us than of them."

"Seems reasonable for him to be," said Annie. "We can be scary. Everyone knows we're evil bastards who go around fitting up innocent people to fudge the crime statistics."

Banks smiled. "Of course. I'd forgotten."

"Alex already knows what to be afraid of. I'll bet her finger still hurts."

"He knows what they're capable of, too, if he witnessed Morgan Spencer's murder."

"Terry Gilchrist saw a car matching the description of Michael Lane's Peugeot driving away from the scene."

"Which also means he could have done it."

"Oh, come on, Alan. You're playing devil's advocate for the hell of it. Where's that famous gut instinct of yours? That kid's no killer."

Banks scratched his chin. He needed a shave. He had gone a couple of days without. His gut instinct did tell him that Michael Lane hadn't killed anyone, Lane could help them find out who had and his girlfriend had persuaded him to talk. Now they had to act.

"OK," said Banks. "We send Gerry Masterson over to babysit Alex Preston, and we go in with an open mind. We don't waste time throwing accusations at him. All right?"

"Fine with me," said Annie.

"And Alex and Ian are our trumps. You saw the two of them there; he'd do anything for her. Even lie."

"Look," said Annie, "maybe he helped Morgan occasionally. I don't know. But are we going after him for that, or are we after the people who killed Spencer?"

"Mainly the latter, of course. But we'll take what we can get."

Annie stood up. "Fine. I'm ready."

Banks followed suit. "Let's go, then."

THE LIBRARY at Eastvale Police HQ wasn't much more than a standard-size office with a few bookshelves mostly full of law reference books and a desk and chair. There was no librarian, and everyone was responsible for reshelving whatever reference they had used. As a result, the shelves were chaotically arranged, and it was hard to find anything. Winsome sometimes even wondered how many of her colleagues knew the alphabet. The library did, however, boast a magnificent selection of local Ordnance Survey maps in just about every scale you could imagine.

Winsome knew she could access maps on her computer, that digital was all the rage these days, but she still preferred the real thing: the well-worn folds, the thick and serious texture of the older cloth maps, the colors, contours, dots and dashes. She had a strong memory of the detailed map of the Springfield area on the wall of her father's office back in Jamaica, showing just about every homestead. Winsome could still remember gazing at that map as a child and naming in her mind the people who lived in every marked dwelling. She had learned to read other maps only later, in the potholing club at university, and it was a skill that occasionally came in useful in the course of her work. Homicide and Major Crimes covered the whole of North Yorkshire, as opposed to the smaller patch of the old Western Area, and that meant a lot of moorland and open countryside as well as a few larger towns, such as Harrogate and Scarborough. She certainly couldn't name everyone who lived at every farm, but the two-and-a-half-inch-to-a-mile map should show her some possibilities as to where Caleb Ross may have been during the missing hour before his death.

With the map unfolded and covering the table, she stood and leaned over it, pinpointing Garsley Farm with the magnifying glass that hung on a chain from the table. That was Ross's last stop, only about a fifteen-minute drive from Belderfell Pass. She had driven that road just yesterday, and there was nothing on it to detain anyone: no houses, no farm, no shops, no pub. She also ruled out everywhere east of the farm. If Ross had wanted to make a longer stop anywhere there, he would most likely have done so *before* visiting Mr. Wythers to avoid retracing his tracks. She concentrated on the western and northern moorlands.

There wasn't much to see. She could follow the heights of the various mountains from the way the contour lines grew closer, traced the dotted lines of footpaths that seemed to disappear in the middle of nowhere, spotted ancient stone circles, deep gullies, old riverbeds, abandoned lead mines and slate quarries. She saw Woadly Edge, which she knew to be a rock face rising steeply at a right angle from the landscape and framing an entrance to the cave system she had explored on numerous occasions. She knew the place well and didn't remember any buildings in the vicinity, which was why the tiny words "High Point Farm" caught her attention. When she looked more closely at the map, the contours showed it was hidden from Woadly Edge and the access road the club had used by a small hill, perhaps a drumlin left by the retreating glacier thousands of years ago. In fact, the farm was set in a hollow all of its own, a sort of dimple in the landscape, or so it seemed on the map. It was odd to call a farm in a hollow High Point, but then Winsome realized the hollow itself was on fairly high ground.

Carefully, Winsome scoured the map within the range she estimated Ross could have driven in the time he had, perhaps picked up an unauthorized load, and stopped for a brief chat, then made it to the point on Belderfell Pass where he met his death. High Point Farm was the only place that fit the bill. It hadn't been on Ross's official pickup list, but that didn't mean he hadn't had business of his own there. Ross smoked marijuana, Winsome remembered, and there were plenty of hydroponic growers tucked away in the rolling dales and remote moorland. Maybe High Point Farm was such a place.

A quick check of the land registry, also kept in the library, revealed that High Point Farm was owned by one Kenneth Atherton, a name unfamiliar to her.

A quick jolt of excitement throbbing through her veins, she went back to the squad room. Gerry was gone, so Winsome left a brief note on her desk, checked her mobile batteries and left the building.

"I SUPPOSE you were listening in back there, when Alex and I were talking," said Michael Lane. They were in a different interview room, and Banks and Annie sat opposite him at the battered metal table. He didn't look much the worse for his few days of sleeping rough, Banks thought, a stubbly beard and tangled hair that needed a good wash and brush being about the only obvious signs. He was a handsome kid, and he looked mature for his age, though he still had the aura of youth about him. Banks could understand what Alex Preston, eternally hopeful, saw in him: perhaps someone she could change and forge a future with. Someone who might lack ambition and wealth but who would cherish her and treat her with kindness and love. Someone who would look after her and Ian. Wouldn't we all want someone like that?

They had already cautioned Lane, who had refused a legal aid solicitor since his talk with Alex, and set the tape machine running. "We were offering you a courtesy by allowing you a few minutes with Alex Preston," Banks said. "We didn't have to do that. In fact, it's against regulations. We were just being nice."

"Sure."

"Can we proceed with the interview, Michael?" said Annie. "The sooner we get it over with, the sooner you can be with Alex and Ian again."

Lane studied her. "You're the one she talked about, aren't you?" he said. "Annie something?"

"DI Cabbot to you."

"Have it your way. She said you were all right."

"You'll have to make up your own mind about that, won't you? Why don't you start by telling us about what happened last Sunday morning at the abandoned airfield near Drewick?"

"You don't mess about, do you?"

"Michael," said Banks. "It won't do any good stalling or making offensive comments. It won't make things go any quicker. We have a few ideas of our own, and you might not like some of them, but here we're giving you a fair chance to tell us your version. Contrary to what you said earlier, nobody's going to 'fit you up' with anything you didn't do, and running away in itself is no crime unless you're running from a criminal act you committed."

"It doesn't mean you'll believe me, though, does it?"

"That remains to be seen. At the moment all I know is that you were observed fleeing a crime scene, and I'm on the verge of holding you for that, lacking any reasonable explanation. Only you can talk me out of it."

"I wasn't fleeing a crime scene!"

"What were you doing, then?"

"I was running for my life."

"That's better," said Banks. "Tell me what happened."

Lane appeared to go through a brief inner struggle with himself, apparent from his changing facial expressions and nervous twisting of a silver ring. "All right," he said finally. "Morgan Spencer was a sort of mate of mine. I mean, we weren't that close, didn't hang out or stuff like that. He was a few years older than me, and he liked to do the club scene in Leeds or Manchester or Newcastle. That's not my thing at all."

"So what did you do together?"

"Worked, mostly. Morgan's got a removal van, and I'd help him shift stuff for people. We'd have the occasional jar or pub lunch together."

"What sort of stuff did you move?"

Lane looked at Banks as if were backward. "Furniture, of course."

"OK, go on."

"And we did odd jobs around the dale. Bit of roofing, general fixing things up. He was good with motors, too, was Morgan."

"What else did you do to make a living?"

"I happen to be not bad at sheep shearing. It was something my dad taught me. I just seemed to pick it up easily. But Morgan was no good with animals."

"When did you last see Morgan before you went out to the hangar on Sunday morning?"

"Friday. We were doing some work on a barn out Lyndgarth way."

"Did you tell him that Beddoes was in Mexico?"

"Why would I do that?"

"So he could steal Beddoes's tractor. I'm sure you knew about the holiday, either from your dad, who was looking after Beddoes's farm, or from Alex. He booked the trip at the agency where she works. Did it come up in conversation, you know, idle chatter while you were working?"

"I might have mentioned it. It was a cold day. I might have said something about some lucky bastards getting to go to Mexico. But I had nothing to do with stealing the tractor."

If that was when Spencer had first heard about the Beddoes farm being empty, it explained why he had stolen the tractor so late in the week. If he'd known earlier and done it Monday or Tuesday, it would probably have been safe at its destination by the time Beddoes got back and missed it. As it was, it had ended up near Dover. "OK. Let's move on to Sunday morning."

"Right. Well, Alex was just getting ready to go to church with Ian. She's not really religious, like, but she thinks it's a good idea to bring him up right, you know, and he likes the Bible stories." Lane smiled to himself. "Probably the violent bits, like his video games. Anyway, Morgan texts me and says to meet him at the hangar, that he might need help with something."

"What sort of help? Did he mention the tractor?"

"No. He doesn't say. It's just a text, you know, not an explanation."

"What did you think he meant?"

"A removal job or something."

"Go on."

"Well, as I said, he's a sort of mate, and he's helped me out from time to time, so if he needed me in a bit of a hurry, I could hardly say no, could I?"

"Didn't you at least suspect that it might be something illegal?"

"No. Why should I?"

"Had you ever met him at the hangar before?"

"No. I knew where it was, like, but it wasn't somewhere I'd been. No reason."

"Go on."

"When I got there, I couldn't see his van or his bike, but there were a couple of cars I didn't recognize outside in the yard. I left my car just down the road, by the turnoff south of Drewick. That was the road someone must have seen me on later. It leads to the Thirsk road and the A19."

"Why did you leave your car there?"

"I don't know. Just a gut feeling. I didn't know who was there, did I?"

"But why would you be worried if you didn't suspect anything criminal was going on?"

"Something felt not quite right. And by the way Morgan talked sometimes."

"What way?"

"Like he was in on things, knew people."

"Criminals? Gangs?"

"That sort of thing, yeah. He talked big. Liked to impress. That gangsta rap stuff. Said he met people in the clubs, contacts, people who could help him if he helped them. He wanted to be a rap singer."

That was an oxymoron as far as Banks was concerned. "So you were nervous about who he was with, who might be in the cars, so you stopped short and made a silent approach?"

"That's right. I was being careful. Maybe he really did have gangsta friends."

"What kind of cars were in the yard?"

"There were two. An old Corsa and a red pickup truck."

Ronald Tanner drove a Corsa, Banks remembered. He didn't know who drove a red pickup truck. Montague Havers drove a BMW 3 Series, but they already knew he didn't arrive in the area until Sunday afternoon, after the deed had been done. The CSIs hadn't done very well with tire tracks from the crime scene, but they had got a couple of partial fingerprints, one of which was a close match to Ronald Tanner, but not good enough for court. Maybe the other matched whoever had driven the red pickup truck. One of them, Tanner or the mystery man, must have brought a passenger, because after Spencer's murder, three vehicles were driven away from the hangar compound. It also made sense that two of them held Spencer's arms while the third, perhaps Kieran Welles, shot him between the eyes with the bolt gun. He wondered whether they were expecting that, or did it surprise and shock them? Banks put his money on Tanner bringing Utley, the crooked ex-lorry driver they still hadn't found, and Welles driving the red pickup truck. "What did you find when you got to the hangar?" he asked Lane.

"I didn't get there, did I? You know how open it is there, on the airfield. They were all inside. I could hear voices, so I figured it was safe enough to creep up, using the cars for cover. Then the voices got louder, people shouting, arguing."

"Could you hear what they were saying?"

"Not at first. The voices got lost in the hangar."

"But later?"

"I started backing off. I mean, it sounded really bad. I didn't know if Morgan knew he was walking into something dangerous and wanted me to fight with him, or what, but I'm no fighter. I suppose I was torn. I mean, we were sort of mates, after all. I didn't like to think I was leaving him."

"But you were scared?"

Lane looked down at the table. "Yeah."

"How many voices were there?"

"I can't say. Mostly it was Morgan, and he was arguing with someone, protesting about something, and occasionally someone else would chip in. Maybe three altogether."

"So what did you do?"

"Like I said, I was backing off by then. I mean, if he was mixed up with a dangerous crowd, I thought they might have knives or something. I thought the best thing I could do was get away from there and call the police."

"But you didn't."

"No. I didn't get the chance."

"What happened?"

"The shouting stopped, and there was silence for a moment. Then I heard this explosion like . . . I don't know . . . It sounded as if someone was firing a gun. I legged it fast as I could. One of them looked out of the hangar. Maybe he'd heard me, or maybe he was just checking there was no one around. He shouted something, and two of them started chasing me."

"Did you get a look at them?"

"Are you joking? I was praying that rust heap of a car I had would start. Thank God it did. First try. Then I was away."

"Did they chase you?"

"I don't know. They didn't shoot at me, and I didn't look back. I mean I didn't see them when I checked the rearview mirror after a couple of miles, so I suppose they didn't know which direction I'd gone."

There was a pause, then Annie said, "I still don't understand, Michael. You'd got away. You thought Morgan might be hurt, or dead. You weren't involved. Yet you still didn't call the police. Why not?"

"It was what he said last, the bloke who was arguing with Morgan. Maybe the bloke who shot him, for all I know."

"What was that?" Annie asked.

"I don't know if—"

"Please answer DI Cabbot's question," said Banks.

Lane looked from one to the other, the fear obvious in his eyes. "He said, 'You've done it this time, haven't you, kid? You've gone too far. You've just gone and stolen the boss's fucking tractor.'"

15

W HEN WINSOME PULLED INTO THE LAY-BY UNDER
the shelter of bare trees just a couple of hundred yards above
High Point Farm to get the lie of the land, it was already beginning to
snow, white flakes swirling in the air, melting on the car windows, not
settling on the earth yet. The forecast promised several inches by
nightfall, and drifts in the high Pennines. Whatever she was going to
do, Winsome realized, she had better be quick about it.

She took her binoculars from the glove compartment and leaned her
elbows on the dry stone wall to steady her grip. As she brought the scene
into focus, she could see that there were four buildings in the hollow, a
small farmhouse, or cottage, a large barn with pens for animals attached
to one side and two smaller outbuildings for storage. It was a typical
Dales barn, part wood, part stone, and it seemed to be shut up tight, as
did the farmhouse. There were no signs of a car in the yard or drive,
though Winsome supposed one might be locked in one of the buildings. Nor was there any smoke coming from the chimney. He could
have electric heating, radiators or a storage heater. Gas was unlikely in
such a remote setting, but whoever lived there would surely have elec-
tricity. Though the building was registered to a Kenneth Atherton,
Winsome realized that he may well have rented it out to somebody else.
Was this where Caleb Ross stopped between Garsley Farm and Belderfell Pass? If so, why? Who lived there, his drug supplier or a killer?

No backup had arrived yet, so Winsome took out her mobile and tried to call the station. No signal. It was after noon, so she also had to ring Terry and postpone lunch. She thought of going back to Garsley Farm, where she had got a phone connection—and Wythers had a landline—but as High Point looked deserted, and help should be on the way, she thought she would take a quick look around first. She didn't expect any trouble. Most people were far more likely to try and lie their way out of compromising situations than use force against the police. Admit nothing and stick to your story seemed to be the code of most of the criminals Winsome had interviewed of late. Besides, she knew how to take care of herself.

She continued along the access road, turned down the drive and pulled up in the farmyard in front of the house. If anyone was at home, he would have heard her arrive.

The snow swirled around her as she walked up to the front door and knocked. Nobody answered. She waited, listening, hearing nothing but the wind howling around the buildings, snow blowing all around, her ears freezing. She knocked again. Still no answer. She tried the door, found it locked, and drew the line at breaking and entering. The wind was really gusting around the hollow now, and the snow was getting heavier. Winsome knew she would have to get out of there soon, before it started seriously drifting, or she'd never get back to Eastvale. She thought about Terry. He probably wouldn't forgive her for standing him up, and she couldn't blame him. She peered through the windows of the cottage. They were streaked and dirty. One of the curtain rods had come loose on one side and the moth-eaten curtain hung diagonally across, so she could look over it into the room. It was sparsely furnished, with a flagstone floor and a large empty fireplace. Dark and gloomy. No light showed, no signs of recent habitation at all. Perhaps Atherton, or whoever he was, had done a bunk already?

Winsome walked over toward the barn. The outside pens were caked with animals' feces, which Winsome could smell despite the near-zero temperature. She wasn't squeamish—growing up in rural Jamaica, you couldn't afford to be—but she wasn't an English farm girl, either, so the smell made her feel vaguely sick. The barn door wasn't locked, and when she opened it, the smell was even worse: feces first, but something else, something deep and rotten underlying it. She had no idea what it was. She felt for a light switch but couldn't find one.

With some light coming in from outside, her eyes became used to the semidark, and she could make out a channel running along the center of the barn, a hook dangling on a rope from an overhead rail that ran the length of the building, various pens that seemed somehow connected to the outside holding areas. It didn't take her long to figure out that she was in a small abattoir. When she turned to head back to her car, she saw a man's silhouette filling the doorway.

"Can I help you?"

He didn't completely block the doorway, but as long as he was standing there, Winsome knew she couldn't get past him. Where was Gerry? Hadn't her note been clear enough? Winsome cursed herself for a fool for not making a more serious attempt to call for backup before heading into the hollow, but she had really thought the place was deserted. Where had he been? Deliberately hiding from her? Why? How had he turned up here so silently? Now she was well and truly stuck. Brazen it out, girl, she told herself. Something her mother had never advised her to do.

She took out her warrant card and held it out. He wasn't close enough to read it, and he didn't move from the doorway. "DS Jackman, Eastvale CID," she said. It wasn't quite true, but she didn't like the idea of using the word "homicide" just at the moment. Remember, she told herself, you brought down "The Bull." You're famous for your dropkick that wasn't a dropkick. But the man before her didn't know about her fame, or he didn't care. Either way, it was unnerving how he just stood there, so calm, so relaxed.

"I take it you have a warrant for entering my property, then?" he said, expression not changing.

Winsome noticed a slight Irish accent. Northern, she thought, not the Republic. "Not exactly."

"Not exactly means not at all, I guess. That's a pity."

"Move away from the doorway and let me pass."

He stood his ground and cocked his head to one side. "And if I don't want to?"

"I'm warning you," she said, with more confidence than she felt. "Interfering with a police officer in the performance of her duty is a serious offense."

He laughed. "I haven't *interfered* with you at all. Not yet. It's trespassing, you know, what you're doing. The Lord tells us to forgive others their trespasses, but I'm not exactly a religious man. In America a person can shoot someone for trespassing on his property."

"Not a police officer. And we're not in America."

"That just means you ain't got no gun," he drawled, in an imitation American accent.

He started to move toward her, but not before shutting the door and slipping a bolt home. He pulled a chain, which Winsome had missed, to switch on the lights. They revealed the abattoir in all its gruesome glory, the floor and channel coated in congealed blood and slippery bits of innards, what might have been a kidney or a piece of liver, bloodstains on the walls. She took it all in at a glance, then her eyes fixed on the man.

He looked like one of those wholesome blond farm boys from Minnesota or Wisconsin she had seen in American movies, wearing jeans and a checked shirt, a shock of blond hair almost covering his left eye. Almost. He ought to be chewing on a blade of straw, but he wasn't. The smile on his lips and the menace in the eyes didn't match, and as far as Winsome was concerned, he might as well have been wearing a leather face mask and carrying a chain saw. He was large, broad-shouldered, muscular, and about the same height as Winsome, which was a bit over six foot.

He headed slowly toward a padlocked metal box, fixed to one of the side walls, not taking his eyes off her as he walked, like one of those trompe d'oeil paintings that looked at you wherever you stood. Winsome took the opportunity to edge farther away from him. He got to the box and unlocked it. Winsome now stood across the channel from him, a little closer to the door. She knew that she couldn't simply make a dash for it, so she didn't even bother trying. She could see only one slim chance. He opened the box and took out what she guessed to be the bolt gun.

"It can be quick," he said. "But it doesn't have to be. It all depends on the animal."

"**WHAT DID** that mean to you at the time?" Banks asked Michael Lane. "That Morgan had stolen the boss's tractor?"

"Mean?"

"Yes. Why did it frighten you? It obviously did."

"Well, it was the way he said it, menacingly like, and they knew I'd heard them, so I thought they'd be after me."

"But how did you know who the boss was? They didn't name him, did they?"

"I . . . no . . . I don't think they did. It was all a bit of a blur, to be honest. I was running for my life."

"But you were quite clear earlier," Annie said. "Why should they care what you heard if you didn't know who the boss was, or who they were?"

"I was scared. I wasn't thinking. For crying out loud, I thought they'd just shot Morgan and I was a witness. Do you seriously think I stood around to talk it over or think it out?"

"Calm down, Michael," said Annie. "Who is the boss? Do you know?"

"How could I?"

"Indeed," said Banks. "That's just what we're wondering. Maybe it's time to come clean and tell us *everything* you know. It'll turn out better in the long run, believe me."

"I've told you. I was hiding behind the car. One of them said, 'You stole the boss's fucking tractor.' There was a silence. Then the sound of a shot. I legged it. End of story."

Banks shook his head. "You disappoint me, Michael, you really do. For a moment, you know, you almost had me believing that you cared about that girl of yours and the bairn. That you really loved them."

"I do love them!"

"Then we want names," Banks shouted back.

Lane appeared to consider his options and perhaps, Banks thought, to try to come up with a way to make his story sound acceptable without implicating himself. He licked his lips and his eyes flitted from one to the other and back. "OK," he said finally. "Look, maybe Morgan did talk a bit more about some of the things he was up to. After he'd had a couple of drinks, like. But you have to understand, I thought it was all just stories, tall tales, bullshit, and I never had anything to do with any of it."

"That's better, Michael," said Banks. "What sort of things did Morgan tell you? What names did he mention?"

"I know who the boss is," Lane said. "Morgan bragged about the tractor, that he was going to steal it while the miserable bastard was on his holiday."

"We know that, too," Annie said. "He's John Beddoes. The point is that if Morgan knew he was the boss, why did he steal his tractor and set up an exchange meet with the others in the gang? It doesn't make sense. Were they all in on it?"

"I don't think Morgan knew who the boss was," said Lane. "I mean, that's the way it sounded in the hangar. When the other bloke mentioned it, he said something like, 'What the fuck? Beddoes?' It was muffled, so I'm not really sure, but he sounded surprised."

That made sense, Banks thought. Spencer is so low level he doesn't even know who the top men are, and he steals one's tractor by mistake. He reports to Tanner and only Tanner deals directly with Beddoes. The typical sad story of a loser's life. But was a tractor really worth killing for? Was it a viable motive for his murder? Why couldn't they just give the tractor back to Beddoes and give Spencer a good hiding?

Then Banks realized why. Beddoes was due back early Sunday morning. They couldn't know that his flight had been delayed. As far as they were concerned, he'd come home, found his tractor gone and done the only thing he could do under the circumstances: call the police to report it stolen. Any other course of action would have looked odd. Even if they had tried to phone him to check and he didn't answer, they would most likely assume that he was down at the police station describing the tractor. Spencer's theft had caused them a lot of trouble and put them all in a difficult position. The gang had had to continue behaving as if they *had* stolen the tractor even after they knew who it belonged to. The best they could do was have someone— the driver Utley, most likely—dump it down south somewhere and hope it was found and returned in good condition before too long.

Still, Banks wondered, was it worth the hue and cry of a murder investigation? On the other hand, perhaps the killer enjoyed his work. Perhaps he also had a grudge against Spencer. After all, Spencer's body wasn't supposed to turn up in a car crash at the bottom of Belderfell Pass. It was supposed to be incinerated in Vaughn's yard with the fallen stock. Someone, probably Tanner, had searched Spencer's caravan for anything that might incriminate the gang and then burned it down just to make sure. People would assume that Spencer had simply moved on after his caravan had burned down. But the gang hadn't reckoned on Lane overhearing the murder and going on the run. That set everything in motion, with Beddoes, who had no doubt been quickly informed about Spencer's mistake, calmly playing the injured party, the victim, knowing it would make him appear blameless, invulnerable.

"Beddoes was an arsehole," said Lane. "He had it in for me right from the start."

"So I've heard," said Annie. "He called you a tearaway and a juvenile delinquent. What sort of things was Morgan up to?"

"He was never very clear about it, but obviously stealing tractors was a part of it. He had the removal van, see, and he knew what was going around the dale."

"Who else was involved in this?"

"I don't know. Honestly, I don't know. Morgan didn't know the people in charge. I never heard him mention Beddoes. He did mention a bloke called Ron once, a club bouncer or something who liked to beat people up. Morgan liked to show off about being around dangerous guys. He was a hothead. He talked big. Said he was going to show them. But he didn't know any of the real bosses."

"Ronald Tanner was the one who broke Alex's finger and frightened her half to death," said Annie.

Lane turned pale. "Oh, God," he said, and put his head in his hands.

"We haven't finished yet," said Banks. "Time for tears and recriminations later."

Lane wiped his eyes and gave Banks a truculent glare. "You're a hard bastard, you are."

"You say Morgan Spencer mentioned wanting to steal Beddoes's tractor while its owner was on holiday, and that he knew a thug called Ron. Did he ever mention Caleb Ross?"

"Not to me."

"Ross smoked pot. Do you know where he got it from?"

"No way. I'm not into that sort of thing. Alex wouldn't have it in the house even if I was, not with Ian around. A few drinks when we can afford them. The occasional bottle of cheap wine in front of the telly. That's all the drugs we do."

"Very domestic," said Banks. "Did Spencer mention any of his other partners in crime to you?"

"There was one other bloke. Morgan didn't like him much. Even sounded a bit frightened when he talked about him. Like, he was a psycho or something. Lived way out on the moors all by himself. Come to think of it, he might have been growing some pot out there. He had his own private abattoir. Used to be a slaughterman, only he got fired for some reason or other." Lane gave a shudder. "Like I said, I thought he was just bullshitting me."

"Did he give this person a name?"

Lane frowned, then said, "Let's see . . . Ken . . . Ken Atherton, or something like that. All I know is he sounded really scary."

AS ATHERTON advanced toward her, Winsome calculated the distance she would have to go and the estimated time she would have to do it. She thought she could probably outrun him, but she didn't think she could take him on in a fight. Even outrunning him depended on the weather out there. There was certainly no chance of getting to her car and driving off, even if it started, even if drifts weren't blocking the drive already. If she ran, she had to run somewhere, had to have a plan. There was only one possibility that came to her mind, and it was a desperate one. But first she had to get out.

"It'll be easier if you just relax," Atherton said. "Sometimes the animals got overexcited, and I had to kick them or stub a cigarette out in their eye to show them who was boss. I can do that with you."

He looked down to fiddle with the gun and Winsome seized her chance. She grabbed the hook and hurled it toward Atherton. It swung fast, but he was faster and moved his head out of the way in time. He was disoriented enough to forget about the return, though, which came quicker than expected. The hook hit one of the low rafters and bounced back unexpectedly fast, and this time it connected directly with the back of Atherton's head. He dropped the gun, which skittered far away down the channel, and fell face forward onto the filth.

Winsome wasn't sure how stunned he was but she had no desire to hang around. He was stronger than her, and he could easily turn the tables in a fight. She decided that running was still the best option.

She slid back the bolt, hauled the door open and ran outside. It was hard to see far beyond the cottage, but the rock face of Woadly Edge stood out dramatically, dark against the whiteness of the snow. Winsome could hear Atherton moving inside the abattoir. She headed for the rock face as fast as her legs could carry her. She had been an award-winning sprinter at school, and she hadn't done badly over distances, either, so she thought she had an advantage. It was a gamble. She couldn't run forever, and she didn't intend to. Much of what happened to her in the next while would depend on whether Atherton knew the caves as well as she did. And on the cavalry coming, of course. Where was the cavalry?

BANKS AND Annie sat in the former's office after the Lane interview to draw up a plan of attack. Lane hadn't been able to tell them anything more about Ken Atherton except that he lived on the remote moorland. First they needed to find out where. They had put Lane back in his cell for the time being, but neither of them thought they could make anything stick against him. Banks also had the feeling that Annie's heart wasn't in putting Lane behind bars.

"Look, he's been a bloody idiot," she said, "and I've no doubt he was a bit more involved in Spencer's doings than he led us to believe, but for the most part I'd say his story holds true, and I'll bet you he's learned his lesson."

"If he hasn't," said Banks, "I have no doubt that Alex will make sure it's drilled into him."

"And what would the CPS make of it?" Annie added. "They'd laugh us out of the office."

"Ronald Tanner might implicate him, if he talks," Banks said. "Or Carl Utley, or this Atherton character, when we find him."

"But that's not proof," Annie said. "Anyone could argue they'd be doing it to save their own skins. When it comes right down to it, do I believe Lane made a bit of extra money from helping Morgan Spencer with his dirty deeds, maybe fingering likely victims, helping with the heavy lifting? Maybe. But do I think he was really *involved*? No, I don't. And did he hurt or kill anyone? No."

"It's just possible he was the one who egged Spencer on to steal Beddoes's tractor in the first place. There was bad blood between them. He knew through Alex that Beddoes was going away, and he did admit he might have mentioned it to Spencer on Friday. That explains why the tractor was stolen so close to the time of Beddoes's return. It was a brief window of opportunity."

"Maybe," Annie admitted. "But that's still just speculation. And he wasn't trying to get Spencer killed. Anything we could charge him with would be vague at this point."

"Let him stew for a while," said Banks. "We'll see what else we can dig up."

"I think Alex really needs him."

Banks studied her for a moment. "Why, Annie," he said, "I do believe you're becoming a bit more like your old self."

"You mean you thought I was soft?"

"Compassionate. You've been a lot harder lately."

"Getting shot will do that to you."

"And now?"

Annie smiled. It reminded Banks of her old smile, though it wasn't quite there yet. "Getting there," she said. "But don't push it. You're the hard bastard now, according to Michael Lane."

"Someone has to be. Cut him loose. Police bail. But tell him not to go wandering off. And you can bring Gerry back in."

"Aren't Alex and Ian still in danger?"

"Keep the surveillance going. I don't think they are, though. I think it's all unraveling, and it's every man for himself. Rats deserting a sinking ship. It's just a matter of who talks first."

Annie left for the custody suite to set Lane's release on police bail in motion. Alone in his office, Banks picked up the phone and dialed Burgess's number. Dirty Dick answered after the fourth ring. "What were you doing?" Banks said. "Shagging your secretary?"

"That only requires three rings," Burgess retorted. "What can I do for you?"

"I think you should close in on Havers. The whole kit and caboodle's falling apart."

"The center cannot hold," said Burgess, after Banks had told him the story. "We'll move in the heavy artillery. I've got something for you, too. You know those blokes you were looking for: Kieran Welles and Carl Utley?"

"Yes. We haven't been able to catch up with them yet."

"Carl Utley caught a ferry from Dover to Calais last Sunday evening. You can get Interpol on him, but I'd guess you'll have a hard time finding him now. As for the other one, a mate of mine in intelligence has been keeping tabs on him as best he can. Seems he changed his name to Kenneth Atherton and moved to North Yorkshire. Remote place called High Point Farm."

Banks had never heard of the place, but that didn't matter. He would find it. He felt the excitement he always felt when he was closing in. He thanked Burgess and went to the squad room to see if Winsome was back.

The room was empty, the desks littered with pieces of paper, some ringed with coffee cup stains. On Gerry Masterson's desk he saw a note in what looked like Winsome's writing. It said: "Got a lead to a place called High Point Farm. Owner: Kenneth Atherton. Gone out for a look around. Can you send a squad car for backup, just in case. Thanks, Winsome."

Being Winsome, she had even noted the time at the top: 11:35 a.m. Banks looked at his watch and saw it was now after three. His heart began to race. She must have left the note after he had sent Gerry to babysit Alex Preston, and Doug Wilson was out keeping an eye on the Beddoes farm. Christ, she should have been back by now.

Just as he was leaving, the phone on Winsome's desk rang. Banks picked it up. "Winsome?" the voice said.

"No, it's DCI Banks here. Who am I speaking to?"

"Oh, DCI Banks It's me, Terry Gilchrist. Can I talk to Winsome? Unless she's really busy of course. I'm afraid it's a personal call."

"She's not here."

"It's just that she said she'd meet me for lunch and . . . well, Winsome's a woman of her word. She didn't turn up. She hasn't even phoned."

"That's not like her," Banks agreed.

"Do you know where she is?"

"I'm afraid I don't, Mr. Gilchrist." On impulse, Banks asked, "By the way. Do you know of a place called High Point Farm?"

"No," said Gilchrist. "Never heard of it. Why?"

"I'm afraid we're in the midst of a bit of a crisis here right now, so I'm going to have to hang up on you, sir."

"Is it Winsome? What's happened? I—"

Banks had no time to worry about Winsome's boyfriend now. The first thing to do was get as many squad cars out to High Point Farm as he could, if it was possible in the snowstorm, then head out there himself immediately. He dialed dispatch and gave the orders. Then, just for a moment, he turned and looked out of the window, and his heart sank. The snow was coming down thick and fast, almost obscuring the market square. He could only imagine what it would be like out on the high moorland. He dialed Winsome's mobile number, though he already had a sneaking feeling that she was in a no-reception zone. He was right.

He needed to get out to High Point Farm himself, but he realized he still had no idea where it was, and satnav was never any use out on the moors. It might as well be on Mars. Then he remembered that one of the custody officers was a walking map of the Dales and hoped he was on duty as he took the stairs two at a time. He nearly stumbled when his mobile chimed. When he answered it, Doug Wilson said, "They're doing a bunk, guv. The Beddoeses. They're doing a bunk."

"Stop them." Banks explained the situation to Wilson as quickly as he could, then he said, "Call for backup and hold them there. They're not going anywhere. Then join us at High Point Farm, if you can find it."

Banks dashed into the custody suite in the basement, where he was relieved to see Annie chatting to the walking map of the Dales.

16

THOUGH THE SNOW WAS PILING UP AGAINST THE ROCK
face, it was easy for Winsome to get through the opening into the
large cavern. She risked a quick glance behind her and saw that Atherton was stumbling in pursuit, about two hundred yards down the
hillside, but he didn't seem to be carrying the bolt gun.

About thirty feet inside the opening, which was high enough for
even Winsome to enter without crouching, three caves ran deeper
into the system, but only one led to the cathedral-sized chamber
where Winsome wanted to go. Another dead-ended, and the third
became so low at one point that hardly a mouse could squeeze through.
You had to know which tunnel to choose, and Winsome did.

To throw Atherton off the scent, she made sure she had her mobile
and wallet and keys, but took off her quilted jacket and lay it outside
the central cave before she took the one to her right. If he didn't know
the caves, it might fool him into picking the wrong entrance.

It was cold inside the cave, especially without her jacket, but while
the stone acted as a natural coolant, it also insulated the place from the
worst of the cold. And the snow couldn't penetrate here, no matter
how hard the wind blew it. The walls were slimy, cool and moist to
the touch, veined with minerals and crystals. It was getting darker
with every step she took from the main entrance. Soon she was bending over to keep going, and as yet she had heard no signs of Atherton

following her. He had seemed out of shape as he made his way up the hill, despite his sturdy build, and he was probably pausing to catch his breath and try to work out which way she had gone. At least, that was what she hoped.

Soon, Winsome knew, the ceiling would hang so low that it would look impossible to get under. A novice would turn around and go back. But Winsome had been through more than once, and she knew it was higher than it looked, even though you had to crawl on your belly for such a long way that it was easy to panic if you were the slightest bit claustrophobic. And if you panicked, you got stuck.

The trick, she remembered as she lay on her belly and slid forward into the clammy darkness, was to pretend that you were a snake and could squeeze through the narrowest of spaces. She cursed the few pounds she had put on since she had last been potholing and vowed to go to the gym regularly if she survived this ordeal, but even with her arse feeling much bigger than she could ever bear it to be, she managed.

She slithered along on her stomach, oblivious to the sharp bits of rock and quartz here and there that cut into her. At the worst moments, she felt as if she were being crushed by an almighty weight, the breath squeezed out of her. For a few seconds, about halfway along, she stopped. There was silence except for the wind and water dripping somewhere. Now the rock underneath her was wet. About an inch of water had accumulated in the passage, soaking through her blouse and jeans, chilling her to the bone.

When she turned a slight bend in the passage, she knew she was almost there, and soon the rock above her seemed to draw up, like a press after it had done its work. In no time she was on all fours, the jeans around her knees shredded to rags. She had grazed her elbows and they hurt like hell. But she was almost there. It was pitch black now, and she was far enough away from any possibility of the light being seen, that she finally risked taking out her mobile and using its light to show her the low entrance ahead. It was just a hole in the wall, really, but Winsome knew that it led to a ledge about forty feet from the bottom of the enormous cathedral-like cavern so many intrepid visitors had oohed and aahed over. She bent forward and squeezed through. After about five feet, she found herself on the ledge, which was wide enough to sit comfortably on.

The light from her phone didn't have the power to illuminate the full glory of the cavern, but it was better than total darkness. If Atherton did follow her, if he chose the right path and made it under the overhang, then she would hear him coming and have time to stand in wait against the wall by the edge of the entrance and use his momentum as he came through the hole in the wall to hurl him forward over the edge. Whether the forty-foot drop would kill him, she had no idea. It would certainly incapacitate him, and there would be no way he would be able to climb back up and get at her.

Winsome turned off the phone to conserve battery power and huddled against the wall, shivering, arms locked around her drawn-up knees. As her eyes grew used to the darkness, she could just make out the shapes of stalactites and stalagmites and sense the cathedral vastness of the space she was in. She would stay where she was until she was certain Atherton had given up, or her backup had arrived and caught him, then she would crawl and slither back out again, hoping to God the drifting snow hadn't completely blocked the exit.

Now there was nothing to do but wait. Water dripped. The wind moaned and whistled through the interconnected passages and made a deep humming music in the chamber. She heard a loud cry followed by what she thought were curses, swearwords. *Atherton.* She couldn't tell where they were coming from, but they froze her blood. Again she heard howls and curses echoing around the vast space, as if she were being hunted by a pack of hounds, and she hugged herself tighter and tighter until she almost turned into a ball.

BANKS AND Annie signed out one of the police four-by-fours from the car pool for their journey. Neither Banks's Porsche nor Annie's Astra would handle the present conditions well. It was tough going, and Banks gritted his teeth as he drove every inch of the snow-swept roads out of town. Neither said a word. Banks didn't even put any music on. He needed all the concentration he could muster for the driving.

Out on the main dale road, through Fortford, Helmthorpe and Swainshead, the conditions were much worse, as Banks had expected. It hadn't yet got to the point where any stretches were completely impassable, but it sometimes felt close to that, and once Banks skidded on a drift and clipped the dry stone wall before regaining control of the steering. Annie held on to him. It was hard to see. The windscreen wipers couldn't keep up with the volume of snow. The only piece of good fortune was that there was hardly anyone else out on the roads.

For a while after they turned off the main road, which branches toward Belderfell Pass to the left and the high Pennine moorland beyond the source of the river Swain to the right, Banks thought they might have to stop and continue on foot. But the drifting was patchy and for every deep and difficult stretch to plow through they would get a few hundred yards of relatively easy driving.

Eventually, taking much longer than he would have liked, Banks pulled up in the yard of High Point Farm, happy to see that two squad cars had somehow managed to beat him there. Even better, one of the officers said he had used his police radio to send out for a snow plow from Crowborough, the nearest village, about seven miles north. There were telegraph wires leading to the farmhouse, Banks noticed, so Welles/Atherton clearly had a landline.

Winsome's Polo stood in the yard, half covered by snow. Without touching it, Banks glanced through the windows. No Winsome. No keys in the ignition, no signs of a struggle. The snow had covered up any tracks that might have been in the yard, except their own. There were no indications of where Winsome and Atherton might have gone.

One of the uniformed officers told him there was also a red pickup truck in one of the outbuildings. Its engine was cold, which meant Atherton had probably been at home when Winsome arrived. Banks pulled up the collar of his three-quarter-length overcoat and surveyed the scene. Snow had drifted up against the front door of the low-roofed farmhouse and one side of the barn. He thought there was something odd about the place when he looked closely. "What are those?" he asked Annie. "Those pens on the side."

"That's not a barn," said Annie. "At least, it probably was once, but it isn't now. They're called lairage. They're used to keep the animals waiting for slaughter. It's an abattoir, Alan, a private bloody abattoir."

Banks hurried over to the building, with Annie not far behind. The front door stood open, and the long fluorescent lights shone on the inner workings of the small abattoir, the motorized rail running lengthways along the ceiling, the dangling hook with its bloody curve, the central trough, boilers and spray hoses for skinning. They stood just inside the doorway, wary of contaminating what might be a crime scene. Not to mention frightened of catching something. Whoever owned the place certainly had no interest in cleanliness and hygiene. It stank to high heaven and the floor was caked in shit and blood and worse. Banks almost gagged; Annie held her nose and breathed through her mouth. She pointed, and Banks saw an object on the floor, a bolt gun. They would leave it for the CSIs. At least Winsome wasn't here, though she might have been, Banks thought. There could have been a struggle, and Atherton had dropped the bolt gun. But where were they now?

Banks and Annie left the abattoir as it was when they found it and walked back to the farmhouse. The front door was locked, but one of the officers soon got it open with his mini battering ram, the "red door knocker" as it was affectionately called. Nobody gave any thought to a warrant. A police officer's life was in danger, and they had every reason to suspect the person who lived there of serious crimes.

The inside of the farmhouse was almost as unsavory as the abattoir. Cups, pans, plates, knives and forks stood piled in the stained sink, unwashed for days, or weeks. A plate on the small table with mold growing out of what had once been food on it, mouse droppings everywhere, signs of rats, too. On the wall was a rack of knives, and not Henckels cookware, either. These were nasty blades, clearly designed for the skinning and gutting of animals, or people. They were the only clean objects in the place, sharp blades so lovingly polished you could see your face in them.

Though Banks and Annie wore latex gloves, they were careful not to touch anything as they went methodically through the place, the bedroom, with its unruly mess of sheets, like the apparition from the adaptation of M. R. James's "Oh, Whistle, and I'll Come to You" Banks had seen on television at Christmas. The toilet was a pigsty, the rest of the upstairs drab, bare and dusty. And nowhere were there any signs of Winsome or Atherton.

Banks supposed that was a good thing. At least they hadn't found her tied to a bed with a bolt pistol wound between her eyes. That meant there was a good chance she had escaped, or was at least on the run. If she had headed for the moors with Atherton in pursuit, Banks would put his money on Winsome. He had seen her in chases, and she was fast and strong. Whether either had the stamina to get very far under these conditions, however, remained doubtful.

It was down in the cellar where they found the hydroponic setup. Marijuana plants, lots of them, along with about a kilo of hash and a similar amount of cocaine, clearly from elsewhere. Drugs were another of Atherton's little sidelines. He had no doubt supplied Caleb Ross with the wacky baccy he had smoked.

"We'll seal the cellar off for now," Banks said. "It's more important to get search parties for Winsome organized. They can't have got far. Have a word with the patrol officers. They might know the area a bit better than we do. I don't suppose there's any chance of getting a helicopter out in this weather, but it's worth asking, too."

Annie walked over to the nearest patrol car, leaning down to speak through the window. Banks looked around. The snow showed no signs of abating. He imagined Winsome caught in a drift, slowly freezing to death. He put away such disturbing thoughts when he heard a car approaching. It turned out to be a dark blue Focus, and it appeared around the bend in the drive and pulled to a halt behind the police four-by-four.

Though he had never met Terry Gilchrist before, Banks recognized him from the car he drove, his limp and Winsome's description. "Oh, bloody hell," he said as Gilchrist advanced through the snow. "What are you doing here?"

"I thought you might need some help."

"It's a police operation," said Banks. "We don't normally involve civilians, not even ex-military."

"So that's all the thanks I get for fighting for my country? Not to mention driving all this way in a bloody Ford Focus?"

Banks shrugged.

"What exactly are you doing that you don't want my help on?"

"Why don't you just get back in your car and head for home, Mr. Gilchrist. Leave it to us."

"It's Winsome, isn't it? I knew something was wrong when she didn't call."

"Yes, it's Winsome," said Banks, losing his temper. "She's a friend and a colleague and I'd like you to clear out of here and let us do our job."

Gilchrist stood his ground and looked around the farmyard. "It doesn't look to me as if you're actually doing very much."

"That's your opinion."

Gilchrist sighed. "Look, Chief Inspector, you may not like me, or you may simply not like the idea of someone telling you your business, but if you're looking for Winsome, I might be able to help. And if I think what's happened is true, the sooner the better."

Banks was suddenly interested. "Oh? And what do you think happened?"

"Do you know where you are?"

"High Point Farm. You said you'd never heard of it. I blame myself for letting it slip."

"I hadn't, but it was easy to look up. You're within a quarter of a mile of Woadly Edge, though you can't see it from here in this weather. It's up that hill and across the moors a couple of hundred yards or so."

"So?"

"Winsome and I have had a few conversations. I wouldn't say I know her well, but I do know one or two things about her that I think you ought to consider."

"Those being?"

"First off, Woadly Edge is one of the main access points for the Swainsdale cave system. And second, Winsome used to be a keen pot-holer. She'd know the caves like the back of her hand."

"So you're saying . . ."

"You're catching on. If she was in trouble out here, the odds are she'd run for the caves. It would give her an advantage."

"And her chances once she'd got there?"

"Depends on whether someone was after her, and whether that someone also knows the system. It's not for novices, though, so he'd have to be an experienced potholer. The odds that he's not are good. There aren't that many."

"From what I know of him, I doubt he goes potholing in his spare time. More like pulls the legs off flies. What would you advise us to do, assuming this is true?"

"Get up there right away and find out if I'm right."

Banks said nothing.

As if sensing and understanding his indecision, Gilchrist said, "Look, I know you don't want people like me interfering, but I assure you I also have experience of the caves. I have military training, too. I can handle myself, despite the injury." He held his arms out. "Look, no stick."

"You don't need it?"

"Actually, it's in the car, and I could certainly use it to get to Woadly Edge. But once I'm inside, no. As long as I don't have to run."

"This is against my better judgment," said Banks.

"Come on, we should get going. Bring the others. We might need some help clearing the entrance."

Banks spoke to Annie and two of the patrol officers while Gilchrist got his walking stick and torch, along with two spades they found in the yard, then the four of them set off up the rise toward Woadly Edge. It didn't take long to get there, and the drifts had not covered the entrance. A gaping dark hole showed in stark contrast against the white surroundings. The snow was light enough that they could walk straight through it.

"That's her jacket," said Banks, pointing his torch toward the middle of three cave entrances. "That's Winsome's jacket."

His voice echoed. They were standing in a sort of stone hallway or foyer with a high ceiling, or so it seemed to Banks, and Winsome's quilted jacket lay on the ground in front of the central of three openings. There was no trace or sign of Atherton.

"That's a dead end," said Gilchrist. "She was trying to misdirect him."

"Which means she knew he was after her, and he wasn't far behind," said Banks. "She must be bloody freezing."

Gilchrist bent forward and went into the right-hand tunnel.

"What are you doing?"

Gilchrist looked back. "If she went anywhere," he said, "it was down here. She'd know as well as I do about the left-hand entrance."

"What about it?"

"It gets too narrow. This one's narrow in parts, too, but it's the only way in from here."

"Into where?" Annie asked.

"I don't have time to explain," said Gilchrist, edging forward even as he spoke, "but it's a large system of passages and caverns, one of the biggest in Europe. There are miles and miles of connected caves in there, but it's a bit like a maze."

"Can you get through?" Banks said, bending in the entrance after him.

"Yes," Gilchrist said, then vanished into the darkness.

Banks caught up with him and tapped him on the shoulder. "Be careful," he said. "Don't forget, Atherton might be in there, and we believe he's a killer."

"I've encountered killers before," said Gilchrist. "I'll make sure I see him before he sees me."

Banks went back outside to Annie. "Shit," he said. "I don't like this at all."

"Well, do you want to go in after him?"

Banks looked at the dark tunnel. Even when he shone his torch on the walls they looked slimy and uninviting. He felt a sense of claustrophobia envelop him. "No way. But if it's for Winsome I will."

He started to move forward.

Annie grabbed his sleeve. "Don't," she said. "Leave it to Gilchrist. He might be a civilian, but he's a trained soldier and potholer. He knows what he's doing. You don't. You could get stuck in there or something."

"I hate just waiting around."

"You and me both. But like you said, it's Winsome. He's her best chance."

"What if Atherton is in there?"

"At least he doesn't have his bolt gun. And if he is, I'd say it's already game over, one way or another, wouldn't you? You can't turn back the clock."

"You're a real comfort."

SHE WAS back at Spring Hill walking home from Sunday school and a man in a battered hat and a dark moth-eaten coat was following her. Only it was snowing and she remembered thinking, in the dream, that it never snows in Maroon Town. But it did, and all the flame trees were covered in it, all green and white and red like Christmas trees. But she was frightened. The man was following her. She thought he was probably the "Skinner" people were talking about. He skinned his victims after he'd had his way with them. But there was another man on the scene, her father in his best Sunday suit, not his uniform, and they were fighting. The Skinner was going to kill her father and skin him. She had to get back to them and help but she couldn't get through, she was slipping and sliding and getting stuck up to her knees and she knew she just couldn't make it in time, a knife flashing . . .

Winsome gave an involuntary twitch and her eyes opened wide with fear. She realized that she had fallen asleep. She was waking from a dream. Moving carefully, she curled up into a ball against the cold. It wouldn't do to fall off the ledge after all she had been through. She had no idea how long she had been there. Using her mobile light, she checked her watch and saw it was going on five o'clock. About four hours, then. Had she waited long enough? Would the cavalry have arrived at High Point Farm? Of course, they would have no idea where she was. Maybe Banks and Annie vaguely remembered her mentioning potholing, but they probably didn't know about the cave system here, or its access points. They'd be searching for her around the farm and the open moorland, hindered by the snow.

Where was Atherton? She wasn't certain that the shouts and screams she had heard earlier were human or just a trick of the wind, but she hadn't heard anything for some time now. He certainly hadn't got through to her in two hours, but that didn't mean he wasn't waiting at the exit. He could even have gone back to the abattoir and picked up his bolt pistol. Or perhaps he imagined there were other exits, that she must be long gone, and had given up the ghost and scarpered. She just didn't know. Was it worth the risk of going back to find out?

Despite the insulation of the rock, she was freezing. She wished she hadn't left her jacket behind to try to fool Atherton. She rubbed her hands together and held her knees tighter to her chest. There wasn't much she could do about her feet. They were like blocks of ice.

She would give it an hour longer, she decided. If no help had come by then, she would make her way back out as slowly and quietly as she could. Even if Gerry and the backup had no idea that she was in the cave, they would surely have got as far as High Point Farm, and she could outrun Atherton back down there.

Just when she had made herself as comfortable as she could again on the ledge, she thought she heard a slithering sound from the tunnel.

Atherton.

She strained, but heard nothing for a few moments, then she heard it again, a light scraping, like someone crawling on his stomach.

As quietly as she could, she stood up and pressed her back against the wall by the entrance. When he came out, he would be bent forward. Just one quick tug on his arm was all it would take, and his own momentum would take him over the edge. She had rehearsed the possibility time after time in her mind during her first anxious minutes in the cavern.

He was getting closer, up on his feet now. She could hear muffled footsteps, though there was something odd about them. If he had a torch, he must have turned it off, because the opening was still pitch-black. Winsome tensed. It wouldn't be long now. Just one quick pull, she told herself, then let go, or she'd be following him over the edge and end up impaled on a stalagmite. The shuffling got nearer and she was just about to reach out when she realized why it sounded so strange. *He was limping.* She relaxed just as she heard a familiar voice say, "Winsome? Are you there? Are you alone?"

Terry. She let herself fall back against the wall and slide down so she was sitting on the ledge again.

She had tears in her eyes. "Yes," she said, laughing or crying as she spoke. "Yes, I'm here. And yes, I'm alone. Very bloody alone." She never swore, and when the word came out it shocked her. She put her hand to her mouth, but she couldn't stop laughing. "I swore," she said. "I can't believe it. I swore."

Then he was standing there, his torch on again, illuminating part of the cathedral vastness before them. "Wash your mouth out," he said.

"Help me."

He reached down to help her to her feet, and as soon as she was standing she leaned forward and kissed him full on the lips, far far longer than she had even planned on doing.

.

"SORRY WE'RE so late getting around to you, Mr. Beddoes," said Banks. "We had a bit of a crisis to take care of first." It was nine o'clock and the Beddoeses had been in a holding cell at the station since four, complaining all the time. Patricia Beddoes had been demanding to see Cathy Gervaise, but even when one of the custody officers thought he should at least inform the AC about what was happening, "Cathy" Gervaise made it clear that she wasn't available.

Cassandra Wakefield had turned up half an hour ago, and while her associate represented Patricia Beddoes in another interview room with Annie and Doug Wilson, she stuck with John Beddoes, sitting opposite Banks and Gerry.

"I can't believe this," Beddoes complained. "My wife and I are quietly going about our business and some hooligan of a police officer blocks our way and drags us all the way down here."

"Where were you going?" Banks asked.

"It's none of your fucking business."

"Swearing won't help, Mr. Beddoes," said Cassandra Wakefield.

Banks looked at his notes. "According to our preliminary analysis of recent activity on your laptop computer, you had just completed a number of large financial transactions, money transfers, in fact, to offshore bank accounts in the British Virgin Islands."

"So what? They're legitimate accounts. I pay my taxes."

"I'm sure you do, Mr. Beddoes, but don't you think it's a bit soon for another holiday? I mean, you've just got back from Mexico. Think of all that ultraviolet radiation."

"What business of yours is it where and when we go for our holidays?"

"You also had a lot of luggage. How long were you planning on being away for?"

"I don't know. A while."

"Don't you think it looks a bit suspicious? Just after I visit you and let you know I've talked to Malcolm Hackett, an old business associate of yours, and that we've found Michael Lane, a witness to the murder of Morgan Spencer, you and your wife make a run for it."

"We weren't 'making a run for it.'"

"It looks like that to me," said Banks. "Wouldn't you agree, Gerry?"

"Certainly would, sir. I mean, it's not everyone takes a fragile vase off the mantelpiece on holiday with them, or a pair of antique silver sugar tongs."

"That vase happens to be a valuable antique, too. And given what occurred last time we were away, I'd say we were more than justified in taking a few valuables with us."

"Really, Chief Inspector," said Cassandra Wakefield, fingering her pearls, "it does seem a remarkably thin context for detaining my client and interfering with his basic freedom of movement."

"Morgan Spencer stole your tractor, didn't he?" Banks said to Beddoes.

"Did he? I can't say it surprises me."

"You know Morgan Spencer, then? Earlier you said you had no idea who he was."

"I didn't know him well. Not personally. Only that he was a mate of the Lane boy. I've seen him around. Thick as thieves. Look, you know all this. Why am I here?"

"You're here because we believe you're one of the men running a lucrative international criminal activity dealing in stolen farm equipment and livestock. Your partner Malcolm Hackett, aka Montague Havers, who is currently being questioned by my colleagues in London, took care of the export side, and you supplied the raw materials from the North Yorkshire region. That is, tractors, combines, Range Rovers, lambs, whatever. You employed a number of people at various levels, including Ronald Tanner, Carl Utley, Kenneth Atherton, aka Kieran Welles, Caleb Ross and Morgan Spencer. Your wife, Patricia, may be involved. Police have also picked up Mr. Havers's chief operators in Lincolnshire and Cumbria. More arrests are expected to follow. Plenty of people are talking."

"Really?" said Beddoes. "Where's your proof of all this?"

That was a thorny issue for Banks. He didn't really have any proof. A deeper dig into Beddoes's finances would probably turn up anomalies, but that would take time. Michael Lane's word alone wasn't good enough, but it was a place to start.

"We also believe," Banks went on, "that Morgan Spencer was murdered partly because he stole your tractor, and partly because his colleagues, especially Atherton, had got fed up with him. He talked big, wanted a bigger role, more money, and he thought he was demonstrating his ability to get creative and play with the big boys by stealing an expensive tractor. Unfortunately, it turned out to be yours."

"So someone steals my tractor and I'm the criminal?"

"Kenneth Atherton killed Morgan Spencer with a bolt pistol he stole from Stirwall's Abattoir around the time he was fired nearly two years ago. He has also committed an earlier murder with the same weapon. We have matching prints from the weapon."

"This is fascinating," said Beddoes, "and nothing you can tell me about Spencer surprises me, but it has nothing to do with me, apart from the fact that the little creep stole my tractor."

"Why did you do it, John?" Banks asked. "Why did you get into the business in the first place? Surely you had everything going for you. The life you always dreamed of. Enough money not to have to struggle like real farmers. Was it *just* the money? You weren't that badly off, surely? Did Havers make you an offer you couldn't refuse? Did he have something on you from the old days? Insider trading?"

Beddoes laughed.

Cassandra Wakefield shot Banks a puzzled glance. "Are you going to charge my client with insider trading in the eighties? I fear that may be even more difficult a case to bring than the one you're struggling for at the moment. Go ahead, though. I'm sure the trial would be a lot of fun."

"Someone heard Atherton say to Spencer, 'You went too far. You stole the boss's fucking tractor' just before he killed him. What do you make of that?"

"Nothing," said Beddoes. "I was probably somewhere over the Atlantic Ocean at the time."

"But why would he say it? It's an odd thing to say just before you kill someone, isn't it? 'You stole the boss's fucking tractor.' Now, neither Morgan Spencer nor Michael Lane, who overheard this, and whose return had you packing your bags and running for the British Virgin Islands, knew who this boss was until they heard that, of course. After all, it was *your* tractor Atherton was referring to, and Lane had an inkling that Spencer might try to nick it to prove himself to his masters. The problem was, Spencer didn't know you were his master. You were too high and mighty to rub shoulders with the hoi polloi. Your orders went through Tanner."

"Lane's a lying little bastard, always has been," said Beddoes. "He had every bit as much to do with . . ."

"To do with what, John? Your business enterprise? As much as Morgan Spencer?"

"Spencer was a pushy little half-caste. He—"

Cassandra Wakefield tapped her client on the shoulder and whispered in his ear.

"They're trying to pin a murder on me," Beddoes protested, turning red. "I'm no killer. All right, I'm no saint, either, but if Atherton killed Spencer, it was because he was getting too big for his boots. And Atherton is a fucking psycho. It was a private vendetta, nothing to do with me."

"The *boss's* tractor, John?"

"He must have misheard. Lane. He's had it in for me ever since I moved to the farm. His father wanted the land, but I outbid him."

"I can see that might give Frank Lane a motive for killing you, but he hasn't. Why would Michael care? He was just a kid then."

"I don't know. Some kids are born evil. You can tell. All I ever did was give him a clip around the earhole."

"If Spencer didn't know you were the boss, then Lane probably didn't, either. The problem was that he knew who the tractor belonged to. Spencer had told him he was going to steal it while you were away in Mexico. Lane just put two and two together. What it added up to scared him, and he made off."

"This is nothing but speculation," said Cassandra Wakefield.

"We've got a witness statement from Michael Lane."

"Not enough."

"They never accepted me," said Beddoes.

Cassandra Wakefield narrowed her eyes. Banks and Gerry looked at him quizzically.

"What?" Beddoes said. "Why are you looking at me like that? You're just the same. You're just like the other bloody farmers. They laughed at me behind my back, called me a 'weekend' farmer, made fun of me. I was better than the lot of them put together. I was a Master of the Universe."

"It was a long time ago, John," said Banks.

"I'm saying they didn't respect me. My own neighbors. And I'd grown up on a farm. It was in my blood."

"Is that why you did it? Went into business with Havers."

"I knew I'd show them somehow."

"By stealing their livestock and equipment?"

"It's all they bloody care about."

Cassandra Wakefield dropped her pencil on the table. "Enough," she said. "I think we should end this interview right now."

"Getting a bit too close to the bone for you, is it?" Banks said.

"My client needs a break. He's been under a lot of stress lately. PACE regulations call for—"

Banks raised his hand. "Fine. Fine," he said. "Interview suspended at 9:27 p.m. To be continued." He called to the uniformed constable at the door. "Take him back to his cell, Nobby."

"Yes, sir."

The constable took Beddoes by the arm. He stood up and went without resisting.

Cassandra Wakefield looked at her watch. "You've got another nineteen hours or so to come up with some real evidence, otherwise my client walks."

"I don't think so," said Banks. "He's already admitted to theft of farm equipment."

Cassandra Wakefield snorted, then she followed Beddoes and the constable out of the room.

Gerry let out a long breath. Banks smiled. "Get used to it," he said. "It's the way of the world."

One of the female PCs stuck her head around the door. "Phone call, guv," she said.

"I'll take it in my office."

Banks told Gerry to hang on back in the squad room and walked down the hall to his office. He picked up the phone and engaged the line.

"Hello, Banksy," said the familiar voice. "Any luck?"

"We're getting there. Unfortunately we had Cassandra Wakefield representing Beddoes."

"She gets around, doesn't she? Mind you, I'd hardly call that bad luck. Have you seen the tits on her? Nipples like chapel hat pegs. What I'd—"

"Yes, yes, I can imagine what you'd do," said Banks. "But she happens to be a bloody good solicitor."

"Nobody's perfect. Anyway, it's your lucky day. I've got news'll make the hairs on your arse stand on end."

"Go on. I can hardly wait."

"Havers coughed. The lot."

Banks gripped the receiver tightly. His palm was sweating. "He what?"

"He cracked. Easy-peasy."

"What did you do, bring out the rubber hosepipes?"

"Didn't need them. He did it to save his own skin and to protect his overseas bosses. He's more scared of them than he is of us. Basically, you could say he fell on his sword. He knew the northern operation was fucked. They knew it, too. Word came down. They were cut off. Finished. They're falling over one another to avoid a murder charge. They'll take tax evasion, handling stolen goods, you name it, but not the murder. Havers wasn't going to go down by himself, so he gave us Beddoes, Ronald Tanner and Kenneth Atherton. And Carl Utley as a bonus. He was hiding out in a farmhouse in Provence. We're sending him up to you, but he was so shaken by what he saw Atherton do in the hangar up there that we can't shut him up. He and Tanner had to hold the poor bastard's arms. They thought Atherton was just going to rough him up a bit, but before they knew what was happening he pulled out the bolt gun and shot the kid. At least that's what Utley says. Apparently there was history between them, bad blood. It was all a rush job. Utley says Spencer didn't contact Tanner about the tractor he'd nicked until early Sunday morning. They had no time to get the usual crew up from London for a transfer so they arranged to meet at the hangar to figure out what to do: Spencer, Tanner, Utley and Atherton. Then they discovered whose tractor it was and all hell broke loose."

"That sounds about right," said Banks. "What about Michael Lane?"

"That name never came up. But it's airtight, Banksy. It's being faxed to you as we speak. Next time you get Beddoes and little Miss Melons in the room, you'll have times, dates, amounts, bank accounts, an eyewitness statement from Utley. Everything but the cream, of course. We know there are people pulling Havers's and Beddoes's strings, we even think we know who some of them are, but they're good at protecting themselves. There are no money trails leading to them, and nobody dares talk. Welles/Atherton isn't the only psycho killer they've got strutting around. But we've got the northern mob sewn up. Not too bright, none of them. Get down to the fax machine, then read it and weep. Beat you again, Banksy. And hold the party. I'm coming up for it. You can invite Cassandra Wakefield, too, if you like."

Banks thanked Burgess, then hung up and sighed. For a moment he felt defeated. He hadn't got as far as he had wanted with Beddoes, while Burgess had broken Havers, obviously the weakest link. Then he realized that it was just as he had said to Gerry, the way of the world. Get used to it, mate, he told himself. There'll always be a Cassandra Wakefield, and there'll always be a Dirty Dick Burgess. He smiled at the thought of what a couple they would make. And Burgess was certainly right about her charms.

This was no defeat, it was a win, and it called for champagne, or at least beer. Maybe they wouldn't get Beddoes for murder, but they would get Atherton, if they could find him. Tanner, Utley and Beddoes would get time for various offenses, too. And Michael Lane could probably live happily ever after with Alex and Ian, if he kept his nose clean. That would please Annie, but Banks still found himself wondering to what extent Lane had egged Spencer on to steal Beddoes's tractor simply because he didn't like the man who had once given him a clip around the ear. Lane couldn't have known Spencer would get killed, of course. If he had instigated the theft, he had done so to get at Beddoes, and perhaps at his father. The rest was just pure irony. That Lane had helped Spencer with certain jobs of a criminal nature, Banks had no doubt. He only hoped the kid had the sense to realize what he'd got in Alex and Ian, and what a lucky escape he'd had. Some people learn, many never do. It was a toss-up.

It was a mopping-up exercise now. Compile the evidence, get the forensics right on Atherton's farmhouse and private abattoir. Spencer's blood was sure to be among the sticky mess Banks had seen in the central trough, and Atherton's prints were all over the bolt gun. He'd clearly had his own little business on the side there, which explained the disappearance of stock around the dale over the past year or so.

Banks ran his hand over his head. He was tired. And hungry. He looked at his watch: 9:45. Time to go down to the fax machine, then home for some microwaved chicken tikka masala and a bottle of red. Maybe not champagne, but a good red, one from the "cellar." And thinking of a good red got him thinking of Australia and Oriana. He wondered what time it was over there. He was whistling "You Win Again" as he picked up his coat, turned off the light and left his office.

"MINE'S A pint of lager, Banksy," said Burgess in the Queen's Arms a week later.

"As if I'd forget," muttered Banks, heading to the bar to buy the round of drinks. It was the "official" celebration, mainly because the CPS had reviewed the evidence and agreed that there were strong cases against Beddoes, Tanner, Utley, Atherton and Havers. Vic Manson had also managed to get some prints from Spencer's removal van, and they matched Carl Utley's. Caleb Ross's tox screen had come back clean. Banks didn't think Ross knew it was human remains he was collecting. Atherton, who supplied him with marijuana, probably told him it was the carcass of a sheep or a pig he'd slaughtered and didn't want to go through official channels.

Cyril was playing his oldies playlist in the background, Amen Corner belting out "If Paradise Is Half as Nice." The whole team was there: Annie, Winsome, Gerry, Doug, Burgess up from London, Stefan Nowak, Vic Manson, even Terry Gilchrist, under special dispensation from AC Gervaise, who had bought the first round. She was looking a bit put out, Banks thought, perhaps because Patricia Beddoes had screamed blue murder at her when her husband was charged, accusing her of being a false friend. Patricia also swore blind she had no idea what John was up to, that he had just, on the spur of the moment, suggested they take another holiday, and she didn't see why not. That rankled with Gervaise, too. It was patently untrue, but they couldn't prove her guilt, and none of those who had talked had ever mentioned her name.

The only problem was that Atherton wouldn't be able to stand trial. His frozen body had been found in the caverns the day after Winsome's ordeal, when the search parties went in. He had taken the left passage and managed to get himself stuck where the ceiling reached its lowest point. He must have thought he could wriggle under it, because he appeared to have got his head and shoulders through and pushed on, then got stuck around his midriff. In trying to shake his body free, he had managed to wedge himself firmly between the rock bed and the overhang. The doctor who examined the body, once the rescuers had managed to chip away enough rock from above to pull him out, said that he had clearly panicked, as his body was covered in bruises and abrasions, and his back was broken. Nobody could have saved him. He was probably dead by the time Banks and the others arrived on the scene to rescue Winsome.

It was a horrible way to go, Banks thought with a shudder, but so was Morgan Spencer's death and its aftermath. He couldn't dredge up a great deal of sympathy for a killer who liked to stub out cigarettes in a pig's eye. Looking on the bright side, Atherton's death saved them the expense of making a case against him and keeping him in prison for the rest of his life.

Annie appeared at Banks's side to help him carry the drinks back as Bobby Vee came on, singing "Take Good Care of My Baby."

Back at the table, Burgess was chatting up AC Gervaise, so that ought to take her mind off Patricia Beddoes for a while, Banks thought. The thing about Burgess, Banks knew from experience, was that however crude and blokeish he was with the lads, he was still a handsome devil in his way, and he had the sort of manly charm that many women found attractive. Not exactly a bit of rough—he was too sophisticated for that—but world-weary with a hint of danger and a definite dash of the bad boy.

Banks and Annie handed out the drinks and sat down again. As Banks sipped his pint, he started to feel himself drifting away from the crowd; the voices became distant, blending into one another, just meaningless sounds. It happened often these days. Even Bobby Vee sounded faraway and distorted, fading in and out.

He thought about Oriana. He had phoned her the other night in Sydney, after working out what he thought would be a good time. She hadn't sounded exactly over the moon to hear from him, had seemed distracted, as if she had somewhere to go, something else on her mind, things to do. She was busy, she said, and still tired from the jet lag. He understood that, but he couldn't shake the feeling that she had resented his intrusion into her other life, and in the end he had hung up feeling much worse than when he had dialed the number.

"Penny for them," Annie whispered in his ear.

"Oh, nothing," he said, snapping back to the giddy world of the group celebration. "Just life, you know."

"Life, the universe, and everything?"

"Something like that. You doing OK?"

Annie smiled and clinked glasses. "I'm doing OK."

Burgess had just finished telling a funny story, and everyone was laughing. At that moment Joanna MacDonald walked in and flashed him a quick smile. She'd been invited, but Banks had assumed she wasn't coming. But there she was, looking lovely as ever with her blond hair loose, her powder-blue tailored jacket over the crisp white top, and the skirt that ended just above her knees. Everyone moved over and made room for her. Banks asked her what she wanted to drink and she said a gin and tonic. Off he went to the bar again.

As he waited to be served, he looked back at the table, at his team, deservedly wallowing in the feeling of a job well done. Bobby Vee gave way to Fleetwood Mac's "Man of the World." Winsome looked hale and hearty despite her terrifying experience of the previous week. She leaned in close toward Terry Gilchrist, smiling at something he was saying. Banks was pleased for her. It was about time she found someone who recognized her rare and precious qualities, and Gilchrist seemed like a decent, solid bloke. Why Banks felt so protective, he had no idea. Annie, too, deserved someone, but that might take a bit more time, he thought. She was prickly to start with, and there was still some residue from the shooting, however well she was doing. He cared about them all, he realized. Sometimes it was a feeling of heart-swelling pride; other times it was a burden. Tonight it was a joy to share their joy, even though he felt distant and more than a little melancholic.

Burgess switched his attentions from AC Gervaise to Joanna Mac-Donald, turning up the charm a notch. Banks could see Joanna responding, smiling a little flirtatiously, then laughing easily at his jokes. Their shoulders were touching, and it didn't seem to bother her. Now she was looking serious and nodding, engaged in something Burgess was saying. As Banks walked back to the table with the gin and tonic and a double Laphroaig for himself, he experienced something that, if he were to be honest with himself, felt very much like jealousy. He sat down and shrugged it off, then picked up the whisky and knocked it back in one.

ACKNOWLEDGMENTS

I WOULD FIRST LIKE TO THANK SHEILA HALLADAY FOR reading the manuscript when I thought it was finished and pointing out that there was still work to be done.

At Hodder, my thanks go to Carolyn Mays for such a terrific job on the editing, especially given the time constraints. Also thanks to Katy Rouse for all her assistance and to Justine Taylor for clear and clean copyediting. At McClelland & Stewart, I would like to thank Ellen Seligman and Kendra Ward for their editing, and at William Morrow, Carolyn Marino and Emily Krump.

Thanks to my agents Dominick Abel and David Grossman for their continuing support. Also thanks to the publicists—Kerry Hood at Hodder, Ashley Dunn at McClelland & Stewart, and Laurie Connors at William Morrow. Thanks are also due to Debby de Groot in Toronto and Jane Acton at Four Colman Getty, London.

A special thank-you to Nicholas Reckert for the interesting walks that somehow always seem to suggest a possible crime scene.

Last but not least, thanks to the sales teams who make the deals and set up the special promotions, to the reps who get out on the road and sell the book to the shops, and to the booksellers themselves, without whom you wouldn't be holding this volume in your hand. And thanks, of course, to you, the reader.

Here is a chilling excerpt from
Peter Robinson's Inspector Banks novel

WHEN THE MUSIC'S OVER

Coming Summer 2016

PROLOGUE

They threw the naked girl out of the van on the darkest stretch of road. First she felt the wind whip as one of them slid open the door, then she was in free fall, tumbling through space. Her hip bounced on the hard road surface and she felt something crack. Then she hit damp grass and rolled into a ditch full of stagnant water. She could hear their laughter and whooping over the loud music, but soon even the music had faded into the distance and there was nothing left but silence.

She lay in the ditch winded, her hip hurting, head spinning, and tried to take stock of her situation. She had no idea where she was. Somewhere in the countryside, obviously, miles from civilization. She struggled to push herself up out of the foul, muddy water. As soon as she moved, she gasped at the pain, which shot first through her hip, then seemed to diffuse through every atom of her body, as if someone were pushing red-hot needles into her flesh. The stuff they'd given her back in the van was wearing off, the last couple of hours fading like a dream as she awoke into pain, but even as it faded it rushed through her when she least expected it, distorting her senses. There was a whooshing sound in her ears, like big waves crashing, and her vision was blurry.

She had also cut her shoulder on something, a broken bottle in the ditch, perhaps, and she became aware of other cuts and bruises as the pain started to focus on more specific parts of her body. She tried to clean the mud and blood off her skin as best she could with water from the ditch, but it was too dirty, and she only succeeded in spreading the filth all over her body. She felt that she resembled some primeval creature crawling out of the slime.

She limped into the darkness and stumbled in the direction from which the van had traveled. There was nothing she could do about her nakedness except hope someone decent came along, someone who would wrap her in a blanket and take her to the hospital. Being naked and muddy were the least of her problems. Her brain wasn't working properly, for a start. The road surface seemed to be undulating beneath her, and the overhanging trees were assuming threatening shapes. She shook her head to try to make it all go away, but that only made things worse. She felt dizzy and had to support herself against a tree trunk for a moment. The bark was pulsing under her fingers like the dry scaly skin of a reptile. Her hip hurt so much that she was certain it was broken. And she felt terribly torn up inside. She was certain she was bleeding internally. She needed a doctor. He would give her painkillers, maybe even morphine. Then her pain would disappear and she would drift on warm soft pillows without a care in the world. But they would want to take swabs and samples. They'd call the police and then she would really be in trouble. The police wouldn't believe her. They never believed people like her. Besides, in her experience, such kindness was unlikely. No Good Samaritan would come along and give a lift to a naked girl covered in mud. That wasn't what the sort of people she knew did with naked girls. It wasn't the kind of thing that happened in her life.

It was late July, but a long week of rain had just ended. The night was muggy, and a gauzy mist hung over the dark landscape. No street lamps, only the hazy light of a haloed half-moon. Somewhere in the field beyond the drystone wall a sheep bleated, and she thought she could see a lone light shining in a farmhouse upper window. Should she head for that? Would they help her? There was the ditch and a stone wall topped with barbed wire in her way, but there might be an entrance farther ahead. If she found a gate, she decided, or a gap in the wall, that's what she would do. Head over the field toward the light.

How late was it? Or how early? She had no phone or watch. She couldn't remember how long she had been in the van. Surely dawn couldn't be far off. The sun rose early these days. But everything was still dark, and the trees and walls were silhouettes of scarecrows and demons closing in on her. The road was narrow, and there was no pavement, so she walked on the hard surface. Stones dug into the soles of her feet with almost every step. If a car came she would have plenty of warning. She would hear it and see its headlights from far away. If a car came . . .

She hadn't been walking for more than ten or fifteen minutes when she thought she heard the distant drone of an engine and saw lights playing between the shadows and trees ahead, refracted in the mist down the winding road. A car! It was traveling in the opposite direction she was walking, the same direction the van had been heading, but that didn't matter. As the car came closer, she at least had enough sense to stand back, near the edge of the ditch, so it wouldn't hit her by accident. She threw away her dignity and waved her arms in the air. The headlights dazzled her, and the small van shot straight past. She watched it in despair, then she saw it stop with a screeching of rubber about a hundred yards ahead. She couldn't make out what sort of van it was. The engine purred and the red brake lights glowed like a demon's eyes in the mist. Shaking off the feeling of apprehension that came over her, she started hobbling toward the van as quickly as she could.

ONE

Detective Superintendent Alan Banks stood in front of the mirror in the gents and studied his reflection. Not bad, he thought, tightening his mauve-and-gold-striped tie so that it didn't look as if the top button of his shirt was undone, which it always was. He couldn't stand that claustrophobic feeling he got when both button and tie pressed on his Adam's apple. There was no dandruff on the collar or shoulders of his suit jacket, and his dark hair was neatly cropped, showing a hint of gray, like a scattering of ash, around the temples. He had no shaving cuts, no shred of tissue hanging off his chin, and he wore just a faint hint of classic Old Spice aftershave. He straightened his shoulders and spine, noting that there were no bulges in his jacket pockets to spoil the line of his new suit. His wallet and warrant card were all he carried, and both were slim. He fastened the middle button, so the jacket hung just right, and decided he was ready to face the world.

He glanced at his watch. The meeting was due to begin at nine sharp, and it was about three minutes to. He left the gents and took the stairs two at a time up to the conference room on the top floor of the old mock-Tudor building. Timing was an issue. Banks didn't want to be the first to arrive, but he didn't want to be the last, either. As it happened, he ended up somewhere in the middle. Detective Chief Superintendent Gervaise and Assistant Chief Constable McLaughlin stood outside the room chatting as they waited outside. Banks could see through the open door that some people were already seated.

"Alan," said McLaughlin. "New duties not proving too much of a burden, I hope?"

Banks's promotion to detective superintendent had come through a short while ago—a bloody miracle in this day and age, or so he had been told—and he had spent the last few weeks learning the ropes. "Not at all, sir," he said. "I had no idea how much I was getting away with before."

Gervaise and McLaughlin laughed. "Welcome to the real world," said the latter. "Shall we go in?"

McLaughlin went ahead. Banks turned to Gervaise and whispered, "Any idea what this is about?"

She gave a quick shake of her head. "Very hush-hush," she said. "Rumor has it that the chief constable himself is going to be here."

"Not crime stats or more budget cuts, then?"

Gervaise smiled. "Somehow, I doubt it."

The conference room was sparsely furnished, nothing but an oval table, tubular chairs and institutional cream walls. They took their seats around the table, and a few minutes later Chief Constable Frank Sampson—soon, it was whispered, to be *Sir* Frank Sampson—did indeed arrive. When he was followed shortly by the new police and crime commissioner, Margaret Bingham, Banks knew that something important must be brewing.

But the last person to arrive, a minute or so after everyone else, was the biggest surprise of all.

Dirty Dick Burgess was now some sort of deputy director or special agent at the National Crime Agency. More commonly known as the British FBI, the NCA dealt mostly with organized crime and border security, but it also worked against cyber crime and the sexual exploitation and abuse of children and young people. Burgess flipped Banks a wink before sitting down. Even he was wearing a suit and a crisp white shirt instead of his trademark scuffed leather jacket, though he could have done with a shave and a haircut, and he had foregone the tie completely. Clearly the British FBI didn't bother dressing up for a visit to the provinces.

There were eight people seated around the table when the chief constable opened proceedings by introducing them all to one another. One of the people Banks didn't know, by either name or sight, was the lawyer from the Crown Prosecution Service. Her name was Janine Francis, and she was not one of the CPS lawyers that he usually dealt with. The eighth person, still only vaguely familiar to Banks, was the county force's new media liaison officer, Adrian Moss, an ex-advertising agency up-and-comer and political spin doctor with a flowered tie, fresh-scrubbed youthful appearance and a breezy, confident manner. A motley crew, indeed, Banks thought, as he tried to imagine why they might all have been brought together under one roof. It had to be something big.

BOOKS BY PETER ROBINSON

 **NO CURE FOR LOVE**

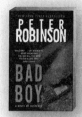 **BAD BOY**

 **IN THE DARK PLACES**

 **THE PRICE OF LOVE AND OTHER STORIES**

 **CHILDREN OF THE REVOLUTION**

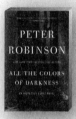 **ALL THE COLORS OF DARKNESS**

 **WATCHING THE DARK**

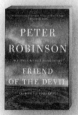 **FRIEND OF THE DEVIL**

 **BEFORE THE POISON**

 **PIECE OF MY HEART**

 **STRANGE AFFAIR**

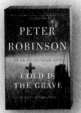 **COLD IS THE GRAVE**

 **PLAYING WITH FIRE**

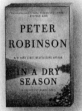 **IN A DRY SEASON**

 **THE FIRST CUT**

 **BLOOD AT THE ROOT**

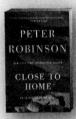 **CLOSE TO HOME**

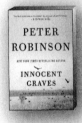 **INNOCENT GRAVES**

 **AFTERMATH**

 **FINAL ACCOUNT**

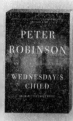 **WEDNESDAY'S CHILD**

 **A NECESSARY END**

 **PAST REASON HATED**

 **A DEDICATED MAN**

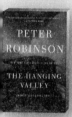 **THE HANGING VALLEY**

 **GALLOWS VIEW**

Discover great authors, exclusive offers, and more at hc.com.

Available wherever books are sold.